Praise for the Nightkeepers Series

"This series goes right to your heart! Jessica Andersen is a must read for me!" —#1 *New York Times* bestselling author J. R. Ward

"I love the whole Nightkeepers world." —Night Owl Romance

Magic Unchained

"[Andersen's] storytelling talent has been honed to a fine art."
—*Romantic Times*

Storm Kissed

"A superb thriller . . . fast-paced and character-driven. . . . Fans will relish this exhilarating tale." —Genre Go Round Reviews

"Thrilling. . . . With this tale of prophecy and curses, Andersen really shakes up her series. Love, loss, passion, and drama are all here. You won't be able to put this one down." —*Romantic Times*

"Andersen's tight writing style and ability to build tension on both the romantic and action sides of the story lines is never better." —Fresh Fiction

"*Storm Kissed* is a fantastic part of the Nightkeepers journey. I can honestly say that it rendered me absolutely speechless."
—Romance Novel News

Blood Spells

"For readers with a hankering for a fascinating and intricate foray into the Mayan world, the Nightkeepers series is just perfect." —The Romance Readers Connection

"Andersen has created a compelling cast of characters whose personal travails add richness to these highly entertaining novels. Another excellent job." —*Romantic Times*

continued . . .

Demonkeepers

"Andersen ramps up the danger . . . mix[ing] action and elements of Mayan myth—from a voyage to the underworld to a fantastic high-stakes ball game—with soul-searching, lust, and romance. Jade's inner journey is particularly engaging, and while the background makes more sense to returning fans, even new readers will find plenty to latch onto." —*Publishers Weekly*

"Intense . . . thrilling . . . a world that fans of any genre will enjoy." —The Romance Readers Connection

"Fabulous . . . will have the audience appreciating the skills of master magician Jessica Andersen." —*Midwest Book Review*

Skykeepers

"An exciting, romantic, and imaginative tale, *Skykeepers* is guaranteed to keep readers entertained and turning the pages." —Romance Reviews Today

"Will knock you off your feet, keep you on the edge of your seat, and totally captivate from beginning to end." —Romance Junkies

"A gripping story that pulled this reader right into [Andersen's] Final Prophecy series." —Romance Reader at Heart (top pick)

"The Final Prophecy is a well-written series that is as intricate as it is entertaining." —The Romance Readers Connection

"The world of the Nightkeepers is wonderful, and I love visiting it. It is intricate, magical, and absolutely fascinating. . . . Step inside the Nightkeepers' world and prepare to be swept away!" —Joyfully Reviewed

"If you're looking for a book to read, one that has an intricate, inventive, and well-researched world with characters that are fully realized, might I suggest *Skykeepers*?" —Romance Novel TV

Dawnkeepers

"Prophecy, passion, and powerful emotions—*Dawnkeepers* will keep you on the edge of your seat begging for more!" —Wild on Books

"This strong new series will appeal to fantasy and paranormal fans with its refreshing blend of Mayan and Egyptian mythologies plus a suitably complex story line and plenty of antagonists." —Monsters and Critics

"This exhilarating urban romantic fantasy saga is constructed around modernizing Mayan mythology. . . . The story line is fast-paced and filled with action as the overarching Andersen mythology is wonderfully embellished with this engaging entry."
—Genre Go Round Reviews

"Using the Mayan doomsday prophecy, Andersen continues to add complexity to her characters and her increasingly dense mythos. This intense brand of storytelling is a most welcome addition to the genre."
—Romantic Times

"Action-packed."
—Romance Junkies

Nightkeepers

"Raw passion, dark romance, and seat-of-your-pants suspense all set in an astounding paranormal world—I swear ancient Mayan gods and demons walk the modern earth!"
—New York Times bestselling author J. R. Ward

"Andersen's got game when it comes to style and voice. I loved the kick-ass series . . . a fun mix of humor, suspense, mythology, and fantasy . . . a series that's sure to be an instant reader favorite, and will put Andersen's books on keeper shelves around the world."—New York Times bestselling author Suzanne Brockmann

"Part romance, mystery, and fairy tale . . . a captivating book with wide appeal."
—Booklist

"[A] nonstop, action-intensive plot. . . . Ms. Andersen delivers a story that is both solid romance and adventure novel. If you enjoy movies like Lara Croft . . . or just want something truly new, you will definitely want this."
—Huntress Book Reviews

"Intense action, sensuality, and danger abound."
—Romantic Times

"If Nightkeepers is any indication of her talent, then [Jessica Andersen] will become one of my favorites. . . . [The book] brought tears to my eyes and an ache in my heart. I read each word with bated breath."
—Romance Junkies

"[A] terrific romantic fantasy . . . an excellent thriller. Jessica Andersen provides a strong story that . . . fans will cherish."
—Midwest Book Review

Also Available in the Nightkeepers Series

SPELLFIRE

A NOVEL OF THE NIGHTKEEPERS

JESSICA ANDERSEN

A SIGNET ECLIPSE BOOK

SIGNET ECLIPSE
Published by New American Library, a division of
Penguin Group (USA) Inc., 375 Hudson Street,
New York, New York 10014, USA
Penguin Group (Canada), 90 Eglinton Avenue East, Suite 700, Toronto,
Ontario M4P 2Y3, Canada (a division of Pearson Penguin Canada Inc.)
Penguin Books Ltd., 80 Strand, London WC2R 0RL, England
Penguin Ireland, 25 St. Stephen's Green, Dublin 2,
Ireland (a division of Penguin Books Ltd.)
Penguin Group (Australia), 250 Camberwell Road, Camberwell, Victoria 3124,
Australia (a division of Pearson Australia Group Pty. Ltd.)
Penguin Books India Pvt. Ltd., 11 Community Centre, Panchsheel Park,
New Delhi - 110 017, India
Penguin Group (NZ), 67 Apollo Drive, Rosedale, Auckland 0632,
New Zealand (a division of Pearson New Zealand Ltd.)
Penguin Books (South Africa) (Pty.) Ltd., 24 Sturdee Avenue,
Rosebank, Johannesburg 2196, South Africa

Penguin Books Ltd., Registered Offices:
80 Strand, London WC2R 0RL, England

First published by Signet Eclipse, an imprint of New American Library,
a division of Penguin Group (USA) Inc.

First Printing, November 2012
10 9 8 7 6 5 4 3 2 1

Copyright © Jessica Andersen, 2012

SIGNET ECLIPSE and logo are trademarks of Penguin Group (USA) Inc.

Printed in the United States of America

PUBLISHER'S NOTE
This is a work of fiction. Names, characters, places, and incidents either are the
product of the author's imagination or are used fictitiously, and any resemblance to actual persons, living or dead, business establishments, events, or
locales is entirely coincidental.
    The publisher does not have any control over and does not assume any re-
sponsibility for author or third-party Web sites or their content.

ACKNOWLEDGMENTS

My heartfelt thanks go to Deidre Knight, Claire Zion, Kara Welsh, Kerry Donovan and others too numerous to name for helping me bring these books to life; to J. R. Ward for being my sounding board; and to my family, friends, and many e-friends for always being there for a laugh or (cyber)hug. And most of all to my husband, Greg, for showing me that soul mates, spontaneous combustion and true love do exist, and that they're so very worth waiting for.

Finally, as we reach the finale of the series, thank you, dear reader, for being part of the Nightkeepers' world!

In three weeks, the barrier that separates the earth and underworld will fall and the vicious Banol Kax, lords of the underworld, will emerge from millennia of torture and damnation with one goal burning in their blackened blood: to destroy mankind. Our only hope rests with the Nightkeepers, a group of magic-wielding warriors who live among us in secret and who have—maybe, hopefully—enough skill, power and conviction to defeat the Banol Kax and restore the barrier between the earth and the underworld.

With their numbers decimated, the last dozen surviving Nightkeepers and their allies have managed to defend the barrier so far. Now, though, they are at a crossroads . . . and the strongest and most unpredictable among them has done the unthinkable: in a world of magi who draw their greatest powers from bonding with the other halves of themselves, he has cruelly betrayed his lover. In the end he sacrificed himself to save her, but that has put him in the demons' clutches and destroyed his magic.

As the days count down and he suffers the tortures of the damned, the Nightkeepers widen their search, hoping for a miracle . . .

CHAPTER ONE

December 1
Three weeks until the zero date
Somewhere in the Gulf of Mexico

Red-Boar had always said that someday Rabbit would get what he deserved . . . and it turned out the old bastard had been one-hundred-per-fricking-cent right. Shit, Rabbit could practically picture his father standing in the arched stone doorway, glaring from beyond the grave with a big-assed "See? I told you so" plastered on his mug.

Then leather whipped through the air and the brined lash cracked across Rabbit's back, laying open another bloody ribbon. The image exploded into white-hot pain, and he twisted against his shackles as if it was the first time he'd been whipped rather than the thousandth. He might even have screamed. Maybe not, though. He wasn't sure. He wasn't sure of much these days; his world had gotten condensed down to the circular stone prison, and Phee, the pale-haired bitch who kept tormenting him, torturing him, trying to make him give up something that was already gone.

"Turn him around." At Phee's order, talons scraped on stone and he was hit with a foul stench as claws swung him on his chains, and he went from having his battered face pressed against the putrid wall to staring into the equally putrid visage of a *camazotz*.

Nearly eight feet tall, with the body of an overendowed man and a face cursed with ratlike red eyes, a smashed-in nose and a triangular mouth that held way too many fangs, the bat demon was ugly from a distance, and really fucking gnarly up close. It kept its ragged wings and barbed tail curled around its body in the narrow confines of the cell, but the oily drool and the way its beady-assed eyes went over Rabbit's body said it was thinking about taking what little was left of his skin for wing patches.

Earlier in his captivity—a month ago? two months?—he would've told it to fuck itself, and maybe even described the process. Now all he could do was groan as his spine grated against the stone.

"Back off," Phee said from behind the creature, and the *camazotz* ducked its head and gave way, returning to its post beside the door with a hiss that was its version of *Yes, mistress. Anything you say, mistress.* Which left Rabbit with a view that—to him, at least—was worse than a chorus line of *camazotz* doing *The Pirates of Penzance*.

He didn't know what the demoness's natural form looked like—the *Banol Kax* could take on many shapes, from humans to three-story-tall winged monsters that breathed fire. This one appeared to be a woman in her twenties, with light, almost colorless hair, high cheek-bones and blue-gray eyes that were unnervingly like his own. She had the trefoil mark of a dark-magic user on the inside of her right wrist, and wore a long silvery-white robe.

All that was the same as it had been before, when she had slipped through the protective wards around Skywatch to speak to him in visions. Back then, though, she had seemed ethereal and ghostly. Now she was flesh and blood, or at least pretending to be.

It was all a lie.

As she approached, he forced a sardonic smile through split lips that hadn't even bothered swelling, as if his body had given up on any hope of repair. "Hello, Mother."

She wasn't, of course, but she had played the hell out of the role, getting inside his head and offering him what he'd most wanted: a mother who had loved him and a reason to think that his old man had given a shit at one point in time. She had sold him on the fantasy of having a real name—Rabbie—and a real family. She had cooed over him, coddled him . . . and then she had turned him, gradually and irrevocably, until he believed with every fiber of his twisted being that she was his only ally and all the others were his enemies. Even the one person who had loved him.

"Rabbie . . ." Phee tutted sorrowfully. She stayed in character even now, with him imprisoned and the charade unnecessary. He had a feeling she liked the pretty shell. She might not be able to get inside his head anymore—his mental powers had vanished along with his magic—but she had to know it was a bitter reminder for him to see her like this. Cruel enjoyment gleamed in her eyes as she leaned in close, brushed her fingertips along his swollen jaw, and whispered, "My poor, poor Rabbie. Why are you making me do this? You're hurting us both, you know."

His flesh quivered, triggering muscle spasms that had him twisting away and then swinging back when he hit the ends of his chains. He groaned as the shackles bit into his wrists and ankles, and his shoulders and arms screamed from having supported him for too long. His healing powers might not have deserted him entirely—some things, it seemed, were coded into his DNA—but the longer this went on, the slower he healed.

Her eyes were falsely warm, her voice a purr. "Just give me what I want, and all of this stops and I set you free."

If he'd been another guy, in another place and time— some other Rabbit who lived in a parallel universe that wasn't a few weeks away from D-day—he probably would've taken the deal, even knowing that freedom was her word for "death." Anything had to be better than this . . . except that he wasn't a different guy in a different place and time, and in this universe with him being who he was, death wouldn't put him out of the demon's reach. Given his track record, he was headed straight for hell. Xibalba. Whatever the fuck you wanted to call it. So he was keeping his ass alive and stonewalling the demoness, figuring that if he couldn't escape, the least he could do was stall.

His former teammates would never know about his sacrifice, but it brought a spark of grim satisfaction to dredge up bloody saliva and spit in her face. "Kiss my ass, bitch. You want what's inside my head? Come and fucking get it."

She hissed, her eyes flaring briefly demon-red, and the air around them crackled with the oily rattle of dark magic. The power was useless against him, though, at least for her purposes. Turned out he would have to give her his magic voluntarily for this particular spell . . . if he still had any magic, that is. She didn't realize the gods had already taken back their gifts.

Biting off a vicious curse, she snapped, "More. I don't care what it takes—I want him *broken*, damn you. We're running out of time."

Rabbit braced himself, knowing the first few blows were going to hurt like a bitch. He didn't close his eyes, though—it was worse not knowing when the whip was going to hit. Instead, he glared at Phee, hating her for what she'd done to him. And hating himself for what he'd let her turn him into.

An animal. No, worse—some subhuman creature that couldn't tell truth from lies, couldn't recognize love and loyalty when he had it.

He still knew what hatred felt like, though. Knew it very well. It was his blood, his bones, his very existence.

The lash whined, then cracked across his shoulder and chest, and agony slapped at him, bright and brilliant. He kept his eyes fixed on the demoness, using the rage to weather the pain. Little by little, though, blow by blow, agony whittled away at his humanity, his capability for rational thought, until he became no more than a whipped dog that refused to die, living only because it dreamed of escaping its chain and tearing into its captor.

By the tenth blow, the hot agony of each whip strike had turned cold and his body was shaking with chills. By the twentieth he was nearly numb, his eyes going unfocused as his consciousness threatened to take a hike.

And then the weirdest fucking thing happened. He saw his father, in all his hatchet-faced, pissed off, Wes Studi from *The Last of the Mohicans*–channeling glory.

It wasn't a memory or even a vision. It was more like Red-Boar was really there, sitting in midair near the doorway with one booted foot crossed onto his opposite knee. He was a little on the transparent side, but he was wearing brown fatigues and a camo-green T-shirt, and scowling at whoever sat opposite him, giving them his trademark don't-be-an-idiot look. It was so real that even knowing his old man was dead and gone, anger lashed through Rabbit.

But then the image wavered and disappeared, leaving a faint tingle of magic behind.

Son of a— He roared and went after the vision, surging against his chains and hitting the ends with a body that was still big and strong despite his captivity, though marked now with new scars. The manacles bit into his wrists and ankles, giving only slightly against the pins that held them in place. And as blood flowed from the cuts, old, unloved memories came at him from someplace deep inside, a flip-book of remembrance that battered at his inner defenses and threatened to turn the beaten dog back into the boy he'd once been.

He was a kid—six, ten, sixteen, whenever, it was all pretty much the same—watching his father turn away from him with that same old don't-be-an-idiot look because he'd fucked up again.

He was nineteen, seeing his old man do real magic for the first time as he brought the Nightkeepers' desert home out of its magical shield and back to earth with Strike and Anna's help. Not Rabbit's, though, because he was only a half blood and his father didn't trust him with the magic.

He was in a dark tunnel beneath the ruins of Chichén Itzá, fully a magic user now, though not by his old man's doing. He raced ahead of a fiery lava creature and then darted into a side passage to hide, but tripped over a limp, yielding body. When he lit its face, he saw Red-Boar's slashed throat and open, staring eyes.

He was torching his old man's pyre and watching it burn, not sure how the hell he was supposed to feel, and feeling nothing, really.

After that, the time blurred into a gooey mess of mental sameness—not because the months and years had been the same as he had grown and aged, his powers accelerating the process until he was huge and looked closer to thirty-three than twenty-three—but because his old man had been the little devil that rode his shoulder and whispered in his ear: You're an idiot, a moron, useless, unworthy.

Gods knew he'd spent those years trying to prove Red-Boar wrong. But maybe his old man'd had a point there, too. Just look where he'd wound up.

Gasping, gagging, Rabbit went limp in his shackles, numb to the outside world as he cursed the place where his old man's ghost had been.

Or maybe there hadn't been anything there at all. Maybe he was finally losing his grip on sanity. Gods knew it was past time.

"Enough!" The word cracked in the air, yanking him back into his body. He groaned as the agony of the beating flooded back through him, only then realizing that the flogging had stopped, that Phee was scowling at him. "This isn't working, and we're running out of time." Her lips curved. "I guess we need to take a little trip and pick up that leverage we've been talking about."

"No!" Rabbit bellowed with a force that turned his throat raw. "Don't you fucking touch her!" The demon

bitch meant it this time. Where before she had used the taunt to twist him up inside and make him bleed, now it was for real. He had stalled too long.

But Phee just laughed and swept out on a buzz of dark magic. The *camazotz* followed without a backward glance, dropping the blood-soaked whip into the small pool of salt water that collected near the door. Its barbed tail was the last to leave, lashing with a force that sent the wicked, knifelike point skittering across the stone floor.

Rage hazed Rabbit's vision. He hated Phee and her *camazotz* minions, hated the part of him that had allowed itself to be poisoned by her lies, the part that hadn't ever outgrown feeling unloved and unwanted. He hated this fucking cell, with its line of stone skulls carved up near the ceiling, watching him with empty sockets, and he hated the trickle of seawater that ran from a crack near the door to fill that blood-tinged depression, bringing the smell of the ocean and taunting him with the hint of the outside world. But most of all, he hated knowing that Myrinne was once again in danger because of him.

Maybe he'd been wrong to steal the resurrection skull and try to bring her back from the verge of death. But after what he'd done to her, betraying his teammates had been all too easy. The spell hadn't worked, though, and the Nightkeepers had come after him, leaving him with just one option: a life for a life. He had offered himself to the gods in exchange for her, and had wound up in Phee's hands instead. It was a sacrifice he would make again, though, a thousand times over. He would do anything for her, damn it. Give anything.

"You can have the magic!" he roared, straining to the ends of his shackles. "Come back. You can fucking have it!" But there was no answer.

He went mindless, berserk, lunging against the chains over and over again, howling threats, curses, pleas, words that stopped having any meaning beyond the fury in his veins and the roar of the creature he had become, which lived only to rip into his enemy and protect what had once belonged to him. The chains clattered *rat-a-tat* like automatic fire and then snapped taut with grenade *crack-booms*. Agony howled through him, but he didn't care about the damage or the pain; the whipped dog had finally reached its breaking point.

"Come back, damn you!" He slammed to the end of the chains—*crack-boom!*—and then fell back—*rat-a-tat*. "I'll give you the magic. I'll give you whatever you want!" Shouting, foaming at the mouth, he kept flinging himself forward, and then falling back. *Crack-boom*, *rat-a-tat*, three more times, four. But then the noise went *crack-clunk*.

It took a second for the difference to penetrate, another for him to feel the give in the manacle holding his right wrist. Whipping his head around, he saw that one of the bolts had sheared off where it held the chain to the wall, and another had bent partway. Sudden visions of freedom hammered through him—images of the ocean, the desert, Phee screaming as flames consumed her—and something like panic closed around him, galvanizing him to escape. He hurled himself to the end of the chain, then tore at it, yanking with every bit of strength he possessed. *Crack-clunk, crack-clunk, crack-clunk-crack-clunk*, the blows vibrated through him, rattling his clenched molars, until with a final *crack-crunch*, he wrenched the chain free from the wall.

Shaking now, breath whistling between his teeth, he tore at the lock pins on his wrists. Then, hanging on to one of the chains to keep himself upright, he undid his ankles, kicked away the clinging irons, and was free!

Son of a bitch. He was fucking free.

Letting go of the chain, he stood for a second in the center of his cell with his feet braced so his body wouldn't reel the way his head was doing.

He had thought he was going to die there, strung up against the fucking wall.

Apparently not. Or at least not right now.

Cobbling together some semblance of his former self, he did a once-over of his body and supplies, like he would've done back when he was a warrior. His shoulder and hip sockets howled and his skin felt strange on his body, as if gravity had changed now that he was standing on his own two feet. He was still wearing the jeans and boots he'd had on when Phee took him—or what was left of them. That was all, though. He didn't have any weapons, backup, or way to contact the Nightkeepers. He wasn't even sure he could copy whatever magic the demoness was using to get to Skywatch—although he could still feel the stir of dark magic in his blood, it, too, had deserted him, as if not even that half of his heritage wanted to claim him anymore.

But he was alive, damn it, and he was free.

And he had demons to kill.

Grabbing the fallen whip, he staggered through the door and into an unfamiliar tunnel that was lit by a string of bare lightbulbs on a Home Depot–orange cord. The smell of the ocean was stronger here, and he could hear the rise-and-fall hiss of the surf. All around him, the softly ridged limestone and the cold slick of moisture told him the tunnel had been a subterranean river at some point, while the carvings—more screaming skulls along with the trefoil hellmark of the Xibalbans—said he was in what was left of an ancient dark-magic temple, somewhere in the former Mayan empire. On the shore of the mainland, maybe, or one of the sacred islands.

Tightening his grip on the whip—the lash might work as a garrote, the bone handle as a bludgeon—he headed toward the sound of the ocean. It felt strange to be walking, stranger still to have the scenery move past him, but even as part of him registered the disconnect between now and a half hour ago, he scanned his surroundings, searching for his enemies. The tunnel curved up ahead; he slowed as he reached the bend and heard telltale scraping noises that fired his blood.

Camazotz!

Snarling, Rabbit surged forward, moving low and fast. He whipped around the corner and slammed into a *'zotz*. The lone bat demon shrieked and backwinged in shock, causing it to rake its wings bloody on the stone around it.

It wasn't Phee's favorite toy—this one was wearing a necklace of bones and teeth, signifying some sort of rank, and it was a big son of a bitch. Eyes flaring, it screeched beyond Rabbit's hearing and lunged for him, claws outstretched. He tried to dodge, but the 'zotz slammed into him and they both went down. Red eyes gleamed from its pug-assed mug, and the stench swirled like sewage as they wrestled on the tunnel floor.

Rabbit jammed an elbow under the thing's chin and reversed the whip butt for a club blow that bounced off its cement-hard skull. The 'zotz gave a piggy, pissed-off squeal and raked his torso and upper thigh with its claws. The venom couldn't knock him out—not anymore—but the scratches hurt like a bitch.

Cursing, Rabbit grabbed the thing's wrists and rammed a knee into its oversized genitals. The batdemon keened in pain but wasn't incapacitated. Instead, it twisted around, hissing, and snaked its ugly mug in to bite him.

"Fuck you!" Fury surging alongside the knowledge that he needed to hurry, Rabbit jammed the whip butt into its gaping maw and shoved, putting his weight into it.

The whip handle pierced the back of its throat and up toward its brain, something went *crack* up inside, and the 'zotz went limp.

Rabbit lurched to his feet and took a couple of steps

away, but then turned back, knowing the fucker was going to regen—

A heavy weight slammed him into the wall and the battered 'zotz loomed over him, spraying his face with the oily black ichor that pumped from its throat wound. *Fuck!* Somehow, Rabbit tore free from its grip. The creature's claws bit through skin and sinew, though, leaving him limping. He reeled around and shook out the whip, cracking it for good measure when the demon squared off opposite him with a blood-chilling snarl.

"Son of a bitch," Rabbit got out between ragged, painful breaths. So this was what it was like to fight without magic . . . it fucking sucked.

He was still bigger and stronger than the average human, still thought, moved and healed faster, but that was it. He didn't have the warrior's explosive magic or protective shield, didn't have his own pyro skills or telekinesis. Worse, the 'zotz could regenerate way faster than he healed, and it could be banished only by magic . . . or by him getting up close and personal, sawing off its dick and cursing it back to the hell that had spawned it.

Rabbit was outmassed, outgunned, didn't even have a knife, but he didn't give a shit what the odds were. He didn't know if this was one of the fuckers that'd whipped him to the bone, but that didn't matter. Anything that kept him from going after Phee and saving Myrinne was the enemy right now.

Roaring a vicious curse, he raised the whip and charged.

The next minute or so was a slippery, bloody blur of Rabbit getting his shit torn loose while returning as many blows as he could with the whip butt, like some mad, beaten-down Indiana Jones. He blocked a blow with his forearm and lost his grip on the whip, grabbed for it and came up with the end of the *camazotz*'s tail instead.

The demon screeched and tried to yank away, but Rabbit hung on. It was like holding a rattler—hot, scaly, dangerous and way stronger than it looked. The *'zotz* roared and reared back, and its eyes went deadly cold, like it was saying, *No more fucking around. You're finished*.

But Rabbit wasn't letting it go down like this. No way.

Shouting as the oily fangs came at him, he blocked the incoming bite with that pissed-off rattler. The *camazotz* chomped down on its own tail. And screamed bloody fucking murder.

Black ichor flew, pumping oily gouts that made Rabbit's grip even slipperier. Instead of letting loose, though, he dug in. And, turning his fingers to claws of his own, he wrenched off the barbed end of the *'zotz*'s tail.

The bat demon's screams went supersonic, no doubt calling in every reinforcement within earshot, but Rabbit didn't care. Hissing between his teeth, he grabbed the *'zotz*'s dick, set the barb's edge to the base of the

thing's cock, and started sawing. And, as the bat demon sank its claws into the back of his neck, he grated,
"Go back to hell where you belong, motherfucker."

It was JT's quasi-spell, JT's discovery that a non-
mage could kill the bat demons with a sharp knife and
a curse. For a second, Rabbit remembered the *winikin*'s
face and his go-to-hell attitude loud and clear, and the
memory pushed the animal instincts back down inside
him, making him feel for a second like a mage, like part
of a team. Sudden heat flared, turned the red-gold of
Nightkeeper magic, and then—*whump*—the *camazotz*
puffed to a cloud of oily smoke.

And all of it—dick, tail barb, ichor, the whole mess—
vanished, leaving behind only greasy smudges of char
and ash.

In the aftermath, the stone hallway rang with silence.

Rabbit lay there for a second, sprawled and gasping,
barely able to believe that he'd done it—he'd freaking
done it! More, the silence said that the other *camazotz*
weren't close by, that maybe he had a chance to get out
before they showed. He didn't know how the hell he
was going to get to Skywatch, but he knew one thing
for damn sure: he needed to get his ass out of this fucking tunnel.

Cursing, he dragged himself up. It wasn't until a
sharp pain in his palm worked its way through the
other discomforts that he looked down and saw new
blood flowing, red and thick, from a deep gash that ran
along his lifeline, scoring through the tough layers of

sacrificial scarring. More, the buzz he'd gotten from the 'zotz's banishment hadn't totally faded—it was still there, feeling more like Nightkeeper magic each second. It was weaker than his old fighting magic, more like his healing powers, deep-seated and cellular. And as he headed along the tunnel at a shambling run, it flared outward as if it were seeking a distant connection.

CHAPTER TWO

Skywatch

One minute, Myrinne was sitting in the mansion's main room, listening in on a strategy session with seventy or so of her nearest and dearest—aka the Nightkeepers and their human consorts, the *winikin*, who had gone from being servants to possessing fighting magic of their own; and whatever the hell she was.

But then in the next second, without warning, she was staring into her ex-lover's eyes.

Her. Heart. Stopped.

On one level, she was aware that it wasn't Rabbit suddenly standing up from a straight-backed chair on the other side of the room. But where, in the months since the resurrection spell had shocked the Nightkeepers by bringing Red-Boar back to life, she'd gotten used to seeing the resemblance between him and Rabbit, now it was more than that. It wasn't just that the older man looked like his son or sometimes moved like him.

No. In that moment, he *became* him.

Rabbit's eyes looked out from Red-Boar's face, hollow and haunted, and his wide-shouldered, go-to-hell stance showed in place of his father's slightly stooped frame. The sight of it—the painful *reality* of it—hit Myr in the gut and she lurched to her feet, barely aware that she and Red-Boar were suddenly the center of attention.

Then he blinked, and Rabbit was gone.

For an instant she thought she might have been wrong, that it had been a trick of the light. Then Red-Boar's face lit and he spun to face the king. "I've got him." He slammed a fist into the opposite palm. "I've fucking got him. I've got a blood-link!"

And right then, with his features sharp and intense, his body vibrating with leashed energy and violence, the father looked very like the son. Enough to have Myr sinking back into her chair while the air rushed out of her lungs and a complicated sort of shock—part horror, part relief—raced through her.

It was happening. Oh, shit. She wasn't ready for this. Because as Dez asked if Red-Boar could lead the teleporters to the place and got a "Fuck, yeah," her heart thudded sickly against her ribs with the knowledge of what was coming next.

They were going to try to rescue Rabbit from the demoness who had corrupted him. And if the rescue succeeded, they were going to bring him back to

Skywatch . . . because the gods had sent Red-Boar back from the dead, not just to find Rabbit, but to reunite him with the Nightkeepers.

Apparently the Xibalbans weren't the only ones who believed that Rabbit was the key to winning the end-time war—the gods did, too, and now the Nightkeepers. And where before their opinions toward him had ranged from "how could he?" to "good riddance," now along with the wariness and mistrust there was scattered relief and a few "thank the gods," because they were that desperate for something to believe in. They were pinning their hopes on Rabbit's rescue and Red-Boar's promise that he could be redeemed.

The irony seemed lost on everybody but Myrinne.

Then again, she was used to being the outlier.

You can deal with this, she told herself, swallowing hard to keep the growing churn of nausea at bay. *You knew it was going to happen one of these days*. But now she realized that while her head might've known there was a good chance that they would find him and bring him back, her heart hadn't believed it, not really.

"You okay?" Anna asked from beside her.

Myr just stared at her friend, feeling like she was drowning.

The two of them had nearly two decades between them in age and were miles apart in looks, with Anna's red highlights, cobalt eyes and ex-professor sensibility contrasting with Myr's straight dark hair, brown eyes and Goth-goes-coed clothes. Their temperaments were as opposite as their looks, too, but they had bonded recently over their dubious distinction of being Red-Boar's two least favorite people in the compound—Myr because she was only human and thus worth less than earwax in the old mage's mind, and Anna because she couldn't use the seer's magic of her bloodline.

It took a moment for Anna's words to get through, another for Myr to nod. "I'm . . ." she began, but then trailed off, suddenly aware that although most of the others were already on the move, getting geared up for the rescue, there were more than a few sympathetic looks—and outright pity—being shot her way. Her spine stiffened. "Don't worry about me. I can handle myself."

"I know you can. I just wish you didn't have to."

"I'm not afraid of him." Things were different now, and not just because the gods had sent Red-Boar back with an explanation of Rabbit's brainwashing and a spell to ensure that he wouldn't betray his king and teammates ever again.

"That's not the only thing you're going to be up against, living here with your ex." Anna's smile went crooked. "Ask me how I know."

Maybe it was ridiculous to flinch at the word "ex," but she'd never had one before. Besides, it sounded weird to call him that. There should be a distinction between a relationship that ended, say, because of infidelity or general assholeness, and one that flamed out in the midst of accusations and attempted murder. And that was when it hit her: after today—assuming the Nightkeepers pulled off the rescue—she would be dealing with Rabbit on a daily basis. Even fighting alongside him.

A dull headache took root, pounding with the beat of her heart. "I'll be fine." *I don't want to talk about it. Not with you. Not with anyone.*

When Dez called for the teleporters to get into position, Anna hesitated. "I could stay."

"Don't. Not on my account. I'll just . . ." Myr made a vague gesture. "I don't know. Go take some Tylenol or something. Maybe drink myself stupid."

Dez might not be the soul of sensitivity—the former gang-leader-turned-Nightkeeper king was more of the club-and-drag variety—but he didn't ask if Myr wanted to go on the rescue mission. The answer would've been "no," of course. In fact, she didn't want to be there to see the warriors in their black combat gear, with their loaded weapons belts slung around their hips, didn't want to wonder what they were going to find when they reached Rabbit, didn't want to care.

Moving on legs gone far wobblier than she wanted to admit, she headed out of the main room with no real destination in mind just so long as she didn't have to watch the rescue team 'port away. To them, this was the gods' will, the next step in the battle plan, and Rabbit was just another mage run afoul of dark influences. Lucius had spent more than a year possessed by a demon and working for the Xibalbans; Brandt had turned away from his wife and children because of a decades-old curse; and Dez had spent ten violent, lawless years under the influence of a dark-magic idol. Each of them had come back and redeemed himself, and the Night-keepers were hoping Rabbit would do the same. They wouldn't trust him easily—he had gotten plenty of second chances already—but they were willing to give him the slim benefit of a doubt.

Myr, on the other hand, had no intention of giving him anything, ever again.

Just leave, whispered her inner, smarter self. *Just grab a Jeep and go.*

It wasn't the first time she'd considered it—she even had a plan, and had stashed some cash and liberated one of the remote controls that the *winikin* used to de-activate the blood ward and open the main gates. Before, she'd always wound up staying, telling herself that the world needed saving and she could help. Now, though, she realized that she wasn't nearly so tough as she'd wanted to think, because when it came down to saving the world or avoiding her ex, she was all about plan B.

"So what are you waiting for?" she asked when she found herself in front of the door leading to the garage wing. "An invitation? Permission?"

She wasn't going to get either, she knew, and she shouldn't have needed them. She was supposed to be a loner, an independent contractor who did what she wanted, when she wanted to. That was what she'd told herself back in New Orleans when freedom had finally beckoned. But almost immediately after the disappearance of the Witch—foster mother, fake tea shop psychic, and general evil bitch—she had fallen in with Rabbit, then fallen *for* him, hard. He had rescued her, brought her to Skywatch, and offered her everything she'd been raised to want: magic, power, a greater purpose. She had thrown herself into the Nightkeepers' world, marveled at it, fought for a place in it, and earned the right to call herself a warrior, even if only a human one. And through it all, she and Rabbit had been a team within the team, a pair of misfits who fit perfectly together.

Or so she had thought.

When tears fogged her vision, she swiped them away with her sleeve. "Get over it. He's gone."

The others could welcome him back if they wanted to, but as far as she was concerned, the demoness had taken Rabbit away from her long before he'd physically disappeared. In those last few weeks, he had been moody, suspicious and angry, entirely unlike the man she had loved. And that last morning. That horrible morning . . . *No.* She blocked the memories, not wanting to remember how his eyes had been cold, his voice a double-edged blade, his—

"Fuck this." She was moving before she was aware of having made the decision, pushing open the door into the garage and beelining for the wrecked Jeep Compass that sat in the corner, waiting for some body work and a new motor—or a decent burial. The cash and remote were right where she had hidden them, as were the keys to the oldest and most nondescript of the Jeeps, which didn't have GPS tracking installed. Given that the teleporters couldn't lock on to her with their magic—so long as she kept herself out of trou-

ble, at any rate—she would be off the Nightkeepers'
grid.

Heart drumming in her chest with a cadence that
seemed to say *hur-ry, hur-ry, hur-ry,* she fired up the
vehicle, hit the override for the garage doors, and
aimed for the widening patch of sunlight and desert.
She was doing twenty when she burst from the garage,
thirty when she flew through the wrought iron gates
that guarded the front entrance of the compound. And
by the time she hit the first downhill dune leading from
Skywatch, she had the pedal to the metal and the Jeep's
engine whining in protest. She didn't know where she
was going, didn't care, just so long as she disappeared.

The Nightkeepers could save the world. She was
saving herself.

Somewhere in the Gulf of Mexico

Rabbit was just short of making it out of the tunnel
when a dozen *camazotz* suddenly dogpiled him, jamming the tunnel and coming at him like a fucking
swarm.

Cornered, he fought hard, swiping at his enemies
with the broken-off whip handle, which had cracked
on an angle that gave him a weak-assed excuse for a
blade. But it was something. By the gods, it was something.

"Go to hell!" The snarl tore at his throat and drew
stabs from his tortured ribs, but the grab-yank-dick-
hack move that accompanied it melted another *'zotz* to

a stinking pile. It was his fourth kill with only eight, maybe ten left to go, but that didn't matter fuck-all when another rat-eyed bastard took its place almost immediately.

He was wedged in a narrow spot of the tunnel, where the 'zotz were forced to come at him one by one, like something out of a freaking Spartans-versus-everyone-else movie. Beyond the next curve, sunlight shone in, gleaming white off the limestone. When was the last time he saw the sun?

"Come on, motherfuckers. Bring it!" He stepped out of his niche and the two nearest creatures screamed and closed on him. He stabbed one in the eye, got a splatter of ichor in his mouth, spat it out and turned on the second just as it wound up to bitch slap him with razor-sharp claws. He cursed and ducked, but he was too damn slow. Fiery pain slashed across his cheek and throat, but he straightened, jammed his makeshift knife straight into the thing's screeching mouth, and shoved until stone grated on bone.

As the 'zotz headed for the floor, he spun back to the other one and did a Lorena Bobbitt, in some dim corner of his brain wondering whether he should be worried that it wasn't even freaking him out anymore to grab on to a demon's dick, hack it off, and have it puff to dust in his hand. *Don't think. Just do it.* Ah, a Nike commercial by way of ancient demondim, he thought, and knew he was brain-babbling. He was losing it—losing steam, losing coherence, losing everything except the driving force that told him he didn't have time to lose anything. So he turned to the sixth *'zotz* he'd taken down—seven if he counted the one back in the tunnel—and did his thing. Grab, yank, hack, gone.

Eight . . . eleven . . . he was kneeling on number thirteen when it vaporized, dropping him to his knees on the stone with a vicious *crack* that made him see stars. Bleeding heavily, he dragged himself to his feet and came around to face . . . nothing.

The tunnel was empty.

Sunlight beckoned up ahead.

New energy burst through him, and he hurled himself around the corner. But then he skidded to a stop and yanked up a hand to shade his eyes.

The arching cave mouth opened to a brilliant white sand beach that gleamed so bright that it hurt. A breeze stirred nearby palm trees, and beyond that, turquoise water stretched like glass to a distant blue-sky horizon. It was beautiful. Incomprehensible. More, it was a fucking "wish you were here" postcard come to life, a few hundred feet from where he'd been tortured. There were even folding chairs, a cooler, and a couple of towels laid out on the beach, as if a swimsuit model had just stepped out of the picture.

Spurred on by the thought of Phee hanging out there in between his torture sessions, catching a tan while he bled, he tightened his grip on his blade, and headed outside. "Okay, you bitch. How did you—*Fuck.*"

The stone monoliths were all too familiar, though on a different scale than the carved eccentrics he'd once carried in his pocket. The wickedly curved half-moons—one black, the other a deep, red-streaked amber—were three times his height, with their bases set together, deep in the sand. Their inner faces matched perfectly and could magically interlock to create a transport spell. They were separated right now, so the stone slabs formed a huge, jagged V, but they would have been joined all too recently. That was how Phee traveled the earth, damn her, just as she had used the smaller stones to send her image into Skywatch to contact him. To corrupt him.

And right now, there was no fucking way he could use the stones without his own link to the dark magic.

But he had to follow her. Had to find a way.

Tightening his grip on his makeshift weapon, he advanced on the stones as a cloud covered the sun, throwing him back into the shadows. The temp dropped and the palm fronds rattled in a sudden downdraft, sounding like giant wings and making the back of his neck crawl, just like—

"*Shit!*" Rabbit flung himself to the ground and rolled.

A huge *camazotz* hit right where he'd been, with its wings and claws outstretched and its tail scything the air. The creature wore a stone yoke tied around its hips, which didn't just make the demon damn tough to banish; it signified that it was a '*zotz* leader. Bigger and meaner than the soldiers, they were tough as shit to kill . . . and they rarely traveled alone.

Sure enough, as Rabbit ducked a tail-swipe and missed a grab for the barbed end, the sky went dark, clouding over with more huge *camazotz*, dozens of the fuckers, all zeroing in on their leader.

Grim reality broke over him. He was screwed, finished. He couldn't get to the stones, couldn't get back to the cave, couldn't do a godsdamned thing except bare his teeth at the hoard, brandish his puny-assed knife and shout, "Come on, motherfuckers. You want a piece of me? Come and fucking take it!"

"Rabbit, get *down*!"

The sound of Dez's voice froze his brain, but his body obeyed the king's order, pancaking him face-first in the sand. Then the ice cracked and his mind raced. That hadn't just happened, couldn't have happened, he hadn't heard—

A salvo of fireballs blasted right over him, crackling red-gold and burning like fury and proving that the impossible was real. The Nightkeepers had found him, they had come for him.

The fireballs hit the '*zotz* line and detonated. Flames roared, and the demons shrieked as Rabbit lifted his head and squinted through watering, disbelieving eyes at the carnage. And carnage it was—a dozen of the enemy were down and smoking, including the leader. But the sky was still dark, the air still full of the leather-boom of wings and the screams of incoming demons.

He wasn't alone anymore, though.

Lurching to his feet, he started to turn toward the others, choking out, "How in the hell did—"

"Save your questions," said a deep, grating voice

behind him, nearly drowned out by sudden bursts of gunfire, which went ripping into the oncoming *camazotz*. Rough hands spun him back around, shoved a heavy machine gun in his hands, and jammed a sheathed knife in his ragged waistband. "Fight!"

Then a hard spine slammed into Rabbit's and he was back-to-back with something he never thought he'd have again: a teammate.

Holy shit. Holy, holy shit. The Nightkeepers were all around him—huge, strong, beautiful and so damn glossy it almost hurt to look at them. There were dozens of *winikin*, too—smaller, lighter and more agile than the magi, they fired machine guns filled with jade-tipped ammo from behind shield spells as if, while he'd been gone, they had somehow turned into an actual magic-wielding army. At their core, Sven and Cara fought shoulder to shoulder—a Nightkeeper and a *winikin* teaming up, aided not just by Sven's huge coyote familiar, but also by a smaller, darker coyote that stayed close to Cara's heels.

Rabbit's head spun. Jesus fucking Christ. How long had he been gone?

A second round of fireballs detonated, biting into the enemy line and filling the air with fury and pain, but he barely flinched. He was too busy staring.

He saw Anna and Strike, huge and regal, and the closest thing he'd had to siblings; Patience and Brandt, who had taught him what a real family could feel like; Lucius, the human researcher who was more of an outsider than Rabbit had ever been, yet had somehow become one of them. And so many more . . . all familiar, yet suddenly seeming like strangers.

But there was no sign of the one person he was looking for, the one person he needed to see. Where the hell was Myrinne?

A bony elbow jabbed his ribs. "Fight, damn you!"

He didn't know who he was backed up against—JT, maybe, given the attitude and sneer-laden voice—but the order cut through the shock and triggered what was left of his warrior's instincts. Sudden adrenaline seared through Rabbit, pushing the other stuff aside. He raised the machine gun—how the hell had they known he would need it?—and sighted on an ugly brute that was swooping through the dissipating fireballs and beelining straight for him. Leaning into the solid weight behind him, he shouted through split lips and hit the trigger.

The jade-tipped bullets ripped into the approaching demon and then detonated, sending fragments of the Nightkeepers' sacred stone deep into its flesh. The thing screamed, spasmed and crashed into another, sending them both slamming to the ground. More gunfire spat from behind Rabbit as he lurched forward, yanking the knife from his belt. It was a plain military-issue blade, not the ceremonial stone knife he'd left behind at Sky-watch, but it would do the job.

He went down on his knees, feeling the impact thud all the way to his jaw as he yanked at the 'zotz's dick, hacked it off and grated, "Go to hell."

The thing puffed to oily smoke and a funk at the

back of his throat. After that, his vision narrowed and he went into overdrive, bringing down demon after demon and dispatching them with a hack and a curse, over and over again. And then . . .

Silence. Suddenly there weren't any more demons to fight, only gritty ash mixing with the churned-up white sand and the gentle lap of waves. But his blood still raced with battle madness.

Furious and unsteady, caught between his prisoner self and the warrior he'd been, Rabbit whirled on Dez. "Where is she? Where's Myr?"

That rasping voice snapped from behind him, "How about you start with a fucking 'thank you for saving my ass'?"

Without the muffling gunfire, the tone was suddenly all too familiar, yet impossible.

Rabbit's blood chilled as he spun around, then froze solid when he saw who he'd been fighting with.

His godsdamned father.

Red-Boar.

It was another fucking ghost. Only it wasn't, because sure as shit it was his old man standing there in flesh and blood, looking exactly like he had right before he died—dark-eyed, sharp-faced and condemning, with a thin line of a mouth and a salt-and-peppered skull trim. He was wearing his usual drab brown, though in combat camo rather than the ceremonial robe he'd favored, saying that brown was the color of penitence. Not that Rabbit had ever heard him apologize for shit. If anything, it was the people around him who were constantly sorry.

Red-Boar's death had been a shock, but in reality it hadn't left much of a hole—at least Rabbit hadn't thought so. Now, though, an old, ugly fury kindled in his gut. "You're dead."

"I was. And I would've stayed that way if it hadn't been for you." Red-Boar spat on the ground, in a gesture that either meant respect for the gods or disgust for his son. Probably both. "The gods sent me back to find your ungrateful ass."

Suddenly, the flash of magic Rabbit had felt when he killed the first 'zotz made far more sense. That didn't stop the thudding pulse of what-the-fuck in his veins, though, didn't make it any easier to say: "You used a blood-link." Which was ironic, given that his old man hadn't ever wanted to admit they were related.

Red-Boar nodded curtly. "I don't know how the gods knew you were going to get your shit in trouble like this—history repeating, I guess—but rather than send me to the afterlife, they warehoused me in the fucking in-between for a while, and then gave me my marching orders and sent me back here. The reanimation spell will keep me going until after the war, and then *poof*." He pointed to the sky. "Up I go."

"They sent you back to find me." It didn't make any sense. He and the gods had forsaken each other long ago.

"Yeah. That was my first job—that, and letting the others know what happened to you, so maybe they could find a way to trust you again." Red-Boar's eyes were like his voice, hard and harsh. "After that, I'm supposed to bind your ass to your bloodline and fucking babysit you until the war, making sure that you've got your priorities straight this time, and knock off this shit about the demons being the good guys." He made a disgusted noise. "For fuck's sake. I—" He clamped his lips together rather than saying, "I taught you better." Which would've been a joke, because they both knew he hadn't taught his son a damn thing about the magic, or about being a man.

Before, Rabbit would've gotten in his old man's face, not caring where they were or what else was going on as long as he got to defend himself and take a few hacks. Now, though, he shoved his anger deep down inside, and turned his back on Red-Boar.

He had more important things to worry about.

The others were ranged shoulder to shoulder in a defensive formation, like he was as much an enemy as the *camazotz*. Even Strike—who had practically raised him, for fuck's sake—was looking at him cold and hard, as if he'd finally given up. That hurt like hell, but Rabbit couldn't deal with that now, either.

Instead, he did something he'd never done before, never thought he would do. He knelt in front of the king and bowed his head. He heard a murmur of surprise, hoped it would be enough.

"Look," he said, "I'm a piece of shit, and I fucking know it. I was wrong about the underworld, about all of it, and I'm sorrier than I can say. You probably don't believe me—shit, I wouldn't if I were you. But you've got to believe me on this one: Myrinne's in danger."

He looked up, praying that Dez saw that he meant every word when he said, "I'll take whatever vows you want me to, the second I'm sure she's safe and Phee is dead. Once that's done, I'll be your fucking slave."

The king scowled down at him, every inch the hard-assed serpent mage. "Myrinne is fine. She stayed back at Skywatch."

But there was a stir in the crowd and JT stepped forward with a satellite phone in his hand. "No, she didn't. She left the compound right after we 'ported out. Took the oldest Jeep and bolted."

Dez's breath exploded. "What rocket scientist let her through the gate without double-checking?"

"She let herself out." JT's eyes narrowed. "And nobody said she was supposed to stay put."

Rabbit surged to his feet. "Screw the blame. We need to find her!" Then, wincing, he tacked on, "Sire."

Dez shot him a black look, but said to Strike and Anna, "Can either of you get a fix?"

Anna shook her head. "She's off our radar, remember, unless—"

"I've got her," Strike said, eyes going grim. "Which means she's in trouble."

Rabbit didn't know why that followed, but there wasn't time for an explanation. His fingers tightened on his machine gun, and he grated, "Take me there."

"We'll all go," Dez said. "But first we need to destroy this place." He gestured to the warriors, and within seconds, the air hummed with Nightkeeper power. When the vibration peaked, Dez gave a curt "Now!" and fireballs flew.

The fiery bolts slammed into the stones with a rending *boom* and sent them toppling into each other, sheared off at their bases. The noise was deafening, underscored by the sharp pings of shrapnel deflecting off a shield spell that sparked with Dez's signature lightning sizzle.

"Again!" the king commanded, and the Nightkeepers sent a salvo into the tunnel. The ground beneath them rolled and shook, and a gout of limestone ash erupted. "Last one!" Dez called, and they hammered the tunnel mouth with a final round of detonations that blazed and blasted, collapsing the dark-magic portal in on itself and sealing off the threat.

Rabbit had to lock his legs to keep from stumbling— not just because the ground was moving, but because of the flat-out fucking power the Nightkeepers had just unleashed. Before, he had been the strongest of the magi, the only one with multiple talents and the wild magic of a half blood. Now, he had almost nothing, yet it seemed that the old legends had been right about the Nightkeepers' powers increasing exponentially as the end date approached.

"Link up!" Strike called, and the teammates scrambled to form an intricate network of clasped palms and other handholds that would connect them to the teleporters' magic.

Shaken, Rabbit moved into the uplink. He found himself flanked by Dez and Michael, two men he would've called friends before, but who now acted as an implied threat: *Don't try anything, or we'll fry you*.

Michael wielded death magic. If anyone could kill the crossover, it was him.

The crossover. Shit. The label had gotten slapped on Rabbit thanks to his dubious bloodlines and an enemy prophecy, but nobody had a clue what the name meant. Unless . . .

He looked over at Red-Boar, and found himself caught in the steel of his old man's stare. Something twisted inside his chest, a logic-fuse that said *no way, impossible, he can't be alive*. But he was there, flesh and blood, and maybe he would have some answers.

Then Strike and Anna triggered the 'port magic, and Rabbit was surrounded by the familiar-strange sensation of moving while staying still. And alongside the urgent need to get to Myrinne, it hit him like a ton of fucking bricks that he was leaving the island. He wasn't going to die there, wasn't going to be sacrificed to the *Banol Kax*—at least not yet. Instead, he was going to get another chance. More, he was going to get an opportunity for revenge . . . and maybe, if he was really fucking lucky, some sort of atonement.

CHAPTER THREE

Chaco Canyon, New Mexico

When the Nightkeepers materialized in the badlands northwest of Skywatch, rapid-fire impressions slapped at Rabbit like physical blows: He felt the cooler, drier air of New Mexico, saw the yellowed-out sun, the wind-tortured rocks, and the jagged outline of a stone-block Chacoan ruin. Its upper levels had fallen in, but the ground floor was relatively intact, with rows of tall, dark windows the width of arrow-slits and a single narrow door. An older Jeep leaned at a drunken angle in the sand some thirty feet from the road, near the turnoff to the ruin.

Stomach dropping, Rabbit stepped away from the others. "Is she—"

He broke off as a white-robed figure darted around a corner and swept through the narrow doorway into the ruin, followed by a dark, winged blur.

"No!" He bolted for the ruin, not waiting for orders or permission.

His boots skidded in loose grit and pounded over rock, and if Dez yelled for him to wait the hell up, he didn't hear it over the hammering of his pulse. The machine gun was an awkward weight that banged as he ran, but he flipped the clip and slapped it home, and then did his damnedest to be quiet as he reached the ruin and slipped inside.

The single door led to a narrow hallway. He headed for the far end, where the fallen-through roof let in the fresh air. The room beyond stank of dark magic, making him want to howl and fling himself into the attack. Instead, he paused in the shadows, pulse thudding. He might get only one chance. He had to make it good.

The far doorway opened to a larger space, where several rooms had fallen in to form one. There, Phee and the *'zotz* stood shoulder to shoulder with their backs to him. Faced opposite them, cornered, was Myrinne.

The first sight of her in so long punched a fist beneath his heart, and he felt a twisted mess of relief, guilt, love, shame and a thousand other things that he couldn't deal with right now. But there was also surprise, because she didn't look like he had expected, like he remembered. She had her dark hair swept back in a soft, loose braid, but there was nothing soft about the set of her jaw or the anger in her eyes. She was wearing low-slung jeans he recognized and a curve-hugging hoodie he didn't, and she was brandishing a small wooden stick, a freaking magic wand, like it was going to do something against Phee and the '*zotz*.

The last time he'd seen her, she had been weak and broken, barely alive. Even before that, she had wanted to fight but hadn't always trusted her skills. Now she looked strong, capable and somehow brilliant, like she was in sharper focus than everything around her. But she wouldn't be for long if he didn't get in there and save her. *Please gods.*

His prayers had gone unanswered for so long that he almost didn't feel the click at the back of his brain, almost didn't recognize it. But then the heat of battle readiness changed inside him, gaining a subsonic hum and suddenly feeling like magic. Liquid energy flowed from deep inside him, bubbling up to fill the empty spaces, and the air around him glistened with red-gold sparks.

His heart clutched. Holy shit. This was really happening.

Through suddenly numb-feeling lips, he whispered, "*Pasaj och.*" And, as if it had never been blocked, the barrier connection formed.

Power hammered through him, lighting him up and making him feel like he could do damn near anything. He didn't stop to question why or how. He just summoned the magic into him, knowing there wasn't a second to lose.

Phee hadn't sensed him yet; she was too focused on Myrinne. Dark energy crackled in the air as the demoness raised her hands to cast a spell. "*Xibal*—"

"No!" Rabbit shouted, lunging through the doorway, out of the shadows and into the light. And, as Phee and the 'zotz spun toward him, he slammed a thick, fiery shield spell around Myrinne, protecting her.

The flame-threaded shield blurred the details, but he saw her jolt and heard her cry his name in a tone of horror. But then, without warning, emotions blasted through him: shock and anger, followed by a sharp lash of resentment.

What the fuck? His senses spun under the sudden onslaught, which was coming from the magic, from Myrinne. It was like they were mentally connected all of a sudden, like his mind-bender's talent had fused their perceptions. Only he wasn't using that part of his magic. This was something else.

Focus! His self-directed snap was almost too late, because Phee quickly shook off her shock, and when she saw that he was riding high on the Nightkeeper magic she coveted, her eyes went bright and brilliant. Her arms swept wide and she flung a bolt of dark magic at him.

Rabbit raised his hands, spread his fingers and shouted: *"Kaak!"* And for the first time in months, the fire came at his command. Pure and cleansing, it poured from him in a brilliant stream of Nightkeeper power.

Dark magic met light and detonated, hammering him back with its shockwave. The 'zotz screeched and took wing, narrowly escaping the blast. But the bat demon recovered almost immediately, and beelined straight for him with its fangs bared and its talons outstretched, attacking before he could call more fire.

Shit! He threw himself flat and rolled aside.

Without warning, a streak of green fire—like his, only not—seared through the place where he'd been, hit the *camazotz* and blasted it back. The strange flames clung like napalm and spread, engulfing the bat demon, which fell to the ground and lay writhing, emitting shrill shrieks.

As it died to ash, a suddenly wild-eyed Phee cast a shield spell around herself, yanked a pair of carved stones from her robe, and started a transport spell. The bitch was trying to escape!

"She's mine!" he bellowed, not sure which of the others had taken out the *'zotz* or how they'd summoned the green flames, but not really giving a shit as long as they gave him a clear shot.

The knife was suddenly in his hand, his palms bleeding, though he didn't remember making the sacrifice. It added to his power as he called the fire magic, gathering it from the depths of a soul he'd thought was dead and gone, used up and kicked aside when he'd betrayed his teammates. Now, though, he felt whole in a way he hadn't for a long time—farther back even than his imprisonment. He wasn't the whipped dog anymore, wasn't the betrayer, the prisoner or the mage.

He was all of those things and none of them.

Magic pumped harder and higher, flowing through his synapses and setting fire to neurons long unused. He could do this. He could.

Raising his bleeding palms, he drew breath and shouted the command again: *"Kaak!"*

Sound, heat and fury detonated; flames speared from his outstretched fingers and hammered into the demoness. Her dark-magic shield cracked and then imploded, sucking back into its maker as she screamed, flung her arms wide, and caught fire.

"*Rabbie!*" she cried. The word trailed up at the end, going to an inhuman screech as she began morphing away from the human form she'd flaunted. Her fire-wreathed shape stretched, blurred, elongated . . . and became a huge dark shadow, with glowing green eyes that blazed with hatred and pain.

"Son of a *bitch*," Rabbit grated. It was a *makol*, a soul of such terrible evil that it had descended to the lowest of the nine levels of Xibalba, to be tortured there, honed by fire and pain until it emerged as a green-eyed wraith.

The luminous eyes dominated his vision, locking him in place as her voice spoke deep inside his head. *In time you will know me for real . . . Son.*

"No!" He poured himself into the spell, into the flames, aware that the others had arrived and were adding their magic to his as he shouted a final: "Go to hell!"

The fire flared higher and the *makol* writhed, screeched and clawed the air, fighting hard enough to make him think it wasn't simply being dumped back in the underworld, but was being destroyed utterly. And who knew? Maybe it was. The rules were changing as they got closer to the end date; the magic was stronger, the stakes higher. Good fucking riddance.

Her face appeared in the flames, human once more, and tortured as it screamed, "Rabb-ieeeeee!" Then the luminous green eyes winked out, the shadow disappeared, and the flames guttered and died. And Phee was gone, leaving behind only a few char marks scored deeply into the stones.

Rabbit stood, staring at the scorched spots.

Phee was gone.

Dead. Kaput. No more.

The burning need for revenge drained suddenly, leaving him hollow and aching, with no clue what he was supposed to do next. He could hear the thud of his own heart, the rasp of his breathing. He was very aware of the others standing behind him, partly as backup and partly—no doubt—to protect Myrinne from him. Which was a hell of a thought. *I won't hurt her*, he wanted to tell them, but history said otherwise, driving home the fact that one part of the battle might be over, but another had only just begun.

Taking a deep breath, he turned his back on the Nightkeepers—on his resurrected father, his king, all the people who had every right to hate him—and faced Myrinne. Who had the most right of all of them to hate his ass.

She was standing at the midway point between him and the far wall, at the edge of where he'd set his shield spell—gone now, though he didn't know when or how it had fallen—and very close to the smudgy ash pile that was all that was left of the *camazotz*.

As their eyes met, she lowered her ridiculous magic wand. And his power went out—*poof*, gone.

"I didn't need your help," she said coolly. "I had it under control. So, hey, thanks for nothing, don't let the door hit you on your way out."

Shock seared through him and he took a step toward her. "Myr?" There were a dozen questions in that one word, but he couldn't articulate a damn one of them, not when she was staring at him the same as he'd stared at his old man, like he had come back from the dead and wasn't all that welcome. And when a gesture from her had severed his link to the magic.

What was he supposed to do now? What was he supposed to say? An apology would be a good place to start, but there was really no way to apologize for what he'd done to her. Still, he wiped his freshly healed palms on his grubby rag-pants and started toward her, holding out his hands in a gesture of *no harm, no foul*, and hoping to hell that was the truth. He had harmed her, he knew, had fouled their relationship beyond repair. But if he could just—

She flicked the wand up and a shield spell slammed into place an inch from his nose.

He froze as another shock piled up on top of the others. "What the *hell*?"

The force field was clear, but threaded through with an almost imperceptible gleam of the same green he'd seen in the flames that had killed the *camazotz*. And suddenly things started lining up, sort of. His magic had come back when he got near her. He had sensed her emotions, felt a connection. Green fire magic—like his own, only not—had taken out the 'zotz. And his magic had cut off with a flick of her magic wand.

Holy shit. Had he somehow transferred his barrier connection when he traded his life for hers, linking their energies and giving her some of his magic?

Impossible.

"Not. One. More. Step." Her eyes were hard now, implacable. "In fact, how about you just back the fuck off?"

He started to say something—anything—but then she pushed up her right sleeve and the air vacated his lungs with a quick *sayonara* at the sight of four marks in stark black on her forearm: the warrior, the fire starter, the telekyne and the mind-bender.

They were Nightkeeper marks.

More, they were *his* marks. All of them, save for the dark-magic trefoil.

"Holy shit, Myr," he blurted, forgetting himself, forgetting the situation in the sheer impossibility of it all. "You got my magic!"

Myrinne hated how her nickname came out differently in his voice somehow, becoming more important, more intimate than it should've been. Hell, *everything* was too important and intimate all of a sudden, because— damn it—the magic had reached out to him. And now, even though she'd cut the connection, she couldn't stop herself from looking at him and feeling an unwanted pang.

He was filthy and ragged, his hair grown out from its usual buzzed Mohawk to punkish spikes. The magic had healed him and kept his broad frame covered with a warrior's muscles, but whip marks formed an X on his bare chest, as if a single arm had wielded the lash in an unvarying pattern. His back was even worse. More, the deep creases beside his mouth and the haunted strain in his pale blue eyes said that he had suffered over the past two months, and badly.

Part of her—dark and vindictive—whispered, *Good, I'm glad*. But the rest of her knew there was nothing good about any of this.

She wanted to tell him to fuck off, wanted to walk away. Unfortunately, she knew damn well that the magic was going to force her to deal with him. More, she didn't want the others to see her wimp out. So, keeping her voice level, she steeled herself and said, "After you disappeared, I was unconscious for almost three days. When I woke up, I was wearing the marks and hearing voices in my head, reading minds." It had been terrifying, yet illuminating, as if a whole new world was opening up in front of her. "The other talents came online soon after. Our best guess is that the gods wanted to keep the crossover's magic with the Nightkeepers, and somehow managed to shunt the power into me when you went bad."

The new lines beside his mouth deepened, but whatever pain she'd just caused him wasn't nearly enough payback. He had accused her of spying for the demons when he was the one being influenced, and he had nearly offered her up to them as a sacrifice. *Bastard*, she thought grimly, because while he'd believed her in the end, saved her in the end, she'd had to let him into her mind to prove her innocence.

Having him see so deeply inside her had been bad— a tearing, rending invasion by the man she had loved. Worse, the mind-bending had stirred up old, unwanted memories—of watching tourists out on the street or from a small, cold closet adjoining the teashop, listening for details the Witch could use in her "readings," knowing she would be beaten if she failed. *You're gone*, she had told the Witch's memory, over and over again. *You're nothing to me now*. But then again, she'd told herself the same thing about Rabbit, yet here he was. And the painful thud of her heart against her ribs said that whatever he was to her now, it was far from nothing.

"Anyway," she said, making herself keep going. "After some experimenting, we discovered that I needed to use the accessories of my 'magic' to channel the power." She bracketed the word with finger quotes, because he'd never really taken her Wiccan-style rituals seriously. None of them had, until she'd gone out to meditate in the cacao grove and nearly started a forest fire. After that, things had gotten seriously shaky for a few days, with her trying to adjust to the idea of suddenly being a mage while the others waited to see if she'd inherited Rabbit's problems along with his magic.

Dez had been the first one to really stand up for her, believe in her. Guilt tugging, she shot a look at the king. "I'm sorry I bolted. I just needed . . . I don't know. Distance." Yet the very person she'd needed to escape from was standing a few feet away, looking at her as if she'd just sprouted wings.

Or stolen his magic.

The muscles in Rabbit's throat worked as he swallowed. Then, voice hoarse, he said, "I haven't been able to use my powers since I left Skywatch . . . and now they're gone again."

Dez's eyes went from her to Rabbit and back again. She didn't know how much the others had witnessed, how much they had guessed. Hell, she didn't want to admit to any of it . . . but with only a few weeks left in the countdown, there was no time for secrets. "The magic reached out to you." She rubbed her inner wrist, where the marks ached, though that had to be the power of suggestion.

"And now?" It was Dez asking.

"I'm blocking the link. The connection caught me by surprise just now. That won't happen again."

With a gesture from her ash wand, she killed the shield spell around Rabbit. It had mostly been a symbol anyway, a sort of in-your-face "look what I can do now."

Apparently taking that as an invitation, he closed the distance between them with three long strides, in a move that had several of the magi bristling. She shot them an *it's okay* look, even though it was far from okay. But if she was going to have to deal with Rabbit, they might as well get this reunion over with. Better to do it in public, too. That way there wouldn't be any sidelong looks, any pity.

Or less of it, anyway.

As he squared off opposite her, she told herself she was imagining that she could feel his body heat. There was no mistaking the reek of sweat and blood, though. The stink of captivity brought a pang, but she refused to give in to it. She glared at him instead. "Well? What have you got to say for yourself?"

"I think the real question is 'Where the fuck do I start?' "

CHAPTER FOUR

Myr's chest tightened at Rabbit's question, because it didn't have an answer, not really. There was no way he could make up for what he'd done—not in the time they had left. And after that it wouldn't matter; they'd either all be dead, the earth enslaved by the *Banol Kax*, or the world would be saved and they would all go their separate ways.

Forcing herself to breathe past the sudden lump in her throat, she said, "Red-Boar explained what happened with the stones and the demoness, so we can just take it as a 'yeah-I-know' and move on, I guess."

That had been how she and Rabbit had sometimes ended their fights. The shorthand had allowed them to walk away from the dispute without really settling it, because it could mean anything from "this is stupid and I don't want to fight anymore" to "I'm sorry, I love you and I won't ever do it again." It didn't matter, as long as the other person's expected response would be: "Yeah, I know." It had gotten them out of a few of their more serious fights—over her rituals, his secrecy, her ambition. And it would work now, not because it would really solve anything, but because they didn't *need* to solve anything. They just needed to find a way to tolerate each other for the next three weeks.

But Rabbit shook his head, expression set. "That's not good enough. Not anymore. Maybe it never should've been."

Nerves tugged at the knowledge that he was talking about their last few months together, when things between them had been strained even before the demoness made contact. "You don't have to—"

"Yeah. I really do." He reached out and took her hand.

"Hey!" She yanked away.

"Please." He held out his hand, palm up to show both his forearm marks and his sacrificial scars.

"If you say 'trust me' I'm going to kick you where it hurts." She was bluffing, though, trying to stay angry when she was suddenly all too aware of the new scars on his chest, arms and back. She didn't want to feel sorry for him, didn't want to feel anything for him.

He shook his head. "I don't want you to trust me. I want you to read me."

"You . . . Oh." The mind-bender's talent was the ultimate human lie detector, after all.

"You don't have to do it," Dez said when she hesitated.

That decided it for her. "I'll do it," she said, reaching for him. She was determined to stand on her own and be a teammate that the others could rely on. She shuddered inwardly, though, when his fingers closed around hers, firm and warm.

He placed her hand flat against his chest, then covered it with his own. "Look inside me," he ordered. "Believe me."

She was acutely aware of the ridged scars beneath her palm, the steady beat of his heart beneath that. Through the mind-bender's magic she could feel his urgency and forthrightness, along with a deep, pained exhaustion. She didn't open herself any further to the magic, though; she really didn't want to know what lay beneath that, and she sure as hell didn't want to read his mind or experience his memories. Her own were bad enough.

So, blocking all but the surface emotions, she nodded, "Go ahead."

"It's not enough to say I'm sorry, not even close." His voice vibrated beneath her palm. "But, I *am* sorry, Myr. I'm so fucking sorry for what I did to you. I've spent the past two months going over and over it again in my head, torturing myself with it, but in the end there isn't really anything more I can say except that I'm sorry."

The apology resonated, though.

Don't, she told herself. *Don't trust him. Don't believe in him. Don't let yourself rely on him, lose yourself in him.* Because that had been the worst of it, really. It hadn't been until he was gone, until she had healed, that she stepped back and realized that she had gotten so involved in being the crossover's girlfriend, she had stopped trying to be herself.

Pulling her hand away, she took a big step back, until she couldn't feel his body heat anymore. "Apology accepted."

His pale blue eyes narrowed. "Seriously?"

"You're not the only Nightkeeper to do shitty things under the influence, and now that I've experienced the magic firsthand, I get how powerfully it can affect the user. And like it or not, we've got more important things to worry about right now."

The brave words rang hollow inside her, though, because it really, really sucked to realize it was the truth. Once upon a time she would've bloodied anybody who'd dared to imply that her and Rabbit's relationship wasn't the number one most important thing in the universe . . . but that relationship didn't exist anymore. And, really, how much did a lover—or an ex—matter when they were facing the end of the world?

"So that's it?" he said. "We're done?"

"What did you expect?" snapped, suddenly very aware that they weren't alone.

"I never expected to see you again. I thought I was going to die in that cave."

Her heart twisted. "Damn it, Rabbit."

"Sorry." He cursed under his breath. "Sorry. I'm the bad guy here, not you. Never you." He squared his shoulders. "Okay. That's it, then. I guess I'll need your

help with the magic. Other than that . . . well, I'll stay
out of your way."

"Yeah. Okay." They stood there for a moment that
probably seemed longer than it really was. A dull headache thudded as adrenaline drained. Pinching the bridge
of her nose, she said softly, "For what it's worth, I'm
glad you made it back."

And she was, really. The anticipation had been
worse than the actual event. Sort of.

"Thanks. And Myr?"

"Yeah?"

"I'm glad you were the one who got my magic. Of
anyone, I'm glad it was you."

She just nodded, doing her damnedest to hold it together. He was really her ex now; it was really over.
Which shouldn't have hurt but somehow still did,
warning that some part of her had hoped, deep down
inside, that when Red-Boar found him he'd be the old
Rabbit, quirky and unexpected, and so thoroughly in
love with her that he made her feel like she could do
anything.

Thing was, she didn't need a lover to be strong.
More, the man standing opposite her wasn't the guy
she'd been in love with . . . but he also wasn't the angry,
strung-out stranger he'd been at the end. He was both
of those men and neither of them, a grim, scarred version with stark, honest eyes that had new shadows,
new secrets. She didn't know this Rabbit, didn't know
how to deal with him.

Just walk away, she told herself. *Be smart this time, and just walk the hell away.* And, forcing her feet to move, she did exactly that.

Rabbit hadn't been lying when he'd said he'd never expected to see her again. But in his deepest, most secret fantasies—the ones he hadn't even really admitted to himself—he'd never pictured her walking away from him.

She still cared—he'd seen it in her face, along with the shadows that said she didn't want to care. Which meant . . . shit, he didn't know what it meant, but he knew he didn't want to leave it like this. Couldn't. He went after her, boots digging into the soft sand outside the ruin as she headed for the bogged-down Jeep.

But the moment he started down the incline, Red-Boar came out behind him and grated, "Hold it right there." And the bastard backed it up with a shield spell that he cast like a damn cage.

Rabbit banged off the invisible wall, cursed, and spun back toward his old man. "Stay out of this," he warned. "It's none of your damned business."

Red-Boar was alone; the others hadn't followed, though Rabbit didn't know what that meant. His old man cast a long enough shadow as it was, as he strode to where the shield enclosed Rabbit, then leaned in close to growl, "It's entirely my damned business. The gods sent me back to make sure you do your duty, and that doesn't have fuck-all to do with patching things up with your girlfriend."

Rabbit's jaw locked. "We were mates."

His father shot a pointed look at his forearm, which was bare of the *jun tan* mark. "Listen up, boy, and listen good. We're both here by the gods' graces, and for only one reason: To figure out what the hell you're supposed to do that's going to tip the balance of the war, and then make sure you fucking *do* it. So you need to focus on what's important, and she's not it."

Which meant Red-Boar didn't know dick about the crossover's supposed powers. "She's got my magic."

"Lucius will find a way to fix that," Red-Boar said, flicking his fingers to dismiss the detail, and Myrinne.

"Do you dislike her because she's human, because she's got access to boar magic, or because she was mine?"

"Me? You're the one who thought she was a spy." The old man's eyes narrowed. "She's always wanted power, after all. Now that she's got it, she doesn't want anything to do with you. Funny how that worked."

"Get. The fuck. Out. Of. My head," Rabbit said grimly, spacing the words between his teeth. In his peripheral vision, he saw Myrinne use her wand to telekinetically ease the Jeep back onto its tires and roll it up to the road.

"You want her, even love her, but you don't trust her all the way when it comes to the magic," Red-Boar said, digging in. "She's always been attracted to it, always wanted it, even when getting it conflicted with the writs and your king's orders. But she's a hot piece of tail, and damn good at leading you around by your dick, so you followed wherever she led. At least until the end."

"Fuck you."

The Jeep's engine fired up, grit spurted from beneath the tires, and Myrinne wheeled off, headed back in the direction of Skywatch and catching air on the first big bump. She went too fast when she was upset, he knew. And also when she was pissed. When she was happy. Pretty much any other time, too. She was a high-octane, life-in-the-fast-lane woman, and there was nothing wrong with that.

It didn't make her a spy or the enemy; it just made her who she was.

Red-Boar stepped up beside him to watch the Jeep speed away. Changing tactics, he said quietly, like they were man-to-man and he gave a shit, "You should leave her alone. You've done enough damage."

And the hell of it was, he was right about that one. Maybe she'd healed up stronger than ever, but that didn't make up for what he'd done.

So he watched her go, and kept watching until the dust cloud disappeared. Then, exhaling, he turned back to Red-Boar, aware that the shield spell was gone and the others had 'ported away, leaving the two of them alone. "What do you want from me?"

"The same thing I've always wanted: for you to get your head out of your ass and behave."

"According to whose rules? Yours?"

Red-Boar made a disgusted noise. "Just follow Dez's

orders, and when we figure out what the crossover is supposed to do, like I said, just fucking *do it*."

Rabbit wanted to argue, but couldn't really. The messenger didn't matter so much as the message. He glanced back along the road, where the kicked-up dust had turned to a faint haze. "Phee showed me a vision of you and her living together in the rain forest."

"Lies," Red-Boar said flatly. "All of it."

"Fine." Rabbit rounded on him. "Then *you* tell me. Who was my mother? How did you end up with her? And why the fuck didn't you leave me in the highlands if you hated me so much?"

Red-Boar spat in the dust near his feet. "Leave it alone, boy. The past doesn't matter worth shit. This is one of the few times that what has happened before won't happen again."

"But—"

"*Enough!*" Red-Boar's sudden bellow reverberated off the nearby ruin and sent a sand-colored lizard scuttling for cover. Lowering his voice to a growl, he said, "Get this through your thick fucking skull, boy. You don't get to make demands here. If you want to get your ass back on the team, you'll do as you're fucking told. More, you'll promise it on your soul. Remember, rescuing you was just the first part of my job. The second is to get you to swear an oath . . . not to the king—that's not worth shit with you and we both know it. No, I've got a spell that'll bind you to the eldest member of the boar bloodline . . . which means I'll have your ass. I'll control you." He leaned in. "I'll fucking *own* you."

Oh, hell, no. A foul taste soured the back of Rabbit's throat. "What if I refuse?"

"Then I'll end it myself." The old man's expression didn't change, like he was talking about supersizing his number three combo, not murdering his own son. "If we can't use you, we're sure as shit not going to let the *Banol Kax* have you."

"Jesus." For all that he'd remembered his old man as a colossal dick, the reality—if you could call a guy back from the dead "reality"—was so much worse.

"Think about it," Red-Boar advised. "But don't take too fucking long." Glancing back at the ruin, he raised his voice and called, "I'm ready to leave."

Moments later, Anna stepped out and headed in their direction. Strike must've taken the others back, leaving her to transport the stragglers. She didn't ask how it had gone. Instead, she held out her hands. "Link up, and let's get out of here."

"He's staying," Red-Boar said flatly.

"Dez said not to let him out of my sight."

"And I'm saying you're going to." The old man's mouth thinned to a grim line. "The spell won't work if his heart isn't in it, and he needs to make his own choice. Besides, I found him once, I can find him again." His eyes went to Rabbit. "And the second time won't be a rescue mission. Understand?"

"Loud and clear." *Asshole.*

Anna's vivid blue eyes gained wary shadows. "Rabbit . . ." She trailed off, shook her head. "I don't know what to say to you anymore. I don't know how to make things better, or even if I should try."

In a way, that stung worse than all of Red-Boar's threats and insults put together. Among the magi, Anna was Switzerland. Years as a researcher and university prof had given her the patience of . . . well, something really freaking patient. So for her not to know how to deal with him . . . yeah. That pretty much summed it up.

Before, he had been the Master of Disaster, always starting with more or less the right intentions but winding up blowing shit up anyway. Now, though, the others didn't even trust his intentions. Hell, he wasn't sure he trusted them himself.

He took a big step back, away from Anna and Red-Boar. "He's right. I need to think." Not about whether he was committed to the Nightkeepers' cause, but whether he could fight effectively—or at all—with his old man up his ass.

"First you need to get some rest and heal up." Her nose wrinkled. "And take a shower. Not in that order."

Now she was being more herself, reminding him of a bossy big sister. But while that brought a wistful tug, it didn't change anything. "Go on without me. I'll hike in later." Probably.

She hesitated a long moment, seeming unperturbed when Red-Boar started muttering under his breath. Finally, though, she nodded. "Okay, I guess. But Rabbit?"

"Yeah?"

"Don't disappoint yourself."

Her quiet command stuck with him long after she and his old man disappeared in a hand clap of inrushing air. More, really, than any of what Red-Boar had told him in between the four-letter words, because he'd spent most of his life trying to live down to his father's opinion. Now, though, it was just him, the badlands, and a whole lot of empty scenery stretching on as far as he could see. Hell, the fact that he could see more than a few feet in front of him without coming up against a rock wall should be enough. Breathing fresh air should be enough. Having a choice—any choice—should be enough.

It was, too. He was grateful for his freedom, grateful that he'd gotten a chance to kill Phee, grateful that he'd gotten to see Myr, no matter how much it had hurt to watch her walk away. And he wanted to think that if the gods were asking him to swear himself to any of the others—or, shit, all of them—he would've sucked it up and done it. Red-Boar, though, would be all over him, telling him when to eat, when to sleep, when to shit . . . and what to do with the powers of crossover magic.

Fuck me, Rabbit thought when that one put a quiver of "so there you have it" in his gut. Because when he came down to it, he didn't trust his father any more than he trusted himself. Less, in fact. Which under the circumstances left him up shit's creek and paddling with his damn hands. The thought had him scowling down at the baked ground near his feet.

He jolted as a winged shadow glided past.

Pulse bumping, he looked up, reached for the machine gun, found it gone and went for the knife instead. But it wasn't a *camazotz*; it was an eagle—or maybe a falcon?—circling in for a lazy landing. The bird was a rich brown color, with golden eyes that fixed on him as it backwinged to perch on a jagged wall nearby. Up close it was a big bastard—way bigger than he wanted to tangle with—but it seemed to be content to sit up there and stare down at him like he was a rabbit of the ears-and-tail variety, and a good option for a snack.

He didn't know his raptors all that well, couldn't tell if this one was a local resident or something more— eagles had been sacred to the ancient Maya, after all, symbolizing the freedom of the sky, the rising and setting of the sun, and even the start of a war. Which was all pretty damn relevant to the here and now, thankyou- verymuch.

"Got any advice?" he asked. Because if he couldn't trust the gods, then who the hell *could* he trust?

The bird just cocked its head to look at him out of one eye, then the other. Nate Blackhawk—the Night- keepers' hawk-shifter—had once told him that it was like seeing a different plane with each eye, then a third with both together. Rabbit didn't know what the eagle was seeing now, though.

"Anything?" he prodded.

It looked away, fluffing its wings a little in a move he took to mean, *Screw you, bub. I'm just an eagle. And besides, this is your call. Either you can handle your old man or you can't. What's it going to be?*

"It's not about handling him. It's a question of whether it's a good idea to give him that kind of power. What if he goes off his fucking rocker and starts following his own agenda, using me as his weapon?" It wasn't unthinkable—Dez's *winikin* had tried to use him that way, convinced he was doing the gods' work. And Red-Boar himself had tried to kill Strike's human mate, Leah, thinking he knew the gods' plan better than the rest of them.

And your other option would be . . . ?

"I could disappear, hole up underground somewhere that the blood-link can't find me, and then . . . shit, I don't know. Figure out a way to help the Nightkeepers from there, I guess. I'm supposed to be the crossover, right? If the gods want me to help, they'll find a way to tell me how."

You're reaching.

He shot the bird a baleful look. "Oh, shut up." But the eagle—or, rather, whatever inner voice he'd given to it—had a point. If he was going to do things differently this time, he didn't get to pick the easy changes, even when the hard ones had the potential to suck donkey dick.

Then the eagle gave an unearthly screech and launched itself into the air. It didn't buzz him or look back or anything as it powered into the sky with steady sweeps of its wings. Still, though, it felt like the bird's visit had been a sign. Even more so when it banked and headed for Skywatch.

"Shit," Rabbit muttered, knowing what the answer had to be.

Sign or no sign, it hadn't ever been a debate, really, because all the logic in the world couldn't trump the one thing he'd left out of his inner argument: Myrinne was at Skywatch. And while she probably didn't want his protection—probably didn't even need it anymore—she was going to get it anyway.

CHAPTER FIVE

December 2
Nineteen days until the zero date
Skywatch

The next morning, Rabbit woke groggy as hell, and blinked up at the ceiling. Which in itself was disconcerting after spending so long chained to a damn wall.

The wall's gone, he reminded himself, reorienting. *Phee is dead and Myrinne is safe.*

And he was back at Skywatch.

Granted, he'd spent the night in one of the basement storerooms that had been retrofitted as a cell, with a narrow bunk, a squat-pot, and a small bookshelf stocked with a few dog-eared paperbacks, bottled water and a six-pack of energy bars. The door was locked and faint crinkle of magic said it was warded, too. Which meant that he was as much a prisoner here as he had been on the island . . . except that now he was a willing prisoner.

By the time he'd hiked to Skywatch yesterday afternoon, he'd been shakier than he'd wanted to admit, knocked on his ass by the aftereffects of captivity, rescue, Red-Boar's return, seeing Myrinne, finding out that she had his magic now . . . all of it. And after a shower—which had been a weird cross between orgasmic and something out of a sci-fi movie, with all the chrome and gadgets feeling unfamiliar and futuristic—he'd willingly crashed in the basement, knowing the others wouldn't trust him until he'd made his vow to Red-Boar. And maybe not even then.

I'll do whatever you want, he was trying to signal by being a good prisoner. *You name it, you've got it.* Anything was better than the chains and being utterly alone except when he was being beaten. And having an opportunity to kick some demon ass and help with the war . . . yeah. He'd do whatever it took. Even stay away from Myrinne.

Probing the idea like an aching tooth, he rose and padded to the chair by the door, where someone had left him clean clothes. He reached for them automatically, but then hesitated at the sight of a familiar pair of jeans, his backup combat boots with the knotted laces and scarred toes, and a black cartoon tee he'd bought off CafePress.

He hadn't thought much about his stuff while he'd been strung up in that cave—it was just stuff, after all—but the clothes hammered things home.

Christ. What a fucking difference a day could make.

Twenty-four hours ago, he'd been a beaten animal, practically inhuman, living only to kill his tormentor. Back then, if a big-assed foam finger had come down out of the sky and a booming voice had told him he was going to get another chance, he would've said it would be enough to kill Phee and do something to balance the scales. Now, though, surrounded by the trappings of civilization, he was coming back to himself—or maybe, hopefully, a better version of the fuckup he'd been. He wanted the chance to prove that to the others, to himself . . . and he'd give anything to be able to make some real restitution. Even promise himself to his old man.

As if on cue, magic sparked, a heavy fist banged on the door and Michael's voice said, "You up? It's time."

A chill walked down Rabbit's spine, but he shook it off, dredged up a shadow of his old swagger and called, "Give me a minute to get dressed. Unless you're planning a cavity search?"

"Been there, done that."

"You're kidding, right?"

"Just get your ass dressed." But there was a thread of amusement in the ex-assassin's voice that said he, at least, might be willing to give Rabbit one last chance.

Then again, Michael knew better than most just how bad a guy could get under the influence of the dark magic.

But any optimism that might've brought died off a few minutes later when Rabbit found himself following Michael to the last fucking place he would've chosen for a meeting, the last fucking place he would've chosen to be, period: the sacred chamber at the center of Skywatch.

He hesitated in the doorway, becoming the sudden focus of way too many eyes as a couple of dozen team members—Nightkeeper, *winikin* and human alike—all looked at him as if to say "Hey, asshole, remember what happened the last time you were here?"

Myrinne stood at the edge of the crowd. She had one foot out the far door and looked as trapped as he felt, but she was there. He wasn't sure what that meant, didn't know what he wanted it to mean.

He nodded to her as he stepped into the open center of the room. The gesture was for all of them, though, including Red-Boar, who stood front and center before the *chac-mool* altar. Carved of red-tinged limestone and mortared in place with the ashes of generations past, the statue was a human figure, reclining with its body forming a zigzag shape and its blank-eyed face turned toward him, like it, too, was saying, "*Hey, asshole . . .*"

Yeah, he remembered what he'd done here, in this room. How the fuck could any of them think he would forget?

The glass ceiling had been replaced, and the floor, walls and altar all looked pristine. Still, though, he saw the scene as it had been, with blood everywhere and Myrinne's torn body folded up against the foot of the *chac-mool*. He hadn't struck the blow that had hurt her—that had been the demons—but he might as well have, because she had taken a blow meant for him. After everything he'd done to her, she'd saved his ass.

Christ, Myr, I'm sorry. He tried to send the words to her, but she was blocking the one-way magical link that had connected them the day before. Which left him standing there, wishing to hell he could warp time and go back to knock the shit out of himself before he fucked up things between them, before he fucked *her* up.

Only she didn't look fucked up. She looked fierce and competent in dark jeans and a black tee, and at his glance, she stepped all the way in the room and glared at him, as if to say "I'm not afraid of you."

"You come here freely to take the Boar Oath?" Red-Boar asked, eyes glittering as he put himself in Rabbit's line of sight. He was wearing a worn brown robe, tied with a rope. It probably should've made him look like Obi Wan, but instead brought memories of him spending most days stoned and pissed off, and not much use to anyone, especially himself. Now, though, his voice was clear and strong as he added, "Once you've taken the oath, you'll be bound to obey three orders given by the eldest of the boar bloodline. Me."

"They'll be my orders," Dez said with a warning look at Red-Boar.

The brown-robed mage tipped his head. "Of course."

Rabbit swallowed hard, though, because even if the content originated with Dez, he'd still be bound to his old man. But it had to be done. He crossed to the altar, squared off opposite his father, and said, "I'm in."

"We'll see." Red-Boar pulled a stone knife from

where it had been tucked into a twisted knot in the rope belt. Rabbit recognized the blade—he'd inherited it from his father and carried it into battle for years before leaving it behind at Skywatch when Phee took him. The sight of the knife back in his old man's fist dug at him, but he supposed it was fitting.

Sunlight glinted on the blade as the old man lifted it to the sky, where the sun shone through the glass ceiling. Then, in a move so quick it felt like that of a predator snatching up its prey, killing it before it even knew it was in trouble, Red-Boar grabbed Rabbit's wrist and yanked his hand palm up. The knife flashed down and cut deep.

Rabbit hissed, but the feeling of being palm-cut was familiar, almost cleansing after so damn long. He was more aware of his old man's hard, hot grip than the pain as blood pooled in his cupped palms, then spilled over and splashed on the stones of the sacred chamber.

Magic gathered around them, sparking red and gold, and filling the air with an expectant hum as Red-Boar yanked him close, eyes going narrow. "Listen up, and listen good. This isn't like any oath you've taken before. It's not some weak-assed compulsion spell; it's the real deal. If you break your word, you break your connection to the boar bloodline, understand? So be really fucking sure."

"What do you care if the bloodline rejects me?" Rabbit said, voice low enough that only the closest onlookers would hear. "You never wanted to accept me in the first place."

"This isn't about what I want. It's about saving the godsdamned world."

"So what are you waiting for?"

Glaring, Red-Boar reached into his robe and withdrew a familiar leather pouch. It was worked with crimson and gold threads that twined together to outline the boar bloodline's glyph, along with the sigils of the warrior and the mind-bender, just like the marks on the old man's wrist. They were his damned ashes. Rabbit should know; he was the one who'd filled the bag and ritually sealed it into a hollow at the base of the altar. His eyes went to the spot, where now there was a darker smear of new, damp mortar, and his gut tightened.

He wasn't just going to be swearing on his own blood. He was going to be using his father's ashes.

"Pretty fucked up, huh?" Red-Boar looked at the bag for a moment, then said, "Hold out your hands."

Rabbit reached his bloody fingers to take the bag, but instead of handing it over, Red-Boar upended the thing and dumped its contents. The ashes were gray and crumbly, and the whole mess hit Rabbit's palms and poofed up in his face as he drew in a startled breath. And sucked up his father's remains.

There were exclamations from the others, a couple of gags and lots of shifting feet, but Rabbit forced himself to hold it together as a dark taste hit his sinuses and the back of his throat, making him want to cough. His palms burned where the ashes mixed with his blood, and strange magic ate into him like acid, roughening his voice when he grated, "Get on with it."

Red-Boar tucked the empty leather pouch into his robe, used the knife to slash his own palms, and then took both of Rabbit's hands in his, letting their blood mingle. And, whether or not the old man liked that they were related, the blood-link formed instantly. Red-Boar's power poured into Rabbit and flared through his veins, until he could feel the old bastard in every damn corner of his being. It was the first time he and his old man had linked up, the first time he'd felt the extra resonance that came from shared DNA. Which was ironic, really, considering that his old man was dead and he didn't have magic of his own anymore.

"Concentrate on your bloodline mark and repeat after me." Red-Boar rattled off a spell in the old tongue, one that Rabbit normally wouldn't have been able to remember, never mind repeat. But somehow the words translated themselves in his head, grabbing on to him, burning themselves into his mind: ". . . by my own blood and the bones of my ancestor, I swear to obey my Keeper's three demands." His stomach clutched but he said the words, putting himself under Red-Boar's command. Making the old man his fucking Keeper.

As he said the last of it, lines of fiery pain burned across his palms and then caught, flaming blue for a moment before they guttered and died, leaving his skin scoured clean of ashes and blood.

"By the Boar Oath, here is your first order," Red-Boar said without preamble. "Obey your king without exception." Rabbit felt the order take root, dig in, and twine itself into a hard little knot at the back of his head, where his magic used to be. It wasn't painful so much as intrusive. Unsettling, knowing the threat was there. His old man continued, "By the Boar Oath, here is your second order: Do not physically hurt any of your teammates—Nightkeeper, *winikin*, human, it doesn't matter. Don't hurt them." Which only went to prove that Dez had written the orders, because Red-Boar wouldn't have bothered to add the humans and *winikin*.

The second order settled itself in his brain, making him feel invaded, controlled. "What's the third one?" Rabbit asked, his voice sounding strange in his own ears.

"We're going to save that one for now," Dez said. But while the answer had come from the king, Red-Boar's eyes glinted with satisfaction.

Bastard, Rabbit thought, but squelched the anger. This was his punishment, after all. More, despite the oath, his onetime teammates were all looking at him with varying degrees of wariness and skepticism, warning that he still had a long way to go with them. All except Myrinne, whose level gaze said it didn't matter what he said or did, she didn't intend to trust him ever again.

Ah, baby. He wanted to get her away from the others and tell her that he wasn't that guy anymore, that he'd finally learned his lesson. But no matter how important Myr might be to him, she couldn't be his priority right now. It didn't take the Boar Oath to tell him that.

So, focusing on Dez but talking to all of them,

really—and especially her—Rabbit said, "I've taken the vow, and I damn well mean it. You don't have to trust me, but the gods seem to think you need to use me . . . so let's get started."

The king looked at him for a few seconds, weighing his sincerity. Then a gleam entered his eyes, and he nodded. "Well, then. Seems to me that we need to figure out how the magic works between you and Myrinne, what the crossover is supposed to do . . . and why the hell the gods want you on our side when all you ever seem to do is blow shit up."

As the crowd in the sacred chamber started dispersing, Myr slipped out the back door and headed for an empty apartment wing–turned–storage area that had little to recommend it except a side door that would get her back to her quarters in the mage's wing without having to stop and talk to anybody.

In the deserted hallway, cloths were draped over sideboards and chairs, protecting them from stacks of boxed ammo and other gear, and dust motes hung in the air and swirled in the light coming from the curtain-hung windows. Her stomach churned as she walked, but while she'd skipped breakfast, it wasn't hunger talking—it was her better sense, the part of herself she had learned to listen to over the past few months. Right now, it was telling her to get back to her routine and do her damnedest to pretend that nothing had changed . . . even though as of yesterday, everything had changed.

"Myr. Wait up."

Damn. It was Rabbit's voice, Rabbit's bootfalls suddenly sounding in the hallway behind her.

Which was partly her fault—she would have sensed him through the magic if she hadn't blocked him so thoroughly, been so determined to ignore the faint tickle of warmth that had kindled at the base of her skull with his return.

She stopped and turned back to face him. He halted a few paces away, eyes dark with lingering exhaustion, along with the pain of having just sworn himself under his father's thumb. Refusing to feel sympathy, she said, "What do you want?"

I want you, Myr. I came back for you. The words came in his voice and sent a shiver down her spine, but they weren't real. They couldn't be, not with the magic blocked off. But that meant they came from inside her, from the weak, wistful part of her that kept thinking how Michael, Brandt and Lucius had all overcome the influence of the dark magic to become better men—and mates—than ever before.

But her smarter self said that Rabbit wasn't any of those guys. He was the crossover. And the one thing they knew about the crossover was that he was supposed to wield both light and dark magic. Maybe he was channeling only his Nightkeeper powers right now, but that wouldn't last. Soon, he would have to embrace the darkness again. And she didn't want to be anywhere near him when he did.

Eyes level on hers, he said, "I want you to know that

I won't hurt you, ever again. Even without the oath, you don't have to be afraid of me."

Jamming her hands in her pockets, she scowled. "I'm not afraid of you, but that doesn't mean I want to hang out, either. You said yesterday that you'd leave me alone. So how about you start now?"

But he shook his head. "During the spell, the blood-link sent my old man's power into me, but it didn't flip the switch on my magic. You're the only one who can do that, Myr . . . which is why Dez wants us to do some experiments and figure out what's going on with my magic, the sooner the better."

"It's not your magic." Temper sparking, she slipped the ash wand from her pocket and felt a faint hum enter her bloodstream. "It's mine now."

A flick of her wrist opened a nearby box of jade-tipped bullets. Even though she'd practiced endless hours with the magic, the move still sent a burst of energy and wonder through her. *Telekinesis. Gods.* Power flowed through her, thick, rich and glorious, and making her feel like she could do anything. Using her mind to direct the energy now, she plucked a single bullet from the box, sent it skimming through the air like a special effect in an unscripted movie, and then brought it to a halt, so it spun gently in midair between them.

Rabbit watched the bullet. "It doesn't have to be all or nothing, Myr. We can work together, fight together, just like we did yesterday. I'm not asking for anything more."

"Yesterday was a fluke." More, she didn't want to

fight with him, connected through the magic; it was too much like she used to picture, pretending they were both Nightkeepers, destined mates who went into battle as lovers and partners.

Back then, she'd had the man and wished for the magic. Now she had the magic and wished the man would leave her alone.

"I don't think it was a fluke . . . and if it was, we need to know that, too." He took another step toward her, so there were only a few feet—and a spinning bullet—between them. "Try it, Myr. Please. Drop the blocks and let's see if the magic comes to me again."

"Damn it." She didn't want to, but what other choice was there? The Nightkeepers needed their crossover, and she had his magic. Or at least the good-guy half of it. "Fine. Okay. Fine, I'll do it."

Gods, she hated this.

Yesterday, the connection had formed spontaneously, unbidden. Now, she concentrated on the place at the back of her skull where she'd blocked the power flow. Stomach churning, she gestured with the ash wand and relaxed the mental blockade, releasing the eager-feeling magic.

It flung toward him as if magnetized; she felt it go, felt it connect, and despair clawed at the confirmation that they were going to be joined more intimately than ever. She might have the magic inside her, but it wanted to be with him, would find a way to get to him, just as it had yesterday. A chill ran through her at the thought that it might leave her utterly. *Please gods, no.*

"Ah, shit." His face smoothed and filled as the magic entered him. "Good. That's so fucking good."

And, without warning, the rasp of his voice reminded her of him saying her name as he came deep inside her, whispering praises, reverent curses. Lust surged suddenly, twisting inside her core and making her want. *This isn't the same, damn it,* said her better sense. *This isn't about sex.*

But that was a lie, because the magic was almost always about sex. Lovemaking was a way to tap into the magic, and the magic invariably sparked arousal between lovers . . . or ex-lovers.

And, oh, shit, she was in trouble. Sweat prickled along her body at the sudden understanding that the mental connection wasn't the worst of the danger. *I can't do this.* Not if she was determined to stay away from him. The raw ache was too potent, too tempting.

They had been good together, physically. Very, very good.

Rabbit reached out with his mind and caught the bullet, then sent it spinning between them, faster and faster until it whined in the air and threw off red-gold sparks. His potent, masculine magic vibrated between them, reaching into her and making her yearn.

Oh, no, she thought as their eyes met and she saw the rising heat in him. *Hell, no.* She tried to block the arousal, but couldn't. It was coming from inside her, a sensual energy that curled in her core, pulsing and shifting, seeking an outlet. She wanted to close the distance between them, wanted to flatten her hand on his chest again and feel his heartbeat. She wanted to rub her thumb along his jaw, where last night's shave had missed some bristles. She wanted—

"No!" She yanked back a step, instinctively slamming the mental blocks into place.

The magic winked out and the bullet fell to the floor, pinged off the hardwood, and skittered under a cloth-covered chair. That was the only sound, though. That, and the two of them sucking ragged breaths as the heat leveled off, then faded.

"I'm sorry," he said, breaking the silence. "Shit. I didn't mean to—"

"Of course not. It was the magic. Sex magic." There, she had said it.

"It . . . yeah." His eyes held a sheen of power, making his expression unreadable. She didn't know what he was thinking, which put a stir of new nerves in her belly.

"This is a bad idea," she said. "There has to be another way for you to use your talents. Maybe your father . . ." She trailed off. "It won't work, will it?"

"No. You're the one I need."

I don't want to be.

"You'll be in control of the link. You can pull the plug any time you want."

"I'm not so sure about that." Not after the way the magic had reached out to him. Not after the way her body had wanted to do the same damn thing.

He looked away. "I hate putting this on you."

"It's not your fault."

"Bullshit."

That startled a laugh out of her, though it quickly threatened to head toward hysterical territory. "Well, when you put it that way." But this wasn't about blame, wasn't even about the two of them, really. And it wasn't like they had a choice. "Okay," she said finally, "we can do this. We can find a way to work the magic together." She could learn to block the sexual stuff, maybe. Probably. "But that's *it*. Nothing else is going to happen."

She wasn't sure which one of them she was trying to convince.

He nodded, though. "Agreed." He held out a hand. "Deal?"

They shook on it. "Deal." She pulled away as quickly as she could, wondering whether she was talking herself into something that would be a big mistake. But there was no running away from the end of the world, was there? And as for the sex magic . . . gods, she didn't know how she was going to stop it—or, worse, endure it. "We'll need to experiment, like Dez said. We need to figure out whether the connection has a cutoff range and how it really works . . . and we need to see whether we're stronger if we work together." She didn't want to think about the possibility, not when she used to fantasize about being his true mate and fighting at his side, their powers joined.

He searched her face. "You want to hold off until tomorrow, give it all a day to sink in?"

Yes. "No." That would be the coward's move. "I'll meet you out at the firing range in an hour." She needed breakfast, needed to pull herself together. And most of all, she needed to find a way to armor herself against the sex magic. Because she and Rabbit might've had their problems before, but sex had never been one of them. And now, with the added connection of the magic . . .

Gods. She didn't know if she could handle this, not really.

She would have to find a way, though. Somehow.

CHAPTER SIX

Chichén Itzá, Mexico

Anna could've told Dez that finding more info on the crossover was going to be far easier said than done. She and Lucius had already combed the Nightkeepers' library for references, and it wasn't exactly the kind of thing Google could help with. So they were back to the drawing board.

In a more perfect world, the Nightkeepers could've asked their *itza'at* seer to tell the future for them . . . but Anna was their only *itza'at*, and her inner eye was busted.

Sighing, she eased back on her heels and let the skull-shaped seer's pendant drop back below the neckline of her tee. The magic flowed out of her, dissipating quickly because she hadn't managed to call a vision, hadn't managed to summon any of the old, blocked-out memories that she suspected were clogging her magic. Hadn't managed to do anything, really, except waste her energy teleporting to the ancient ruin in the hopes that being there would shake something loose.

Granted, there wasn't anybody around to see her fail yet again . . . but, really, that wasn't a good sign either. Up until four or five weeks ago, the Mayan ruins of Chichén Itzá had been crawling with sightseers pretty much from dawn until after dusk. Now, though, the region was in the throes of an infectious outbreak, the area quarantined and the park off-limits.

The quarantine had allowed Anna to teleport directly to the ancient site rather than try to sneak in through the Nightkeepers' hidden tunnels. And it had given her the run of the place, so she could climb up inside the Pyramid of Kulkulkan, touch the ancient carvings of the Skull Platform, and dangle her feet over the edge of the Cenote Sagrada and feel the power that wafted up from the perfect circle of green water a hundred feet below, where the ancient Maya had made untold sacrifices to appease the gods.

Now, though, as she wiped the blood off her nearly healed palms and tucked her knife away in the tough cargo pants she had worn with a cobalt blue T-shirt that nearly matched her eyes—fieldwork garb just in case someone saw her—she was too aware of the echoing emptiness of the ruins, where it seemed not even the ghosts were stirring.

Damn it all.

Exhaling, she folded her copies of the three torn

pieces of notepaper that contained all that was left of the super-secret *itza'at* seer's ritual and tucked them into her battered knapsack. An old friend, the knapsack had been with her since grad school. It had seen her through countless digs and field studies, and nearly two decades at the university, along with marriage, divorce, magic, the Triad spell and onward, all the way to now, with the Nightkeepers running out of time.

As she slung the battered knapsack over her shoulder, she tried not to think that it had been her companion more consistently than anything else in her life.

Well, that and the crystal skull amulet. But it wasn't as if she'd had a choice when it came to the seer's skull. "Keep it with you," her mother had said right before leaving to attack the intersection, her eyes bright with what Anna had thought was excitement but had probably been tears. "I'll show you how to use it when I get back."

Only she hadn't come back—none of them had. They had all died in the tunnels below Chichén Itzá, leaving behind a dozen surviving children, one grumpy-assed old mage, a handful of *winikin*, and the mandate to save the world in 2012 but no clue how.

Instead of reaching for the amulet or begging for help—been there, done that—Anna sighed and turned to head back the way she had come.

She found herself facing a man who most definitely wasn't a ghost, but seemed like he'd appeared out of thin air without any magic.

"Oh! I'm sorry. I didn't . . ." Her words trickled off

when her instincts kicked in, telling her not to say too much to the guy, who just stood there, eyebrows hitting his shaggy hairline.

At about six foot and one eighty, he wasn't much taller than she. With brown hair, faded hazel eyes and an aquiline nose that had a bit of a once-upon-a-time-broken left-hand crook to it, he looked reassuringly forty-something and human. His bush pants and scarred boots were much like her own, and his open-throated shirt had a medical logo embroidered on the pocket.

"You shouldn't be here." His voice was smooth and mellow, with the faintest hint of an accent—British? Australian? She couldn't quite place it, but it tagged him as nonlocal, while the logo said he was part of the outbreak response. Which made him official, and therefore someone she needed to handle carefully.

She was tempted to say she was a Red Cross volunteer or something, and use the opportunity to pump him for info on the progress—if any—the humans were making against the *xombi* virus. Gods knew the Nightkeepers hadn't been able to make a dent against this wave of the cursed disease, which was part magic, part biochemical and wholly vile. They had tried, but there had been too many hotspots popping up all at once, warning that the barrier was on the verge of collapse, the demons amassing to pounce. The *Banol Kax* had sent their hellspawn virus to create a chaos that would be ripe for their plucking, and damned if it wasn't working.

Dez had pulled the magi off the virus and made a few calls, tipping off the CDC to the disease and what little the humans could do to manage it—which amounted to quarantining the hot zones and restraining the infected people so they couldn't pass the soul-stealing disease, rabieslike, by biting others.

Since then, the Nightkeepers' info on the virus had been limited to news crawls, blogs of varying degrees of hysteria, and the occasional stealth drop-in, and Anna had heard the king muttering just the other day about needing some on-the-ground intel. But something about this guy warned that she didn't dare try pretending to be part of the volunteer force and risk getting caught in the lie. Better to go with the truth.

Or part of it, anyway.

"I snuck in," she admitted. "I'm a Mayan studies—"

"Well, shit. You're one of *them*." His eyes hardened and he raked her head to toe with a withering look. "Those big blues aren't going to get you anywhere with the militia, lady. You should get the hell out of here while you still can."

Australian, she thought. A pissed-off Aussie, and one who wasn't making much sense. "Wait. What?"

"They're shooting looters on sight, you know."

"I'm not—"

"Seriously, what the hell? These people are being slammed with a disease that wipes their minds and turns them into vicious, greedy shells that can't live off anything other than human flesh. So we restrain them, tie them, gag them, whatever it takes to keep them from chewing on us, each other, even themselves while we try everything we can think of to cure them. Only it doesn't work, so they starve to death . . . and in those last few seconds before they die, you can see their souls come back into their eyes. And they die screaming, not because of the fear or the pain, but because they suddenly realize what they've become."

Stomach knotting—she had seen that exact look, time and again, right after she struck the fatal blow—she held up a hand. "Look, I—"

He took a step toward her, seeming to loom, though they weren't far off in height. "And you people sneak in as slick as you please, figuring this is your chance to do some digging without bothering with permits, or maybe pop the locks on some of the tunnels and pull down a carving or two." He made a disgusted noise. "You're just as bad as the docs who come down here just to get data for some paper they're planning on jamming through the review process, not giving a shit about the actual patients they're supposed to be treating."

She agreed wholeheartedly. Or at least she would if she could get a word in edgewise. "If you'd—"

"Maybe you're not even here to steal. Maybe you're doing legit research and think that because you've got a grant application or a paper or whatever due, it shouldn't matter that the site is on lockdown, the whole region quarantined. Hell, if you can bribe your way in, you'll have the whole place to yourself—no paperwork, no bullshit. What could be better than . . . shit.

This is ridiculous." He finally ground to a halt, glaring at her while one hand drifted to his belt, making her wonder if he had a pistol tucked behind him, if he was pissed enough to use it on her.

Hopefully not. She could shield herself, yes, or 'port away. Or even drop him where he stood with a sleep spell. She didn't want to, though.

So she stayed put, heart drumming lightly against her ribs, though she kept her voice steady as she said, "Is it my turn yet?" At his grudging nod, she continued, "Look, I swear on the deity or family member of your choice that I'm not a looter. Hell, I've turned in a dozen or more tomb robbers who've tried to sell me antiquities over the years. Hate 'em."

He narrowed his eyes. "For real?"

"I collect really bad fakes, but not the legit stuff. Never, ever." She paused, exhaling when she saw that he might not have softened, but at least he was listening. "The only thing I'm guilty of is sneaking through the quarantine to get some one-on-one time with the carvings. And I get why that probably seems really, really tacky to you, but it's not like that." She started to hold out her hands in a gesture of innocence, then remembered there was probably blood on them. She clasped them together instead, and said, "We're on the same team here, Doc. I'm just trying to help."

"How so?" He didn't look convinced, but he was staying put, even easing back a little, putting distance between them and decreasing the loom factor.

"When I was here a few years ago doing fieldwork,

I noticed a badly degraded stone panel inside one of the temples. I thought I saw something on it about a strange disease, a plague that swept through the kingdoms and turned brother against brother and father against son. At the time I thought it was a metaphor for a civil war or something, but when the outbreak started"—she shrugged—"I figured it was worth checking out."

One eyebrow went up and his accent thickened slightly with disbelief. "So you got across the border somehow even though they've closed it to tourists, made it through the quarantine and onto the site here, to . . . what, see if this carving mentioned a cure?"

"Is that any dumber than electroshock therapy or partial drowning, trying to get the infected people to 'snap out of it'?" Which, hadn't been part of the official international response, but rumors said that both of those things—and worse—had been tried in the highland villages.

Granted, the near-drowning thing hadn't been the worst idea, as it came straight from the ancient Nightkeepers' practices. She didn't mention that part, though, because she wanted to come off as a dedicated, potentially foolhardy Mayanist, not a doomsday-nut wack-job.

He tilted his head, considering. "You can really read the hieroglyphs?"

"I've spent my whole life studying them." Which was true. She had bolted for college without looking back, swearing she was going to make herself into something far more normal than she'd ever had a chance to be—because normal was safe, normal didn't wake up in the middle of the night hearing screams and seeing flames and blood. But no matter how hard she had tried to get away from the Mayan stuff she had been raised on, it was no use. That was where her talents and interest lay, what her soul kept bringing her back to. So she had studied the culture and the glyphs, and made herself as normal as she could. For a while, anyway.

"Prove it." He waved around them. "Translate something. And no bullshit, because I'll know if you're lying."

That had to be a bluff, of course, but she nodded anyway, because if she wanted to get information out of him, he was going to have to trust her, at least a little.

They were standing in an open courtyard enclosed by lines of rubble where walls had once been. There, generations of ancient Mayan kings had erected row after row of stelae—stone pillars carved with hieroglyphs that recorded major events. Births, deaths, marriages, wars, all the news that had been fit to chisel was there.

Nearest them were three stelae; two were crumbled and fallen, but one still stood, tall and pale, its white limestone worn from wind and blackened with acid rain. The glyphs seemed legible enough, though, so she headed for it, aware of him trailing too close, like he thought she might make a break for it.

She wouldn't, of course, not unless things turned

hairy. But as she got up close and personal, she hesitated, recognizing the stelae too late and wondering if this was the gods at work or just a coincidence.

"Oh," she breathed, tracing her fingertips along a glyph panel that wasn't like any of the others. For one, it was in better shape, preserved by the remnants of a spell that sent shimmering tingles up her arm. And for another, it told a story . . . and gave a warning. One that her father had ignored.

She blew out a shaky breath. *What has happened before will happen again . . .*

"What's the matter?"

"It's just . . ." She shook her head. "Never mind."

"Can't you translate it?"

"That won't be a problem." In fact, she knew the story by heart, though she hadn't consciously thought of it in nearly three decades. Not since her father's advisers had tried to use it to talk him out of his plan to attack the demons on their own turf, at the intersection beneath Chichén Itzá.

"That's enough!" he thundered, and shook off her mother's restraining hand. "The next person who quotes the writs or an old legend at me better have something new to add to the discussion, because by the gods I'm getting sick of repeating myself." He glared around the royal suite, eyes skipping past where Anna had shrunk back in the hallway, out of sight.

That was all she got, just a flash, there and gone in an instant. But it was a real memory, one that imprinted itself on all of her senses, so much so that for a moment she could hear the rumble of her father's voice, feel the nap of the hallway runner beneath her Reeboks and smell the faintest hint of lemon furniture polish.

But when she blinked she found herself in the here and now, with her parents long gone, her boots planted on limestone dust, and the doctor regarding her with a glint of challenge in eyes that, up close, were a mix of green and brown rather than real hazel.

It was ironic, really, that this man, this *human*, would be the one to shake loose a memory of those last few days when all her spells had failed. Not that the memory in question would do a damn thing to help her summon the visions, but still.

Letting out a long, slow breath that didn't ease the tightness in her chest, she said, "Okay, here goes. You see this one?" She touched a glyph that showed a peccary with curlicue tusks beside the line-and-dot notation for a number. "It refers to King Ten-Boar. This one means there was a war or a fight, but this symbol over it means it had gone on for a very long time. And this one . . ."

Realizing that he probably didn't care about the exact translation of each glyph and phoneme—and that she was stalling—she shrugged. "Basically, it says that King Ten-Boar had a dream he claimed the gods had sent him, telling him how he could defeat his enemies once and for all. His advisers tried to talk him out of it, but he wouldn't budge. Instead, he ordered his entire army to march, leaving the women and children behind to guard the city." Her voice went flat, her insides hollow. "The dream was a lie, or maybe just wishful thinking. Either way, Ten-Boar's enemies ambushed him, slaughtered his troops and then marched on the city and imprisoned everyone there. Some they used as sacrifices, others as slaves."

She had dragged her fingertips along the glyphs as she'd told the story, not as it was written—in an ancient, stilted style—but as she had heard it too many times in the days leading up to the massacre. Now, her fingers rested on the last glyph in the string. Worn almost indecipherable, she knew what it was without squinting, as her fingers found the familiar sockets and gaping mouth.

It was the screaming skull, the symbol for the end-time war. A warning to those who, a thousand years later, would do their damnedest to hold the barrier when the zero date came.

What are you trying to tell me? Something? Nothing? What?

There was no answer from the gods, though.

He was watching her intently. "It bothers you. It happened centuries ago, but it still bothers you to put yourself in their places and think of what it must've been like."

She shifted, glancing toward where part of the tent city was just visible beyond the ruins, fenced off and plastered with KEEP OUT signs in three languages, along with biohazard symbols and a spray-painted skull and crossbones. "It bothers me to see what's happening to their descendants right now, and to know that none of us are safe."

"So you snuck down here, thinking maybe you could help." The suspicion had leached from his expression.

She shrugged. "It seemed worth a shot."

"Any luck?"

"No. But I'm not giving up." She didn't dare, with the countdown ticking toward its end.

"You're staying in the area?"

"Pretty close," she said, deliberately vague. "I'll keep out of the hot zone, though." More or less. Then, remembering her plan to gather intel, she said, "What's it like in there?"

He grimaced. "Brutal. Frustrating. Heartbreaking." Seeming to catch himself wanting to say more, he drew back and stuck his hands in his pockets as he looked out over the rows of crumbling stelae. "We can't even figure out how the disease really works. Part of it acts like a normal virus, like the flu bug or whatever. Or maybe rabies is a better comparison, since it's transmitted through saliva bites, rapes, that sort of thing." He shot her an uncomfortable look. "Sorry."

"Don't be." Though it was nice to be treated like a woman rather than a warrior for a change. Which made her, just for a second, wonder how he saw her. With her hair pulled back in a practical ponytail, zero makeup and field clothes that had seen better days—

Doesn't matter. Get your intel and get out. She didn't

have time to pretend she was normal, didn't even really have the time she had taken for this trip.

But the doc stayed silent, still looking off at the middle distance, where the Pyramid of Kulkulkan rose with its iconic silhouette. That was why he had come out here, she realized—he'd needed to get away from the tent city, away from the frustration of not being able to find a cure.

You can't cure it, she could have told him. *All you can do is try to contain it.* The humans were doing a good job of slowing the spread . . . which was helpful, because the fewer *xombis* there were, the weaker the demons' reinforcements would be on the final day. And the better the humans' chances for survival.

The Nightkeepers and *winikin* would bear the brunt of the end-time war, but there would likely be human casualties, too. Maybe lots of them. Always before, Anna had told herself that even huge losses would be acceptable so long as mankind continued on. Now, though, she thought of the people she'd met over the years in what had become the hot zone, everyone from villagers in thatch huts to executives in high-rise penthouses, all vulnerable now. Some were probably already dead, others infected and dying.

And standing against the demons' vile disease were men like this one—tough and determined. And human.

The doc shrugged and looked back at her, his expression tinged with grief and worry. "To be honest we're running out of ideas. If your research turns up anything at all . . . well, I'd like to hear about it."

"You will." And that was a promise. More, she would put Lucius and Natalie on it, and see what they could turn up in the archives. Granted, they'd been through it all before, trying to get ahead of the first outbreak, far up in the Mayan highlands. But maybe there was something else, some subtle hint that could help the humans fight the *zombi* virus.

This time when he reached behind his back, she didn't tense up. He came up with a battered wallet of leather-edged nylon, and from there produced a business card that he held out. "Call me and we'll meet someplace safe."

It shouldn't have felt like a big deal to take the card. She gave it a glance. "Well, then, Doctor Curtis."

"David. Or Dave." He paused expectantly.

"Anna Catori." She rattled off her phone number, then opened her free hand to show that it was empty. "Sorry, didn't bring a card."

His eyes locked on her palm, where the sacrificial cut had healed to its usual scar, but blood had dried to rusty streaks. "What'd you do there?"

He reached out and caught her wrist before she could yank it back. And he stilled at the sight of her forearm—not the black glyph-marks of her bloodline and magic, which he would no doubt think were tattoos, but the raised white crisscrosses below.

"I nicked myself on a rock," she said, meeting his

eyes and daring him to mention the scars. "It's nothing." Nothing she wanted to talk about. Nothing he could help with. "Just a scratch."

His eyes searched hers, but he said only, "You're sure?"

"Positive."

He hesitated a long moment, then exhaled. "Well, call me if you find something. And be careful, will you? If the militia doesn't shoot at you, then the real looters will."

She didn't tell him she could take care of herself, or that they wouldn't see her unless she allowed it. She just nodded. "I will." But as she reclaimed her hand, she had a strong feeling that they had just agreed to far more than a phone call.

He watched her go, no doubt trying to figure out how much of what she'd told him was a lie—which was all of it and none of it, really. Dez would be pleased. She hadn't gotten anything out of Doctor Dave that they didn't already know, but the possibility was there, and he was someone they could leak suggestions to, if anything came up.

More, she had a feeling that meeting him had been important. Maybe it hadn't been gods-destined, but she had needed the reminder that the outbreak was affecting living, breathing people. Mothers, fathers, children, loved ones . . .

"Hell," she muttered under her breath as she headed down the raised stone *sacbe* that led toward the cenote, where she could use the small temple to shield her from view while she 'ported back to Skywatch.

Her first stop was going to be the royal suite, to report back to Dez . . . but her second was going to be the library. She might not be able to summon the visions, but she was a researcher, a translator, and damn good at what she did. There had to be something more the humans could do to fight the *xombi* virus. And she was going to find it.

CHAPTER SEVEN

December 10
Eleven days until the zero date
Skywatch

In the week and a half following Rabbit's return, Myrinne met with him two, sometimes three times a day, first to figure out the limits of the shared magic, and then to train with him. Because, like it or not, she was the only one who could trigger his powers. There was no sign of his darker side . . . but the sex magic remained a problem. She had learned how to throttle it down, muting the raw lust with meditation, crystals and chants, but the urges remained. It was as if her body cared only that he had been her lover and not why that couldn't happen anymore.

He hadn't been her first—there had been plenty of guys in the Quarter who'd been up for a no-harm-no-foul encounter, and her body had been one of the few things she had controlled back then. Rabbit had been the first who mattered, though . . . and he had been the first to totally consume her world, the first to break her heart. She kept that firmly in her mind as they trained, and did her damnedest not to touch him. The linked magic was bad enough. Physical contact was worse. And when it all got to be too much, she retreated to her quarters and hit the Internet, not to Web surf, but to help search for more information on the *xombi* virus and the crossover's magic.

As the days passed, finding anything new on the crossover started to seem like an impossible quest . . . until she hit the jackpot.

Okay, it was a small jackpot, but still. It was something.

"No shit." She stared at the picture on the page in front of her. It was a purple painting with too many five-pointed stars, but she was willing to bet that it was a reference to the crossover. Courtesy of a kid's book she'd ordered from Amazon's Witchcraft and Spirituality department, no less. Go figure.

The picture didn't look like Rabbit—more like Gandalf with a touch of Martha Stewart—but the figure was clearly straddling the line between day and night, with one foot in the darkness and the other in the light. More, he was wreathed in fire, and the old doomsday standbys—bell, book and candle—were hanging suspended in front of him. Pyrokinesis, telekinesis and a text that talked about a man who was supposed to "build a bridge between the darkness and light on the day of final reckoning"?

Yeah, that was the crossover, all right, smack dab in the middle of a Wiccan-influenced children's story about something called the Gatekeeper's Doomsday. She didn't know whether the story had come from the Nightkeepers and morphed from there, or if it had another, more human origin. Either way, score one for her.

The buzz of discovery didn't last long, though. Not once she read the rest of the text beside the picture.

The Crossing Guard stands at the bridge between day and night. A lone warrior, he can free the armies of the dead when the world rests on the brink of war.

"A lone warrior," she said aloud, chest going hollow. "Damn it. Just . . . damn it."

A few of the other references had hinted that the crossover was supposed to go into the war alone, without a fighting partner at his side. Worse, Lucius had come up with a spell he thought would shift her magic back to Rabbit. So far, Dez hadn't ordered them to make the transfer, but she had a feeling that one more reference—like this one—would tip the scales.

Lose it, said a small voice inside her, and it was tempting. She couldn't, though; she just couldn't. So instead she took the book to the royal wing, holding it against her chest as she knocked on the carved doors leading to Dez and Reese's quarters.

"It's open," he called.

She found the king in the main sitting area, going

over something on his laptop. Holding out the book, she flipped to the right page, and said, "You're going to want to read this."

He took it, skimmed it, and grimaced. "A lone warrior. Damn it."

"That's pretty much what I said." She jammed her hands in her pockets and hunched her shoulders. "I'll do it, though. It's time." Her voice didn't shake, didn't do anything to betray how much she hated the idea of losing the magic.

Dez reached out and squeezed her shoulder in a rare show of sympathy. "I'm truly sorry. And to be honest, I hope the spell doesn't work, because you make a hell of a mage . . . But if it does work, remember that you're one of us, Myrinne. Whether you're kicking ass with magic or a machine gun, I'd want you on my side any damn day, even if it's the last day. Especially if it's the last day."

"Thanks. That matters." She didn't let him see just how much it mattered. "But before you show me too much more love, I need to ask you for a couple of favors."

"Such as?"

"No offense, but I'm done with public performances. I want this to be just me and Rabbit."

He hesitated, then tipped his head in acknowledgement. "I can't say I blame you. And it's not like you can't handle yourself with him. You've made that plenty clear since he got back."

Which just went to show that she was a better actress than she thought. But all she said was, "Thanks." Then, taking a deep breath, she added in a rush, "Next favor . . . I want to do it in the *winikin's* cave."

The cave, which was painted with the strange, ghostly animals that the *winikin* could call from beyond the barrier, was where she had taken Rabbit's prized stone eccentrics, hoping to purify them of whatever evil spells they were casting on him. Instead, he had followed her, held a knife to her throat, and accused her of being the enemy.

She hadn't set foot near the cave since that day, hadn't ever planned to . . . but her gut said that if she wanted to move forward, she first had to go back.

Dez scowled. "That's outside the blood-ward."

"I don't like it, either, but you have to admit that it makes sense. What has happened before, and all that." She swallowed. "I need to bring this full circle, Dez."

More, she had to do whatever the Nightkeepers needed her to do, at least for the next week and a half. And after that . . . hell, she didn't know. Whenever she tried to picture her life after the twenty-first of December, all she got was a blank screen and some static, like her inner Cablevision was on the fritz. She didn't have a clue what she was going to do in the aftermath.

The others had their plans—Patience and Brandt were itching to reunite with their twins, and would probably move to New England, where Jox and Hannah—the boys' *winikin* and current guardians—would reopen the garden center that had long been Jox's dream. VR game designer Nate and fashion-forward Alexis would undoubtedly go somewhere and be creative, successful and disgustingly happy; Jade and Lucius would probably fund an esoteric Mayan dig somewhere and eat weird food; Strike and Leah would get into law enforcement or private security and have a half dozen kids; and Myrinne . . . well, she didn't have a clue what she was going to do. She didn't have a mate, didn't have any real skills or hobbies, didn't have much going for her beyond the magic, and soon she might not even have that.

And she fucking refused to open up a tea shop, sell crappy crystals and illegal voodoo concoctions, pick pockets, and pass off cold reads as fortune-telling. Even if that was all she was really trained to do in the outside world.

"I don't like it," Dez grumbled.

"Me either," she said, then realized he was talking about the cave. Regrouping, she added, "But if we're going to try this, we need to give it the best chance of succeeding." *Duty first*, she thought, *blah, blah, blah and yadda-yadda*. It was the truth, though. Now more than ever, their priorities needed to be to the war, the gods, their leader, and from there on down, with personal wants way at the bottom of the list.

Thus, the cave.

She and Dez went back and forth for a few more minutes, but in the end he agreed to her plan with a few choice expletives and a worried sigh that touched her more than it probably should have, warning her that her emotions were way too close to the surface right now, and she needed to find a way to dial them down before she met with Rabbit.

"Do you want to tell him, or should I?" Dez asked.

"Can you take care of it?"

"Consider it done." Hell glanced down at the book, then closed it and handed it back to her with a scowl of *well, hell.* "Looking at this from an earth-magic angle was good thinking, by the way. Very good thinking. In fact, I'm going to have Lucius and the rest of the brain trust do a broader search along these lines and see what else they can come up with. Okay with you if they give a shout-out with any questions?"

"Of course." The vindication helped some.

The Witch's spells might've been the bastard child of voodoo, devil worship and ancient Aztec rituals, but she'd kept a few Wiccan texts on the shelves for the sake of appearances. Myr had memorized the incantations and practiced them in secret, hiding her small crystals and hoarded scents. And now, at Skywatch, the earth magic was hers alone. More, there was no blood or violence, no sacrificing or swearing away bits of her soul; there was only the peace of incense, the solidity of crystal, the supple strength of wood and a sense of connecting to something far bigger than herself that welcomed her, supported her, and asked nothing in return.

It appealed to the person she sometimes thought she would've been if she hadn't wound up with the Witch. Heck, it still appealed to the person she was, despite everything.

So use it, she told herself, and felt the fear recede a

little. Who knew—maybe she could find other pieces of real magic in the books she'd bought. Maybe she wouldn't be giving all her powers to Rabbit.

Still, though, dread pinched.

"When do you want to do it?" Dez asked.

She wanted to close her eyes and block out the sympathy in his. It would still be in his voice, though, and in the air between them. "Let's get it over with. Say, an hour? Tell him I'll meet him at the cave."

The king hesitated, looking like he wanted to say a whole bunch of things, but in the end settled for, "Wear your armband, park as close to the entrance as you can, and keep your panic button primed." The newer Jeeps were fitted with transponders that could pick up her signal and bounce it to Skywatch, hopefully overcoming the reception problems that had been getting worse and worse as the zero date approached and the barrier flux increased.

"Will do. And Dez?"

"Yeah?"

"Thanks for always treating me like I've got a right to an opinion."

Rather than the platitudes she would've gotten from most of the others—the ones who'd been raised by their *winikin* and had always been given choices—he nodded. "Street smarts recognize street smarts, Myrinne, and ambition recognizes ambition. You've got more than your share of both, and I'm the last guy who's going to ding you for that."

Her spine straightened. "Is that a warning?"

"Nope. I'm not that subtle—if I thought you were heading for trouble, I'd tell you straight out. It was an observation, nothing more."

But as she left the royal suite, she was pretty darned sure Dez was far more subtle than he let on. In his own way he was as much of a manipulator as the Witch had been, though with far better intentions. And right now, those intentions involved protecting the Nightkeepers' agenda—which meant her giving up the magic to Rabbit.

"I'm doing it, aren't I?" she muttered as she headed down the hall. But that didn't stop her from feeling the pressure of being involved in something so much bigger than herself. It dogged her as she stalked out of the royal wing and across the main kitchen, and had her turning away from her suite.

Her rooms were too quiet, too empty and at the same time too hemmed in, sparking a sense of suffocation that chased her out a side door. There, a stone-lined path flanked the garage, but she didn't want to snag a Jeep and keep on driving today. Instead, she headed for the magic-imbued cacao grove beyond the *winikin*'s hall, where the air was rainforest humid, the ground soft and the trees green and fragrant.

She slipped into the grove and picked her way to the open space at its center. There, she sat cross-legged, with her hands open on her folded knees. And—for a little while, at least—she found peace in the whirring sound the leaves made in the faint breeze, and the feeling of the earth surrounding her.

"I'm trying to get it right," she said aloud. "I'm doing my best." Deep down inside, though, she wondered whether that was the truth. Because when she came down to it, she didn't want to give back the magic, not one bit.

It wasn't fucking fair.

At the appointed time, Rabbit sat outside the *winikin*'s cave for a good five minutes before he managed to make himself get out of the damn Jeep. He didn't want to be here. More, he wished he could forget the way he'd acted the last time he'd been at the cave, wished he didn't see the parallels. And he wished to hell his knuckles weren't throbbing like a bitch from punching his damned fridge when he got Dez's message.

It was a dumb fucking idea to go around punching appliances, no matter how pissed off he was. More, he couldn't let himself get pissed off, not like that. For a few minutes, he'd felt like the guy he used to be, the one who'd lashed out without thinking, doing major damage. He needed to be better than that, damn it. He needed to control the part of him that used to take over and make him do dumb things—not the stripped-down creature he'd become while imprisoned, but the angry, unloved kid who wanted to set the world on fire and watch it burn.

Or maybe the two were flip sides of the same anger.

"Pull your shit together," he muttered. He owed Myr his absolute best self, even today. Especially today.

He hated that it had come to this, hated that she was

going to be the one making the sacrifice when she deserved the magic a hell of a lot more than he did. He hated it . . . and he respected the hell out of her for making the call. She would be dreading the mind-meld that the spell required, he knew, and was determined to make it as easy as he could for her, just as he'd done his damnedest to quell the raw gut punch of lust that had nailed him every time he had gotten near her over the past week and a half.

It was his problem that he couldn't be satisfied with what he'd gotten back already, his problem that he wanted more, wanted *her*, with a churning desire that was equal parts magic, lust, history and fascination with the stronger, sleeker, glossier woman she'd become . . . and one hundred percent Not Happening.

It was also past time for him to get his ass down there. Bad enough he was supposed to take her magic, worse to make her wait on him.

He had parked on the bank of the wide wash, where flash floods created a huge river and filled the cave when the rains came. It was dry now, so Myr had parked with her Jeep's nose stuck into the cave mouth, no doubt partly so it could act as a transponder, partly so the trick door—a huge stone slab that was geared to uncertain magic—couldn't slide into place and trap them inside.

As he got out of his vehicle and headed down there, kicking up pebbles and sand with his worn boots, he remembered all too well the fury that had carried him into the cave the last time, the anger and betrayal that had blasted through him when he'd seen her there with his eccentrics. Phee's lies had been whispering in his head, stroking the rage and chaos inside him until he'd let it loose.

Not again. Never again.

Taking a deep breath, he brushed past her Jeep and stepped into the darkness. It took a moment for his eyes to adjust, for the cave to come clear around him as a circular space with a sandy floor and ancient paintings of animals overhead. In the center, near a plain, unadorned stone altar, Myrinne sat cross-legged in front of a small fire that she'd laid in a circle of stones.

Heat seared low in his gut and punched beneath his heart, but he weathered the blows like he'd endured the '*zotz*'s lash, by telling himself he was getting what he damn well deserved. More, he was trying to give her what *she* deserved—the respect of a fighting equal and the room to do what she needed to do, even when it wasn't what he wanted.

The air carried hints of ginger, patchouli and vanilla, making him think of the candles she used to light in her college dorm room, back when things had been so much easier than they were now, though they'd both thought them complicated as hell. It was only a couple of years ago, but it felt like a fucking lifetime. Since then, he'd been to hell and back; he'd destroyed villages, led battles and killed *xombis*; he'd aged a decade in a year; he'd lost one king and gained another. And, though he wouldn't have believed it possible back then, he'd lost Myrinne.

She looked up at him now, eyes dark and determined, and if there was an answering flare of heat deep within them, it was quickly gone.

Ah, baby. He wanted to tell her that she could trust him, that he wouldn't hurt her ever again. And yet he didn't dare make any promises when his knuckles were bruised with temper and the end of the world lay ahead of them. So he didn't say a damn thing. Instead, he crossed to her, boots thudding hollowly on the dried mud.

She watched him approach, expression unreadable. The small fire darkened, though, turning more green than orange, and the smoke thickened and turned bitter, coating the back of his throat.

He drew breath to speak, but she forestalled him with: "How about we skip the conversation and go right to the Vulcan mind-meld." It wasn't a question.

Exhaling, he said, "Yeah, sure. If that's what you want." He told himself to leave it at that. Couldn't. "Shit, Myr, I—"

"Don't. Let's just get this over with." She pointed to the opposite side of the fire. "Sit."

He sat, assuming a cross-legged pose that mirrored hers. "You've got the spell?"

"Yeah. Here." She handed him an index card with the Hooked on Phonics version of the ancient Mayan incantation. "I'll unblock your magic and we'll both jack in. After that, we say the spell, and . . . well . . ." She looked away.

Before, she had forbidden him from mind-bending her, going so far as to have him put mental blocks in there and teach her how to use them to keep him out. And she had, right up until the moment when she'd realized he had lost himself to Phee's lies. Then, to save herself, she had let him in and showed him that she wasn't working for the demons . . . *he* was. He hated that he'd forced her to that point, hated that he'd hurt her. And he hated that he was about to do it again.

He waited until she looked at him, until their eyes met and held over the fire. "Seriously, Myr. I'm sorry about this."

Anger flared in the depths of her eyes. "Yet here you are."

"King's orders."

"Right. Because you've never gone against orders before."

"Hello, Boar Oath." Though he hadn't really bumped up against it yet, wasn't sure what would happen when he did. For the moment, he wasn't having trouble following his old man's orders.

The look she shot him said she knew it. "You want this. If you didn't, you wouldn't be here."

"Myr . . ." He didn't want to go there, didn't want to have this fight. Her glare said she wasn't backing down, though, so he said, "I agreed to this because we need to figure out the crossover's powers. Not because I want to take the magic away from you."

Her eyes narrowed. "And?"

She knew him too damn well. "Fine. I'm also doing this because when the barrier comes down, the *Banol Kax* are going to be gunning for the crossover. And I don't want you standing next to me when that happens." Not when he wasn't sure he'd be able to shield her and still do whatever it was the gods needed him to do.

Her expression flattened. "I don't want you protecting me."

Quelle surprise. Because if he'd learned anything over the past week and a half, it was that she didn't want anything from him anymore. "Deal with it. This is one of the few things I can do to protect you, whether you want it or not. I just wish to hell we could break the connection without you losing your magic." He knew better than to think she would wait tamely behind the lines—she'd be going into battle with or without the magic. Given that, he'd far rather have her fully armed. Unfortunately, the spell Lucius had found was very specific—it would return the magic to its rightful owner.

"You . . . damn it." She looked around, but he wasn't sure if she was seeing the cave or fighting back tears.

"Myr . . ." He reached out to her.

"Don't." She held up a hand. "Just don't, okay? Like I said, it's probably better if we go right to the spell. It's not like us talking about it is going to change anything." She paused, lifting her little wand. "Ready?"

No. "Yeah."

And, as they had practiced a hundred times over the

past ten days, she unblocked the magic, letting it flow from her into him.

Power washed through his head and heart like an old, familiar friend. Suddenly, he was himself again; the cold places were warm, the empty places filling as his magic sizzled through his veins, back where it belonged. The flames changed, gaining red along with the green as his talents came online, his mind-bender's magic vibrating against hers like it knew what they were about to do.

"Breathe in the smoke and cast the spell," she said. But then, echoing along their shared magic, he heard her whisper, *I don't blame you for any of this.*

Ah, damn it, he thought, as a one-two punch thudded beneath his heart. He wanted to call it off, wanted to hold her, tell her everything was going to be okay. That would be a lie, though, because no matter what happened next, things were going to be anything but okay. And this was one of the best chances he was going to have to protect her, or at least get her out of the direct line of fire when the *Banol Kax* came for him. So he leaned in, opened himself to the mind-bending magic, and breathed in smoke that was laden with the scents of patchouli, vanilla and ginger. And, as the world spun around him, going faster with each rev, he said the short spell, his words echoing a nanosecond behind hers.

Magic flared between them, lacing the air with sparks of red and gold. His perceptions went swimmy and indistinct and then lurched, and it suddenly felt as if the universe was moving past him while he sat still, more like a teleportation spell than mind-bending. He braced himself to enter her thoughts, but he didn't.

Instead, he dropped into the mind of a long-dead king.

CHAPTER EIGHT

One second, Myr was diving into the mind-meld . . . and in the next, she found herself in the middle of someone else's thoughts. But she wasn't in Rabbit's head, and she wasn't in the *winikin's* cave anymore. Instead, she was wearing full battle gear and seeing out through the eyes of a Nightkeeper queen.

And oh, holy shit, this wasn't what the spell was supposed to do.

Summer Solstice, 1984
The tunnels beneath Chichén Itzá

"Door," King Scarred-Jaguar snapped over his shoulder, sending his adviser, Two-Hawk, out of the circular chamber to guard the hallway and keep the stone slab from closing. The plan was for the king and Asia to form a blood-link and open the intersection, as the dreams had said. After that, the

others would join in for the spell that they hoped would seal the barrier for good. If they succeeded, there would be no more countdown, no end-time war.

Please gods, *Asia thought, not even sure they would be able to manage the blood-link. Not the way things were between them right now.*

The king watched his adviser leave, then glanced sharply at her. "At least he doesn't think his fealty oath only counts when it's convenient."

"There was nothing convenient about it." *Gods, how she wished she could go back a half hour, to when they had arrived at the site and, seeing how damn worried he looked, she had told him what she had done to protect their children, thinking it would reassure him. Instead, he had taken it as a slap, a lack of faith.*

"Well it wasn't a shining example of loyalty, either," *he growled.*

With the huge chac-mool *altar behind him and a row of screaming skulls lining the ceiling of the chamber above him, he was surrounded by symbols of the war he was determined to prevent. He looked very much a Nightkeeper, very much like a king and the man she loved with all her heart. But he also looked very, very pissed.*

Then again, so was she.

She moved between him and the altar, so he had to look at her. "We're on the same side, damn it."

His jaw locked with the familiar jaguar stubbornness, which had been magnified to near deadly proportions over the past few weeks as he'd become obsessed with following the dreams the gods had sent him. "Then stop trying to undermine me."

"I'm here, aren't I? And I've been right behind you every step of the way. I believe in you, Jag," she said, using the nickname that was hers alone. "But I couldn't let Strike and Anna . . ." She trailed off when he stiffened, eyes going cold.

More, she was all too aware of the minutes passing, the solstice approaching, time running out. She had distracted him—both of them—with her ill-timed confession. Which wasn't the work of a queen or a warrior. Not when they had work to do, a prophecy to fulfill.

"We need to get started," he said, almost as if he'd read her mind. Except he couldn't have caught her thoughts, even through the mated bond. Not with them so out of synch.

Exhaling, she stepped aside and turned to face the altar. Thy wills be done, she thought, and offered him her bloodied hand. "You're right," she said softly, trying to channel the warrior's calm that kept eluding her. "Let's do this."

She had made her choice—she was there, with him. They all were, nearly a thousand Nightkeepers and three times that many winikin, filling the tunnels and spilling out into the ancient courtyards, ready to add to the uplink and block the Banol Kax from the earth, once and for all.

Gods willing.

He looked at her for a three-count, as if measuring her sincerity. Then he nodded and took her hand. "Ready?" His voice was tough and tight, that of her king, not her husband.

No. "Yes." She opened herself to him, added her magic to his, and put her faith in him, in his dreams and his plan.

"Pasaj och," he intoned, his voice resonating through their joined magic. The connection formed, jacking him into the solstice-thinned barrier and bringing her along through *the uplink. Power flared through them, ramping quickly from a hum to a jaw-aching buzz. But it didn't stop there, didn't level off the way it always had before. Instead, it kept going, flooding her and amping higher and higher.*

They hadn't yet opened the intersection, yet already there was more energy here than she'd ever wielded before. Suddenly, the magic was the stuff of legends, the kind of power their ancestors had used to drive the Banol Kax *from the earth plane and create the barrier.*

Wonder seared through her, because the magic had to mean that it was real. It was all real—the dreams, the gods' promises, the potential to avert the war—all of it.

Gods. Tears prickled behind her closed lids, and one hot drop slipped down her cheek.

"Asia." Jag's energy was suddenly different, stronger and more vibrant than it had been, not just since her confession, but for days now, weeks. Heat thrummed through their blood-link, sharp and prickly with desire, but tempered with a deeper, softer warmth that wrapped around her, feeling like his arms. Feeling like love. His voice caught as he said, "Open your eyes. Please."

She didn't want to lose the moment, didn't want to see the coldness in him. But when she looked up at him, she saw the man she'd been missing. "Oh, Jag."

The magic coiled around them, sparking the air red and gold as he moved in and locked his lips to hers.

And his kiss . . . ahh, his kiss.

I love you. *His voice spoke through their mated bond, which was strong and true once more.*

The knots of fear and grief loosened as she leaned into him, feeling the rise of their own special mated magic. I love you, too, she sent back. I'm sorry I told you. I was trying to help.

I know, and you *did* help, and that scared me, because it means I'm not as sure as I need to be that this is going to work.

Maybe—probably—that should have worried her. Instead, it put them back on the same team, shoulder to shoulder. The fear wasn't gone, but they were together. And that gave her the strength to break the kiss and look up at him. "I love you. What's more, I believe in you." She linked their fingers together. "I love you for the life we've had together and the children we've created. And I love you for being willing to make whatever sacrifice is necessary so they can live their lives without a war hanging over them."

His eyes were moist. "Asia . . ."

"It's okay. Really. I'm proud to stand beside you right now. That's what's important, in the end."

"This isn't the end for us," he said with new determination. "I won't let it be. We're going to do this, damn it. We're going to win the war, right here, right now." Tugging her to his side, he said, "Come on. Let's get this intersection open."

Suddenly aware of the solstice power that thrummed up through the stones beneath their feet and the banked energy of the others waiting to begin the spell, she turned so they faced the chac-mool *side by side.*

And, linked by blood sacrifice and the mated bond, they began the spell, doing it as it was meant to be done: together.

Myr was shaking as she came out of the vision. Because that was what it had been—a vision, sent from the gods. The spell hadn't transferred her magic—it was still lodged inside her, still racing through the connection linking her and Rabbit. Instead, the spell had sent them back to the past and showed them the last few minutes before the old king had unleashed the Solstice Massacre. But how? Why?

"Jesus," Rabbit rasped. "That was . . . are you okay?"

She blinked, somehow unsurprised to find that they were on their feet, holding hands in front of the *winikin*'s altar, just like the king and queen had been facing the huge *chac-mool* beneath the pyramid of Chichén Itzá. More, when she locked eyes with Rabbit, she saw a hint of Jag in him—just a blink and then gone, but it was enough. "You saw it, too," she said. "You were there, in the king."

He nodded. "He was so convinced he was right . . . and he was so damn wrong."

"Asia knew. She had seen foreseen their deaths, but she stood beside him anyway, not because of the writs or his orders, but because she loved him and believed in him utterly . . . even though she was furious with him, too."

"She wasn't mad at the end."

"No. Not at the end." Was that what the gods—or the ancestors, or whatever force had guided the vision—had wanted them to see? That when the chips were down, true love conquered even the worst of mistakes? That mated pairs needed to go into battle united, no matter what they needed to forgive in order for that to happen?

Myr looked away from him. She couldn't stop shaking, couldn't quell the heat in her blood that had come from the dream-kiss and the pressure of Rabbit's fingers on hers. More than ever before, she wanted to lean into him, touch him, kiss him, and forget about the outside world, just as Asia had done.

"He loved her so much," Rabbit's voice was rough with emotion. "So damn much, and he didn't know how to fix things with her, how to protect the people he loved and still do what the gods wanted."

Breath hitching, she looked back at him, and found herself caught in the heat of his eyes. They were warm and alive, making her realize suddenly how locked down he'd been since his return. Now, though, there was a spark of the old impetuousness when he tugged on their joined hands and pulled her into him, against him. And when she made a muffled noise, he wrapped his arms around her and held her close. "It's okay. I've got you, I swear."

It wasn't okay, far from it . . . but she couldn't make herself pull away from his body, his warmth, his scent. Her mind went blank, save for a deep-down whisper that said, *Yes*. This was what she had been missing; this was where she was supposed to be.

Only it wasn't.

"Let go of me," she said into his chest. But she held him close.

"I can't. I've tried." He rested his cheek on her hair and breathed her in. "We should've been like them. Partners. Mates. Together to the very end."

"Rabbit . . ." She trailed off, knowing she should push him back. Instead, she pressed her face against his chest, so she could hear his heartbeat, thudding steadily with a rhythm that seemed to say, *I'm alive, I'm alive, I'm alive.*

Was that what the vision was trying to tell them? That life was short? Warmth kindled low in her stomach, weakening her and telling her to take what she wanted now, before it was too late. And whether or not she wanted to admit it, that wasn't just the sex magic talking. It was her body, her heart.

I'm alive, I'm alive, I'm alive.

She levered away, not to escape but to look up at him. There was a faint curve to his lips, which were so often—more these days than ever—set in concentration. "It was your smile," she said before she knew she was going to. "That day in the tea shop, it was your smile I noticed first."

He went still, not even breathing. But his eyes were locked on hers and the magic raced between them.

"You came in with Nate and Alexis to buy that ceremonial dagger from the Witch," she continued, "but I didn't really pay attention to them—they were just marks. Customers. Whatever. But you were different." He'd looked fierce and capable, like he could handle anything. "And when you saw me, you smiled." Just a quick grin, a "hey, hottie, whassup?" like she'd gotten a thousand times before . . . but one that had held empathy, along with a devilish glint that had made her want to see what would happen if he let loose.

"You were hiding behind some shelves." His voice was thick. "You disappeared almost as soon as I saw you, but for those few seconds, it was like you were the only person in the room. Like the light was drawn right to you." He paused. "After we left the shop, it was your face that stuck with me. Not just because you had a black eye, but because you looked lonely, angry, trapped . . . and for the first time in my life, it felt like I'd met someone like me."

Myr's heart bumped in her chest. They'd never really talked about their first meeting, at least like this, and that was probably the most romantic thing he'd ever said to her, damn him.

"You did," she said through a throat gone tight with emotion. "I was. Oh, hell." Her better intentions crumbled in that instant—or maybe they had already been most of the way gone, undermined by the vision and his smile, and remembering what it had felt like to be beaten down for so long . . . and then to suddenly have someone who gave a shit.

She didn't know which one of them moved first, but they met halfway.

Spurred by magic, memories and the crazy desire that hadn't burned out despite everything, she pressed her lips to his, opened her mouth to the plunge of his tongue, and clutched at his shirt as he kissed her.

Yes! said the burn of excitement that flared as his warm strength surrounded her and their bodies lined up, bumping and then pressing together from collarbones to thighs, and everywhere in between. *Finally!*

said her libido as he growled low in his throat and changed the angle of the kiss. *What the hell are you doing?* said her better sense. But even though kissing him went against everything she'd been telling herself for the past ten days, she couldn't make herself stop.

So she didn't stop. Instead, she opened to him, twined around him, and moaned as the sizzling energy pumped from her to him and back again, racing through the connection she had hated before, but now couldn't get enough of.

Then, suddenly, *boom*! The magic flared higher and hotter, not sex magic anymore, but spell-cast magic. It whipped around her, caught her up, sucked her in.

"Rabbit!" She clutched at him, fear surging as her senses pinwheeled and then accelerated, spinning faster and faster. Wind came out of nowhere, screaming suddenly inside the cave to buffet them, circle around them, suck at them.

She screamed as the tornado dragged at her, coming somehow from her and Rabbit's magic. She couldn't block it, though—the connection was wide open, the magic racing between them, and from there into the gaping vortex.

"We have to shut it down!" Rabbit shouted. "We need—" The tornado roar cut him off.

Myr grabbed for her wand. It was gone, though, and the fire had been blown away. She slapped the panic button on her comm device, but the indicator didn't light up; the magic was interfering with the signal, even with the transponder nearby. Rabbit yelled something, but she couldn't hear him, didn't understand. How had they gone from a kiss to this? Fear slashed—she was defenseless, vulnerable—

No! She wasn't giving up. Her wand might be gone, her backup faraway, but the magic was still inside her. Digging down, she fought to summon her powers, just like she would've if she'd had her wand and crystals, if she'd been surrounded by scented oils and sitting in front of a fire pit shaped like a five-pointed star. *They're just props*, she told herself, and tried to believe it.

Rabbit put his mouth next to her ear and yelled through the whirling whip. "Shields on three!"

She nodded, though she wasn't sure she could cast the spell. What other choice did she have, though? Sand blasted her skin, dragging her toward the funnel. They had to stop this!

He counted it on fingers she could barely see. *One . . . two . . .* On "three" she cast the strongest shield spell she could summon, slamming the green-hazed magic into place around her body. And it worked! The force field materialized around her just as Rabbit cast his shield, which was fiery red, and crackled with tremendous power. The two shields met as they had a hundred times before when the two of them trained together—but where before they had melded together, now they repelled violently.

Boom! Energy flared at the point of contact, and a huge explosion flung Myr across the cave. She landed hard and slid in the sand, screaming as something tore inside her—not in her body, but in her mind, at the base of her skull. The shield spell protected her from the shock wave and the pepper of rocky shrapnel, but it didn't blunt the impact, which left her dazed and gasping for breath.

She heard the sizzle of magic and Rabbit's vicious curses, but she couldn't move, couldn't focus. Her head felt terrifyingly empty—had she banged it, injured it? No, this wasn't pain, it was—*Oh, gods*. Her heart raced as she realized that she couldn't feel their connection anymore. She couldn't sense his emotions, his life energy or even the flow of magic between them.

The separation spell had worked!

Maybe it had been triggered by their kiss, maybe by something else, but it *had* triggered, giving him back his magic and breaking the connection between them. More, she had kept her own version of the Nightkeepers' powers. The shield still surrounded her, and magic still pulsed in her veins. Relief and fierce joy hammered through her, brightening the threads of green flame surrounding her. *She was a mage!*

"It worked!" Killing the shield, she lurched to her feet and turned toward him. "We— *No!*" Her heart stopped at the sight of the oily brown cloud pulsing around him.

Dark magic. She stumbled back, lifting her hands to ward off the sight, along with the realization that their bond had been blocking his hell-link. Now that the connection was broken, the evil magic was coming for him. *"Rabbit!"*

She flashed back on the memories she'd tried so hard to forget, or at least move past. Only she hadn't moved past them, she realized now. The terror was still there, the pain still fresh and sharp.

He burst into the cave, eyes brilliant with fury, and for the first time she was truly afraid of him. She didn't know the man storming across the sand toward where she knelt over a small fire. His face was set, unrecognizable, and he had his ceremonial knife in one fist.

"Rabbit." She rose, holding out her hands. "Wait. It's not anything bad. I'm just—"

"Don't!" he thundered. "No more lies!"

"I'm not lying. I—" She screamed as the scented oil she'd been using to purify his eccentrics blazed suddenly red, and the stones erupted in twin sprays and winged to him, landing in his outstretched palm. Flaming oil burned her face, her arms, but the pain was nothing compared to the terror of suddenly hearing the rattlesnake rasp of the dark magic he'd sworn not to use anymore. Her throat closed, strangling her whisper of, "What's happening to you?"

Stuffing the stones into the pocket of his jeans, he advanced on her. "Were you going to destroy them right away, or were you going to summon her first? What were you going to do to her? Damn it, tell me!"

Tears tracked down her face. "I wasn't going to hurt anybody. I was just trying to help. After what you said about the stones, I got this idea—"

His lips pulled back in a feral snarl. "This was what you wanted, right? You wanted me to use the dark magic again.

But why? Who are you working for?" He leaned in to yell,
"Damn it, what are you trying to do to me?"

Mercifully, the flashback cut out, leaving her bent over
and gasping for breath, dizzied by the memory and the
knowledge that it had gotten worse from there. And,
more from the reminder that at one point, she *had*
pushed him to rekindle his link with the darkness.

She hadn't understood what it meant, not really. All
she had known was that the old Xibalban shaman had
named him the crossover and said he would be the key
to winning the war. She had been scared—of the end of
the world, of the way things had been cooling off between them—and she had pushed him to experiment
with the other half of the magic.

Gods. She didn't want to remember that.

She could barely see him now; he was lost in the
greasy brown mist. But then a blue-white light kindled
within the cloud, and her heart leaped. It was a Nightkeeper's foxfire, made of pure light magic. He was
fighting the darkness!

"Rabbit!" She surged forward, calling up her magic,
not as a shield now, but as a fireball that crackled and
seethed green. But could she launch it without frying
him?

"No," he shouted hoarsely through the fog. "Don't,
Myr! I can do this."

Do what? She let the fireball fade, but kept her magic
revved up. She couldn't see him. But the darkness was
threaded through now with sparks of red-gold.

"What are you . . ." She trailed off, throat locking as she got it. She freaking got it. He wasn't trying to fight the magic. He was trying to gain control of it. He wanted to reforge his hell-link and then shut the magic away, back behind the barriers that used to hold it. The ones that had failed before. "Dear gods." Her voice was a whisper, her emotions a hard, hot ball lodged in her throat.

The words from the children's book shimmered in her mind: *The Crossing Guard stands at the bridge between day and night.* This was what the gods had intended; it was part of him becoming the crossover. Again, her head might've known that this needed to happen, but the rest of her hadn't wanted to believe it. Her heart, stupid organ that it was, was clinging to two versions of him—one was the dark, dangerous mage she wasn't supposed to trust, while the other was the man she'd spent the past ten days fighting alongside, the one who had kissed her just now.

Who was he, really?

"I can handle it." Even as he grated the words, the red-gold sparks brightened and the dark fog began to thin. It wreathed around him, sliding along his body and then fading, until she could see his outline again, then the terrifying details—his eyes were rolled back, his face taut and haggard, like he was little more than skin stretched over a skull and animated by the dark magic that shifted and seethed within him. She could feel its poison, hear its serpent rattle.

She took a step back without meaning to.

He blinked, and suddenly he looked like himself again. "Myr, wait." He reached out a hand, though they were too far apart for him to touch her. It wasn't too far, though, for her to see the flash of red on his inner forearm.

The trefoil hellmark had gone from black to scarlet. The hell-link was fully active.

"No." It was a whisper, a moan. A denial of everything they'd been through, everything that had gone wrong. Only she couldn't deny the past, or the sight of the red hellmark.

"Please, wait." But the despair in his voice said he knew it was already too late.

"I can't." Her voice broke on the words, which suddenly meant far more than she had realized. *I can't do this anymore, can't trust you like this, can't be around you.* And, knowing there was no way they could go back, not now, not ever, she did what she should've done the first moment she saw the dark fog surrounding him.

She turned and ran.

Rabbit didn't let himself go after her—not to tell her that he'd blocked off the dark magic behind its old mental barriers; not to reassure her that he had it under control; and not to tell her that she didn't need to be afraid of him. What was the point? She had every reason to fear the magic, and to fear him when he was under its influence.

"Let her go," he told himself, the words echoing hollowly in the cave.

He didn't need to borrow his magic from her anymore—the spell had severed their connection, setting
her free and making her a mage in her own right, having apparently decided that both of them were the rightful owners of the magic. More, he *had* brought the dark
magic under control, shoving it into the mental vault it
used to inhabit, and locking the fucker down tight. But
what if the vault cracked? Hell, what if it ripped wide
open? Just now, it'd felt like the magic wanted to behave, as if it had gone meekly into confinement.

He didn't trust it. Didn't trust himself with it. But he
couldn't refuse it, either. Not if he was going to become
the crossover. Which meant that whatever had happened between him and Myr over the past ten days,
including their kiss—*especially* their kiss—was gone
now, nullified.

"Fuck me." Feeling like his soul was hollowed out
and his damn bones were creaking, he headed to his
Jeep, fired the engine, and aimed the vehicle back along
the dirt track to Skywatch.

He braced himself to find a not-so-welcoming com-
mittee waiting for him at the gate, looking to protect
Skywatch from the dark magic. But the front parking
area was deserted and nobody flagged him down as he
rolled past the mansion toward his cottage. He'd intended to suck it up and go make his report, would
have if there'd been any sign that it was a command
performance. But the lack of an armed guard tempted
him to keep on driving . . . and made him wonder what
Myrinne had told the others.

"Doesn't matter." She might've played things down in her report, but he'd seen the way she'd looked at him.

The memory tightened his chest, making him feel restless and hemmed in. Suddenly he couldn't handle the thought of being inside the mansion, or even his cottage. Instead, he floored it, headed for the back of the canyon.

The others could come after him if they wanted to.

Gravel spurted beneath the Jeep's tires as he bounced along the dirt track, and again when he skidded to a stop at the base of the narrow trail that led up to the ancient pueblo. The footpath was overgrown, as was the wide ledge in front of the pueblo's lower level, showing just how long it'd been since he'd last been up there.

Before, when he'd first come to Skywatch, he had hung out at the ruins for hours, sometimes even days, listening to his iPod and getting high on weed, hard liquor, *pulque*, and anything else he could find that came under the heading of "shit that alters consciousness." Now, as he tugged aside the dusty serape that covered his stash, he saw there wasn't much left. It should be enough to fog things out for a few hours, though. And right now, he'd take what he could get.

CHAPTER NINE

December 12
Nine days until the zero date
Skywatch

Rabbit grogged his way to consciousness near daybreak and stared at the mud-daubed ceiling of his hideout, which had two round openings that let in the light and smelled of the animals that used it for shelter when he wasn't around.

It wasn't the first time he'd woken up in the pueblo, wrapped in the musty-smelling serape, with his head pounding with the "hey, hello" of a hangover. It also wasn't the first time he'd lain there studying the mud daub, with its ancient handprints and carved zigzag lines, and wishing like hell he didn't have to go back down to the compound. But it was the first time he dreaded going back because it would mean facing Myrinne.

"Damn it." He dragged himself vertical anyway. He needed to report in and see how the others were taking the whole dark-magic thing.

At the moment, it was buttoned up safely in the vault, behaving itself. But as he picked his way down the trail, he wasn't so sure he was in the clear, or even that he should be. If the things that'd happened with Phee were any indication, the dark magic wasn't good for him. Or maybe it was that he wasn't good with it, that he wasn't strong enough to control it, his grip on Nightkeeper magic too weak, his moral compass too fucking imprecise. And if some of that started sounding like his old man—*you're not smart enough, not tough enough, not worth my time*—maybe that wasn't an accident.

"Fuck him. You can handle it this time." He'd learned his lessons the hard way, and he was determined not to screw up again.

Still, the whispers dogged him as he drove the Jeep back to his cottage, grateful that he hadn't seen anyone coming or going. Right now, he didn't want to have any conversations that started with "Hey, how are you" or even "What the fuck happened to you yesterday?"

"Damn it." With irritation riding him hard, putting his gut into a knot of what-ifs, he shouldered through the kitchen door . . . and stopped dead at the sight of Red-Boar sitting at the kitchen table, scowling at a couple of Cokes.

Well, that explained the feeling of impending doom.

"Don't even start," Rabbit said, heading across the kitchen for the main room without giving his father a second look. "I need to shower and get some food in me before I can even think of dealing with you."

"Or you could sit the fuck down and listen."

"Blow me." But Rabbit couldn't make himself walk away. Not knowing that the king could've sent his old man to lay the last order of the Boar Oath on him, in the hopes of taming the dark magic. And that maybe that wouldn't be the worst thing. He stopped in the far doorway, and turned back. "Fuck it. What? Did Dez give you an order?"

"Yeah. But not for you." Red-Boar scowled and took a hit of his soda. "When he heard about the dark magic, he leaned on me to tell him where you really came from."

That cut right through what was left of Rabbit's hangover—*thud*, instant clarity, or close to it.

Back when he'd first returned to Skywatch, he had given the Nightkeepers a full report on his conversations with Phee, hoping there might be something in there that could help them figure out what the *Banol Kax* were planning. At the time, Red-Boar had listened, stone-faced, and said it was all bullshit. Repeatedly. That was all he'd said on the subject, though. Until now.

Thumping into a chair opposite his old man, Rabbit reached for the unopened Coke. "You going to tell me or not?" He wouldn't put it past the old bastard to make an announcement like that, then remind him that he'd never sworn an oath to the current king—Dez had taken over for Strike pretty recently—and clam up.

"For starters, everything the demon told you was a

fucking lie. Your mother didn't escape from the Xi-balbans, and she and I didn't fall for each other and live in some godsdamned rain forest paradise until they tracked us down and killed her. And you never had a twin brother. That was all a bullshit fairy tale."

Rabbit didn't give his old man the satisfaction of seeing him flinch. "How about you tell me something I don't already know?"

Disappointment stung, though, warning that some part of him had wanted to think that maybe there had been a romance between his parents, a tragedy that explained why his father hadn't ever been able to love him, or even like him just a little. And that there had been a twin brother whose absence accounted for the holes inside him, the broken, ragged places that not even Myrinne had been able to fill.

"How much *do* you already know?" Red-Boar demanded.

Frustration stirred, old and ugly, but Rabbit didn't let that show, either. "Fine, we'll play it your way. Fucking whatever. Jox told me that not long after the massacre you lost your shit and disappeared into the rain forest, and he gave me the name of a village: Oc Ajal. I went there and discovered that it was full of Xibal-bans—not members of Werigo's sect of wack-jobs, but peaceful dark-magic shamans led by a guy named Anntah. I met him on his deathbed." In fact, it had been his fault Anntah and the others had been murdered. Iago—Werigo's son and Anntah's sworn enemy—had followed him there and razed the village.

Voice thickening, Rabbit continued, "He said that you had stayed with them for a day or so and then moved on. You were looking for Cassie and the boys, convinced they were still alive somewhere." As far as Red-Boar had been concerned, then or now, his real life had ended with the Solstice Massacre, when his Nightkeeper wife and their twin sons were killed. "He thought my mother had probably been part of Werigo's sect, either voluntarily or as a prisoner. As far as he knew, the villagers of Oc Ajal were the last of the pacifist Xibalbans." And because of him, they were all dead now. He drained his Coke, which bit like hundred-fifty-proof *pulque*. "Anyway, that's where the trail went cold for me." He left it hanging, though he didn't trust his old man to pick up the story. Didn't trust him to do anything, really.

But Red-Boar gave one of his "you're an idiot" snorts, and said, "You've got it right up to the part where I visited Oc Ajal, but you're dead-ass wrong about the rest of it. For one, the villagers were far from pacifists. And for another, Anntah wasn't one of the good guys. Fucking far from it."

"But—"

"Do you want to hear this or not?"

Maybe not. Visiting Oc Ajal and meeting the elder had been a turning point for Rabbit. The village was where he'd learned to think twice before giving in to the impulses that had ruled his life up to that point, where he'd started to learn to control himself rather than hurting the people around him. But it was also where he'd gotten one of the two eccentrics that had summoned Phee. Anntah had given it to him, fuck it all.

Closing his fingers around the empty soda can and not letting himself crumple it, he nodded. "Go on."

"When I showed up in Oc Ajal, I was pretty fucking out of it, raving about the massacre, the Nightkeepers, all of it. So it took Anntah and the others about two minutes to figure out who and what I was." Red-Boar glanced down at his forearm, which bore the distinctive black marks of a Nightkeeper warrior. "He got me to admit that I was the only surviving Nightkeeper mage—I didn't tell him about Strike, Anna and Jox, thank fuck. I kept that much to myself. Anyway, he kept saying that the gods had sent me to him, that he could give me what I wanted."

"Your family."

Red-Boar was back to staring at his soda can. "That's what I thought he meant, what he wanted me to think. He said I should eat and rest. My wife was out hunting, he said. She'd be back soon and she'd be so excited to see me." His mouth twisted. "I don't know what he put in the food, but by the time the hunting party got back, I was hammered, horny, and not feeling picky."

Ew. Rabbit didn't say anything, half-afraid his old man would elaborate.

"I didn't know where I was or who I was with. I just went where I was told, did what I was told, and when Anntah put me together with his daughter in a hut some ways away from the village . . . well. Anyway. We did what we did, and I don't remember any of it. All I know was that the next morning, I woke up alone, hungover and feeling like shit. And when I tried to leave, I couldn't. The door was locked, and what I thought was a hut turned out to be a cage." His flat, cold voice gained an edge. "Every night after that for a couple of months, it was the same fucking thing. The food, the drugs, his daughter. Turns out old Anntah had been looking for the last surviving Nightkeeper for a long time. I guess he had a prophecy to fulfill."

Rabbit's Coke can was a crumpled mess, though he didn't remember crushing it. He just stared at it—easier than staring at his old man—for the first time realizing the familiar logo was the color of blood. "He was trying to breed the crossover. Half Nightkeeper, half Xibalban."

Somewhere far away from his conscious mind, his stomach was knotted and his heart thudded a sickly, sticky beat. But inside his brain there wasn't much going on except a whole lot of buzzing and a couple of neon flashes of "Does not compute." In a way it *did* compute, though, which was a bitter damn pill to swallow. Because Anntah hadn't just given Rabbit the stone eccentric, he'd been the one to tell him he was the crossover, the key to the war . . . and he was the one who'd convinced him that the demons were the true gods and the sky gods were his enemies. He'd planted the seeds.

More lies. And Rabbit had bought into every fucking one of them. He'd been so ego-blinded, so ready to believe that he was right and everyone else was wrong, that he'd jumped on the godsdamned bandwagon.

"He wasn't just *trying* to breed the crossover," Red-Boar said. "He succeeded."

All Rabbit could think was: *Don't puke*. Coke in reverse hurt like a bitch, but what other response was there to learning that you'd been bred like a fucking science experiment? "Go on."

Maybe his old man's eyes softened a little. Maybe not. Probably not. "After a couple of months, there weren't any more drugs and she stopped coming around. They kept me there, though, locked up like an animal. A stud dog they were just warehousing in case they needed to rebreed their bitch."

Rabbit made an inarticulate noise as the last of his illusions crumbled. He'd been looking for his mother, thinking that learning about her would help, when, really, it just made shit worse. He hadn't had a loving mother, a twin brother, or a father who gave a crap. And Anntah had been his grandfather, his creator. What the fuck was he supposed to do with that?

"At first I raved," Red-Boar continued, "or just sat there like a godsdamned lump. Eventually, though, I started sharpening up, coming out of the place I'd been since the massacre. I finally wrapped my head around the fact that Cassie and the boys were gone. I knew I had to get away and warn the others that the Xibalbans were real, and, worse, that they were working toward their end-date prophecies even though the barrier was sealed off. So I pretended I was still out of it, and waited for my chance. And I listened. The villagers didn't think twice about what they were saying when they brought my food. That was how I found out what Ann-tah and the others were trying to do. What the cross-over was supposed to mean."

Unable to sit still anymore, Rabbit got up, grabbed a couple more drinks—beers this time, because who gave a fuck that it wasn't even noon?—set one in front of his old man and plonked back down in his seat, feel-ing like gravity was working on him harder than it ever had before.

"Drink," he ordered. "Then tell me. For fuck's sake, it's time to rip off the godsdamned Band-Aid already." Anger fisted hard and heavy in his chest, but there was no point in being pissed that his old man had taken this long to tell him. What was done was done.

Yeah, another beer or five, and I might even believe that. So he hammered his first while his old man was still popping the top.

Red-Boar took a couple of swigs, and said, "Yeah. Fuck it all. Yeah. You're right." Which didn't feel like the victory it once would have, especially when the Nightkeepers had been busting their asses trying to fig-ure out the crossover's secrets . . . and Red-Boar had known them all along. Bastard.

But, bastard or not, he was talking now. "The way Anntah and the others saw it, the crossover was going to be their Messiah. He was going to win the war for them, lead them to the promised land, what the fuck ever. So the first thing they had to do was make sure he was born the way their prophecies said—from the union of a lone survivor with a princess of the blood. Or some such shit." Red-Boar's tone wasn't nearly so dismissive as his words, though, probably because the prophecy had come true. "When I heard that, I knew I couldn't leave you there."

"You . . . oh." The beer hit Rabbit hard, making his head spin.

"I waited until you were a few months old. Then, when the guards started to look at me with enough pity that I knew it was only a matter of time before they killed me, tying up loose ends, I decided to make my move. I saw my chance one night, and I took it. I got out, grabbed you, set a couple of the huts on fire as a distraction, and bolted." He said it matter-of-factly, like he wasn't in the process of confetti-ing Rabbit's whole damn existence. "I should've killed them all. Would have if it hadn't been for you slowing me down."

It was yet another in a long line of the "if it wasn't for you" comments Rabbit had heard all his life, but where it might've stung before, now the dig was indistinguishable from the rest of the shitstorm going on inside him. How could his old man's version and Phee's be so fucking different, yet both fit the evidence? Fact: Red-Boar had flipped his lid, disappeared into the rain forest, and had come out a few years later with a kid in tow. Fact: He'd never been what you'd call an affectionate father. Hell, there had been more than a few times Rabbit had been pretty sure that his own father had hated him, wished he'd never been born. Now he knew why. He hadn't been a baby; he'd been a fuck-ing hybrid. To the Xibalbans, he'd been a weapon, to his old man, a threat.

Swallowing past the aftertaste of a beer he already regretted, he said, "Why didn't you tell anybody where I came from, what I might be capable of? Why didn't you tell *me*?"

The stubborn set of the old man's jaw got harder. "That wouldn't have changed anything."

"You don't know that." Rabbit told himself not to bother, that it was enough that he knew the truth now, but the churn in his gut wouldn't let him leave it alone. Who the hell was he supposed to be? What was he supposed to do now that he knew where he'd really come from? Ignore it? Forget it? Use it? Voice close to cracking, he got out, "Why didn't you just kill me? Fuck knows it wasn't like you wanted me."

If there was ever a time for Red-Boar to say some-thing kind—or even uncruel—this was it. But all he managed was: "Anntah would've known you were gone. He would've tried to recapture me—or find someone else he thought might work—and breed an-other crossover. This way, as long as I could keep us off his radar screen, I could control things and keep you from getting your hands on the magic . . . or at least I thought I could."

Another piece of Rabbit's childhood puzzle thudded into place—it explained why his old man had barred him from the little shrine he'd set up wherever they'd lived, and why he'd refused to tell him any of the old stories, though Jox and the others had. It explained why he'd refused to accept Rabbit as a magic user even when the evidence had been right there in front of him, and why he'd refused to let him go through an official bloodline ceremony. It even explained why his old man hadn't ever warmed to him, even a little.

Didn't make it right, though.

Anger settled, cold and bitter in Rabbit's stomach, and maybe the vault cracked open a little. It was hard to tell when two decades worth of resentment felt so much like the burn of dark magic. "Sorry to disappoint you. I never was very good at controlling myself . . . or being controlled."

Red-Boar looked past him, out the window to where the sun was beating down like it was just another day, not potentially one of the last nine. "You're pissed, and maybe you've got a right to be."

"Maybe?"

He looked back with a glint of anger. "Haven't you learned a godsdamned thing? How about you get your head out of your ass and focus on your damned priorities? The gods sent me to bring you back here for a reason. It's not just the Xibalbans you can help—you can help the Nightkeepers, too. And that means blocking off the dark magic. Whatever you need to do, you can do it with light magic."

Rabbit might've been telling himself the same damn thing, but that didn't stop him from baring his teeth. "Is that what the gods told you when they sent you back? Or are you just making this up as you go along?"

Red-Boar pushed abruptly to his feet. "If I knew what you were supposed to be doing—or how you were supposed to be doing it—I would've told you right off the fucking bat."

"Like you told me about my mother?"

"Does any of that help with what we're up against right now? Dez didn't think so, and neither do I. But he told me to give you the whole story, so there it is."

"Jesus Christ," Rabbit muttered, not just to blaspheme and piss off his old man, but because there didn't seem to be much else he *could* say. As his father turned for the door, though, he said, "Wait. Why did you name me 'Rabbit'?"

Red-Boar turned back, brows drawing together. "Seriously? *That's* your biggest question?"

"No, it's not, but I'll save the rest for Lucius or someone else who gives a shit about figuring this out. Because, guess what? I'm doing everything I can to get this right. I took your oath, I'm training my ass off, and I'm blocking the hell out of the dark magic. What's more, I'm damn well going to figure out what the crossover is supposed to do, and I'm going to fucking do it, no matter what it takes." The words came out with the force of a vow. "Right now, though, I'm asking you this one question, and you damn well owe me an answer. Why 'Rabbit'?"

"I didn't name you. They did . . . and you answered to it, so I didn't bother changing it."

Rabbit didn't mistake that for compassion. "Fine. Why did *they* pick the name?"

There was a long pause—long enough that he thought his old man was going to blow him off. But then, grudgingly, Red-Boar said, "They named you after the Rabbit shadow in the moon. It's an old legend. Xibalban. Aztec. Whatever. Supposedly, the god Quetzlcoatl was on a long journey, but he couldn't find any food. He was damn near close to starving when he came on a rabbit eating grass, and rather than running away, the rabbit sacrificed itself so the god could survive. Quetzlcoatl was so grateful that he put the rabbit's image up on the full moon, etched out in its shadow half. He said that way mankind would always know about the rabbit's sacrifice."

A shiver tried to crawl its way down Rabbit's vertebrae. "So what does that make me?"

"Either a hero, or somebody's fucking dinner. You figure it out." With that, Red-Boar shoved through the door and stumped down the short stairs, leaving Rabbit sitting there staring after him and feeling like . . . shit, he didn't know what he was feeling right now. All he knew was that he was glaring at the kitchen door with his stomach tied in fucking knots in a way it hadn't been in years. Not since the old man died.

Fuck. Don't go there.

He wasn't that pissed-off, lonely kid anymore. He didn't think the world owed him an explanation or even a break. He had to think this through. What had the Xibalbans wanted from him back when he was born? What did the gods want now? *A little help here?*

"Shit." Shoving away from the table, he surged to

his feet and stood there for a moment, seeing the long-gone oinking cookie jar and fridge magnets that'd been in Red-Boar's old cottage when he and Rabbit moved back in twenty-four years after the massacre. The boar-themed dust collectors were long gone, just like his old man should've been, but suddenly Rabbit couldn't stay there one second longer. But he didn't want to be in the mansion, either, and the thought of heading back up to the pueblo made his stomach lurch.

Suck it up. Don't be a pussy. Just fucking deal. The words trickled through his mind, maybe in his own voice, maybe in the old man's. But for the first time in a long time—maybe ever—they didn't resonate. Instead, they chimed faintly wrong, like some part of him was saying, *Been there, done that.*

Yeah, he'd sucked it up, he'd dealt, and he'd ended up wound so fucking tight that it hadn't taken much for him to implode. And maybe what had happened before would happen again, but that didn't mean it had to happen exactly the same. He could do things different, do them better. Which meant finding someone to talk to, someone he trusted to give him a reality check.

Except there was really only one person he trusted like that . . . and she didn't want anything to do with him.

"Leave her alone," he said, the words echoing in the kitchen he and Myr used to share. "She's better off without you, and you need to learn to deal with that." Wasn't like he had much time to make the adjustment, either.

He couldn't do it in the cottage, though—there were too many memories there, too much old stuff pressing in on him from all sides. So he headed out, not following his old man toward the mansion, but turning the other way instead.

If the pueblo was where he'd always gone to embrace a state of temporary amnesia, the cacao grove was where he went to find some approximation of peace. He'd always felt at home in the rain forests and Mayan highlands. Maybe it was because he'd been conceived there, born there, but he didn't want to think about that right now. And as he paused at the edge of the cacao grove, it didn't matter why; it only mattered that his brain slowed down somewhat and the anger dulled as he inhaled the soft, tropical air.

Yeah. This would help.

Exhaling, he entered the grove, pushing past shrubby cacao trees that reached to touch him with leafy fingers. The sense that the sunlight was warmer here came from the power of suggestion, he knew, as did the phantom cry of a parrot and the smell of vanilla.

Except the scent of vanilla wasn't his imagination, he thought, pausing as his instincts went on alert. The smell was really there. More, there was a faint crackle coming from up ahead, along with a skim of magic.

He told himself to walk away. He followed the sound instead, and when it led him to a small grove he hadn't realized was there, he hesitated in the shadows, and stared.

Myrinne sat cross-legged at the edge of a circle of stones that danced with flickering green flames. She was wearing wide-legged jeans, a woven green belt that sparkled in the light, and a green T-shirt that moved with her body as she gestured and then whispered a chant he couldn't quite hear, but that sent the blood thrumming through his veins and made the air around him sizzle with Nightkeeper power.

She stilled suddenly. Maybe he had made a noise, or maybe she had felt the answering surge of his magic; he didn't know. But her head came up, her hand went for the pistol that lay beside her, and she said softly, "Hello?"

"It's me." He moved out of the shadows. "I didn't know you were here. I was just . . ." He trailed off, because it didn't matter why he'd come, or that he suddenly wondered whether some part of him had known she was here. "Never mind. I'll go." He took a step back.

"Wait." The word was low, ragged.

He froze in place as her eyes softened and—incredibly, impossibly—he saw a glimmer of warmth, an echo of the way the girl she used to be had looked at the guy he'd been.

"Sit." She pointed to the opposite side of the fire. "We need to talk."

CHAPTER TEN

Myr cursed herself as he crossed the grove. She should've told him to get lost the moment she sensed him, should tell him that now. Things would be a whole lot easier if they stayed away from each other. Problem was, easier wasn't necessarily better. Especially not now.

As he took a seat opposite her, she murmured a few words and cast a handful of salt into the fire.

Tendrils of darker green threaded within the flames and the scent changed, making her think of the sea. Leaning in, she breathed the salted smoke and felt the sharp edges smooth out. "It's a cleansing ritual," she told him, though he hadn't asked. "It's supposed to help you cast out doubt. The salt represents us anchoring ourselves to the earth, while the flames are the way we move through our fear."

He leaned in and took a deep breath, then held the

scented smoke for a moment before he let it out on a sigh, and said, "You don't need to doubt me, Myr, or be afraid of me. I've learned my lessons when it comes to the dark magic." His voice was low, his eyes intense, and even though they were no longer linked, she could sense that he was telling the absolute truth . . . at least as he saw it, right here and now.

But she shook her head. "It's not just about me doubting you, Rabbit. It's more about us doubting ourselves, and each other." She paused. "I was going to come find you later today."

"Oh?" The word carried a note of wary surprise.

She knew he must think she was afraid of him. Why wouldn't he? She'd run away from him. She had been more overwhelmed than anything, though, and she'd had the night to think it through. And when she came down to it, their past didn't matter right now. The kiss didn't even matter, really. It couldn't. What mattered was that he'd squelched the dark magic rather than give in to it. She didn't sense it in him anymore, didn't see it in his eyes. And he needed to become the crossover.

So she said, "I owe you an apology."

"You don't owe me a damn thing."

"Maybe not on balance, but this needs to be said." She couldn't smell the salt anymore, couldn't taste it at the back of her throat. Her senses had gotten used to it, she thought, just like the two of them had gotten so used to how things were between them that they hadn't noticed when the dynamic had gradually changed.

"Yesterday, when I saw you with the dark magic, I remembered something you said to me that morning."

His eyes darkened. "Myr—"

"No. Let me get this out." She wanted to forget about the attack—of course she did. But maybe this was a necessary sacrifice. "You said I kept pushing you to try the dark magic, and you were right. I *was* pushing you back then. Hell, I was nagging you, even though Dez had made you promise not to experiment with it anymore."

"It's okay," he said too quickly. "I always understood, always knew you were trying to help, even if it was hard to hear sometimes. You don't have to apologize for being ambitious."

"It wasn't ambition. It was fear."

He snorted. "You? Afraid? Bull." But his eyes narrowed. "Since when?"

"Since always." She didn't want to remember. But maybe that had been part of the problem. "How much of my childhood did you see when you were inside my head?" She had been afraid to ask before.

"Not much in the way of details. More flashes." He paused. "I saw a deep, dark place, heard her shouting, felt . . . I don't know. Numb, I guess."

"Close enough." *Numb, helpless, angry* . . . forcing her shoulders square, she met his eyes. *Don't pity me.* "My parents abandoned me when I was a few months old, left me in a booth of a strip club around the corner from the tea shop, with a blanket and a twenty, like that was going to cover anything." The anger had scabbed over through the years, as had any hope that they were go-ing to show back up and claim her. "Nobody there wanted the cops involved, and the owner figured it'd be easiest to just make me disappear. He sent his bouncer to take care of it, but the guy sold me to the Witch instead."

"Jesus, Myr." And, yeah, there was the pity. Or maybe it was sympathy.

She shrugged, telling herself that it didn't matter anymore. "She never let me forget that I owed her my life. More, she told me I couldn't expect better than what she gave me—a bed, some food, and more than enough work to earn it. And it wasn't like anything I saw made me think any different." The more upstand-ing locals had stayed the hell away from the back alleys of bars and black magic, and the Witch's friends— including the grabby-handed strip club owner—had given her the creeps. Add in the clueless tourists who came to the shop and looked away when they saw her bruises, and the drunken man-boys who offered her strings of beads in exchange for a look at her tits, and she'd believed the Witch when she'd said she was bet-ter off in the shop than out on the streets. More, she hadn't dared argue. Not often, anyway.

"You were ready to get out," Rabbit reminded her. "You stole the ceremonial knife Nate and Alexis were trying to buy, and told me I could have it if I took you with me."

"That was just a moment of temporary bravery. One of my few." More, the Witch vanished right after that—

dead, Myr had later learned—leaving the tea shop locked tight, and Myr out on the streets. And being on her own had turned out to be just as bad as her foster mother had threatened—she had been dirty, cold, hungry and scared by the time she saw Rabbit again, recognized him. Latched on to him.

"Still, you took a stand."

"And look where it got me. Out on the streets for a few weeks, and then, when I hooked back up with you, snatched by Iago." She didn't remember much about the imprisonment, only that she had been cold and afraid, and had learned firsthand that all the things the Witch had threatened were nothing compared to how bad reality could get. "It . . . I don't know. Broke something inside me, I think, to realize that the Witch was right about me not being able to handle the world outside."

His eyes blazed. "She wasn't. Not even close."

"I went from being under her thumb to being at Skywatch with you, surrounded by these huge, glittery people who could do magic—*real* magic—and were scrambling to save the world." She shook her head, facing the hard truths that had finally become clear to her last night, when she'd stayed awake, staring into the darkness and making herself accept that she'd played a part in what had happened with Rabbit. "The point is that my nagging you wasn't about the power, not the way you thought. It was about me needing to feel safe. Even though I learned how to fight, how to be a warrior, it wasn't enough. I was still scared. And the closer the end-time got, the more scared I got . . . and the more I tried to make you be strong enough to protect both of us."

"I wanted to," he said, voice rough with emotion. "I still do."

She was suddenly very aware of her heart—how it beat in her chest, feeling heavy and tender. But she couldn't let it run the show anymore. "You can't. You've got to be the crossover, and gods only know what that's going to involve."

A shadow came over him, though the sun-dappled air hadn't changed. "Like the dark magic."

"Don't." She would have reached out to him, but he was too far away, with the fire between them. Instead, she said, "It's part of your powers, and you're handling it. You should be proud of that, proud of everything you've accomplished . . . and I'm sorry for making you feel like you should've been doing more."

"You didn't—"

"I did. Not at the beginning, granted." The first couple of years had been the best of her life. She had been in love, surrounded by magic, and she'd been his champion when the others had treated him like the destructive kid he'd been rather than the man he was becoming. Once the Nightkeepers had accepted him as a warrior, though, she hadn't let up. Hadn't been able to. "But when things started getting serious—with the countdown, the *xombi* outbreaks, all of it—I . . . I don't know. I freaked. I stopped feeling safe, and instead of admitting it, even to myself, I started hounding you about being stronger, better, finding a way to use both halves of your magic." And when he'd refused, she'd pushed harder.

He stared down into the fire, and his voice was hollow when he said, "I could've called you on it. Should have. Instead, I . . . I don't know. Shut down, I guess."

"I don't blame you."

But he shook his head. "I was the one who listened to Phee. You don't need to be sorry for any of it."

"Yeah. I do."

"Then forget it. We're still not close to being even after the crap I put you through."

"Let's call it even anyway."

"Shit," Rabbit said finally. There was more sorrow than anger in the word, though. "What the hell happened to us, Myr? We were perfect together." His eyes were stark and sad . . . but he didn't look all that surprised, letting her know that he'd figured out some of it on his own. He hadn't known how afraid she'd been, but he'd known Phee wouldn't have been able to get to him if their relationship had been in a better place.

Tears stung the backs of her eyes. "I think maybe we just outgrew it. Took it all for granted. Something."

He sighed heavily and looked back into the fire. "Yeah."

Breathing out of synch, they stared into the flames for a long moment in a silence that was both easier than she would've expected and harder than she could've imagined. They couldn't go back—she thought they probably wouldn't even if they could. But how were they supposed to go forward from here? She didn't want to avoid him, but she wasn't sure she dared spend too much time near him. Their relationship might've crashed and burned, but the chemistry remained. Even now, she was acutely aware of his smallest movements, and the way the black marks on his forearm looked even blacker now with the red hellmark among them.

The sight should've scared her, should've reminded her how bad the darkness could get. Instead, it sent new warmth skimming through her veins as she remembered how he'd gotten it in the first place: he'd let Iago bind him to the dark magic in exchange for her life.

It had been the first time anyone had really rescued her. And it had been the beginning of her first crush. Her first love.

Don't go there, she told herself as her heart thudded too fast. "What are you doing out here, anyway?" she asked, needing to break the silence. "Were you looking for me?"

"No. Maybe. I don't know." He paused. "I was just walking, trying to clear my head."

His sudden grimness had the warmth inside her shifting to concern. Which was safer in some respects, but not in others—because if it had Rabbit worried, it couldn't be good. "What happened?"

"My old man ambushed me this morning and told me about my mother finally. The whole fucking story, damn him."

"Oh. Wow." Shock sizzled through her, chased quickly by a flash of anger at Red-Boar, who hadn't been any more of a father to Rabbit than the Witch had been a mother to her. "You want to tell me about it?"

He hesitated, but then exhaled and said, "My mother was Anntah's daughter."

A shiver of instinct worked its way through her, the kind that said, *This is important.* "The old shaman at Oc Ajal?"

Rabbit nodded. "Which explains how he managed to contact me when Iago's red-robes destroyed the village. We had a blood-link, even though he denied it when I asked." His voice was flat, his eyes hollow as he stared into the guttering green flames. He leaned in and took another deep breath. Then, like he was reading off a lame-ass playlist, he repeated Red-Boar's story, describing how the Xibalbans had purpose-bred him, and how his father had kidnapped him so he couldn't be used as an enemy asset. "That was why he didn't want me to get my bloodline mark or learn to use my magic." His lips thinned. "The old bastard never could control me, though. The harder he tried to make me fall in line, the more I busted out."

Oh, Rabbit, she thought, but didn't say, because it wouldn't change anything. She wanted to reach out to him, wanted to touch him, but couldn't do either with the fire between them. Where before it had seemed like a necessary bulwark, though, now it was in the way. So she got up and moved around to sit beside him, letting their shoulders bump.

They sat like that for a minute, watching the flames gutter and send up plumes of vanilla-scented smoke. Finally, she asked, "What else did he say about the crossover?"

"Nothing that we didn't already know, which is why he didn't tell me sooner. At least that's his excuse. There's got to be something more to it, though. Some clue we're missing." He hesitated. "I want to go back to the village."

"You . . . oh." She swallowed. "Right." It made sense, she supposed. They needed more information on the crossover—where better to look than the place where he'd been conceived? Still, though, she inched away as her mind filled with memories of Oc Ajal—bodies, burning huts, the stink of charred flesh. It had been gruesome, loathsome, heartbreaking . . . more, she dreaded the thought of the village itself, the dark magic that still lurked there.

The problems between her and Rabbit might have made him vulnerable to Phee's seduction, but it was the stone eccentric he'd found beneath the center pole in Anntah's hut that had summoned her.

"It's the only thing I can think to do now that I know the truth," Rabbit continued. "I'll get Anna to 'port me down there today, a quick in-and-out, low risk and no bullshit."

She wasn't sure which one of them he was trying to convince. "What are you going to do when you get there?"

"Look around. Maybe pray for a miracle."

Don't go, she wanted to say. She couldn't, though, because he was right. And, besides, she knew he wouldn't listen to her if she tried to talk him out of it. His jaw was set and his eyes gleamed with an anticipation that had her instincts humming. So instead of arguing, she took a deep breath and said, "I'm going with you."

The words hung in the air between them for a moment before he shifted to look at her fully, his eyes dark and unreadable. "You don't have to."

The hum got louder. Was he trying to spare her from the bad memories, or was there something else going on here? Damn it, she didn't know. "I'll go," she said firmly. "I used to be good at watching your back."

He hesitated for a split second, but then he nodded. "Thanks. There's nobody I trust more to have my six."

Damn her throat for closing on a lump of emotion. This wasn't about emotion, though; it was about making sure nothing went wrong. And she still wasn't entirely sure he wasn't playing her—or himself. "Okay, then. You run it by Dez and get the go-ahead."

"Will do. Meet me in the great room in an hour."

It wasn't until he'd melted back into the grove, though, becoming nothing more than a shadow that shifted and then disappeared, that she found herself wondering what the hell she had just gotten herself into, and why. *You shouldn't have said you'd go,* her better sense whispered. *He's not your problem anymore.* But both she and her better sense knew that was a lie. He'd been her problem—her weakness—since the first moment she saw him, and that hadn't changed. Like the *xombi* virus, it seemed like repeated exposure didn't lead to immunity.

More, she knew him better than anybody . . . which meant it was up to her to make sure he wasn't drifting again toward the darkness and telling himself it was the light.

CHAPTER ELEVEN

Oc Ajal, Mexico

The village of Oc Ajal didn't look anything like it had the last time Rabbit was there.

The pathway to the parking area was gone—hell, the parking area was probably gone, along with the road leading in. The rain forest had grown in from the edges of where the double row of huts and the villagers' slash-and-burn landscaping had held back the undergrowth. The green carpet and higher secondary growth had even covered over the charred remains of the huts, which were visible now mostly as lumps of greenery. That, and the chunks of rocks poking up here and there, made it look like any of the thousands of small, unexcavated Mayan sites strewn throughout the territories, ancient rather than just a year or so old.

Overhead, birds called and flitted, splashes of color against the background of breeze-stirred leaves.

"It's like they were never here," Myr said quietly from behind and a little off to one side of him. "Like *we* were never here."

"There's magic, though," Anna said from the other side of him. She'd stayed instead of dropping them off and 'porting back to Skywatch, though he didn't know if she was curious or under orders to keep an eye on him.

"They built on a hotspot and then camouflaged it," he commented, mostly because he needed to say something, needed to pretend that this was just another op.

It wasn't, though, not for him. Because as he stepped through the stone archway and into the hub of the village, he saw what was left of Anntah's hut, where a village woman had been tied, raped and killed. He saw the places where bodies had lain, and the bushes where he had puked up a lung, knowing that Iago wouldn't have found Oc Ajal if it hadn't been for him. And, right in the middle of it all lay the remains of the fire pit where Anntah had died, his soul lingering just long enough to give Rabbit the information—the lies—that had put him on the path to nearly destroying himself, and Myrinne.

Unlike the rest of the overgrown village, the fire pit was bare.

He found himself standing there without really being aware of having moved, his toes nearly bumping one of the millstones the red-robes had used to pin the dying shaman in place. Anna and Myrinne were right behind him; he could feel their wariness, their worry. He didn't know what they were expecting him to do, though. Shit, he didn't know what he was expecting himself to do—there was magic here, yeah, but there wasn't anything really jumping out at him, waving its arms and saying "Here I am. Here's your answer!"

No big foam finger moment. Shit.

Looking back over his shoulder, he met Myr's eyes. "You getting anything?" Although he was jacked in and had his senses wide open, he had a feeling that her version of the magic gave her a different view. More, it gave him an excuse to look back at her, check on her.

She was wearing skintight black combat gear, surrounded by the red-gold sparks of Nightkeeper magic, and carrying a machine gun across her body. She looked deadly, sexy and resolute. As much as he had wanted to leave her back at Skywatch, far away from the memories and the very real possibility that he would have to call on his dark magic to find whatever secrets the village still held, she was right that he needed a partner, someone to watch his back in the *xombi*-infested forest. And if things went wrong, if he started losing control of the dark magic, she would catch it before it was too late.

He hoped.

She shook her head. "I can feel the energy all around us, but I'm not sensing anything specific."

"Same here. Okay. I guess that means we need to search the site, looking for smaller hotspots. Let's—"

The digital bleat of Anna's satellite phone cut him off, sounding freakishly mechanical against the background whirr of the rain forest.

She shook her head. "Damn phone doesn't get a signal half the time in downtown Denver, but picks it up here. Go figure." She pulled out the unit—military, bigger than a regular cell but still pretty streamlined for what it could do—checked the ID, and shrugged. "No name coming up. Wrong number, maybe?"

Moments later it stopped ringing, but then a second tone indicated there was a voice mail. When she punched it up and put it on speaker, a man's voice said, "Anna, this is Dr. Curtis. Dave. Dr. Dave." Her eyes went wide and her mouth shaped an *oh, shit*. The message continued: "Are you still down here? If so, I could really use your help. Please call me back at this number if you can. Or better yet, just come to the camp. I know I told you to stay the hell away, but this is important. I'll leave your name at the main gate and tell them to have all the gear waiting for you. And . . ." He hesitated. "Well, please come if you can, or at least call. I don't know who else to ask."

After that, there was a moment of silence in the grove, broken only by the sounds of the rain forest, which didn't give a crap about a weird-assed phone call coming in the middle of a ghost town.

'Myr turned to Anna. "You gave the *xombi* doctor your real number?"

She flushed. "I meant to have JT change it. Guess I forgot."

"I guess." Myr seemed amused. "Well? You going to go?"

"I . . . damn it. It can wait until we're done here."

But Rabbit shook his head. "Go ahead and go. That's the guy Dez wants to liaise with right? And it sounded important."

"So is this."

"Yeah, but—and no offense intended—whatever happens here, either Myr and I will be able to handle it on our own, or else we're going to need the whole freaking team. Since we've got Strike and the others standing by for our Mayday"—he lifted his wrist, where his comm device was primed and ready to transmit—"we'll be covered. So go. See what the *xombi* doctor wants."

Anna's gaze went from him to Myr. "That okay with you?"

Myr hesitated, but then nodded. "We'll be fine. And if there's anything you can do to help with the outbreak, you should do it."

Rabbit didn't let himself take that as a sign of faith. It was more a sign of just how close they were getting to D-day, which was forcing the Nightkeepers to split up, spread out and do their best.

Anna put in a call to Skywatch and got Dez's okay for the change in plans. She looked a little flustered as she moved away from the fire pit and gave herself a once-over to make sure she was dressed down enough to pass in the human world. Then she fixed her eyes on Rabbit and Myrinne and said, "Behave yourself."

Knowing damn well she was talking to him, he nodded. "Scout's honor."

"Right." To Myr, she said, "Call me the second you think you might need me. Or, better yet, sound the general alarm. These days it's better to overreact than play hero." Then she disappeared, leaving behind only a faint handclap as air rushed in to fill the vacuum her bodyprint had left behind.

When even that noise had faded and the normal rain forest chatter had resumed, Rabbit took a breath and turned to Myr. "Ready to check out what's left of Anntah's hut?"

It was where he'd found the first eccentric, after all. Maybe they'd get lucky and find something else there. He hoped to hell they would, because otherwise they were going to have to go to plan B. And Myr wasn't going to like plan B. At all.

Chichén Itzá, Mexico

As Anna slipped into the quarantine zone, shielded from human view by the faint distortion of a chameleon shield, she wasn't sure which was worse: forgetting to have JT change her cell number, or jumping to answer Dr. Dave's page.

Sure, she had sent him what little she'd managed to put together on the virus, along with Sasha's suggestions on herbal remedies that borderlined on spell territory. Dez had approved it, though, wanting to foster the relationship. Which was all she was doing now, she told herself as she slipped into what looked like a main tent, following right on the heels of a laundry-laden volunteer. But it didn't take an inner "yeah right" for her to know that was bull. She was here because . . . well, she was here. And she needed to make it snappy before Rabbit and Myrinne got into too much trouble.

She checked her wrist, but there was no sign of the yellow flasher that would signal an emergency recall. So she took the few minutes to find a supply area and snag the thin, disposable safety gear she'd seen the others wearing, which was consistent with the *xombi* virus's tendency to transmit through bites rather than by air. The Nightkeepers weren't susceptible to the virus—or any other germ they knew of—but she wanted to blend. More, the pause gave her a few seconds to breathe, and remind herself that she was okay. She wasn't the patient this time, wasn't coming out of a spell-cast coma to discover that Dick had divorced her and sold the house, Strike had given up the throne, and the others were expecting her to step up as a Triad mage and an *itza'at* seer, do not pass go, do not pay two hundred bucks.

That had been another hospital, another time. Practically another lifetime.

You're okay, she told herself, then closed her eyes and counted to five, breathing deeply through the full face mask. Then she dropped her shield spell and stepped out into the busy hallway.

A sea of humanity surrounded her in an instant. Or maybe it just seemed that way because she spent so much time alone. Either way, she found herself adrift in a hustling mass of scrubs, gloves, face masks, sterility, filth, sickness and health. *This*, she thought, tempted to take a moment to feel the energy, this was what the Nightkeepers were fighting to save. This anthill-scurry of humanity—overcrowded and hurry-hurry-hurry.

She stepped in front of a clipboard-carrying nurse, summoned an authoritative I-belong-here voice, and said, "Dr. David Curtis, please. He sent for me."

"Back there," the woman said, gesturing over her shoulder. "Just follow the noise."

"Thank—" Anna didn't bother finishing, because the woman had darted around her. Then again, this wasn't exactly a polite chitchat sort of place. So she followed the high-pitched, babbling howl coming from the hallway the woman had indicated.

As she got closer, Anna distinguished a single voice, female, speaking Spanish with an edge of hysteria. "She's a blue-eyed devil, an abomination! She did this. She'll kill us all!"

Her breath caught as she edged around the door to find a small room crammed with four beds, all occupied. Three held the restrained, motionless bodies of two men and a woman in the final stages of the *xombi* virus—at least the final stage when they weren't allowed to feed on human flesh, and thus starved to death. Their faces were ruddy and dark, the skin sunken over their bones, pulled so tight that their lips had pulled back over their teeth, making them look like mummified corpses.

Or screaming skulls.

A shiver rippled down Anna's spine. Then an unearthly cry yanked her attention to the fourth bed, where three protective-suited figures were struggling to contain a thrashing woman who was early enough in the disease to still be able to screech and fight, and cast curses and threats sprinkled with the words "demon" and "possessed."

"Hold her, for the love of God," said the guy in the middle. "She's going to hurt herself." His accent was Australian, his cuffs rolled up to reveal tanned forearms, in defiance of sterile protocol. David.

"Or one of us," puffed the beefy guy on his left as he struggled to get a strap on one of her wrists. "Or, more likely, the kid."

"Bless her little soul," said the third—a smaller figure, female but still plenty tough as she wrestled with an ankle strap. "Where are the meds, damn it?"

"On their way," said Dr. Dave, followed by, "Got her," as he pulled the last strap snug across the patient's chest. Then, flattening his palm on her sternum, he leaned in and switched to Spanish. "You're sick, Mrs. Espinoza. You're in the hospital, and we're going to take care of you."

Her eyes flashed suddenly, going the telltale red of a *xombi* as the demon spirit pushed the human soul further and further toward death. But there was human terror in her expression as she howled, "You can do nothing as long as that *thing* lives."

The doctor straightened. "Christ. I don't . . . I need the translator."

Anna stepped into the doorway. "She's here . . . I think, anyway."

He spun, hazel eyes lighting behind his plastic face shield. "Good. You got my message." He gave her a quick once-over, checking that she was protected. "No trouble getting in here? I left word with the security guys, but you never know."

"It was fine." Telling herself there was no reason for the low-grade shimmy in her stomach, she added, "I'm not sure why you need me to translate, though. Your Spanish is excellent."

Sobering, he glanced back at the patient, who had sunk deeper beneath the virus, until she was barely tugging at her bonds and taking halfhearted snaps at her attendants while muttering disjointed epithets and warnings. "Poor thing. We'll dose her with our drugs and your herbs, which should slow things down. I didn't call you to talk to her, though. I need . . . well, it's probably better if you see for yourself."

"We've got this," said the linebacker-looking attendant, waving him off. "I'll get the meds into her and set her up for the night."

The doctor nodded. "If you have a chance, try to find some family. If you can learn anything else about her and the little girl, it might help."

Anna was all too familiar with the vague hospital-speak that translated to "don't alarm the patient, but we don't know fuck-all about what's going on here," but the instinctive kick of irritation it brought was dampened by his obvious frustration. "What little girl?" she prodded.

"Follow me." He shucked his gloves and dumped them in an overflowing bin out in the tent-city hallway, then pulled out a fresh pair from the pocket of his light-weight coat, which had an ID badge clipped to the collar and DAVE written on a pocket in faded blue Sharpie. As he led her through the human traffic, dodging laundry carts and gurneys with the ease of long practice, he said over his shoulder, "The cops brought them both in this morning after a neighbor reported hearing screams. They found a man and a woman dead out in the front room—they were infected, but it looked like a murder-suicide. The little girl was locked in the bathroom and the woman you just saw was going at the door with a hammer, screaming that she was going to kill the little devil. The virus must've crossed the blood-brain barrier, though that's not the normal presentation. Anyway, we're guessing she's a relative." He grimaced. "You saw what she was like."

"Scary," Anna said softly. "And very sad."

"Yeah." He stopped outside a closed door near the end of the hallway. There was a hand-drawn biohazard symbol on the door, along with DO NOT ENTER in three languages. Putting a hand on the knob, he said, "This is a rough one. Kids always are."

"I'm tougher than I look." *You have no idea.*

He didn't look convinced, but nodded and pushed

through, paused a moment to survey the patient, and then said, "Come on in."

Anna stepped through into a smaller room, which was hot and stuffy despite a narrow window vent near the ceiling. The space was maybe ten by ten, and held two beds; one was empty, the other occupied by the heartbreakingly small figure of a child.

She was curled on her side as much as a set of padded, too-large restraints allowed, and barely made a lump beneath a soft blanket that was decorated with smiling cartoon teddy bears in jarring primary colors. It had no doubt been a donation from some group or another and designed to cheer up younger patients. Here, though, it just emphasized the gloom of the shantytown hospital and the pallor of the little girl's face, which was a sharp contrast to her dark lashes and the glossy blue-black hair that had escaped from a thick braid.

The sight of a pink ribbon tied at the end of her braid—and the smear of bloody fingerprints on the crumpled bow—had Anna blowing out a steadying breath and telling herself, *You're here to help, not hurl.* The latter was tempting, though, as the antiseptic-laced smell of disease and jammed-together people went suddenly oppressive.

She'd said she could handle a sick child. Maybe she'd been wrong. *Suck it up. You can do this.*

The girl was murmuring something, her lips moving almost soundlessly.

"Hey there, Rosa," the doctor said gently, in English.

"I've brought the lady I told you about. Can you open your eyes and talk to us?"

"I'm still not sure what you need me for," Anna said, equally softly. "If the mother speaks Spanish, and the child understands English, what—"

"Lean in," he said, waving her to the bed. "Listen."

She leaned in . . . and froze as the girl said, in perfect ancient Mayan, *"Ilik oolah. Tun k'eex le ka'ano' tin kaxtik aantah."* *Greetings, seer. The sky is changing, and we need your help.*

Oc Ajal, Mexico

Myr and Rabbit didn't have any big "aha!" moments picking through the overgrown remains of Anntah's hut, and they didn't get anything when they spiraled out around the site, searching for a hotspot, a spike in the force, whatever the hell you wanted to call it. Some sort of evidence that they were on the right track.

There was plenty of dark magic—she could dimly sense it as a greasy shiver down her spine—but that was all. Which left them standing back at the main fire pit, feeling like that was where they'd been heading all along. One look at Rabbit's face and she knew it wasn't her imagination. He was tight and withdrawn, his eyes shadowed as he stared down at the spot where his grandfather had died. Or maybe it would be more accurate to call the old bastard his breeder. His creator. *Gods.*

She swallowed as sympathy warred with uneasiness. "What aren't you telling me?"

He hesitated. "You're not going to like it."

Probably not. "Try me."

"Phee never really mentioned the crossover, or what she was going to do with my magic once she had it. Which makes me think she didn't know everything about it . . . and that would mean the *Banol Kax* don't, either. If that's the case, then we can assume that Anntah's soul never made it to Xibalba, because sure as shit they would've pumped him dry."

"Okay. So you're thinking . . . what, that his soul was destroyed?" It sounded logical enough, but didn't do anything to ease the shimmies in her stomach.

"Not exactly. He used a seriously powerful dark-magic spell to anchor his soul to his body, so he could talk to me when I got here. So I was thinking . . . what if his soul got stuck?" He gestured to the fire pit. "What if he's still here?"

Myr's mouth went dry. "You want to summon Anntah's ghost." It wasn't a question.

He lifted a shoulder in a half shrug, but there was nothing casual in his expression as he said, "It's the best theory I've got right now. Unless you've got another idea?"

"How about anything that doesn't involve summoning another one of your relatives from beyond the grave?"

"It's not like I *want* to do it this way, especially not with you here."

"Because you knew I would argue?"

"Look around you." His gesture encompassed the

village. "The whole place reeks of dark magic. I used it to bring Anntah's soul back the last time, and I'm going to need to use it again."

She lifted her chin. "I won't run away from you this time. I sw—"

"*Don't*," he said sharply. "Don't promise me that, not ever. In fact, promise me that you'll run if you need to, call for help, whatever it takes. Promise me you'll stay safe."

Suddenly, it didn't feel like he was talking about just here and now. She remembered what he'd said back in the cave, about not wanting her beside him during the final battle. She hadn't really thought about it at the time—too many other things had been going on. Now, though, as he faced off against her wearing combat black and bristling with weapons, with his eyes fierce and his jaw set in a stubborn line, she could picture him standing alone in the final battle, so damn determined to make things right that he wasn't thinking of anything else. Even himself. "Rabbit . . ." she began.

"Promise me." He looked away, voice roughening. "I'm not kidding, Myr. I've kept the dark magic under control so far, but it hasn't been testing me. It is now, though. It wants out. And once it's out, I don't know if I'm going to be able to handle it."

Oily brown magic surging in the air, pulsing and writhing as if something was trying to be born from the other side of the barrier. Rabbit looming over her with his ceremonial knife at her throat and dark-magic madness in his eyes. The images came straight from her nightmares.

She shoved them aside. "Stop trying to scare me."

"I'm not trying to scare you. I'm trying to *protect* you, damn it."

"Well, knock it off." She called her magic and cast a crackling green shield around her body. "I can take care of myself. What's more, I can keep an eye on you and make sure things don't go very wrong . . . or I can deal with it if they do." She tapped her armband, indicating the dead man's switch she'd had JT install. "One way or another."

He stilled. "You knew."

"I guessed it would come to something like this. Why would you come to Oc Ajal otherwise? And I figured I was the best one to stand guard, both over you and against you." She paused. "Besides, I think I need to do this. It's one thing to say I can handle myself and another to actually prove it."

Phee's ghost had nearly killed both of them. Anntah's wouldn't get the same chance. Not if she had anything to say about it.

He hesitated, then blew out a breath. "Shit, Myr."

"You can do this," she said, and heard the words echo back to her old self, the one who'd had his back no matter what. "Just remember whose side you're on, okay?"

For the first time in days, she caught a flash of his grin. "Okay." Then he sobered. "Okay. Let's do this." Turning to face the fire pit once more, he pulled his combat knife from his belt and used it to cut his palms.

Red blood welled and flowed, the air stirred around

them, and Myr's heart stuttered. Oh, hell. They were really doing this. Reminding herself that she had asked for it, argued for it, she held her ground as a faint rattle hissed to life, as if a giant snake had been disturbed. Her heart thudded, but where the other day the syncopated beat had sounded like *I'm-alive, I'm-alive*, now it sounded like *oh-shit, oh-shit, oh-shit*.

She stayed put, though. Not because there wasn't anywhere to run to, but because she wasn't going to leave Rabbit behind.

CHAPTER TWELVE

Chichén Itzá, Mexico

Anna's mind raced as she stared at the child and tried not to let Dr. Dave see how thoroughly freaked out she was, or how sudden sharp hope flared through her, making it hard to breathe. "Tell me what to do," she whispered in the ancient language.

The little girl—or whatever entity was speaking through her—said, "There is a ruby skull hidden within the *chac-mool* at the center of your home. It holds the key to your powers and the secret of the true gods."

Anna fought not to gasp. According to the archive, thirteen life-sized crystal skulls had come out of the sinking city with the earliest of the Nightkeepers, the ones who had built the barrier to contain the demons in Xibalba. Four had been sacrificed to the underworld, four had been sent into the sky, and four had been given to mankind. The last and final one had been split into thirteen smaller amulets, one for each of the *itza'at* bloodlines. As far as she knew, hers was the only one left.

What if there was another? What if it could awaken her powers? Excitement whipped through her and her voice shook as she said, "Who are you?"

But Rosa's expression didn't change and she didn't answer. After a moment, she said, "Greetings, seer." And Anna's heart sank as she repeated the message, word for word.

"She just keeps saying the same thing, over and over," David said. "What does it mean?"

Anna jolted at the doctor's question. *Keep it together,* she warned herself. *Don't let him guess what's really going on.* How could he, though? The truth was so far out of normal reality that it wouldn't even compute for most rational humans. He'd think she was insane.

She chose her words carefully. "It's ancient Mayan, sort of. But it's gibberish, like someone taught her a few words, but not their meanings or syntax." There was no reason for her to feel guilty about lying. It was for his own protection.

"You're sure?" Behind the face shield, his eyes were too perceptive.

"I'm sorry." That was no lie. "What were you hoping for?"

"Something . . . more." Expression going rueful, he shot a glance at the now-dozing child and said in an undertone, "The way that woman was calling her the devil and blaming her for the outbreak and all . . . Intellectually, I know she was raving, that both cases are just atypical presentations of the virus. But after reading the stuff you sent over, about bloodletting, rituals, sacred incense and gods and stuff, when one of the volunteers told me she thought Rosa was speaking an old Mayan dialect . . . well, I guess I was hoping she might tell us something useful."

She did. Thank you for calling me. "Like what?"

"More herbal remedies, maybe, or an incantation." At her startled look, he shrugged. "The station where I grew up put the 'out' in outback. I was making potions long before I learned about chemical drugs, so you're not going to get any guff about traditional medicine from me. Some of the other doctors, maybe, but not me."

Rosa was murmuring in her sleep. The same thing, over and over again. *There is a ruby skull . . .*

"It's not a cure," Anna said softly. Worse, the message was specifically for her, which meant she was the reason the child had been chosen. The gods had seen her as a way to get to Anna. *Why not just send me a damn vision?* she thought viciously. But they couldn't, of course, because her subconscious was blocking her magic. Her fault. Swallowing, she asked, "What will happen to her?"

"If she lives? Foster care, probably."

Anna knew she couldn't afford to get any more involved than she already was—not with Rosa, her aunt, or any of the other motionless figures bound to their beds in rooms nearby, and certainly not with the handsome doctor. They were part of the larger fight, not its focus. But she said, "I'll keep looking for cures."

He grimaced. "I didn't mean to put this on you. It's not your fight."

Oh, yes it is. "I'll call you if I find anything."

"Do that. Or, hell, just come to the main entrance and have someone track me down." His hazel eyes locked on hers through the shield, going suddenly intent. "How much longer are you going to be here?"

"I don't know. A few days, maybe longer."

"Where are you staying again?"

"I don't . . . I can't . . . shit." She didn't want to lie to him. He was a good man. Faking a look at her wristband, she said, "I've got to go. I'll call you."

She was through the door before he could say anything else, heading up the corridor at a fast walk as the panel *thunked* shut.

Moments later, it *wonked* back open. "Anna, wait!"

I can't. Pretending not to hear, she ducked through a makeshift decontamination area that led from the inner area to the outer ring of buildings. There, she shucked off her protective clothing and sailed through a half-assed monitoring station, giving a vague wave when the guy called after her in Spanish.

Outside, she dodged around a ragged knot of shell-shocked-looking locals she guessed were the family members of a newly made *xombi*. "Sorry," she murmured as she got around them, apologizing for far more than crowding them, though they would never know it.

"Wait, damn it." A hand grabbed her arm and swung her around, and she found herself with her back against the wall, staring up at David, who looked frustrated and grumpy, and as flustered as she'd yet seen him. He had shucked off his gear, too, and his bare hand on her forearm seemed suddenly very naked, as did his bewilderment. "Anna, seriously. What's going on here?"

She tried to edge around him, but he didn't budge. "This isn't a good time. I really need to go." Her mind raced, but even though she'd spent an entire career—and an entire marriage—playing human, with all the lies that had entailed, now she couldn't come up with a damn thing.

"What aren't you telling me? Are you in some sort of trouble? Damn it, I told you to watch out for the cops."

"It's not . . ." She trailed off, because she didn't know what it was or wasn't anymore, couldn't wrap her head around anything with him touching her.

When was the last time she'd been this close to a man who wasn't one of her teammates? When was the last time someone other than Strike had crowded her overprotectively, trying to make sure she was safe? How sad was it that she couldn't remember? The answer should've involved her ex, and maybe it did, but she couldn't remember how it had felt to have Dick's body this near hers, and he'd never been one to get big and protective, at least not over her.

She had told herself she liked that he respected her independence, and maybe back then she had. Now, though, she was badly tempted to lean into David's warm, solid strength.

Instead, she braced a hand on his chest and levered him back several inches, until their bodies weren't touching anywhere except at palm and wrist. Then she broke those contacts, too, dropping her hand from his chest and using it to pry his fingers off her wrist. He let go immediately, looking surprised to find that he was holding her at all. Which left them standing there at the edge of the hallway chaos, not touching anymore. But not moving either.

"Talk to me," he said quietly, urgently.

She shook her head, denying more than just the question. "You've been on shift too long, doctor, with too many weird things happening. You're imagining things."

"Am I?"

"I'm just a linguist."

"No, you're not." He leaned in, voice dropping. "You're a top-notch Mayanist who hasn't published anything in nearly three years, and who's been on sabbatical for the past year and a half, since not all that long after your grad student protégé got in trouble for defending a thesis on the twenty-twelve doomsday . . . which by my calendar is just over a week away. And that makes this outbreak—and your presence here— look awfully coincidental."

Anna. Couldn't. Breathe. "You had me investigated?"

"If you call spending five minutes on Google the same as having you investigated, then yeah, I did." His features tightened. "Look, I'm not trying to freak you out or come off like Creepy Stalker Guy, but I was interested, okay? Even more so once you sent me the recipe for a wacky-sounding herbal mix that actually worked." He lifted a hand, but then let it fall again without touching her. "That's why I called you when Rosa came in and started spouting ancient Mayan . . . because I need to know what's really going on here. Is this the beginning of the end, an army of darkness, or what?"

Close, she thought wildly. *He's too damn close*. Not just to her, personally, but to the truth. The Nightkeepers weren't sworn to secrecy, granted, and gods knew there were plenty of doomsday theories out there, but Dez would be furious if she blew this contact. Worse, he'd be disappointed.

Play it cool. You can do this. If she didn't, the doctor would have to be mind-bent, and she didn't want that. She just didn't.

They were getting some sidelong looks from the hurry-scurry folk in the narrow strip of space separating the inner and outer tent rings, but nobody seemed to be paying attention to their conversation; they were too busy getting from point A to point B. Anna and David, though, seemed suddenly encased within a strange, human-made shield of privacy.

Think. She had to think. She couldn't, though—not when her head was starting to pound, harder and harder, reminding her of when—

"I had an aneurysm," she blurted.

His face blanked. "You what?"

She took his hand—warm and wide-palmed—and lifted it to her scalp so he could feel the ridged scar. "Surgery, a coma, long recovery, the works. I'm fine now, really. But by the time I was back on my feet, my cheating husband had divorced me, the university had put a perfectly good replacement in my position, and I realized that I wasn't dying to go back anyway. I wanted something more."

"Like what?"

"I'm working on a book about the ruins and their inscriptions. That's why I remembered the carving that talked about a plague." Again, the lies pinched.

"You're writing a book." His face had gone unreadable.

She eased out from behind his big body. This time he let her go, which brought a pang. Facing him now, with her back to the flow of traffic, she said, "I'm sorry, Dr. Curtis. I really need to go."

"Dave."

"Dave, then." His name felt strange coming off her tongue, like it was too close to "Dick," yet nothing at all like it. Not that she should be comparing the two of them, really. They were very different men and the situations were worlds apart. "All I know about the so-called Mayan doomsday is whatever I couldn't avoid hearing from my grad student, Lucius, and the tripe that's been in the media. As for the outbreak, I've told you everything I know, except for the stuff I'm going to go look up now, based on what Rosa was saying." She spread her hands and met his eyes. "Seriously. I'm not hiding anything."

It seemed like an eon before his shoulders dropped and he shook his head, chuckling a little at himself. "Shit. I could've sworn . . . well, maybe you're right that I've been on shift too long. You wouldn't be the first one to suggest I'm pushing too hard."

"You should rest."

"Yeah. I . . . yeah." He raised a hand, hesitated as if surprised to see that it wasn't wearing a glove, and then scrubbed his fingers through his thick hair, leaving it rumpled and standing on end. "Sorry I got weird on you. It was just that, back there in the room with Rosa, it was like there was something else in there with us. Some sort of presence, or power, or something." He rolled his eyes, and his accent thickened. "My ma would say I'd been listening to too many stories again."

Anna made herself ignore the tug of his voice, and the way it made her think of open spaces far away from ground zero. "I really do need to get going, and not because I'm in trouble. I promised to meet friends. *Outside* the quarantine zone," she added when he started to frown. And that much, at least, was the gods' honest truth.

"You're taking proper precautions?"

"I am. I swear." Just not the kind he was talking about.

"And you'll call if you find anything else?"

"Absolutely." Well, once Dez cleared it.

He hesitated, then nodded. "Okay. Well . . . right. I guess I'll see you?"

"I hope so." And that, a little to her surprise, was also the gods' honest truth.

Still, though, as they parted with a wave and one too many over-the-shoulder looks back, her stomach was tied in serious knots over the entire exchange. As she headed for the outer perimeter, she tried to figure out why she didn't feel good about how that had gone down. She had kept him as a contact, talked her way out of a sticky situation, and managed to preserve her cover. So why did she feel like shit? Or, more accurately, why did she hate having to lie to a virtual stranger when she'd been lying to her friends and coworkers—and even a husband—for decades?

It doesn't matter, she told herself. *What matters is getting home and getting your hands on that skull.* The thought brought a renewed buzz of excitement and a stir of magic, along with the nerves that came with the thought that she would need to tread carefully if she wanted to—

A big, bulky form stepped in front of her, and a deep voice boomed, "Excuse me, ma'am?"

She stopped dead, and an "oh shit" zinged through her at the sight of a security guard. It wasn't the guy she'd waved her way past as she'd booked it out of the clean zone, but she had a feeling that had been her mistake. It'd gotten them talking, and they had realized that nobody had signed her in. Faking surprise, she blinked at him. "I'm sorry. Is there a problem?"

He caught her arm and turned her back the way she'd come. "I'm going to need you to come with me, please." His voice was polite, his grip inexorable, and Anna found herself being force-marched past row after row of doors that all looked the same, while her brain raced. What the hell was she supposed to do now?

She had options, of course—she could knock him down with a sleep spell, use a chameleon spell, teleport away . . . But any of those things would send up some serious red flags for her already-suspicious doctor.

A glance at her comm device showed that there weren't any blinking lights, no evidence that anybody needed her. So, as the guard ushered her through an unmarked door into a prefab steel room that held a desk, a couple of chairs, a huge wipe board scrawled with guard shifts and notes suggesting that she was in what passed for their security hub, she followed his orders without question, figuring she would go with the flow, do her best to smooth things over, and talk her way out of starring in an incident report.

Gods knew that in a place like this, with so many people coming and going, the left hand probably wouldn't know what the right was doing half the time. Ten bucks said she could convince this guy that she'd been waved through the checkpoint on the strength of Dr. Dave's name, asked some volunteer for help with her protective gear, and found him on her own. And if they couldn't track down anyone to verify, they'd just figure it'd gotten lost in the chaos.

Last resort, she'd lock herself in the bathroom and put in a call for some mind-bending support—which she was far less reluctant to do on the guards than she had been on David. Either way, she could deal with this. Hopefully, Rabbit and Myrinne could handle things on their end for a little longer without getting in major trouble.

CHAPTER THIRTEEN

Oc Ajal, Mexico

Rabbit faced the fire pit and tried to block everything else out—the rain forest, the remains of the village where he'd been born, the latent hiss of magic surrounding him, the Nightkeeper powers that wanted to flare and combat the darkness—all of it. He was still aware of Myr standing behind him, though, with her shield running hot, ready to protect him . . . and to protect herself against him.

Hoping it would be enough—hoping *he* would be enough—he sent a quick prayer to the gods he'd forsaken. Then, pulse thudding in his ears, he opened his hands and cast his blood into the cold, bare fire pit. *"Cha'ik ten ee'hochen!" Bring the darkness to me!*

Blam! The floodgates slammed open, giving way beneath an onslaught of power. Dark magic hammered through him, terrible yet incredible, and as he staggered back a step, flames erupted from within the stone circle, writhing like serpents.

"Rabbit!" Myr cried, her voice sounding far away.

"Stay back!" he shouted as the darkness surrounded him, swamping him with an incalculable power that gushed up from the depths of his soul. More, emotions tore at him—frustration, impotence, resentment, murderous rage, loneliness, all of it mixing together into a blinding fury that made him want to howl.

No! He fought the impulses, but he wasn't braced for fury, wasn't buffered against one of the red rages that used to grab on to him, making him do stupid, impulsive things. For that was what raced into his mind.

Suddenly, he wasn't himself anymore, at least not the guy he wanted to be. Instead, he was the whipped dog he had become beneath the '*zotz*'s lash. He was the pissed-off teen who had torched Jox's garden center, the frustrated punk who'd wanted to make his mark on Skywatch. He was the impulsive asshole who'd led Iago to Oc Ajal, the gullible prick who had listened to Phee's lies, sucking them up like soft-serve. And he was the stone-cold bastard who'd held a knife to Myr's throat and made her bleed.

He clenched his fists as his soul overflowed with every bad decision he'd ever made, every moment that he'd been unhappy, pissed off, pissed on.

Burn it, whispered a voice inside him. *Burn it all down.*

The fire climbed hotter and higher, sending out billows of dark, oily smoke that tore at his throat and filled his lungs. His heart hammered as his warrior's instincts said to back up, back off and lock himself down. But another set of instincts said he couldn't shut himself off now. Not if he wanted to become the crossover.

"Oh, shit," he said, not sure if he said it aloud or only in his mind. "I get it. I fucking get it."

This was why the Nightkeepers' ancestors had deemed the dark half of the magic too dangerous and banished the dark magi . . . and it was why they had feared the wild powers of a half blood like him—because where the light magic tapped into the good stuff, like love, sex and the power of teamwork, the dark magic drew from all the bad stuff inside its wielder. It concentrated it, encouraged it, made it real.

He hadn't felt these things when he'd used the dark magic before, when the rage had already been at the surface of his soul, ready for the darkness to tap into it. Now, though, he could feel the old frustrations hissing and seething inside him, heard them whispering, *They never believed you, never believed in you. You can show them all just how powerful you really are.*

Sudden images crammed his mind's eye, and anger surged through him, pure and powerful. Screw them. They never liked him, never understood him, had always been afraid of him. They were small-minded, shortsighted, jealous, and—

Rabbit shuddered as he recognized all the things

he'd told himself when he'd been under Phee's spell. But those weren't his words; they weren't his thoughts. And that meant he could ignore them, block them off.

You can do this. You can handle it. He needed to prove it to himself, to the others, especially to Myrinne. He hadn't wanted her to see him like this, and he sure as hell didn't want her to see him fail. More, he didn't have a fucking choice, not if he wanted—needed—to harness the crossover's powers. So, imagining a fierce, cleansing wind blowing through his mind, he swept up the voices, the memories, the taunts and the righteous-feeling anger that wasn't righteous at all, corralling them and stuffing them back into the vault. Then, with a mental heave, he slammed the lid on all of it, leaving the dark magic outside but shutting his own weaknesses away.

The hinges creaked; the door bulged. But it held. It fucking held.

For now, at least. And with the whispers and emotions gone, only the power of the dark magic remained, deep and surging, pulsing an urgent demand through him. *Use me*, it seemed to say. *I'm yours*.

Exhaling, but not daring to glance back at Myr to see how much of that inner battle she had comprehended, he reopened the slashes across his palms and cast a spray of blood into the flames. Then he steeled himself, and said, "*Cha'ik ten nohoch taat*." *Bring me the grandfather*.

Fire burst skyward, turning the day red-orange, scorching his skin and sending the monkeys overhead screeching to higher branches as the noise of the dark magic cycled up to a chain-saw buzz, whipping around him and making his jaw ache.

He felt the spell hesitate, teetering between success and failure, felt the vault door shudder as the other part of the dark magic struggled to break free.

Strengthening his mental hold on his inner garbage, he repeated the incantation. *"Cha'ik ten nohoch taat."*

Pain streaked along the scars that striped his back, turning them raw and new as the smoke swirled and churned, becoming something. A strangled sound tore from Rabbit's throat, but he held in the rest as the smoke twined together, and then, *bam*, whipped into the shape of a gimlet-eyed old man who wore the long robe of a Xibalban priest and had the hellmark on his wrist.

And even though Rabbit had come for this, prepared for it, sick and ugly anger awoke at the sight of the old shaman. His fucking grandfather.

The smoke-ghost looked around, seeming unsurprised at the summons. His eyes lingered on Myrinne, but then moved on. "Greetings, young Rabbit."

"Greetings . . . Grandfather." *You cocksucker.*

The see-through bastard had the gall to smile. "Ah. So you know the truth now."

"I know you bred me. I want to know the rest. I want to understand your purpose for me." He heard Myr's smothered gasp, felt her mistrust, and hoped to hell she would go with it. More, he hoped he wasn't making a big fucking mistake. Because if anything happened to

him, he wasn't sure she'd be strong enough to take
Anntah on her own. Hell, he wasn't sure *he* could do it,
and he'd summoned the bastard. If she got hurt because of him . . .

Over my dead body, he thought, and the mental promise had the force of a blood vow.

Anntah spread his ghostly arms. "Ask your questions."

Rabbit was all too aware that the smoke-ghost had
his own agenda, that he would lie . . . but he was also
the only one left who knew the truth. "How do I become the crossover?"

"You already are. You are the son of a Xibalban princess and the last surviving Nightkeeper mage. You are
the child of prophecy."

A shiver tried to work its way down Rabbit's spine,
but he ignored it. "Okay, let's try it this way. How can
I access the powers of the crossover? Is there a spell, an
artifact, what?"

"There is nothing. Only you."

"Bullshit. Tell me the fucking truth."

"This is the truth. There is no spell or artifact, no
need for you to become anything other than what you
already are. You *are* the crossover, Rabbie. The power is
inside you."

Rabbie. The name echoed in his head, in his heart,
rattled at the vault. "Don't call me that."

"Why not? It's what your mother and I called you,
the name your father and the Nightkeepers took from
you. Just like they told you that you weren't good

enough for them, that your mistakes were too costly, your self-control too weak." The ghost leaned in, eyes lighting. "They were wrong, you know. You're stronger than they are—stronger than any of us. And I can make you stronger still."

"Fuck you." But the whispers urged him on. And he had a feeling the bastard knew it.

"You are the last Xibalban, Rabbie. Swear yourself to the dark gods and all our powers will be yours."

"Swear . . ." He trailed off as shock rattled through him, sounding like the magic. He was suddenly aware that the elder wasn't alone in the mist anymore. There were others behind him, around him, vague shadows that shifted, yearning toward Rabbit like he was their hope, like he was the hero he'd always wanted to be. More, there was a new note to the power—a deep thrumming that vibrated at the edge of his magic, limitless and tempting.

Take it. It's yours. You can show them all, burn them all.

"Rabbit, don't do it. Don't listen to him!" Myrinne's faraway voice was ragged and breathless, like she'd been shouting at him for a while and he hadn't heard.

Ignoring her, Anntah held out his hand, which bled red-tinged fog from a slashing cut across the palm. "Come, son. Take the oath and you will have more power than you ever imagined. And when the day comes, you'll rule the war."

"Rabbit, no!" Myr's magic surged and a fireball crackled to life in the supercharged air.

"We'll do it together," Rabbit said, and reached out

and clasped the ghost's outstretched hand, not just with his body, but with his magic as well. Suddenly, he could feel Anntah's flesh, his cool skin, and even the slickness of his blood. Gripping tight, he summoned a whiplash of Nightkeeper magic, and shouted, *"Kaak!"*

Red-gold fire erupted from his hand and laced up Anntah's arm, and then higher, racing to engulf him. The ghost shrieked and jerked back. "Aiiee!"

Rabbit hung on, body and soul, and poured himself into the flames. "Myr, now!"

A green fireball hit Anntah and detonated, wreathing the spirit with lambent napalm. And then she was there, standing beside him and hammering the ghost with magic.

"No!" Anntah howled. "Noo!" He whipped from side to side as the fire engulfed him, ate at him. "Whyyy?"

"Because I'm choosing my side," Rabbit grated, "and it's not yours." Nightkeeper power sang through him, driving the dark magic back into the vault. Buoyed by that victory—and by the ferocity in Myr's face as she fought beside him—he cast the banishment spell. *"Teech xeen!"*

Power detonated with a huge shock wave and a flash of brilliant red-gold light. Rabbit reflexively spun and yanked Myr against him, and then cast a shield around them both. For a second, furious magic roared over them, around them, heating the air and lighting his senses.

Then it was gone. And the world went silent.

Suddenly aware that he had his arms wrapped around her when she could've shielded herself, he released her and backed off. "Sorry, I . . . holy crap."

He went silent, stunned by the brilliant colors that suddenly surrounded them.

Myr drew in a breath, and then exhaled it on a soft, "Ohh."

There was no sign of the fire, the smoke, Anntah, or the other spirits. But where those things were gone, there was something new, something that very definitely hadn't been there before.

Butterflies.

Everywhere except for the fire pit, the ruined village was carpeted with the creatures—fiery red, sky blue, pale green, brilliant yellow, lacy white—making it look for a second like tens of thousands of flowers had blossomed in the space of a few minutes. Except these flowers had wings and they fluttered and pulsed, bringing the ghost town to life. And then, as if they'd gotten some silent signal, they rose up into the air and swirled like brightly colored confetti.

They danced and spun for a moment, and then began to settle again, many of them wafting toward Myrinne. They landed on her shoulders, in her hair, on her face, until she was dotted with living jewels.

Her eyes shone with wonder. "Look," she said, even though he was already staring at her. She cupped her palms and they filled with butterflies. "Look at them all."

"Fuck me," Rabbit said. It wasn't exactly poetry, but it was all he could manage as the beauty of the moment cut into him, painful in its intensity.

She was radiant, limned in color, and so very alive that it hurt like hell to know they were running out of time, and he didn't have the answers he needed. More, he didn't know what those answers would mean for the two of them. So he didn't say anything, just cupped his own palms together, very aware that there were only two spots in the village that were bare of the insects: him and the fire pit.

After a moment, a big butterfly landed in his cupped palms. Its wings were streaked with red and orange like flames, its body matte black like his combat clothes, and though he didn't know what that meant, it sure as hell felt like it meant something.

The creature fluttered up, deserting him, but a second later, a shiny green one lofted up from Myr's shoulder to join it. The two hovered for a moment at eye level, then headed upward, twining together in an aerial dance that blurred green and red together. Others followed—blue, yellow, purple, pink—as if an entire field of wildflowers had suddenly taken flight. They churned up, swirled once around the ruined village, and then headed into the trees en masse, as if they had somewhere else to be.

Rabbit's throat tightened at how fricking pretty it was, but also with an ache of frustration, this time not coming from the dark magic, but from him. Because moments like this—beautiful, magical—should be protected. And he wasn't sure he knew how.

"Gods," Myr whispered, her eyes locked on the last of the colorful flutters. "That was incredible." The radiance still surrounded her, he realized. It wasn't just the butterflies; it was magic.

"You summoned them," he said, feeling a kick of *holy shit* inside him, because she sure as hell hadn't inherited that power from him. This was something new, something he'd never heard of before.

"Maybe." She hesitated, then nodded. "I think so. Not on purpose, but maybe deep down inside . . ."

"Tell me." *Talk to me.*

Shadows crept into her eyes, but she said softly, "When I was maybe nine or ten, I found a book on one of the shelves. I don't know why the Witch bought it— an accident, or maybe a special order someone had bailed on. Certainly wasn't her style, with flowers and butterflies on the cover. And the magic inside was so different from hers, all about power flows and respecting the earth and all its creatures." She paused. "Anyway, I used to wait until she was asleep at night, and I'd take the book off the shelf and sneak out to the little garden behind the tea shop, where I'd practice the incantations by candlelight. At first nothing happened, but then, one night, a butterfly came and sat near my candle. Then the next night, there were two of them, then more and more." Her voice flattened abruptly. "I was up to a dozen when the Witch caught on."

"She punished you." One of Rabbit's biggest regrets was that Iago had killed the bitch before he'd gotten to her.

"Worse. She used me. She snuck up behind me and netted the butterflies, then locked them in a cabinet so I couldn't set them free. The next day, she pinned them down alive, dried them in the oven, and sold the powder to the owner of the bar next door, telling him it was an aphrodisiac." Her voice was flat, her eyes hollow. "She made me call them again the next night, and the next. Every night for a week, until they stopped coming."

Ah, baby. He hated what she'd been through. Hated even more that he didn't know what to say.

"I tried to tell her I wouldn't do it, and when that didn't work, I tried to screw up the incantation. But she knew. Somehow, she knew, and she made me do it right. I'm not even sure how. I guess I was that afraid of her, that afraid of what would happen to me if it wasn't for her."

"You were a kid."

"Even later, when I was old enough to run away, I didn't. I just wasn't ever strong enough to stand up to her."

"You are now." When she just shook her head and started to turn away, he caught her hand and drew her back toward him. "Hey, look around you. You just helped banish a dark-magic ghost. You could handle fifty of her."

She started to argue, but then hesitated. "You think so?"

Something shifted in his chest. "I know so. You're not just a mage now, Myr, you're a warrior too. You were ready to bring me down if you didn't like what was going on. Instead, you helped me nail Anntah. Hell, I bet you could've taken him on your own— you're that strong now, Myr. Seriously."

"That sounds like something I would've said to you, back in the day."

And it wasn't the kind of thing he'd ever really said to her before, which was his foul—one of many. He should've backed her up better, should have helped make her feel safer. Now, though, the best he could do was say, "I mean it. The Nightkeepers should consider themselves damn lucky to have you on their side . . . I know I do."

Her eyes darkened. "You've got your own magic working now, both halves of it. You don't need me anymore."

He knew he should back off; she'd be safer away from him. Instead, he caught her other hand and leaned in, so she could see the intensity in his eyes when he said, "Fuck that. I need you."

"Damn it, Rabbit," the words were barely a whisper, but she didn't pull away. And suddenly there was a crackle of new energy in the air.

"Tell me to back off and leave you the hell alone." But then, before she could say anything, he closed the

last little distance between them, and said against her
lips, "Don't. Please."

And he kissed her. Because he'd gotten to where he
couldn't *not* kiss her. He needed her warmth and sass,
needed the woman who could fry a demon one moment and call butterflies in the next. Most of all, he
needed the heat that pounded between them, reminding him that he was alive, and that he wasn't just fighting against his mother, grandfather and a whole
shitload of other baddies, he was fighting *for* the good
guys. For moments like this.

He kept his arms loose in case she wanted to break
free, but had no real intention of letting her go. And
after only a moment's hesitation, she made a muffled
noise of surrender, then twined her arms around his
neck and kissed him back. And all he could think was,
Thank fuck.

Sensations rocketed along his neurons: the softness
of her breasts, the curves of her waist and the brush of
her hair contrasting with the hard edges of her weapons; the buzz of lust and magic in his veins; and the
"Oh hell, yeah" he growled at the back of his throat
when she trailed her hands down, latched on to his
weapons belt, and pulled their lower bodies tighter together.

He cupped her breast through her tight combat shirt,
found a peaked nipple, and caught her moan in his
mouth. Then he broke the kiss and trailed his lips along
her jaw. "Myr," he rasped against her throat, needing

to say it. This didn't feel like a dream-vision, but he wasn't entirely sure.

"I'm here." She pressed her lips to his cheek, his ear.

"Thank the gods." He kissed her again, long and deep, steeping himself in her scent and flavor, soaking her in and—

Power surged suddenly, coming from a few feet away, and the air sparked red-gold. Cursing under his breath, Rabbit pulled away. "Incoming."

"I know."

The two of them were standing shoulder to shoulder, breathing hard, when Anna appeared with a *whump* of displaced air.

Seeming preoccupied, she glanced at them, scanned the village, and let out a relieved breath. "Cool. Glad to see you guys didn't get into too much trouble while I was gone. You'll never guess what happened to me . . . Shit. Why are you laughing? What did I miss?"

CHAPTER FOURTEEN

Skywatch

After Myr and Rabbit got back to the compound, the next few hours were a whirlwind of debriefings and "what the fuck?" as the Nightkeepers scrambled to plug the new info—or lack thereof—into their battle plans.

Myr managed to snag some leftover pizza and a Coke in between sitting down with Rabbit, Dez and the royal council; going over what'd happened at Oc Ajal; and hustling to the library, where she was helping Lucius and the other members of the brain trust look for references to the true gods and the ruby skull.

There wasn't much in the way of peace and quiet in the library—Lucius, Natalie and Jade were constantly coming and going from the racks, pulling scrolls and artifacts for quick-and-dirty translations before turning them over to Myr for some database work. But even that frenetic activity was oddly soothing. Or maybe it was just that she needed some space—any space—without Rabbit in it, some time to process what had happened at Oc Ajal.

She had fought a ghost and summoned butterflies. She had stood on her own, ready to face down Rabbit if she didn't like what she saw. And she had kissed him—not because she was needy or afraid, or because the magic had overridden her control, but because she wanted to kiss him. For the first time, it had felt like they were meeting as equals, as partners.

Or was she talking herself back into the fantasy?

"We're on our way," Lucius said as he came around the nearest rack with a couple of scrolls under one arm, using his shoulder to prop a phone against his ear. "Give us five minutes." Ending the call, he said to Myr, "Anna and the others can't find any hidden compartment in the altar. It looks like they're going to have to break it apart to see if the ruby skull is inside."

"Ouch."

The *chac-mool* had been mortared into place with the ashes from generations of Nightkeepers, and the altar had received the blood of practically every mage to come through the training compound since then. It had overseen the marriages of most of the current Nightkeepers' parents, and held enough accrued magic to make it a serious power sink. It was a constant, a link to their past and a touchstone of the present. Busting it up was *not* going to go over well.

"Jade, Natalie and I are going to head up and see if we can help," Lucius said, dumping the scrolls at the far end of the stone table where Myr was working. "You coming?"

"I think I'll keep working on this stuff." She waved at the pile of printouts and artifacts that still needed to be logged, scanned and cross-referenced.

"I'd appreciate it. The more we figure out about these so-called 'true gods,' the better."

"What do you have so far?" She'd heard the others bouncing ideas back and forth, but hadn't heard an outcome.

He shook his head. "Not much. There's plenty on the gods, of course . . . but what makes a god a 'true god'? Are we talking about all of the sky gods, a subset of them, or what?"

"Which leaves us where?"

"Digging a jackhammer out of storage to have a go at the *chac-mool*?"

Myr winced. "I don't like that idea."

"You're not alone. But the message wasn't exactly subtle." He spread his hands, flashing the *jun tan* he wore on his inner wrist, which marked him as Jade's mate, a love match. The sight shouldn't have brought a pang, shouldn't have made her own wrist feel bare, especially now.

"What if there's nothing in there?"

"Don't even think it." But the shadows in his eyes said he was worried too. He paused. "You sure you want to stay here?"

"Positive." She waved him off and got back to work, only half listening to the subdued commotion of the others leaving, followed by the library settling into an empty quiet broken only by the noises she made when she shifted things from the "to do" pile to the "done" pile, and the background murmur of running water coming from the jaguar-shaped fountain near the door. There was peace in the solitude, and she found herself relaxing as "to do" got smaller and "done" got so big that it started sloping off to one side, threatening an information avalanche.

An hour or so later—maybe longer—she was startled to reach for another "to do" and find the pile gone. And when she actually sat back and looked around, she realized she was more than a little woozy from sitting still too long and probably from some leftover post-magic fatigue.

"Time to call it a night," she said. "You might not have solved any of your problems, but at least you got some paperwork done."

Except, as she grabbed the soft leather jacket she'd worn against the almost-winter chill, she realized that she'd come to a resolution of sorts. There was a strange sort of peace inside her that hadn't been there before, one that said if she could go up against a ghost-demon and summon a whole village's worth of butterflies, she could handle starting something new with Rabbit.

Carefully, she told herself. *Very carefully*. Because she wasn't going to make the same mistakes this time. This wasn't about forever after; it was about taking what they both wanted while they still had the chance.

The cloud-hazed night was inky black, with just a glimmer of moonlight to guide her along the pathway to the cottage she and Rabbit had shared for more than two years. She didn't hesitate at the steps, didn't pause before knocking—*bang, bang, bang*—using the sharp, peremptory cadence she'd used back in college, the one that said "move it or lose it, buster." She caught her breath, though, as the knob turned, then let it out as the panel opened to reveal Rabbit standing barefoot, wearing worn sweats and a black hoodie.

His eyes burned into her, resonating with the leftover heat from their earlier kiss. "You came."

Adrenaline buzzed in her veins, making her feel powerful. "Were you waiting for me?"

"I was doing my damnedest not to go after you. I would've lasted another fifteen minutes, maybe less." His gaze skimmed over her, feeling like a touch. "Come in. Please."

She didn't hesitate. This was what she'd come for, after all.

He stepped back so she could move past him into the kitchen, then shut the door behind her, enclosing them in a four-room cottage that suddenly seemed far smaller than she remembered. It should've felt strange, being back there after all this time, but the air smelled of vanilla and patchouli. The twin scents twined together, amping her magic. More, they drew her deeper into the cottage, across the kitchen and living room, and all the way to the bedroom door.

She stopped there, and breathed, "Oh."

Rabbit came up behind her and stood very close, looking over her shoulder into the room they had shared for so long. Two lit candles sat in holders on the nightstand, one white, one red, both hers. The red one was burned down to little more than a nub, while the white was newer, yet set in wax from a prior white candle, now burned away. Together, they filled the room with warm yellow light, showing where the familiar bedspread was dented in the shape of a big, heavy body curled on its side, with a dog-eared paperback lying nearby.

Her eyes misted at the sight. How many nights had they lain like that together, with her reading and him zoned out on his iPod, the two of them fitting together like the pieces of a puzzle? And how many nights over the past few months had she found herself curled up the same way, alone?

"The candles aren't because I miss the way things used to be," he said.

She turned to him, heart lumping in her throat. "They're not?"

"Not tonight. Tonight I lit them because I was hoping you'd come."

He stood in the doorway, filling it. But it wasn't the size of his body or the hugeness of what he was saying that threatened to overwhelm her. It was the excitement that seared through her veins, and the knowledge that she was strong enough to make this work. "A summoning spell, you mean?"

"Hey, it worked on the butterflies." He paused. "Will you stay with me?"

She didn't know whether he meant for the next few hours, the night, or for as long as they had left, but she found that it didn't really matter. "We can't go back."

"I don't want to go back; I want to move forward." He closed the small distance between them, and took her hand. "This can be whatever you want it to be." He leaned in and pressed his lips to her temple, her cheek. "Anything, so long as it means I don't have to stay away from you anymore."

"Was that what you were doing? FYI, you kind of suck at it."

He grinned. "Got you here, didn't it?"

"I guess it did." Taking a deep breath that smelled of her candles, she turned her head, found his lips, and sank into the kiss she had come for. And, for the moment, at least, she was exactly where she wanted to be, doing exactly what she wanted to do. On her own terms.

Rabbit met the kiss as relief slashed through him. Excitement. Pounding need. He couldn't believe she was really there, that this was really happening. Even after everything that had happened today, he hadn't been sure she would be ready to trust him like this again.

That she was seemed like a minor fucking miracle.

His body lit and his heart thudded. His fingers curled around her jaw, then the back of her skull, as she moved against him, bumping her hips and rubbing her belly against his cock, which was already throbbing and hard. But beside that urgency, there was softness, sweetness. Her lips were lush and giving, her breasts gentle curves that were familiar, yet not, like it was new all over again.

In the back of his mind he was more than half-afraid that he might be dozing, drooling on his Clive Cussler. But if that was the case, fuck, he never wanted to wake up, because this was nothing like the nightmares. *It's real*, something whispered inside him, cutting through the wonder and the almost-fear that if he opened his eyes he'd be back alone in the bed, smelling her scent without her being anywhere near. But he wasn't alone, she wasn't far away, and this was really happening. He knew it from the way her fingers curled into his waistband, sealing them together, and from the sexy purr she made in the back of her throat when he changed the angle of his mouth.

He caught her wrist, kissed her fingers, and then parted from her to draw her down to the bed they had shared for so long. They didn't say anything; there didn't seem to be any need for more words.

The mattress dipped beneath him and poor Clive headed for the floor as she followed him down to the bed and straddled his hips, pinning him and rendering him a very willing prisoner. His hands found her waist and slid up as hers reached for the zipper of his hoodie and tugged it down. Her eyes lit when she found he wasn't wearing anything beneath it, and she spread the edges of his sweatshirt wide, baring his chest, with the new layer of ridged scars. She sobered and traced the marks with her fingers, and where before the scar tissue had been numb, now they caught fire and throbbed with a sensation that wasn't quite pleasure, wasn't quite pain.

He caught her hand. "Don't. I got what I deserved."

She flattened her hand over the worst of it, over his heartbeat, but she didn't argue. Instead, she shifted to kiss the spot where the whip marks intersected, and then, looking up so their eyes met, she said, "Moving forward, right?"

"Moving forward." Emotion roughened his voice and gave the words the force of a spell. Sex magic poured through him, buoying his excitement and revving his system into overdrive. And for the first time, her magic rose up to answer his as they kissed—she wasn't holding back anymore, wasn't blocking the buzz of energy. This wasn't the connection they'd had before, when their powers had been joined. Instead, the sex magic spiraled out into the air surrounding them, ramping up the heat and throbbing with the beat of his blood in his veins.

Suddenly he couldn't lie there beneath her anymore. He surged up and over, reversing them so he rose above her, caging her in with his legs and arms.

She grinned and started to wiggle out from underneath him, as she had so often done before, turning her preference for being on top into a game. Now, though, he tightened his arms and dropped his head to nuzzle her neck, kiss her throat, nip at the soft skin behind one ear. She shuddered and moaned, and went pliant beneath him in a sudden capitulation that burned through him.

"Gods, Myr." His voice was ragged, his cock so hard it hurt, wanting—needing—to be inside her.

He braced himself over her as he dragged his teeth to the dip at the base of her throat and kissed her there, lingering until she arched against him. Her hands came up to grip his waist, then dug in on either side of his spine. Snagging the hem of her shirt, he tugged it up and off, then shucked his hoodie, managing the moves with barely a pause in kissing her cheeks, her eyelids, her temples and then, when she dug her nails into his skin and sought his mouth, her lips.

Then, finally, he lowered himself so they were chest to chest, touching along the lengths of their bodies. He groaned as her soft warmth seeped into him, filling the empty spaces and lighting the shadows, reminding him that he might've been doing fine without her, but he was so fucking much better *with* her.

"Damn, I missed you," he rasped, pressing his cheek to hers.

She had been his first, his only, and being skin-on-skin with her after three very long—and very life-changing—months reminded him of the way it had been at the beginning, when he'd first been learning how different an orgasm could feel with someone else involved. More, with *her* involved. Those had been heady, crazy days, first at Skywatch and then at college, where he'd gotten his first taste of feeling like he really belonged somewhere, and belonged to someone special.

Back then, he'd thought he knew it all, could handle it all. Now, he didn't feel like he knew anything, and was just doing his best to fucking cope.

Except for right now. Right now was perfect. It was magic.

"Don't," she said, and reached up to kiss him, not trying to escape now, but curling around him instead.

He didn't know what she was denying—don't think, don't worry, don't what? But then she moved beneath him, sliding down so his aching cock found its way to nestle between her legs, chafing against the layers of cloth that still separated them. And the blood drained from his head, carrying with it the last of his rational thoughts.

Groaning, he took her mouth and stopped thinking, worrying, whatever-ing, and let himself just *feel* as he feasted on her lips, her throat, her breasts. Before, he'd often needed to rein in the magic when he made love to her, as sex tried to bring out the mage in him. Now, though, there was no need for that control, because their powers met and balanced off, ramping up the sizzle yet somehow still leaving it all about him and her, and the slide of flesh against flesh.

He suckled on a pink, peaked nipple and heard her moan, went to work on her hip-hugging jeans and felt her shudder when his fingers found the zipper and tugged it down. She was wearing a slick, soft excuse for underwear, one of the thongs he fucking loved. The feel of it made him hotter, harder, turned him damn near crazy.

He got her jeans down in no time flat, leaving them snagged on her boots, so she was open to him but bound at her ankles. He halfway expected her to hold him off until she'd gotten free; instead, she moaned as he came back up her body, kissing his way up her inner thighs to that thin triangle of satiny cloth, which was a deep, fiery red that seemed to glow in the candlelight, edged on either side by a neatly trimmed strip of hair.

His lips were flush with the taste of her and his senses filled with the scent of her arousal as he traced the tip of his tongue along the line of cloth.

"Oh!" She gasped and arched into him, then purred when he did it again, licking deeper this time, tasting her and using his hands to spread her wider, give him better access. She caught his head in her hands, urged him up. "Come here. I can—"

He kissed her deeply, thoroughly, tonguing her until she went still and silent, her body vibrating around his. "Let this first one be about you," he growled against the soft skin of her lightly muscled thigh.

He'd never before thought of himself as a selfish lover, or an unselfish one—she'd been his teacher, after all, or maybe it was more that they'd learned together. But he was realizing now that while he'd figured out how to please her, it had always been while she took him with her mouth or her body, giving him everything he could think of and more. She'd never asked for anything that was hers alone. More, when he'd offered or tried, she'd always turned the tables, rising over him, taking him, making him come and come until he couldn't fucking think.

Now, though, he wanted to give her that same care and attention. And if she didn't want to take it, she was going to have to say it loud and clear, because he wasn't going to let her shift gears on him this time.

She had come to him, after all. Now he was going to make her come, over and over again. He was going to make her his, if only for this one night, in this one way.

Things were going to be different this time, damn it.

"But don't you want . . ." she began, then trailed off when he nipped her thigh in warning.

"I want this," he said softly. "I want you. Like this." *Forever*. The last was a whisper in his mind, an impossibility that belonged only in his dreams. But maybe this was a kind of a dream, he thought as he traced his tongue along the smooth, soft crease beside the moisture-darkened thong. It was a waking dream. And he never fucking wanted to come out of it.

CHAPTER FIFTEEN

Myr couldn't think, couldn't breathe, couldn't do anything but lie there, open to him and yet trapped there as well, having become a creature of pure sensation rather than logic or thought. He breathed against her and she moaned; he licked his way up her center and she shuddered; he sucked on the tight bud of her clit through the fabric of her thong and she nearly came.

I should . . . don't you want . . . always before, she had maintained a thread of control so she could make sure she pleased him, kept him. Now, her thoughts scattered as the heat coiled within her, sharp and edgy, and almost there. *Yes*, she thought, *Oh, yes*. Maybe she had come to him for release, but she was getting so much more.

Someone moaned—she thought it was her, though she wasn't aware of having made the sound. She was mindless, incoherent. It had been too long; she had been too alone, and all she could do was let her head fall back on the pillow. It was her pillow, she realized with glittering surprise, though she couldn't think right then what it meant that he'd kept it, because he growled low in his throat and quickened the tempo. And when she cracked her lids to look down at the sight of him feasting on her, she found him staring up her body, eyes dark and intense.

The moment their gazes locked, the pleasure snapped tight within her, flaring bright and brilliant. She came in a crazy, unexpected rush that left her helpless to do anything but clamp herself around him—her legs around his torso, her inner muscles around his fingers—and cry out. It was a wordless sound, not his name, not the love words they'd once used. But the feelings were there without the words, as if the past three months—six months? more?—hadn't happened. Or, more, as if they had happened differently. She was in tune with him, fixed on him, totally gone on him, as if they'd been hot and heavy all along. As if they hadn't drifted, hadn't blown up. And even back when things had been the best between them, he'd never taken her like this, never made her feel like this.

Her eyelids shuddered closed as he breathed her name and shifted to tongue the sensitive knot of flesh at the apex of her cleft, then intensified the strokes of his fingers to counterpoint the fading surge of her body. She gasped and arched into the strokes as intense pleasure overtook her in a second wave, one that spiraled up and up, amping beneath the relentless drive of his mouth and hands, and the sensation of being totally at his mercy. Totally connected to him. She came a second time, with a pressure and power that was shocking and unexpected.

Magical.

She felt invaded, taken, possessed. Always before, it had been give and take between them, and if she'd given more than she took—or allowed him to give in return—wasn't that what guys wanted? This, though . . . this was different, unsettling. And so brutally erotic that she was left torn between holding him close and pushing him away as he kissed down her legs and stripped off her boots, jeans and panties. Then he reversed his course, nipping from her toes to her inner thighs, along her stomach and up to nuzzle at her breasts. He kept his full weight off her, but the bulk of his body dipped the mattress and pressed into her, against her, and the fullness of orgasm turned to an empty ache almost instantly.

Then he shifted, slid up on the bed, and sought her mouth with a kiss that felt suddenly familiar and welcome. She knew this part, this rhythm.

She purred against his mouth and curled her legs around his hips to rub herself against him in a cadence that was warm and wet, and promised wonderful things. She levered herself up, confident that now he would let her have her way with his body, with all that masculine skin and muscles, and with the huge, hard part of him that throbbed between her legs. "My turn," she whispered into the kiss, and reached for him.

He evaded and rolled fully atop her, pressing her into the mattress as he grinned fiercely down at her. "Haven't you figured it out yet? It's all your turn, all for you." And then he kissed her with aching tenderness, sending a sliver of new, wondrous warmth through her.

"But don't you want—"

"This is what I want." He shifted, positioning himself so the blunt head of his cock slipped between her slickened folds and pressed at the entrance to her body. "*You're* what I want."

Her body said "yes" before her mind could catch up—her legs parting and accepting him, curving so one heel slid up and crooked behind his knee. "I—" she began, but then broke off on a gasp when he thrust inside her in a single powerful surge, filling her and setting off a sparkling chain reaction of energy, power and pleasure.

As she shuddered against him, he held her close, held her down and thrust into her with a sharp, bright pleasure that stripped away thought and left only sensation behind. She moaned and clutched at him, would have moved to counterpoint his thrusts, but he didn't give her the leeway, didn't give her any choice but to take, and take more. And gods. Oh, gods.

Breathing became unimportant; self-preservation became unneeded, until the only thing that mattered was the pound of his body against hers, into hers. New pleasure gathered, surprising her. She would've thought she was done, spent—she'd come twice already, after all. But as another orgasm built, she arched up into his kiss, then pressed her cheek to his, her lips to his throat, and inhaled the scent of the two of them together.

This. This was what she needed, what she had come to him for.

"More," she whispered against his throat.

"Hell, yeah." His voice was a passionate rasp, his grip on her hips inexorable as he shifted, held her, and intensified the tempo.

Pleasure gathered within her, seeming suddenly huge and important, becoming the only thing she could think of, the only thing she could seek. She widened her legs, tipped her hips and—ahh, *there. Fuck, yeah. There*. She might've said the words aloud, because he growled low in his throat and slowed his thrusts, lingering at the point of contact, pressing into her within and without.

"Oh." She dug her fingers into the strong cords of muscle beside his spine, and the scars beneath her fingertips added a sharp poignancy to the moment as her body coiled in that perfect, breathless pause that presaged orgasm.

She had almost lost him; they had almost lost each other.

Tears stung her eyes as she came.

The orgasm spiraled in and then flared out again, washing through her with a glorious, intense heat. She cried out—his name, a curse, a prayer, she didn't have a clue what she was saying, only that it went on and on, almost blurring past pleasure to something stronger and more insane. He groaned long and low, gasped her name as he came. His hips pumped into her, his arms clamped around her, and he surged once, again and again.

Her inner muscles milked him, pulsing, pulsing . . . and then slowed.

Everything. Slowed. Stopped. And then it was over.

Only it was far from over, wasn't it?

Oh, shit, she thought as she turned her face away from him, grateful that he was collapsed against her, his heart thudding a heavy drumbeat. Ohhhh, shit.

That had been way more than she'd been expecting, way more than she'd been prepared for. She'd wanted sex, but she'd gotten . . . gods, she didn't even know what to call that, what to make of it. Yes, she was strong. But she wasn't sure she was strong enough for this.

"Rabbit," she began, but then fell silent, because she didn't have a clue what to say to him. Not after that.

"Later," he rumbled thick-voiced, already fading into his familiar postcoital coma. "We can dissect things later. For now, let's just fucking enjoy it. Deal?"

Yes. No. Shit. Don't make this into more than it needs to be. "Deal," she whispered.

He was snoring almost before she'd gotten the word out, his big body going lax and warm around her. She couldn't sleep, though. Not when . . .

Darkness. Warm and wonderful darkness.

Sometime later—more than an hour but less than the dawn—Myr startled herself by coming awake from a doze she hadn't meant to slide into. She was tucked tightly against Rabbit's warm bulk, with her arm partway across his chest and her hand on the steady beat of his heart. Their legs were woven together, their breaths coming in synch—at least they had been when she first opened her eyes. Now, though, her breathing quickened beneath a flood of heat, longing and disquiet.

Gods. The things he had done to her, the things he'd made her feel. She'd never done that before, with anyone, hadn't ever wanted to. *And you enjoyed every minute of it,* said her better sense, which had been pretty damn quiet up to this point. *Question is, are you going to enjoy what comes next?*

Holding her breath, she eased out from beneath the covers, and tried not to shiver as the cold air hit her skin and raised goose bumps. Her nipples pebbled, serving only to remind her of his lips on them, his hands. New tingles erupted—of want, of need—but instead of drawing her back to the bed, they spurred her away. Padding on bare feet, she found her jeans and shirt, her boots and one sock.

She slipped on the jeans and shirt, shoved the sock in her pocket and held the boots dangling in one hand as she looked back toward the bed.

Rabbit slept on, undisturbed and magnificent, looking like he'd been cast in gold thanks to the flickering light coming from the white candle. She wanted to crawl back beside him and kiss him awake. She wanted to give herself to him, lose herself in him.

Gods. What had she done?

"Stop freaking out," she said under her breath. "You got what you wanted." She was the one who'd made the booty call. So what if he'd changed things up some? It shouldn't be a big deal that he'd gotten her off rhythm and out of their routine, shouldn't even matter that he'd taken over. It did, though. And that left her feeling far shakier than she liked as she headed for the door, moving silently on her bare feet.

Behind her, Rabbit shifted and muttered something. She tensed but he didn't wake up. He just rolled over onto his side and buried his face in her pillow.

As she slipped through the door, she heard him mutter, "No, Myr. Don't." Seeing that he was talking in his sleep, she didn't answer him. Besides, it was long past time for her to go.

Summer solstice, 1984
Chichén Itzá

"The dreams said that I'm the key, that I can win the war right here, right now," Jag said as he and Asia faced the chac-mool. *Magic thrummed, coming from the shimmering air above the altar.*

She took his hand. "I'm here. I'm not going anywhere."

Gods, was there anything more terrifying than knowing that? He wanted to order her away, wanted to hide her, protect her, surround her in freaking bubble wrap and know she was going to be okay no matter what. Instead, he grated, "Stay behind me. You're in charge of our shield."

And then, facing the intersection, he tapped into the

joined magic of his warriors, and began the second spell. Where the first had opened the portal connecting this world to the next, the second spell would break the barrier, then seal it forever.

He hoped.

Raising his hands, he summoned the magic and let it rip, pouring the energy into the intersection as—

Unexpectedly, horribly, red-orange light flared in the doorway behind him. And Asia screamed.

Rabbit jolted awake at the sound of a cry that wasn't his own, yet echoed in his ears. The blue-gray of dawn was seeping in through the windows, and the other side of the bed was empty.

Myrinne was gone, and he was having visions. This couldn't be good.

CHAPTER SIXTEEN

December 13
Eight days until the zero date
Skywatch

As the sun hit its zenith overhead, Anna stood facing the *chac-mool* with a sledgehammer in her hands. The statue seemed to be looking straight at her, like it was asking, "What are you doing with that big-ass hammer? You're not doing what I think you're doing, are you?" And although she was the one who'd gotten the message about the true gods, the one who needed the magic that'd been promised, she couldn't bring herself to take the first whack.

Her hands shook. What if the skull wasn't inside the altar? What if she'd gotten the message wrong?

Gods knew she'd done it before—she'd sent the Nightkeepers after the resurrection skull with the prom-

ise of the First Father's return, only to have the spell
bring back Red-Boar in all his assholic glory. At the moment, he was over in the corner, arms crossed, glower-
ing at Rabbit, who was ignoring him while darting
glances at Myrinne, who shifted and looked away. They
weren't the only ones there, of course—the small room
and the hallways beyond were crammed with bodies—
but the three-way vibe was a bad sign. Then again, so
was the tension that was strung bitterly tight throughout
the sacred chamber.

The Nightkeepers needed to go into the final week
as a united force, yet here she was, about to bust up
their ancestors.

"I still think we should try some sort of imaging,"
she said to Dez. "There are times when high tech is
called for."

But he shook his head. "I think this is a time for
faith."

Then why am I the one with the sledgehammer? She
didn't say it, though. Instead, she leaned forward,
touched the *chac-mool*'s forehead with her free hand,
and whispered, "Please forgive me."

Then, not looking back to see her own nerves and
horror reflected in the faces of her teammates, she
hefted the sledge over her head and brought it down
right on the place she'd just touched. Metal met stone
with a sickening *CRACK* that reverberated up the
wooden handle to her hands, which stung as if she'd
just opened a dozen sacrificial cuts.

A jagged fissure slashed lightning-like down across

one carved eye and then to the corner of the deity's mouth, tracking like a tear.

Somebody moaned; Anna didn't think it was her, but she wasn't sure.

"I'm sorry." She lifted the weapon again. "Sorry, sorry." Another swing, another *CRACK*, another shot of burning pain, this time reaching up her wrists and singeing her marks. The fissure widened and one side of the *chac-mool*'s face slid down slightly, turning its beatific smile into a leer.

Please gods, she whispered in her soul, but felt nothing—no lift of hope, no connection to the other side of the barrier, as if they had turned away from her.

She couldn't stop now, though, so she said the prayer aloud, heard it echo behind her, and swung with every ounce of her strength, both physical and magical. The sledge hit with a *crunch*, a different sound, a different reverb, and limestone fragmented, clattering to the stone floor as the side of the *chac-mool*'s face crumbled away.

Where it had been, bloodred crystal gleamed in the sunlight that streamed through the glass ceiling.

"Oh," Anna breathed, letting the sledge droop in her hands as she stared. The smooth ruby surface was huge and curved, and amber gleamed from the depths of a socket, a glowing yellow eye partially revealed.

A ripple of shock ran through the crowd. It wasn't an amulet at all; it was a life-sized crystal skull. And somehow, it had been there all along, hidden beneath a limestone shell.

"Holy crap," Dez said, voice low and reverent.

Anna sucked in a rattling breath that burned in her lungs. "Okay, then. Crystal skull. Check."

The *chac-mool* looked decidedly Terminator-esque, with half its face still normal stone, the other gleaming red crystal, its glare not saying "What are you doing" anymore, but instead demanding "Get on with it."

She pulverized the other side with two well-aimed smashes. Chips of stone stung her face and arms, and clattered to the floor around her, but she didn't stop, didn't look back, just kept going as the other side of the skull emerged from the rubble, as if she'd stripped away the deity's flesh to find the bones beneath.

Then, hands burning with a strange mix of numbness and pain, she let the sledgehammer thud on the stone floor, and moved toward the ruby skull. Sitting atop the ragged neck stump it was macabre, grotesque, but it was the eyes that held her transfixed. The amber pulsed with a strange inner light, drawing her closer and closer.

And suddenly, as if the knowledge had been inside her all along, she knew what she needed to do.

"*Tzo'o'keen*," she said softly. *I am ready*.

Her magic closed around her, brushing along her skin and making her blood hum. It suddenly didn't matter that she'd just desecrated the shrine where she'd been named, where her parents and her parents' parents had been mated. For the first time in a long, long time, she felt like she was in the right place at the right time, that she was doing what she was meant to do.

The skull glowed—red crystal, amber eyes. Was that

power or sunlight? She couldn't tell, but she also couldn't look away. Tugging at her chain, she pulled the smaller yellow quartz skull free and cupped it in her hands, feeling it throb with a beat that wasn't quite in synch with her pulse.

"Anna," Dez said, voice low and warning.

"I'm fine. It's fine." She hoped. Deep inside her, though, fear sparked at the thought that she was about to break through the barrier inside her, the one that had blocked her talents all these years. But she couldn't keep going on like this, blind and not good for much except transportation. So, not letting herself hesitate further, she whispered, *"Tz'a teen ich." Give me eyes.*

Throom! Twin beams of yellow light speared from the skull and straight for her. She jerked at the noise and flash, but held her ground as the air around her turned golden and strange.

"Jesus," Strike grated. "Back up, Anna. Back up and look!"

For a second it was as if she was standing inside a ghost that was half again as large as she. She could see its head far above hers, its shoulders on either side of her. Then, shaking, she fell back another few steps, aware that the others backpedaled, too, keeping her front and center before the huge figure that was suddenly revealed.

Awe raced through Anna as she faced an entity, a goddess who glowed golden from the tips of her feline ears to the edges of her long white robe. Her head was that of a golden-furred lioness, her body that of a vo-

luptuous woman, and her vivid blue eyes had the slit-
ted irises and soul-searing stare of a huge cat. She
didn't blink, didn't move; she looked alive, yet stood
statue-still; looked real, yet was translucent. She was
there, yet she wasn't. She was a holograph. A projec-
tion. Something.

Behind Anna, Lucius said, "Holy shit, it's Bastet."
He said it like he was greeting an old friend, not an
ancient goddess of the wrong religion. But that was exactly what they were looking at: Bastet, the cat-headed
goddess who had protected the kings and the land of
the living . . . in ancient freaking Egypt.

There was a connection, of course—the Nightkeepers had lived alongside the ancient Egyptians for thousands of years until the pharaoh Akhenaton had
outlawed the old gods and slaughtered their priests,
including the Nightkeepers. The few survivors had escaped to Mesoamerica, where they discovered a land
with far stronger magic and a much closer connection
to their gods. There, they helped create the Mayan Empire, with pyramids and writing, and a religion that
was so much closer to what their ancestors had believed.

The Egyptian deities had come along millennia before the Mayan gods, it was true. But the Mayan gods
belonged to the Nightkeepers.

So why the hell was Bastet's image coming from the
ruby skull?

"Say something, Anna." The hiss came from Lucius,
as did the poke in her ribs. He was crowded close be-

hind her, breathing down the back of her neck like he used to when they did fieldwork together for the university, and she uncovered something strange and wonderful. That was Lucius, though. He loved information, discovery, and the sheer fucked-uppedness of life.

Anna couldn't share his enthusiasm, though, because she already knew that whatever happened next, it wasn't going to affect just her. This was bigger than her. It was going to be freaking *huge*.

"I . . ." She stopped, swallowing hard. "I don't know enough of the language." Hell, the ancient Egyptian tongue was even deader than ancient Mayan—so many of the sounds were guesstimates, with filled-in vowels and pronunciations that changed from decade to decade.

"Rosa gave you the message in ancient Mayan," Lucius whispered. "Go with that."

"Okay. I . . . okay." *Stop stalling*. She took a deep breath, found the words, and said formally, *"Oolah yuum Bastet. Ba'ax ka wa'alik?" Greetings, goddess Bastet. What do you say*?

Throom! As the shock of a second sonic boom reverberated through the chamber, magic flared and the goddess's image solidified. Suddenly, Anna could see new details of Bastet's fur, her eyes, her robe.

And then the goddess took a deep, shuddering breath and came alive.

Her robes and fur ruffled in an unseen breeze, her whiskers twitched, and then she blinked and focused, looking momentarily startled to find herself in the midst of a crowd, or maybe a crowd like this one. But then she focused on Anna, and her expression cleared. "*Ahh,*" she said. "*Itza'at. I'm glad to finally see you.*"

The words came out in a strange, guttural language that Anna didn't recognize, but somehow translated inside her head, so she understood the words and heard what was behind them—relief, regret and a huge upwelling of power.

She glanced back at Lucius, whose face was lit with wonder. "Did you get that?"

"Yeah." He swallowed hard. "Yeah, I did."

"We all did," Dez said from behind them.

Anna faced Bastet and said in English, "Greetings, goddess." She hesitated, suddenly aware that her knees were shaking; her whole body was shaking. What was she supposed to say? What was she supposed to do? Should she meet the goddess's eyes or look away? *Mother, help me!* Maybe it was real, maybe wishful thinking, but her amulet seemed to warm further in her grip, steadying her. She took a deep breath, looked up and met those blue, blue eyes. "Yes, I am of the *itza'at* line, though untrained. I got your message and will do whatever you ask of me."

"*I ask nothing but that you listen and believe, all of you.*"

Anna nodded. "We will."

"*It will be difficult.*"

There was movement all around her, a shifting of bodies and stances as the others moved up to surround Anna, so they faced Bastet as a united front.

Dez tipped his head in a shallow bow. "We're not

scared of hard going, goddess, or even death. We only fear what will happen if we fail."

"*As well you should.*" Her image flickered, wavering and growing translucent once more.

Feeling the skull's magic hitch and start to fade, Anna clutched the amulet and poured all of her energy into the crystal skull. The world dimmed around her, sparking desperation. She wasn't strong enough, wasn't—

A hand gripped her upper arm and she was flooded with the power of a touch-link, which was gentler than a blood-link, but still effective, especially for this. Then there was another clasp, another increase in the magic flowing through her. Then more. Relief washed through her as she looked back to find Lucius on one side of her, Dez on the other, and the rest of her teammates standing close by, all touching, linking to help her. Together, as a team.

Gathering their joined power, she focused once more on the amulet, sending the Nightkeepers' magic into the spell. A glow kindled deep within the bloodred skull, and the goddess's image solidified.

"*Quickly,*" Bastet said. "*The* kohan *and the* kax *are trying to block this magic. Soon, they will cut it off at the barrier.*"

"*Kohan?*" Dez whispered, lips barely moving.

"Sickness," Lucius translated, sotto voce.

"Shut it!" Anna hissed in her do-it-or-die prof's voice.

"*The* kohan *rule the upper plane, just as the humans control the middle plane and the* kax *control the lower plane.*"

"The sky gods, then." Dez nodded. "Go on."

Bastet's eyes flashed. *"No. Not gods. Kohan. They are no more gods than you are, or the* kax. *All are equal in the eyes of the true gods. The upper, middle and lower planes are just places, realms where the magic exists. Your many-times-great ancestors understood this, just as they knew that the* kohan *and the* kax *each wanted the middle plane and its inhabitants for their own—a playground, with powerful playthings."*

"That's . . ." *Impossible*, Anna wanted to say, but couldn't, because the sudden elevator drop of her stomach said otherwise.

"Holy crap." Lucius's whisper was dull with shock, but his eyes were alight with wonder. "Rosa was right. There are other gods out there. True gods."

"There are six of us," Bastet confirmed. *"Three belonging to life, three to death."* Images flickered rapid-fire across Anna's brain, imprinting themselves on her mind's eye. *"Your ancestors knew us, worshipped us. But the* kax *corrupted one of the ancient kings and turned him against us, breaking our hold on the middle plane and destroying almost all of our guardians. Those who survived moved to a new land, one that was poised at the juncture of the three planes. There, they lost faith, falling prey to the whispers of the* kohan, *then the* kax. *They split the magic and lost their way, becoming fragments of what they once were. Until now, until you."*

"No." Anna shook her head, denying the awful possibility of it all. But even as her heart tried to reject what the goddess was saying, she saw how it dovetailed

with the Nightkeepers' flight from Egypt and the way
their magic had changed in the Mayan territories, becoming chaotic and unpredictable, and eventually
splitting into its light and dark halves, wielded by the
Nightkeepers and the Xibalbans. "It's not true," she insisted, too horrified to worry about arguing with a goddess.

"Or is it that you do not want to know the truth?" The
goddess's image grew until it filled Anna's vision, her
senses. She didn't know if Bastet had leaned closer, or
if the goddess had simply locked on to her magic, but
in that moment she couldn't move, couldn't breathe,
couldn't do anything *but* see, hear and feel the horrors
of the past.

Terrible visions raced through her, reminding her
finally of the things she'd seen during those last few
minutes of chaos during the massacre, while Jox had
dragged her and Strike down into the shielded, hidden
bolt-hole beneath Skywatch. She hadn't been there,
though—her mind had been in the southlands, dying
with her kinswomen in the narrow tunnel system beneath Chichén Itzá.

Anna let go of the amulet and covered her eyes, trying to shut it out. But the images flowed through her,
awakened her. *A woman screamed as a* boluntiku *rose
above her, dripping with the fiery energy of lava and going
solid in the last moment before it killed her. Another wept as
she unleashed terrible fireballs into the smoking spot where
her mate had been only seconds before. A man cried; another
screamed and held his own entrails. It was all dim and dark,*

cloaked in carved stone and blood, closing in on her, suffocating her.

"Enough," she whimpered. "I get it."

"It's not nearly enough," said Bastet, uncompromising. *"Know the rest, and believe in it. Believe in me."*

More memories, more terror, this time coming from her mother's mind. Her blessed, beloved mother. *"No!"* *the queen screamed as the shimmering bubble of the barrier tore down its center and a terrible blackness poured through, exuding evil and horror as it became a winged serpent—a perverted, wronged form of the great creator god, Kulkulkan. "For gods' sake, Jag, stop the spell!"*

He didn't, though. He couldn't. And they had died.

Anna cried out when her mother's perceptions ended in a flash of brilliant, lava-born orange, then moaned when she was battered by echoes of other horrors, other deaths.

And, as the inner barriers came crashing down and she remembered everything, she had a feeling that they hadn't been barriers so much as her subconscious mind protecting her from what it knew, deep down inside, was another kind of enemy: the *kohan* she had prayed to. The ones that had tried to get to her, tried to send her visions that would only confuse the Nightkeepers further.

Or was she buying into the logic too quickly, too fully? How was this any different from what Rabbit had gone through with the demoness?

"Use your senses and know the truth." Bastet's command was inviolate, inarguable and aimed at all of

them. *"Use the talents given to you by the true gods."* Sudden images flashed in the air around Anna, coming from her magic, but projecting for everyone else to see.

The smoky picture was distorted at the edges, as if seen through a fish-eye lens, but the scene of utter destruction was all too clear. There was rubble, fire . . . and the skeleton of a massive tree that had fallen into the steel-fab building below it.

Anna sucked in a breath on a low moan. Skywatch!

Bastet said, *"This is what will be if you do not act now, all of you."*

"It can be stopped?" Dez demanded. "I thought an *itza'at*'s visions were immutable."

"That was what the kax and kohan wanted you to think, for they wanted to play with you, knowing that the itza'at were meant to be the voices of the True Gods here in the middle plane. And they wanted to prove their superiority by making our guardians—all of you—do as they wished, wanted to improve their chances now by weakening you, over and over again. So they sent corrupted visions to the seers . . . and even to the old king."

"Father." The word came out of Strike on a low groan, once again lining up with what they knew, what they believed . . . yet requiring a leap of faith like none they'd ever been asked to make before.

"They believe you are no longer a threat to them. We believe you can be." Bastet's blue eyes narrowed at Anna. *"Are you willing to try, warrior?"*

"I'm not . . ." she faltered and turned to Dez. "Help."

The king's face had gone to granite, gray-pallored

and hard as stone. It was Reese who said, "What do you want us to do?"

Some of the others muttered darkly, and even Dez shot her a sidelong look. But Reese wasn't just their ultra-practical, tough-girl queen; she was also human, like Lucius and Leah. They had already given up their religion in the face of evidence. They weren't being asked to do it now on faith.

Which didn't mean the Nightkeepers were going to. *No way*, Anna swore to herself, trying to ignore the twisting disquiet deep inside that kept whispering, *What if it's real? What then?*

"Your godkeepers must break their bonds, and all of you must renounce your allegiance to your so-called sky gods on the morning of the Cardinal Day. Only then will you be free to fight for the middle plane."

There was a moment of profoundly unhappy silence.

After a moment, a shaken Reese said, "How can the godkeeper bonds be broken?" It had taken near-death by drowning, along with devastating magic to link Strike, Leah, Alexis and Sasha with their gods.

Prophecy had said those bonds were crucial to the war . . . but those prophecies had come from the *kohan*.

Or had they?

"Cut your marks from your flesh and cast the blood in the fire, and the earth will reclaim its children." Suddenly, Bastet's magic dimmed, and the low *throoming* sound rose up once more, vibrating the stones beneath them. Eyes dimming, she said, *"I must go."*

"When can we summon you again?" Anna said quickly, taking a step toward the apparition.

"You cannot. This is your war to fight, not ours."

"Wait!" Anna cried as the light flickered, then faded. "Why—"

"The three planes must remain in balance. That is how we created them. If one falls, they all fall." Then . . . *flicker-flicker-FLASH!* And the goddess disappeared.

Anna stood swaying, blinking into the amber eyes of the crystal skull.

Someone in the back muttered, "Fucking hell."

"Well," Lucius drawled, voice rough with emotion. "That was . . . unexpected." He was still hanging on to Anna's arm, but now he drew her toward the altar. "You should sit."

"Not there." She couldn't handle seeing the ragged neck stump or the bloodred skull that had been inside the *chac-mool*'s head all along. She could only guess that one of her ancestors had put it there, that the women of the *itza'at*'s line had somehow known it was important to keep it a secret, but not why.

Or was this the trick, and the other the truth?

Her head spun and she leaned into Lucius for a moment, drawing strength from their long history together. They had been friends in the outside world and were friends now. And he was going to be a valuable voice of reason now, in a time when she could pretty much guarantee that the rest of them—Nightkeepers and *winikin* alike—were going to have a hard time being reasonable.

It had been bad enough when Rabbit had tried to convince them that the Nightkeepers had it wrong and the *Banol Kax*—or the *kax*, apparently—were somehow the good guys. That, at least, they had been able to ascribe to Rabbit's flair for the dramatic, his mix of dark and light powers, and his constant quest to find a place where he felt like he fit in.

This, though . . . *gods*, she thought, and felt a twinge at the prayer, a quick spurt of fear that she'd been praying to the wrong entities all along.

"Then let's get you out of here." Lucius steered her toward the door, through a parting sea of shell-shocked teammates who stared at her, wide-eyed, as if seeking a reassurance that she couldn't give. "Let's everybody get out of here and take a breath, okay?"

"No!" Red-Boar put himself between her and the door, his earlier glower gone to a near-manic snarl. "This is bullshit! The demons are trying to trap you just like they trapped Rabbit, godsdamn it. And you're fucking walking right into it!"

Anna snapped back, "Nobody's walking into anything."

"You bought it, though. Didn't you?" Red-Boar grabbed her. "Didn't you!"

Lucius stiff-armed him in the chest, sending him back a couple of steps. "Back off. Right fucking now."

Red-Boar sneered. "Easy for a *human* to say." The air cracked with sudden magic; it wreathed the senior mage, crisping the air with the threat of a fireball. "Especially one who's been on the other side. Tell me, do you still dream of the things you did when you were a *makol*? Have you ever—"

"Enough!" Dez's roar drowned out the rest of the question. The king got big and loomed over Red-Boar. "That's enough. We're not deciding a damn thing right now. We've got work to do before that. Research."

The older mage sneered. "Research. Right. That'll win the war."

"A full-on frontal assault didn't do your generation much good."

Red-Boar flushed a dull, furious red. "You son of a bitch. You have no idea . . ." His eyes flicked to Reese. "Well, I guess you're in line to find out, aren't you?" He spat at the king's feet. "Fuck this. What do I care? I'm already dead." He spun and stalked out, leaving a crack of angry magic in his wake.

Nate started after him, but Dez waved him back. "Don't. Let him be. This is . . . Shit. Just let him go." He sent a look around the room. "In fact, I think Lucius is right. We all need to get out of here, clear our heads a little."

Anna couldn't help it. She looked back at the ruined altar, and the skull that sat atop it. "What do you want to do about that?"

The king's eyes didn't show a hint of his thoughts. "It's your skull. You tell me."

She winced, but then nodded reluctantly. "Yeah. I should work with it. Even if it can't get through to . . . well, whatever that was, maybe I'll finally get control of my visions." Her attempt at a smile fell flat, though, as she pulled away from Lucius and forced her legs to carry her all the way to the altar.

Her heart tugged at the sight of the sledgehammer lying on the floor near a chunk of limestone that showed the curve of a cheek and one kind eye. She didn't apologize to the *chac-mool* again, though, because she didn't dare pray, not even to it. Not when she didn't know who she was talking to anymore.

Where before the air had hummed with magic, now it was as flat and dead as the skull's dull yellow eyes. Still, though, their facets seemed to watch her.

Do you dare? those eyes seemed to ask her.

"I already did," she said softly. Then, steeling herself, she stuck a thumb in one ear hole and a finger in the nasal cavity, and lifted the skull from the last of the enclosing limestone, holding it like some sort of demented bowling ball.

Trying not to let the others see how much its cool, slick surface made her skin crawl, she tucked it under her arm and made for the door. And, as she headed down the hall toward the royal quarters and the childhood suite she'd redone as her own, she did her damnedest not to picture how the thing was going to be staring at her while she slept.

Then again, given what they'd just learned, nightmares were going to be the least of her problems.

CHAPTER SEVENTEEN

"I won't let you do it."

Rabbit stopped at the sound of his old man's voice, surprised to feel a bump of compulsion coming from the Boar Oath. He'd been so damn well behaved that he'd almost forgotten about the fucking thing.

He turned back on the pathway leading out to the cottages. He wasn't even sure why he'd gone that way—it wasn't like he wanted to be back home right now. Not when every last square inch of the place would remind him of Myr and leave him wondering what the hell came next for the two of them. Should he go after her? Leave her alone? He didn't have a clue. She hadn't just been his first lover; she'd been his first everything. He didn't have any practice with breakups, post-breakup hookups, or whatever the hell that had been last night. And it wasn't like he could ask one of the others. They all had bigger, badder things to think about right now—like whether or not they'd been praying to the wrong gods all along.

Which left him and his old man squaring off opposite each other on the beaten-smooth footpath, with the sun coming down on them and no breeze to stir the dust. If they'd had revolvers, he would've been tempted to count down the draw.

Rabbit shoved his thumbs in his pockets but didn't slouch, mostly because he knew it would annoy Red-Boar that he was a couple inches taller and wider. "You won't let me do what?"

His old man closed the distance between them, got in his face and glared. "You will not revoke your allegiance to the sky gods. Do you hear me? You. Will. Not. Do. It."

"Be interesting to see how that goes up against my oath to follow Dez's orders, if he decides to follow Bastet's lead." But although Rabbit kept his voice level, he wasn't nearly as in control as he wanted his old man to believe. Because suddenly the inner darkness was straining against his hold—twenty years of insults, anger and hatred jonesing to go after the man who'd raised him but hadn't ever been any sort of father.

Red-Boar's eyes flicked to the side, as if he was looking for witnesses. Then, in a low growl, he said, "That can be dealt with."

The third order, Rabbit thought. Was the old bastard really so convinced of his own infallibility that he would use it to go up against the king? "Bullshit."

"Don't forget, I fucking *own* you, boy."

Bile soured the back of his throat. "You own my bloodline connection. I'll break it if I have to." Pain sliced through him, racing from his forearm to his heart, as if the oath was warning him just how bad it could get.

Red-Boar's eyes blazed. "You wouldn't *dare*."

"Fucking try me."

The old man flushed an ugly, murderous red. "Back atcha, asshole. You do it and you'll find out what it means to watch your woman die."

Fury hammered through Rabbit in an instant, not coming from the dark magic, but welling up from inside the man he wanted to be, the one who'd fallen asleep last night with Myrinne in his arms. Because that was no idle threat. As far as Red-Boar was concerned, humans were little better than clever pets. Expendable.

He had his hands on his father's throat before he knew it, lifting the old bastard onto his tiptoes and snarling, "You so much as go near her and I'll fucking end you. Oath or no oath, you're dead."

Put. Me. Down.

The words shouted inside his mind and headed instantly for his central nervous system, short-circuiting the whole damn thing. His arms came down, his hands opened.

Red-Boar sucked in a ragged breath as he stepped back. And if Rabbit had thought before that he'd seen his old man in a rage, now he knew different. This was true rage, he thought. It was hatred.

Dark eyes narrowing to evil slits, his father sent into his brain: *Choke. Yourself*.

Rabbit's mind fought, but his body obeyed the commands like a fucking puppet. His own hands closed around his throat and bore down hard, thumbs digging into the vital veins.

His vision went blurry almost instantly, though he didn't know if that was real or the power of suggestion. He went for his mental blocks, tried to figure out where the old man was getting through, but couldn't. Tried to cast a counterspell, but couldn't do that, either. He couldn't move his legs. Couldn't move anything. He tried to . . . shit. What was he trying to do again? Panic had his heart thudding even as rage coiled inside him, useless against the magic.

He tried to break his father's hold on his mind, tried to stay on his feet when he swayed and gray closed in from the edges of his vision.

Tried . . . to . . .

"Enough." Red-Boar snapped his fingers and the compulsion was gone.

"You son of a bitch!" Rabbit lunged, but ran face-first into a shield spell. His nose crunched, making his eyes water. He reeled back, yelling, "Godsdamn it. I hate you!" like he was fifteen again.

His old man stood, implacable behind his shield. "I won't have to go near her. You'll do the job yourself."

Fury roared through Rabbit, but he held it together, barely, because going off on the old bastard wasn't going to change a damn thing. Glaring, he rasped, "I'd kill myself before I'd hurt her again. But first I'd kill you."

"Or you could just fucking do as you're told and we won't have to find out which one of us has a bigger dick. And by the way, it's me."

A few months ago, Rabbit would've gone for a tape measure. Now, though, he wrestled the ugliness down, shoving it deep behind the enemy lines he'd drawn inside his head. Because what was he proving by being pissed? Nothing, except that he could be just as nasty as his old man.

"Jesus Christ," he muttered. "I thought you were bad before. What the fuck happened to you on the other side? I thought death was supposed to give a guy some godsdamned perspective."

To his surprise, his old man took a step back and exhaled a long, slow breath. "This *is* my perspective, shithead. I didn't come back here to watch the Night-keepers go off the godsdamned rails."

That had just enough logic to pinch. Jamming his hands in his pockets, Rabbit shrugged impatiently. "Fine. Whatever. But I'm not in charge here, remember? You want to swing the decision, then talk to Dez. Whether you like it or not, he's the king."

"True. But you're the crossover."

"Which doesn't mean a fucking thing unless I can figure out what I'm supposed to do." And if he believed Bastet, there was a good chance that the whole crossover thing was just another distraction, one that both the *kohan* and the *kax* had used to confuse the Xi-balbans and Nightkeepers.

"How about having some fucking faith?" Red-Boar growled. "When the gods want us to know something, they always find a way to get through."

"Seems to me they just did."

"That Egyptian horseshit was a lie, just like Phee's ghost was a lie."

"I didn't feel any dark magic when Bastet projected herself. Did you?"

"The *Banol Kax* lie about every-fucking-thing. Why not about the magic, too? The barrier is barely hanging on. What's to say they couldn't hide their magic, make it look like something else?"

And the damn thing was, as much as Rabbit wanted to argue with anything that came out of his old man's mouth, he couldn't. Not this time. "I don't. . . . Shit."

Red-Boar's eyes took on a satisfied gleam. "That's better." He didn't move a muscle, but seemed suddenly closer, bigger in Rabbit's field of vision. "Think about it. What's the distraction here? Why did Bastet appear now, this late in the game?"

"Because it took this long for Anna to be ready to receive the message."

"Bullshit. If I could get through to her off and on over the past few years, then sure as shit a god could do it."

It shouldn't have kicked up a spurt of resentment to know that Red-Boar had contacted Anna from the other side. Clenching his jaw, Rabbit ground out, "Fine. Let's say you're right. I'm not saying I think you are, but if you are, then Dez is the one you need to be working on."

"I am. I will. But you're the crossover, damn it. You're the key."

"So you keep telling me. So how about telling me what the hell you want me to do right now. Why even come after me?" His lips twisted. "Or are you just blowing off steam at someone you figure has to stand there and take it?" Now that was an old, familiar pattern.

"Poor you," Red-Boar sneered. "You always had the basics and then some. Cry me a fucking river."

"Don't," Rabbit said flatly. "You really don't want to go there."

His old man must've seen something in his eyes, because he cursed and turned away. "Screw this. I've got a meeting with the king. Think about it, though, boy. Think long and hard before you do something really fucking stupid."

"That's one of the few lessons I think I *have* learned."

Red-Boar just growled back over his shoulder. "Use your head, for fuck's sake."

Rabbit didn't mean to watch him walk away, but his old man always could twist him around and tie him in fucking knots. Which left him standing there for a minute, debating. Logic said he should warn Dez how bad his old man was getting. Instinct, though, had him gravitating toward the path that led to his cottage . . . and beyond that to the firing range.

At the thought of the range, warmth kicked in his chest and an ache tugged low in his gut, letting him know that he hadn't been heading for his cottage, after all. He'd been heading for Myrinne.

His body knew where she was. His magic knew.

What it didn't know was what he was supposed to say to her.

"Fuck it." Deciding to let Dez and Red-Boar go the first round without him, he headed for his cottage, but ducked in only briefly to grab a couple of things. Then he kept going along the path, all the way to the range.

When the Nightkeepers had first returned to Skywatch, the weapons training area had consisted of a boring-ass indoor range of the cubicle-and-paper-target variety, plus an outdoor sniper range that wasn't much better. These days, thanks to Michael's background as a government-trained assassin and his lust for gadgets, the training area included a faux Mayan ruin built in cement and rebar, along with a second indoor range inside a prefab steel building. There, trainees could work their way through an urban-jungle training course, blasting away at pop-up targets and holos, with a digital scoreboard in the corner tallying their speed, kills and collateral damage.

Rabbit made for the big steel building, knowing that was where she would be even before he saw a flicker of reflected light and heard the generator kick on. The setup was like a full-scale video game. He couldn't think of a better place for someone like him—or Myrinne—to burn off some aggression.

As he approached, he heard a muffled *pop-pop-pop* from one of the holo-enabled training weapons, then the crackling roar of a fireball. The surge of magic lit his senses and tightened his skin as he stepped through the main door and into the small locker room that acted as an antechamber. The lights were off in the windowless room, creating a warm darkness that wrapped around him as he paused in the shadows and looked into the main room, seeing without being seen.

Myr had changed out of the jeans and soft sweater she'd been wearing earlier, into close-fitting black workout gear that moved as fluidly as she did when she spun and snapped off a "shot" of laser light into a glowing lava demon, flung herself to the ground to avoid a hologram claw-swipe, and came up firing. Wearing her weapons belt along with the gizmos that made up the badass laser-tag system, with knives strapped to her thigh and calf, she looked deadly as hell, and twice as sexy. Her face was set in concentration, her eyes gleamed with reflected holo-light, and her moves showed the hours she'd put into her train-ing, and the athleticism—and sharp edge—that had made her a natural at this from the very beginning. She didn't think she was brave, didn't think she had fought enough against the Witch, but he knew different. And could've stood there watching her all damn day.

She crouched and spun, flattened three hologram *camazotz* in rapid succession, then nailed a fourth with a bolt of crackling green magic that surged and spit with a dangerous, feminine power that hardened his flesh. More, it brought his own fighting instincts to the fore, making him want to challenge her, tussle with her, make love to her, right here and now.

Question was, what did she want?

Steeling himself, he stepped out of the shadows and into her peripheral vision.

She checked her next attack and spun to face him, cheeks flushed with exertion, eyes going wary and brittle at the sight of him. She raised her weapon but didn't holster it, and didn't let the magic ramp down. "I'm a little busy here. And really not in the mood for company."

"It's a pretty night." He lifted the six-pack that was the first of the bribes he'd grabbed from the cottage. "I was hoping we could sit out and watch the stars for a bit."

Her eyes didn't give a damn thing away. "Why?"

Because last night was amazing, but you still snuck out. Because you're the one I want to be with, the only one I trust, even when I don't trust myself. Especially then.

He kept those answers inside, though, and went with the one that'd come to him as he'd stood there at the pathway's fork, knowing he should go up to the mansion but wanting to be with her instead. "Because the first time around, we just sort of happened. We met, we liked each other, made sense together—at least as we saw it—and we got together and had some damn good times." He paused. "But the thing is, I was so caught up in being a Nightkeeper, so convinced that we were destined mates that I coasted. I didn't work for it, didn't work for *you*."

Maybe she paled a little, but she didn't back down, didn't lower her defenses. "And now?"

"Now I want to make it up to you. Hell, I don't know what that even means, just that I hated waking up alone this morning, and I hate not knowing if you'll be with me tonight, or ever again. What's more, I know damn well that there's not anybody else I want to be with right now, nobody else I want to talk to about the things that're going down." He reached into a pocket, pulled out a Ziploc half full of Sasha's death-by-cacao brownies and held it out to her. He wasn't even entirely sure what he was asking for, but he asked it anyway. "What do you say? Are you willing to give me another chance?"

Myr stared at him for a beat, telling herself not to be an idiot. Problem was, she didn't know which answer counted as idiocy: accepting his peace offerings and risking what little hard-won balance she'd managed to get back after their night together . . . or telling him to get lost.

The fact that she could come up with a laundry list of why she should send him away probably should've made the choice for her. She hesitated, though, and not just because of the brownies. It was the mix of hope and "I dare you" in his eyes, and the shimmer of heat that snapped in the air between them, one that she couldn't quite ascribe to the fighting magic that was pumping in her veins. And, to be honest, it was the shame of knowing she had wimped out this morning.

Tell him to stay? Tell him to go?

It would've been easier if he'd been just another guy, like the ones she'd hooked up with in New Orleans. But there were millions of those guys out there, and only one Rabbit. He awed her, impressed her, sometimes scared the hell out of her. He had the potential to save them all . . . and the potential to destroy her. She wanted him, yearned for him, and after last night she knew damn well it would be far too easy to submerge herself once more in a relationship with him.

But he'd brought her brownies and beer, which had been a Friday night ritual during their year-plus together in college, a way to celebrate the weekend back when they'd thought they had it so tough and hadn't had any idea what tough actually felt like. Now, she knew exactly how it felt . . . and it was asking her for a chance to get back with her, and to let things between them go deeper than she'd had any intention of going.

She should tell him to get lost. Instead, she nodded to the six-pack. "Vitamin B?"

The tense set of his shoulders eased slightly. "Something like that." He jerked a thumb over his shoulder. "Wanna take a walk?"

She really, really shouldn't.

She did it anyway.

They ended up at the pueblo. Nostalgia tugged as she crested the narrow, winding trail leading up and saw the wide, flat ledge and familiar round doorways.

This was where Rabbit had gone when they fought, where they had gone together to get a little drunk and make love under the stars, and—although she hadn't told him—it was where she had hidden out in the weeks after he disappeared, while she recovered from his attack and tried to come to grips with what had happened between them.

She hadn't been back since she gained control of the magic. It didn't look any different, though. She was the one who was different . . . or at least trying to be.

Sitting on the very edge of the cliff, she let her legs hang and felt the shimmy in her stomach that said there was nothing to keep her from falling. Rabbit sat beside her, with a few inches separating them, extinguished the foxfire he'd used to light their way, and stared out as the night closed around them. The lights of Skywatch shone in the distance, but everything else was dark, save for the glimmer of stars up above.

"About last night," he began after a moment.

"I'm sorry I wimped out and did the tiptoe thing," she said, knowing she owed it to both of them, especially after what he'd just said about wanting to make more of an effort with her. Wanting to, in effect, court her, even though they both knew the timing couldn't be worse, and she wasn't even sure it was what she wanted. "Look, last night was great. Better than great. It was incredible . . . but I didn't want us to wake up together and be back where we started." She paused. "I need some space, Rabbit. I went from living under the Witch's thumb to being your girlfriend. Not that I'm saying the two are equivalent. I loved what we had to-gether, loved learning about the magic and how to fight . . . but I never really learned how to be myself. I'm starting to figure it out now, and I don't want to lose that."

He hesitated, then nodded. "Yeah. Okay, yeah. I get that." But the lines beside his mouth deepened.

"I'm sorry," she said again.

"Don't be." He took her hand, lifted it to kiss her knuckles, and shot her a crooked smile. "Like I said, I didn't really work hard enough for you the last time around. You want space, you've got it. But that doesn't change the fact that I want you in my bed—or your bed, one of the Jeeps, a closet, all of the above . . . your call."

Her skin heated at the low rasp of his voice. She didn't believe for a second that it was going to be that easy. Even if he stuck to a no-pressure, whatever-you-want arrangement, she wasn't sure she would be able to stick to it, despite all her newfound determination. If the old Rabbit had fascinated her and made her feel like she wasn't alone anymore, the man he'd become compelled her, made her yearn.

Forcing herself to stay casual, she bumped him with her shoulder. "Does that mean I can still have a beer and one of those brownies?"

"You can have whatever you want," he said simply. "Whatever, whenever, if it's mine, it's yours."

"Rabbit . . ." *Don't say stuff like that.* She wanted too badly to hear it, to believe it.

"Don't worry, no pressure. We'll take things as slow as you want." He paused, smile fading. "It's not like we won't have other things to focus on for the next eight days. And after that . . . well, there'll be plenty of time for us to figure things out." He looked away as he said that, though, making her think he was just saying the words, or maybe trying to believe them. Was that because he didn't think they could work things out, or because he thought it would be a moot point, the earth destroyed? *It doesn't matter,* she told herself. *What matters is the next eight days.* And after that, well, he was right. If they made it through, there would be time to figure out whether to stay together or go their separate ways.

The thought made her want to scoot closer to him and cling. Instead, she pulled her hand from his, balanced a brownie on her knee and reached for a beer. "That's true enough, I guess. Unfortunately, we don't have much time when it comes to figuring out what to do about the gods."

Like it or not, it was easier to talk about battle plans than it was to talk about what was happening between them.

He shot her a sidelong look that said he knew what she was thinking. But then he took a swig of his beer, leaned forward and braced his elbows on his upper thighs. "I'm trying not to let this be an easy choice. It shouldn't be."

Before, back when she'd been pushing him to reach the full potential she saw in him, she probably would've jumped right in with all sorts of opinions, probably none of which would've been "have faith in the sky gods." Now, though, she hesitated. Over the past few months, she had prayed to the gods for her magic and talked to them when she was alone and uncertain. It was unsettling to think that she might've been praying to the enemy all this time.

"Maybe Dez is right," she said. "Maybe we should hold off on making any decisions until we've looked into the info Bastet gave us." It felt weird to call the goddess by name, but was that any weirder than the message itself? Probably not.

"Maybe." Rabbit flicked a couple of pebbles off the ledge, tilting his head as they clinked and clanked on the way down. "The whole Egyptian thing feels right to me, though. It makes sense. But what if that's because I'd already talked myself out of the sky gods once before? I don't trust myself on this one. Not after what happened with Phee."

"Well, for better or worse, it's not really going to be about what we believe, is it? Dez is going to have the final say."

"I hope so."

"What?"

"Nothing. It's . . . nothing. Just something my old man said." He paused. "Did you ever imagine your parents showing up one day, putting the smackdown on the Witch, and whisking you away to your real life?"

She lowered her beer in surprise. "Where did that come from?"

"I was thinking about what Bastet said about the *kohan* and *kax* conspiring against us, and how it would help to think that there was a reason for all the bad luck we've had. Not just now, but in the past, too. The rise of the Aztec, the Spanish conquest, the Trail of Tears, the Solstice Massacre . . . all those times the Nightkeepers were just starting to flourish in a new land, when *wham*, something knocked them back down again."

"Which got you thinking about being an orphan." The word tried to stick in her throat. It was true, though. The surviving full-blooded Nightkeepers had grown up without their parents, though in most cases their *winikin* had filled in as best they could. And Rabbit himself might've been better off if both his parents had been out of the picture. "What about you?" she asked him. "Did you ever imagine your mother showing up and taking you away from Red-Boar?"

"Not really." But then he sighed. "Okay, maybe. More over the past couple of years than when I was a kid, though. Back then, I more or less believed that I was a disaster, good for nothing, all the stuff my old man kept telling me. So why would my mother—who, of course, I pictured being gentle, kind, generous and the exact opposite of him—want anything to do with me? Worse, what if she actually *did* come, and was disappointed?"

"Rabbit . . ."

"No." He took her hand, threaded their fingers together. "No sympathy necessary, no pity requested. I haven't been that kid for a long time. That didn't stop me, though, from chasing after her ghost over the past few years, thinking there was no way she could be as bad as Red-Boar." He snorted, though his fingers tightened on hers. "Just my luck she turned out to be worse."

"Luck," Myr said softly.

"Yeah. There's that word again. Like I said, it's tempting to think that a whole lot of what's gone down has been because our so-called gods have been fucking with us. Which makes it really damn cool to think that there's an even higher power out there somewhere that wants us to succeed, and is trying to get through and help us."

"Bastet as Daddy Warbucks?"

"More like some sort of superhero who's been blocked from the planet, and could help us out if we can manage to open up the lines of communication."

"In eight days."

He glanced up at the night sky. "Almost down to seven, now."

"Scary," she said, going for wry but aware that her voice shook. It hit her like this sometimes, the knowledge that they were coming up on the end date, and that she was going to be right there on the frontlines. For all that she was a warrior and a mage, sometimes she still felt very much like a frightened little girl.

His shoulder bumped against hers. "Yeah. Scary."

They sat like that for a few minutes in silence.

"I thought about it," she said then, surprising herself. "My parents showing up, I mean. Sometimes, I would hide out and watch customers come into the shop, and I would pretend they were my parents, and that they'd come to take me back. Now and then I would picture them having the Witch arrested, but mostly all I cared about was getting out of there." She paused. "I guess it was one thing to picture it, another to do something about it."

"Don't be ashamed of staying. Kids are programmed to believe their parents, wrong or right."

She toyed with her brownie. "You're saying I stayed because of inertia, just like some of the Nightkeepers and *winikin*—maybe a lot of them—are going to want to stick with the sky gods because they're familiar."

"What if they're right?"

"Was I better off letting the Witch use me as a punching bag?"

"Ah, baby. Don't do that to yourself." He wrapped an arm around her.

"I won't. I'm not. I've moved on, damn it." But she let herself lean into him for a few seconds. And, when she felt his breath on her cheek, his lips on her ear, she tipped her head to accept the kiss, then sought his mouth with her own.

The churn of unease in her belly warmed quickly to desire, and she slid her hand up his chest to press over the steady thud of his heart. This was what she needed; it was why she had gone walking with him, why she couldn't stay away from him.

He made her feel important.

He broke the kiss, to press his forehead to hers, so

their breaths mingled when he said, "Will you come home with me tonight?"

She nodded but said nothing, not sure she trusted what would come out of her mouth right now, with her emotions too damn close to the surface.

They climbed down from the pueblo, pausing at the flat spots to kiss. And as they headed back toward the cottage, hand in hand, with her head on his shoulder, she didn't let herself think about tomorrow. It would be enough to go home with him, make love to him. She wouldn't let herself give in all the way like she had last night, though, and she wouldn't stay the night.

CHAPTER EIGHTEEN

December 19
Two days to the zero date

With fewer than forty-eight hours on the clock, the Nightkeepers sat in the great room while Lucius used his laptop to flash pictures of Egyptian paintings and carvings on the big screen. He'd already gone over Bastet; the ram-headed creator god, Khnum, who made the bodies of men from mud and then breathed life into them; and the sun god, Amon-Ra, who had the head of a hawk and ruled the lands of the living. All the good guys Bastet had mentioned.

"Now for the not-so-good guys," he said. "This is Anubis." He clicked to a statue of a pointy-eared, pointy-nosed dog cast in gold and painted black. Lying on its belly with its front paws outstretched, it was positioned like the Sphinx and had gleaming gem eyes that seemed to scan the room even in 2-D. "And so is this." The next slide showed a tomb painting with the same foxy head, but this time on the body of a bulky, muscular man. "Since jackals were often seen scavenging near the dead and their tombs, the ancient Egyptians worshipped them as the guardians of the dead. Anubis here is the god of death and the dying." He hit the button again, skipping a slide and stopping on another animal-headed man. This one, though, had a strangely elongated nose, almost a beak, along with square-tipped ears, and what looked like scales. "And this is Seth."

As Rabbit frowned, trying to figure out what the hell it was, Myrinne leaned over and said in an undertone, "They had armadillos in ancient Egypt?"

He exhaled a soft snort. "That's good news for us—if we poke it with a stick, it'll roll into a ball and wait until we go away."

Her grin warmed him, as did the press of her thigh against his where they sat together at one end of the big sofa. Quarters were tight with the full seventy-seven-person team crammed into the mansion's great room, but he wasn't complaining. Ever since that afternoon up at the pueblo, he and Myr had been hanging out pretty much every day, and things had been going well. The sex was incredible and having her back in his life was even better, though she still wouldn't spend the night.

Even that was probably for the best, though, because it meant he didn't have to explain why he spent almost an hour each morning sitting cross-legged in front of the altar in the spare bedroom, burning incense and staring down at the carved stone surface while he made sure the dark magic stayed contained. And it meant he didn't have to let on that it was getting harder each day.

"It's called the Seth beast," Lucius said with a "shut it" look in their direction. "Seth is the lord of chaos, thunder and the desert. He's roughly equivalent to the Christian's devil, though he does his damage on earth. And this is Osiris." He clicked to a tomb painting of a sharp-featured pharaoh-type guy wearing a tall white hat and the outer wrappings of a mummy. "He rules the underworld and resurrection." He didn't quite glance to where Red-Boar leaned against the back wall, doing his arms-folded-scowl thing.

The resurrected mage had spent the past week lobbying on behalf of the old gods, making it damn clear he thought the Nightkeepers were headed for disaster.

Lucius kept going, sketching out the Egyptian's upper- and underworlds, and finishing with, "I think it's worth mentioning that the Mayan religion didn't have a good-versus-bad afterlife the way that we've been treating it. In fact, the Mayans believed that the sky and Xibalba were two planes that were equally populated with both good and evil gods, just like there are both good and evil people on earth."

"Hold on," Nate said. "You're saying that they had it right and the Nightkeepers had it wrong? The Maya learned the religion from us in the first place!"

"Not from us," Lucius countered. "They learned from

our many-times ancestors, long before things started evolving and the Xibalbans split from the Nightkeepers, separating the light and dark magic."

"So you believe Bastet."

Lucius spread his hands. "Experience tells me that the *Banol Kax* are evil and that the sky gods oppose them. But that doesn't rule out what Bastet told us." He paused. "Not to mention that we found a new treatment for the *xombi* virus . . . in an Egyptian pharmacopeia."

There was a restless shifting of bodies in the jam-packed room.

Anna said, "I passed it along to my contact inside the quarantine zone a couple of days ago, and as of this morning, most of the existing cases have stabilized. In addition, there haven't been any new infections reported in the past five days."

"Which suggests it has nothing to do with a treatment that started two days ago," Red-Boar interjected. "For all we know, the demons just put the poor bastards in a holding pattern so they'll be ready to use as a standing army when the calendar hits zero."

Rabbit wanted to roll his eyes, but couldn't. Because even though Red-Boar was looking seriously strung out these days, he was still making sense. That was the problem, in fact: the arguments were almost perfectly weighted between "it's a trap" and "it's for real." Which meant that somebody needed to be the one to make the call, flip the coin, or what-the-fuck-ever.

"I guess that's my cue." Dez stood.

This time the rustling was louder, lasted longer. Rabbit found himself edging forward in his seat, and Myr's nails dug into his palm. This was what they were all there for, not Lucius's info or Anna's report, but to hear what Dez had decided to do about Bastet's command that the Nightkeepers reject the sky gods.

The king met Red-Boar's narrow-eyed glare. "Don't worry. We all know how you'd vote if this was a democracy." To the rest of them, he said, "The thing is, it's not a democracy. Our ancestors set things up with a king and a fealty oath . . . maybe because they knew it would come down to this. I don't know. It's a hell of a decision to put on one guy, king or not."

"Shades of 'eighty-four," somebody muttered from up near the kitchen, where most of the *winikin* were gathered.

A shiver crawled down Rabbit's spine. He'd had another of the dreams last night, where he was inside Scarred-Jaguar's head in the minutes leading up to the Solstice Massacre. He was pretty sure it was a warning, a pointed reminder that one wrong decision by a powerful mage could make the whole fucking world go *boom*. It wasn't as if he needed the reminder, though. The knowledge haunted him, gnawed at him, and had him staring at the ceiling each night while Myr's pillow cooled beside him. And when the dawn broke, it drove him into the spare room, determined to lock his brain down tight.

When the time came, he would use the dark magic. But he would do it on his terms, and he wouldn't give in to the anger and chaos that came with it. The magic was just magic; the other garbage belonged to the parts of himself that he'd left behind.

"There's one major difference between the old king and me." Dez shot a sharp look at the *winikin*, then scanned the room, so it was clear he was talking to all of them when he said, "I'm not going to force anybody to do anything."

There was a startled silence. Rabbit glanced at Myr, got a "no clue" headshake, and looked back at the king. His own warrior's talent was humming, amping his senses and sending adrenaline into his bloodstream. It was time. Whatever came next, it was going to change the course of human history.

After giving that a moment to sink in, Dez continued. "I realize that our ancestors intended for the king to order his troops into battle . . . but we're not our ancestors. We're the last survivors, the children of the massacre. We didn't ask for the lives we were born into, but each and every one of us stepped up and answered the call when it came."

His eyes went around the room, and when they hit Rabbit, he felt a bit of the old "holy shit, this is real" that he used to get when they all first gathered at Skywatch, back when the whole save-the-world thing had felt so damn faraway. Myr's fingers tightened on his fingers, as if she felt it, too.

When he'd locked eyes with each and every one of them, Dez reached for Reese's hand and brought her to stand beside him. "Now I'm going to ask all of you to step up once more, this time going against so much of what we were taught." He paused while a murmur went through the room—one that seemed, to Rabbit anyway, more resigned than truly surprised. Then the king said, "In forty hours, Reese and I are going to 'port to Coatepec Mountain, stand at the intersection and renounce the *kohan*. I'm asking all of you to join us. More, I'm asking the godkeepers to break their bonds. I believe what the goddess told us. I believe that it's up to the Nightkeepers to defend the earth against both the sky and the underworld."

"You're asking us?" Red-Boar's eyes narrowed. "Not ordering us?"

"You heard me." Dez swept the crowd once more. "If you choose not to join us, you will be released from your fealty oath and given weapons, cash and a 'port wherever you want to go." He dropped his voice. "Wherever you think you can defend yourself best."

From up near the kitchen, JT called, "You're assuming the deserters—"

"Not deserters," Reese put in. "Just no longer allies."

"Whatever. You're assuming you won't wind up fighting them."

Dez shook his head. "I'm not assuming anything. I'm hoping that won't happen, but I'll be damned to the hell of your choice if I lock people up in the basement just because they believe differently than I do, and I'll fucking step down before I conscript an army the way Scarred-Jaguar did." He nodded to Strike, then Anna and Sasha. "Sorry."

"Don't be," Strike rumbled. But his knuckles were white where he gripped Leah's hand.

Dez continued. "It'd be stupid for me to tell you to think about it—gods know that's all I've been doing for the past week and I'm sure you've all been doing the same. But if you figured I was going to make the decision for you, you're out of luck. You've got twenty-four hours to let me or Reese know if you want us to arrange to teleport you out, forty if you don't."

"Who's going to be doing this 'porting?" Strike asked.

Anna said, "I'm already in. The message, the skull . . . I have no doubts."

"This is strictly voluntary," Dez reiterated. "But I hope you'll all step up and keep the team intact. I believe with all my heart and soul that this is the right thing to do."

There were more questions after that, especially from the *winikin*, who seemed to be looking for loopholes in the king's offer to release them. They might have their magic now, but some still didn't trust their freedom.

While those questions and answers were pingponging, Myr leaned in and whispered, "Dez has balls of steel."

Rabbit nodded. "And a legacy he's trying like hell not to live down to."

"Rabbit?" Dez called. "A word?"

The meeting had started breaking up around them, so he rose, caught Myr's hand and tugged her with him when he headed toward where the king was standing with Reese and his advisers. Rabbit didn't miss the way Red-Boar's eyes tracked him, seeming to say: *Remember your loyalties, boy . . . I won't even need to touch her.*

Fury spurted through him, lighting his senses and bringing a surge of magic. Tensing, he fought it down. Deep inside him, though, his own voice whispered, *You can take him. You're better than him, stronger than him, and—*

"What's wrong?" Myr's voice echoed strangely in his ears, and when he looked down at her, all he could see were her eyes, gone dark and worried. When he focused on her, though, the fog cleared and the magic receded. Within a few seconds, it was as if it hadn't ever been there at all.

More, his inner vault was still secure, sealed shut by this morning's meditation. So where the hell had that come from?

Or was he fooling himself with the whole vault thing? Was the dark magic playing him?

"I'm okay," he said, even though he was anything but. "Come on."

They joined Dez, who said without preamble, "Okay, Rabbit. Here's the thing. You know how you're usually the exception to every rule? Well, the same thing goes here. I'm sorry, but I can't give you the same choice as the others."

"You're ordering me to renounce the sky gods?"

The king snorted. "I don't care what kind of spell your father cast, I don't believe for a second that I could force you into betraying something you truly believe in." He paused. "I'm asking you to renounce the sky gods and fight with me . . . but if you choose not to, I'm going to lock you in the basement for the duration. I just can't risk having you running loose."

"What makes you think I'll stay put if there's no spell that'll hold me?"

"Welded cuffs with a shield spell will."

He couldn't picture himself in the storeroom. But he couldn't picture himself renouncing the gods, either. "How long do I have to decide?"

"Forty hours, just like the others."

"Right." Because there wouldn't be any 'port escape for him. "What about Myr?"

The glint in Dez's eyes might've been sympathy. "It's her decision."

And although Rabbit had been the one to say he didn't want her fighting beside him when the time came, now he wanted the king to say that he and Myr were a pair, that they needed to stay that way, fight that way. Hell, he wanted to say it himself.

Instead, he nodded woodenly. "Yeah, good. That's . . . good." He caught Myr's frown out of the corner of his eye, and squeezed her hand.

"Forty hours," Dez repeated, then paused. His voice roughened. "I don't know if this'll mean much—you and I aren't tight like you and Strike or some of the others. We just don't have that kind of history. But as one former fuckup to another, I hope you'll fight with me. I'd really, really like to know you're on my side, and not just because you're the crossover, but because you're a hell of a warrior. A good Nightkeeper."

Rabbit heard a muttered oath behind him, from where his old man was standing. Ignoring that, he stuck out a hand. "For what it's worth, I think you did something good here today. Something very, very worth saving. And I'll have an answer for you in a few hours." More, he would catch the king in private and warn him about Red-Boar. He'd been putting it off, waiting to see what happened. He couldn't put it off any longer, though.

Dez turned away to face the growing line of Night-keepers and *winikin* who had massed behind him, wanting to ask questions. Or maybe they were there to get their payouts and get a place on the Teleport Express.

Gods, Rabbit hoped not.

"Want to take a walk?" Myr was looking at him side-long, as if measuring his mood.

Well, that made two of them. "Yeah. One minute. I've got to take care of a little problem first."

But when he turned around, expecting to see that problem breathing down his neck and raring for a fight, there was nobody there. His old man had disappeared.

CHAPTER NINETEEN

A couple of hours after the meeting broke up, once Leah had gotten done easing the mob-mentality panic as best she could in her officially unofficial role as the keeper of morale at Skywatch—a role she blamed squarely on her old boss in the Miami PD, who had been a big believer in trust circles and desk yoga—she went looking for Strike, following the faint trickle of energy coming from their *jun tan* connection.

She found him in their private shrine.

When Dez took the kingship and she and Strike had moved out of the royal suite and into an apartment in the Nightkeepers' wing, they had converted the hallway walk-in closet to a shrine almost identical to the one they'd had in the royal suite, with stone veneer, motion-sensitive fake torches, and a highly polished disc of black obsidian on the back wall that showed their reflections. Below the disc was a small *chac-mool* altar.

Ever since the day Anna had beheaded the statue in the main ceremonial chamber, the altar in the closet had looked different to Leah, sort of grim and accusatory. Strike had seen it, too, but they had put it down to guilt and the power of suggestion. They hoped.

Now, as she opened the door and let herself into the shrine, her view of the *chac-mool's* face was blocked by Strike's bulk. His gaze met hers in the reflection, and although the polished black stone robbed his gorgeous blue eyes of their color, there was no mistaking the grim resignation. "I can't get through."

He said it matter-of-factly, like he was doing a "can you hear me now?" on his cell phone, but she knew he meant that he couldn't connect with the gods, couldn't pray. And she could see the grief beneath the "it's going to be okay" shell, felt its twin inside her. She'd been holding it together up to now, needing to put on a brave face for the others rather than spark a stampede, but now, with him, her bravery threatened to falter, her "it's okay" face starting to crumble. Because by the gods, this was a terrible decision they were being asked to make.

She hadn't grown up with the Nightkeepers' gods, but she'd sure as hell become a convert—and fast— when she'd seen the sky gods and their demon foe up close and personal, and she and Strike had become the joint godkeepers of Kulkulkan, a huge feathered serpent that flew high above the earth and carried their spirits with it to fight the *Banol Kax* on the Cardinal Days.

If they did what Dez was asking, they would be giving that up. More, they would be betraying a creature—entity?—that had been one of their strongest allies. They shared a special bond with Kulkulkan, and through the winged serpent to each other. The godkeeper spell had brought them together, made them into the warriors and mates they were today. Had that been part of the true gods' plan, or part of the distraction? Had they truly been destined mates, or was that whole concept some game of the false gods? What were they supposed to believe when faith itself turned out to be a lie?

She must have made some sound, because Strike turned and drew her into his arms, and then leaned in to rest his cheek on the top of her head. They stood like that for a long time, holding on to each other, holding each other up. She didn't let herself cling too hard, though, didn't let herself think that this might be one of the last times they stood like this. Because once she started thinking like that, she wouldn't be able to stop herself, and right now they needed to deal with the issue at hand.

As if following her thoughts, he sighed against her hair. "I'm blocked—question is, who's doing the blocking? If the true gods have been hearing me all along, shouldn't I still be able to get through to them?"

"The true gods," she said softly. "Are we sure we know which ones those are?"

He pulled back to look down at her. "I'm sure. Are you?"

"I'm not backing out of what we already agreed . . .

but that's not the same thing as being sure." She wished she could tell him she was as confident as he was. Despite the way he'd challenged Anna and Dez back in the meeting, he had been ready to renounce the sky gods almost from the beginning. Maybe it was his warrior's instincts talking, maybe faith in his sister's magic . . . Leah hoped to hell it wasn't because it could explain his father's behavior as *kohan*-induced madness.

That question was there, though, inside her even when she wished it gone.

He didn't say anything for a minute, just held her close and breathed her in. She let herself relax into him, trying to believe that they were on the right track, that it was all going to be okay. After a moment, he turned her toward the mirror and the altar, tucking the two of them together in the small space and letting the door swing shut.

When it did, he said softly, "Will you stay with me for a bit, my beloved detective?"

Her lips curved. "Of course, my king." She wasn't a detective anymore and he wasn't a king, but gods willing, they would live long enough to be something else. They had talked about it, of course, planned for it—dreams and realities, and a whole lot of "what do you want to be when you grow up?" But now, as she stood beside him, all that mattered was that they were there, together.

Normally, she didn't feel anything much when she prayed—she was only human, after all, though a godkeeper. Now, though, as she faced the mirror and the *chac-mool*, she felt a faint tingle of a magic not her own, as if Kulkulkan himself was reaching through the barrier to warn: *You don't want to do this.*

And the damn thing was, he was right. She really, really didn't want to give up the one piece of the magic that was hers, the connection to the god who had taken her and Strike flying together. Who had saved them from the *Banol Kax*, over and over again. But that was the point, wasn't it? The enemy of their enemy wasn't necessarily their friend anymore.

Please gods, let us get this right.

"Did you get it?" A blond bundle of energy and nerves whipped through the door and homed in on Brandt. "Was it there?"

He grinned and lifted the thick yellow envelope, then shook it a little so the flash drive made a noise. "Got it."

"Oh!" Patience stopped halfway across the sitting area and clasped her hands, eyes filling. Then she covered her face and gave a watery laugh. "Shit. I told myself I wasn't going to cry. It makes me feel like a . . . a . . . I don't know."

"Like a mommy?" Brandt suggested. "Hey, roll with it." He sure as hell wasn't going to ding her, given that he'd watered up a little when he'd gotten the end of the scavenger hunt Jox and Hannah had set up so only he or Patience could reasonably find the drop box, and he'd reached in to grab the envelope, knowing that the twins had no doubt touched it. Plopping down onto the couch, he patted the cushion beside him. "Sit.

Christmas came early this year, so let's open our presents."

He'd meant it as a joke, but wished it back even as he said it.

The Nightkeepers didn't celebrate the holiday per se, but most of them had fudged it to one degree or another in order to fit in with the lives they'd lived in the outside world, and they had kept up the tradition at Skywatch with a festival to honor the *wayeb* days at the end of December, when there were five "forgotten" days in the Mayan calendar, blanks that didn't have any names. Either way, it had looked suspiciously like Christmas, with gifts, feasting and decorations, especially that first year, when Harry and Braden had lived at Skywatch. The presence of two active little three-year-olds had made it easy to appreciate the whole Santa thing, or a version thereof.

In the years since the boys had gone into hiding with the *winikin*, the holidays hadn't seemed nearly so important—or fun—but Skywatch had still celebrated them. Last year, Brandt had taken Patience away for a long weekend, just the two of them and a familiar cheesy hotel room in Cancun, with mirrors every damn place and all the tingles and romance they could've wanted.

It was a hell of a thing to think that they might not live to see another Christmas, especially when it was less than a week away. Worse to think that the boys might not, either. The *winikin* would keep them as safe as possible, locked down somewhere off the beaten track, in a doomsday bunker with all the amenities . . . but that wouldn't protect them forever.

He didn't want to think about them coming aboveground to a blasted, empty wasteland or, worse, a demon-occupied earth and a populace that had been enslaved, turned to *makol* and *xombi*. He hated, too, picturing them showing up at the prearranged meeting point on the morning of December twenty-second . . . and waiting in vain. Or having only one parent show up. Or—

"Don't." Patience wrapped her arm around his waist and put her head on his shoulder. "You'll drive yourself crazy."

"Hello, pot? This is the kettle." Gods knew that they had both been struggling with their decisions—not just to follow Dez's lead and renounce the sky gods, but also to post an online personal with prearranged keywords that counted as their good-bye, rather than setting up another drop box, as they had planned. They had decided they couldn't risk it, though. Not when they couldn't even trust their own prayers not to give them away.

She nudged him in the ribs. "Just open it already!" But when he started to, she grabbed his wrist. "Wait."

He started to laugh at her, but the impulse died when he saw the tears welling in her eyes. His voice went to a rasp. "Ah, baby. Don't."

"I won't. I'm not." She reached out a trembling hand to touch the envelope. "I just . . . gods, Brandt. Tell me that we're going to make it. You, me, Harry, Braden,

Jox . . . even if you have to lie, tell me we're all going to be okay."

"Hey." He shifted, caught her chin and turned her to face him. "We're going to be okay." Tears broke free and trailed down her cheeks, and he forced determination into his voice, forced *himself* to believe it when he said, "We're a team, Patience, you and me. Until death do us part, right? Well, that's not happening this week."

"Promise?" she whispered, then shook her head. "Sorry. Forget I said that." A vow carried the force of a spell for him, after all, and she'd told him it was okay to lie.

He wanted to. He wanted to promise her that the Nightkeepers were going to win the war, that both of them were going to survive. He wanted to swear that four days from now they would be standing on the Cancun beach where they'd first met, watching Harry and Braden run toward them with the *winikin* walking more sedately behind them, hand in hand. He wanted to say all that, wanted it to be true. But he couldn't make it a promise.

So instead he said, "We're going to be okay, Patience. We're going to win the war and make it through, and four days from now we're going to hold our boys again. And after that, we're never going to let them go, ever again. Because we're a family. And I don't care what the writs say, there's nothing more important than family."

There was a time when he wouldn't have said that, and she wouldn't have believed him if he had. It was a sign of how far they'd come since the bad days between them, how solid they were together, that she relaxed against him, letting out a watery sigh. "I know. I just . . . I needed to hear that. I needed you to say it."

He brushed his lips across her cheek and then, when she leaned in, he found her lips. The kiss started soft, more an affirmation than any effort to incite, but then she touched her tongue to his, and things got more serious. Magic kindled low in his gut and flared out from there, making him very aware of his own body, and hers, and the fact that they were alone in their suite, with nobody expecting them to be anywhere for a couple of hours.

Hello, afternooner, he thought, and grinned into the kiss.

But at the same time, he knew that could wait. The heat was always there between them, more now than ever before, and the anticipation would only add to the thrill of making love. So, easing away, unable to wait any longer, he tore open the envelope and dumped the contents onto the coffee table, next to the laptop he had there, ready and waiting.

Smaller envelopes cascaded out—those would be letters from Jox and Hannah, updating them on the more serious stuff the twins didn't necessarily need to know about, along with the flash drive and a fat folder, which would contain printed-out photos, schoolwork, and letters from both boys.

Each care package had a different theme, which was announced by artwork on the carefully selected folder.

Last time around, Braden picked Transformers. This time, Harry had gone with dinosaurs. The folder had an ominous background of darkness, ferns and mist, with a cartoon T. Rex giving a big cartoon "Rawr!" Across the raging Rex's stomach, two very different hands had written *I want a brontosaurus burger* and *Look out for the meteor!*

Brandt chuckled, though the sound cracked at the end, catching against the lump in his throat.

"Oh," Patience breathed, and reached for the folder. But then she stopped herself, and pulled back. "No. Let's do the video first."

"You sure?" Usually they eased into it with the photos, so it wasn't such a shock seeing the boys, and realizing all over again how much of their childhood they were missing.

"Positive," she said, but he was already fitting the flash drive into the laptop, and feeling his heart bump unsteadily as they waited for the video to open.

Moments later, the window popped up and a boy's face filled the screen—just a nose and a gap-toothed grin. Then he pulled back from the in-computer camera to reveal unruly dark blond hair and a face that looked so much more grown-up since the last video they'd gotten. His green tee had a cartoon T-Rex on the chest and a smudge of something on one sleeve.

That, and the off-kilter collar made the ID a cinch. "Braden," they said in unison, and shared a quick grin.

Then the image shifted and Harry's face came into view—each feature was identical to his brother's, the both of them a mixture of the best of both their parents. His blue brontosaurus tee was clean and perfectly adjusted, his hair neatly combed, his features solemn. His eyes, though, glittered with excitement and the devilishness that appeared in him just often enough to keep his brother on his toes.

The two leaned in together and mugged for the camera, giving a ragged chorus of, "Hi, Mommy! Hi, Daddy!"

"They're so handsome," Patience murmured tightening her grip on his hand. "Just like you. But oh, they're growing up so fast."

"I know." He brushed his lips across her temple. "But they've got plenty of growing up left to do, and we're going to be right there with them."

Harry disappeared from the screen while Braden launched into a story about a winter festival at their school, and how his class had done face painting, while Harry's had done a ball toss.

Pulling Patience closer against his side, Brandt settled in to enjoy the show, which the ticker at the bottom said was twenty-four minutes long.

Twenty-four minutes to spend with their boys. Gods, how they needed this.

The prior videos hadn't had any real pattern. One had been shot at a nameless country fair, and had included a now-famous scene of Jox wobbling his way off a roller coaster and doing a near-violent "cut the camera" motion as he headed for some bushes. Another had been on a white-sand beach that could've been anywhere on either of the coasts. That was one of the keys to the video editing, that nobody—not even Patience or Brandt—should be able to use the images to figure out where the *winikin* were hiding with the boys.

This was a rare indoor-set video. The background seemed to be their current home, though all that was really visible was a wainscoted wall and a mantelpiece sporting family photos—including one Brandt recognized as having been taken the last time the boys had been at Skywatch, with the whole family in the frame— along with a couple of trophies and Hannah's trademark bric-a-brac, heavy on the lavender.

Braden was still talking, going on about a bake sale table with huge brownies and the mean lady who had been taking the money, when there was a scuffling noise in the background, then the *thud-thud-thud* of footsteps.

"Got 'im," Harry's voice said from off camera. "Didja tell them about the booth?"

"I was waiting for you," Braden said with an eye roll, but then grinned maniacally into the camera. "Like he said, there was a booth at the fair, from the human society. They were doing a 'doption drive!"

"Ahem," said another voice, interrupting. Braden looked up and shifted aside, and Jox came into view. The former head *winikin* looked good, wearing a longsleeved green polo, a green baseball hat made to look like a dinosaur's head, complete with fierce eyes and cloth fangs coming down off the bill, and a shit-eating grin that didn't look anything like the tense, stressed expression he used to sport 24-7. There were shadows there, yeah—hell, they all had shadows these days. But there was an evil sort of pleasure, too.

Jox leaned in to the camera and said in a stage whisper, "In case you're wondering, that would be 'humane society.' And you can probably guess the rest. For the record, Hannah was the one who caved."

"Baloney!" An elegant, purple-manicured hand came into the screen and poked him in the shoulder. "You were just as bad as the boys, with the big sad eyes and the 'we'll take good care of him'!"

"Uh-oh," Patience said, covering her mouth with her free hand. "They didn't."

Jox disappeared as Harry and Braden both came back into view, hauling between them the squirming body of a half-grown black dog. It looked to be about the size of a cocker spaniel, but had the wiry hair of a schnauzer. Or maybe a Brillo pad. Its feet were fuzzy, its head triangular, and its belly was unappealingly naked.

"They did," Brandt confirmed.

Harry, who was in charge of the front end, had been holding the pup's muzzle shut. Now he let go, and the animal let loose with a string of half-hysterical yips, while thrashing its head side-to-side in an effort to lick Harry. Or maybe consume him.

Probably lick, Brandt decided. Jox and Hannah might've succumbed to puppy breath, but only if they thought it was safe.

And, what the hell. It seemed like they had a dog, like it or not.

Not that he had anything against the critters. He'd just figured it would be more of a family decision, maybe even a way for them to celebrate all being back together. Not to mention that he'd been envisioning something more along the lines of a Rottweiler.

"I was going to talk to you about getting them a dachshund," Patience said mournfully.

Brandt's opinion of the black mutt notched up significantly.

"We were gonna call him Wolfie," Harry chirped, "but the first day he was here, when we went to buy him a collar and stuff, he got out of his cage, broke Hannah's big bowl and the purple vase Jox got her for her birthday, ate the garbage out of the kitchen, puked under the dining table and then chewed up Jox's boots."

"Only one," Braden said defensively, hauling the pup into his arms in an awkward hug that left its face smooshed off to one side and one ragged ear sticking straight up. The puppy didn't look like it cared, though. In fact, it looked like it was having the time of its little life. Either that, or its doggy smile meant it was planning to eat the computer next.

"Jox can't wear only one shoe," Harry said with a serious tone of "duh" in his voice. "Anyway, after that, Jox said we should name him after Unc' Rabbit."

Now it was Brandt's turn to say, "Oh, no, they didn't." But there was a laugh in his voice.

After Red-Boar's death, Rabbit had lived with them and had become the boys' favorite playmate. And to everyone's surprise, he had taken to them in return. He'd played with them, hung out with them, told them all the old stories, and become their unofficial uncle. So for Harry and Braden to name their puppy after him was a sign of love. For Jox, it was more along the lines of passive-aggressive revenge. And more apropos than ever, now, though the *winikin* wouldn't know it.

Brandt paused the video and glanced at his wife. "Well," he said, torn between amusement and horror. "That was unexpected."

"Yes, it was." She paused, lips turning up with wry acceptance. "Apparently we've got one more dependent to add to the list."

"Yeah." He kissed her cheek, tucked her tighter against his side, and tapped the touchpad to unpause things. And, as the video kept going with the boys talking over each other in an effort to describe their efforts to housebreak the new puppy, he inwardly promised the true gods that he was going to do his absolute best to honor his creators and ancestors, fight the enemy, defend the barrier, the earth and mankind . . . and protect his family. Which apparently now included a terminally destructive mutt named Rabbit.

CHAPTER TWENTY

Quarantine camp
Chichén Itzá, Mexico

"Only a couple have left so far, both older, more traditional *winikin* who just couldn't give up on their gods."
Anna tugged at the edge of the teddy bear blanket,
though it wasn't really wrinkled. She needed to do something, make some sort of contact, yet she didn't feel like
she had the right to hold Rosa's hand, given that she'd
'ported straight into her room in the middle of the night.

Not that the little girl minded. She was still unconscious and nonresponsive. Waiting for a miracle.

In the soft bluish glow of Anna's foxfire spell, the
child's face was soft and sweet, yet it carried a trace of
hidden mischief that promised a bright and lively little
girl, if only she could fight off the virus.

Guilt tugged. "We're going to do it," Anna said,

keeping her voice down so nobody out in the hall would hear her. "We're going to renounce the imposters and promise ourselves to the ancestors' gods, right at Coatepec Mountain, where the bad guys are going to come through the barrier. And then . . . well, I guess we'll pray for a miracle." There was a chance—backed up by a couple of papyri—that once they were free of the *kohan*, the true gods would be able to help them.

Maybe. Possibly.

"I know I should be back in the library right now, working on more translations or helping Leah keep up morale, but I just . . . I needed some peace."

It probably should've seemed strange that she would find her peace here, in the middle of illness and death. But it was partly her fault that Rosa was here, and it helped to sit at her bedside, helped to be able to whisper, "I'm going to protect you. I'm going to do everything I can to make sure you're okay after all this." One way or another. "I'm going to—"

A muffled exchange reached her through the door, bringing her to her feet. She doused the foxfire and ramped up her magic, but her gut—those instincts the warriors swore by—told her not to 'port away this time. Her pulse kicked up a notch. Had her magic sensed danger on the other side of that door? Were the *xombis* mobilizing now that the time was near?

With sudden energy sizzling along her skin, she cast a chameleon spell and stepped into the corner on the other side of the door, where the deepest shadows would be cast by the small camp lantern. Right now, it sat unlit on the cardboard box that had been set up as a nightstand, attesting that the little girl had become a favorite of more than a few staffers.

In a flash, Anna had cataloged the contents of the room and their potential as a distraction or a weapon, and where before the thought process had so often felt awkward and ill-fitting, now it came naturally. And, as the hallway conversation cut out and the doorknob turned, she braced to defend the defenseless.

She didn't know if the intruder was *xombi*, *makol*, human or what, but it wasn't getting past her without a fight.

Hidden behind the chameleon shield, she bared her teeth as the door swung open and a small flashlight beam cut into the room, swept it in a casual look-see, and then fixed on the small bump beneath the teddy bears. The door swung shut and the beam headed for the bed . . . and in its reflected light, Anna saw a camp shirt rolled up over strong, tanned forearms, and a body that was sturdy and compact, and moved with an unswerving determination that said "Everything's okay. I'm here."

She relaxed and blew out a silent breath. She knew that shirt, knew that arm and that way of moving. *Ah*, she thought. *David*. She didn't know why she was surprised, why he hadn't been her first thought when she'd heard the voices out in the hallway. Or maybe he had been and she hadn't let herself go there. Because now her pulse was drumming with a different sort of adrenaline.

She had seen him a couple of times in the past week, keeping up her pretense of being in the area while deflecting his curiosity. They had also exchanged a half dozen or so e-mails, notes that had started as quick updates on Rosa's condition and had evolved to snippets of each of their days, with Anna telling half-truths that fit into the life she was supposed to be living, while he talked about being frustrated by the virus, the politics, the buzz about the coming doomsday. And eventually about himself, too. She now knew he'd been divorced for ten years, loved his work, and wasn't looking to change his lifestyle. She also knew he still wondered about the scars on her wrists and the way Rosa had stopped talking after she'd passed along her message, but he didn't ask about it. In fact, he didn't ask anything, really. He just shared himself, slowly and cautiously, but with a quiet openness that drew her in.

It was a very different flirtation than any she'd ever had before, and she was all too aware that most of it was lies, at least on her part. David thought he was talking to an academic on sabbatical, a woman in search of meaning in the wake of a life-changing event. And gods, how she wished that she could've been that woman, that it could've been that simple.

It wasn't, though. And she should go.

There wasn't any danger here; exactly the opposite. She could leave, knowing that Rosa was almost as safe as she would've been under Nightkeeper watch. But as David sat in the chair she'd just vacated, not giving any indication that he'd noticed its butt-print warmth, she stayed put, looking at him. Spying on him, really. But this might be the last time she saw him, so she would let herself look her fill.

"See?" he said to the little girl, "I told you I'd be back. You ready to write her another little letter?"

A thrill raced through Anna. Did he mean her?

He dug in the pocket of his lab coat and came up with the little foldaway computer he used—a clever machine with a decent-sized keyboard and the ability to get a satellite uplink almost anywhere, at least according to him. He woke it up, tapped a few keys, and gave a little laugh. "It's only been twelve hours since the last one. Too much, do you think?"

The thrill turned to giddy, excited warmth, though Anna told herself to take it down a notch. This wasn't the time to be crushing on her human contact.

If not now, then when? her inner voice of reason asked.

"Ah, heck," David said, laughing at himself. "Nothing ventured and all that." He patted the teddy bears near where Rosa's hand would be. "I hope you're taking notes, little one. You'll need to know this stuff in another ten years or so. And don't think it's irrelevant because I'm, well, not as young as I was the first time around, or as young as you're going to be when you start trying it out for yourself." He looked down at the scant paunch that just barely overhung his belt, sat up straighter until it went away, and grinned. "Well, anyway. Love makes you goofy, no matter what age it hits."

Anna's breath whooshed out, loud enough that she

was very glad the chameleon shield cloaked sounds as well as her image. Love? She had been thinking of it as a crush, infatuation, interest . . . but love?

Part of her backpedaled hard and fast, saying, *No way. This is just . . . I don't know. A distraction. At most, it's the potential for something more, something to look forward to.* But another part of her yearned toward the word, and toward the idea of a man who wanted her enough to suck in his gut and worry about how long it'd been since his last e-mail.

She stared, drinking him in as he said, "Ah, well. In for a peso, or however that goes," and started typing out a message.

Her phone weighed suddenly very heavy in her pocket. When was the last time she'd been wanted? When was the last time she had wanted in return? When had she thought about loving and being loved, rather than about the war?

She didn't remember . . . and she didn't remember it feeling like this before.

With Dick, it had been more about being awed by his quick mind and caustic wit, and feeling so very *normal* when she was with him. Their love had evolved in a series of kite-flying dates—he designed and built them when he wasn't being a brilliant economist—and their marriage had stayed solid for more than a decade. Eventually, though, infertility had undermined the foundation, boredom and lack of communication had knocked out more of the bricks, and his infidelity had eventually brought down the walls. Or maybe her being a Nightkeeper had more to do with it than she wanted to admit. She didn't know anymore, wasn't even sure she cared.

She had truly loved Dick while it lasted. But even back when she'd been falling for him, her feelings for him hadn't been anything like this. They hadn't hit her like a funnel cloud of champagne, surrounding her with fizzy, tickling bubbles and making her head spin. And they sure as heck hadn't made her want to tell him the truth about her, about everything.

Don't even think it.

Maybe she was projecting. Maybe this was one of those, "I'm being deployed tomorrow, let's shag," impulses she'd heard about. Maybe when the day after tomorrow dawned—and, damn it, she would let herself believe there would *be* a day after tomorrow—she wouldn't be dying to catch him alone and really touch him, more than just the casual brush of bodies in passing. It was so frustrating to feel that contact through the protective gear he still insisted she wear, even though the virus appeared to have entered stasis. She wanted to lose those layers, wanted his hands on her, his mouth on hers, and—

Down, girl.

She blew out a steadying breath as her pulse thudded in her ears. Maybe in forty-eight hours, with the world's problems solved and her whole life opening back up in front of her, she would look at him and see just a guy who appeared to own three shirts, one pair of shoes, and no comb.

She didn't think so, though. And for right now, when she needed to believe in so many new, scary things, she would give herself permission to believe in this one, too.

"Too much?" he asked, tipping the small display toward Rosa. "Yeah. I thought so." He tapped a key, muttering, "Delete, delete, delete," under his breath.

"I shouldn't be here," Anna said softly. It didn't matter that he was thinking about her, writing to her; he didn't know she was there, and would certainly be acting differently if he did.

She should go.

And she would. In a minute. Right now, though, she couldn't pull her eyes from the intense concentration in his face as he typed one-handed, or the way his other hand rested on the teddy bear blanket, including Rosa in the moment. The camp light cast strange shadows, making him look larger than himself, larger even than the room itself.

"How about this?" He tipped the screen again. "I think that's better. Don't you?"

Rosa didn't answer, but the image of the two of them together engraved itself on her mind, looking somehow both fragile and rock solid, and so very worth saving.

Just go, she told herself. *You can see them both later. Maybe. Hopefully.*

When the thought threatened to depress the shit out of her, she closed her eyes and made the 'port. And as the magic closed around her and yanked her from the room, she told herself not to think about the two people she was leaving behind, not to hash over something that shouldn't be—couldn't be—her main concern.

Still, once she was back at Skywatch, alone in her suite, she checked her phone every thirty seconds or so until David's e-mail came through. When it did, the ringtone made her jump and sent her pulse into overdrive.

Her hand shook a little as she hit the key to bring up the message, and she made herself look away for a moment, partly to prove that she could, and partly to enjoy the anticipation. It was real. *He* was real, and he was interested in her for real.

Finally, she blew out a breath and let herself look.

Dear Anna,

I hope this message finds you away from the doomsday craziness, perhaps even back in the States. Not that I want you gone, but I'd rather have you safe, even if it means I won't have my favorite translator to call on, at least not in person. At least not right now. Granted, we're safe here inside the zone, but the crowds are growing and small riots have already broken out beyond the perimeter. I've been out to tend some of the wounded, and I don't want to see you among them. Please don't make me.

Ah, I'm messing this up, aren't I? I don't mean to be a downer, or to order you around. Blame it on the hours, I guess, or the frustration of knowing that although the virus has stalled, it did it on its own terms, and could, for all I know, kick back on at a moment's notice. I hate that we're not making any progress in curing it. Rosa is here with me right now, but there's been no change. We're just sitting here, waiting it out. But for how long? Will tomorrow really be the turning point? As much as I've tried to level off the doomsday rumors, it's hard not to think that the tide is poised to turn. I just hope—pray, though I wouldn't know what god or gods to pray to under the circumstances—that if things do turn around tomorrow, they turn in our favor.

Blah, blah, blah, me, me, me. Like I said, I don't mean to be a downer. So how about I move the heck on, and tell you something you don't know, giving you one of the little vignettes we have begun to trade, which I look forward to more than you can know. You have started to show me a little of your life, and I respect you more with each small insight. I hope the same is true in reverse. Since I last wrote about my childhood, now I'll give you a snippet of the present instead. Or, rather, the present I'd like to return to, for a day. A week. A month. However long I can manage.

Which is the long way of saying that I'm attaching a picture of my cabin back home, where I go on the rare occasion that I can pull myself away from work. It's small and basic—in fact, the amenities aren't much better than here at the quarantine camp, come to think of it—but the views make me glad to be alive. I don't know that I could live there full time, at least not at this point in my life—I need fast food and a challenge—

*but it helps me get through the dark times—like now—
knowing that when they're over, I can go there and just
be.*

*So have a look. I'm not sure what you'll see in the
picture, or even really what I want you to see. All I
know is that I need a pick-me-up tonight, and wonder
if you might not need one, too, so I'm sending you my
happy place.*

*Be well, Anna. Take care of yourself and watch out
for the doomsday crazies.*

Yours,
David

It was the longest note he'd yet sent her, and the first
that openly acknowledged that they were doing more
than exchanging just updates on the virus and Rosa's
condition. Breathing through an emotion-choked throat,
Anna read it twice, and found herself nodding as she
read. *Yes, I know. Yes, I feel the same way.* Then she clicked
on the attachment, and caught her breath. "Oh."

The picture showed David standing by a rustic cabin
that was exactly as he'd advertised—small, simple and
neat, with a lake edge nearby, a gorgeous mountain
view and a huge sky spreading behind it. But although
the scene was a postcard, she was far more interested
in the man. His clothes were very much like the ones
she'd seen him in when he was out of his scrubs—a
long-sleeved shirt rolled up over his forearms, with
worn jeans and battered boots. But although he was
dressed the same, nothing else looked familiar.

He was smiling broadly, looking relaxed and happy as he held up a stringer of fish and mugged for the camera.

Looking at the picture, she yearned all over again, not just for the man she'd been getting to know, but for the same man entirely in his element. Or one of his elements. He hadn't invited her to go with him, but the hope was there, she thought, between the lines. And oh, how she wanted to go.

Yes, she could 'port herself there right now. But she didn't want to go alone, and she didn't want to cheat. She wanted to wait for him, to go there with him and see it through his eyes and her own.

"Don't get ahead of yourself," she warned, but it was already too late.

So, knowing she was playing a potentially dangerous game, she sent the e-mail to her desktop and printed out the picture in full color, and then folded it and tucked it into the combat gear she would wear tomorrow. And for the first time in a long, long time, she felt like she wasn't going to just be fighting against the enemy . . . she'd be fighting *for* something, too. A future. And, maybe, a new life.

Gods willing.

CHAPTER TWENTY-ONE

December 21
Six hours until the Great Conjunction
Skywatch

Myr woke when the sunlight shone on her face, all too aware that today was the day. She had been dreading this solstice for so long . . . but now it was hard to believe it was finally upon them.

Yeah, she could've bailed to hide out in a bunker somewhere and pray, but that hadn't been an option for her any more than it had been for Rabbit. They both believed in the Nightkeepers and the war . . . and Bastet's message had struck major chords. So they were both still at Skywatch, both ready to renounce the sky gods, and then fight the *kax* and the *kohan* when the barrier fell.

We might even die. She'd been trying on the concept

for the past few days, trying to imagine how it would happen, what it would feel like. Sometimes picturing it made her weep, other times she just went numb. Right now, the terror was a dull throb.

Maybe if she went back to sleep, when she woke up it would be tomorrow.

Or not.

Murmuring a protest, she turned her face into Rabbit's warm bulk beside her, letting herself snuggle up against him a little tighter, with her head beneath his beard-shadowed jaw, her thigh over his.

Yeah, she had stayed the night. So sue her.

"Hey." His voice was a warm rumble, his hand gentle when it skimmed up her arm to her throat, then to brush across her cheek. "Don't." It wasn't until she felt the chill of cooling moisture that she realized there were tears on her cheek.

"I'm not. I won't." She rolled away.

"Don't do that, either. Seriously." He snaked out an arm, wrapped it around her waist and rolled her back into him in a smooth move that didn't seem to take any effort for him, but wasn't something she could fight. Not that she tried all that hard, because for a moment it almost felt like a regular morning, the kind they used to have.

The kind she wanted to have more of.

She had gone into this saying they had to keep it casual, that she wasn't going to fall back into old patterns, but this wasn't an old pattern—it was a new relationship, a new love affair. They spent their days together training, their nights together loving each other, talking about everything and nothing, holding each other, just freaking *being* together, a way they hadn't before. And as the barrier grew thinner, their powers—and their feelings—grew.

This time around, being with him didn't make her weaker. It made them both stronger.

So she let herself be snuggled back against his side, but poked him in the ribs. "You're full of orders this morning, mister. Okay, what *do* you want me to do then?"

"Pretty much just lie there," he said with a chuckle in his voice as he rolled partway atop her, pinning her with his warm, sleepy weight.

"Oh, that's charming. Really." But she arched beneath him, looped her legs around his hips, and ran her feet up the backs of his thighs while he settled against her, hard and ready for action. Her blood heated, then burned, because she was ready for him, too. More than ready. And where they had kept things to the darkness this past week, with no time for daylight trysts and her slipping away well before the dawn, now they could see each other in the morning light. It glowed in the air, haloing him with sparks of red, green and gold. His magic. Hers. Gods.

The solstice was amping their powers already. But would it be enough?

He kissed her deeply, rocking his hips against her so his hard flesh slid against the wet, wanting place between her legs. Moaning his name, she tried to set aside the fear, focusing instead on the man in her arms, the heat they made together, and the way her magic intertwined with his, making the air around them come alive.

She kissed him, stroked him, and then curled around him and angled her body so he could slide into her, putting him exactly where they both wanted him to be. A sexy groan rumbled in his chest and he began the thrust, but then he stopped with just the tip of his thick cock inside her.

Her eyes came open, and she found him braced over her, looking down at her. Expression tender, he stroked her cheek, brushing a few strands away from her forehead. "I'm glad you stayed. There's nobody else I would want to wake up next to on a day like today. Only you."

Throat tightening, she said, "I needed this. I needed you." Then she reached up, tugged him down, and poured herself into a kiss. Groaning, he shifted and slid all the way into her, filling her, stretching her and sending pleasure caroming through her. And for the next few minutes, he kissed her, held her, moved against her, stripped her down to need and sensation and then gave her more, thrusting hard and sure until her entire universe coalesced to the feel of his body inside hers, and the hum of magic that surrounded them.

Spurred by the sudden, sharp desperation of knowing that this might be it, this might be their last time together, she surged up beneath him, twisting up and over to reverse their positions. As she rose above him, his hands clamped on her hips and his eyes brightened with heat and lust, and an edge of *Hell, yeah. Bring it on, baby.*

Blood racing, she leaned in to kiss him, letting her hips rise up as she did, so she slid up along his thick cock, until only the head was inside her. He groaned and tightened his grip, then groaned again when she slid back down. And again.

As the magic sped through her veins, she set a hard, fast rhythm. Her breath stuttered and then caught when she moved against him, around him, reveling in the slap and slide of flesh, but also the way his eyes stayed on hers, the way their powers mingled in the air surrounding them. "Yes," she whispered, angling her hips to ride him just the way she wanted, with his hard flesh rubbing her center exactly right. "There. Yes."

"Hell, yeah, there," he grated, and shifted beneath her, surging up as she came down, the two of them racing together to the peak. She got there first, coiling and crying out as the orgasm gripped her tightly. It went on and on, wrung out by his thrusts and the glorious friction they made together as he hammered toward his own release and then came, gripping her hips and groaning as he thrust up into her again and again, prolonging the pleasure.

She stayed over him for a moment, shaking with the aftershocks of her own orgasm. Then she curled forward to press her cheek against his as the intense sensations faded away, leaving magic thrumming in their wake.

After a moment, he shifted, rearranging them so they were cuddled together with her face in his shoulder and her thigh thrown across his, almost exactly the way she had awakened. She kissed his stubbled jaw and inhaled the scent of their lovemaking, trying to imprint it on her senses. Trying not to let everything feel desperate and final.

He tightened his arms around her, his voice very serious when he said, "Myr, I want to tell you—"

"Not now," she interrupted, lifting a hand to cover his mouth. Her heart bumped, because she knew what he wanted to say, knew that she wanted to say it back. "We'll say it later. After."

His eyes darkened, but after a moment, he nodded. Then he reached up, caught her wrist, and pressed a kiss to her palm. "Are you sure?"

"No. But it'll give us something to look forward to, something to fight for."

"I'll always fight for you." It was low, intense, and carried the force of a vow. "Always."

Her throat closed, so all she could get out was, "Same goes." Then, because she knew if she didn't leave now, she would still be there in an hour when they were due to meet up with Dez, she eased away from him. "I'm going to go shower and change. It just seems wrong to show up for battle wearing yesterday's clothes. Talk about a cosmic walk of shame."

"I'll see you at the rendezvous?"

She swallowed hard at the thought that this could be the last muster, the last group teleport. "You bet."

As she headed out of the cottage, she found herself memorizing the familiar rooms, the furniture, the memories of the good times they'd had there. Outside, she stared for a moment at the flower boxes she'd installed a few months after moving in with him. They held only dirt and a few dried leaves now, and the sight brought a pang.

You'll be back, she told herself, and did her best to believe it as she headed down the path to the main mansion. Still, though, she couldn't stop herself from turning for one last look.

She froze at the sight of Red-Boar gliding noiselessly up the steps to Rabbit's cottage. As she sucked in a quick breath of surprise, he took a quick look around and—not noticing her in the shadows of the farthest cottage—slipped through the door without knocking.

Oh, that wasn't good. Not good at all.

Flashing on an image of Rabbit being surprised awake by his crazy-ass father, Myr didn't hesitate. She headed back the way she had come, moving fast and staying out of view as she heard the kitchen door shut. *Don't freak,* she told herself. *He's probably just going to try and talk him out of renouncing the* kohan.

Heart thudding, she eased up to the side of Rabbit's cottage, near where the kitchen window was cracked to let in some fresh air. She heard Red-Boar's voice loud and clear, suggesting he hadn't gotten beyond the kitchen.

"I talked to Dez," the old mage said, sounding more disgusted than usual.

"And?" Rabbit's question was followed by the clink of a glass on the kitchen counter, then the glug of some milk or juice or something.

Okay, Myr thought. Red-Boar hadn't gone after Rabbit in his bed or anything else particularly psycho-stalkerish, despite the robe and weird behavior. They were just talking. Which meant she was eavesdropping, which wasn't cool.

She eased away, intending to slink into the shadows behind the next cottage over and head back to the mansion. But then Red-Boar said, "He refuses to do the right thing. So I'm going to do it for him."

Myr's blood iced. *What!?*

She wanted to jump up and shout the question, along with "the hell" and "do you think you're doing?" Instead, with a sick mix of dread and guilt churning in her gut, she hit the recorder on her comm device, got it up as close to the window as she could, and peeked around the corner, knowing she would be hidden by the half-open blinds and the cottage shadow at her back.

She could just see the two of them, sitting at the table with glasses of OJ in front of them like it was a break-fast meeting. Since when did Rabbit and Red-Boar have breakfast together, or even freaking juice?

Rabbit eyed his father with a hard, steady gaze. "You know the deal."

The breath froze in Myr's lungs. What was he up to?

Red-Boar nodded. "Dez hasn't left me any choice." He held out his ceremonial knife. "Do it."

"Fine." Rabbit knocked back his juice, set the glass on the kitchen table and took his father's knife. His expression didn't change as he sliced his palms and let the blood fall on the table. Then, sounding flat, like he'd rehearsed the words over and over again his head, he said, "I swear that if you use the last Boar Oath to countermand the two orders you've already put on me, then I will refuse the false gods today."

"*No!*" Myr whispered soundlessly as she felt the magic of the blood oath ripple in the air.

Red-Boar rose and loomed over his son for a second, then said, "Fuck it. By the Boar Oath, this is my third command: I order you to disregard the two prior orders."

This time the ripples were stronger, the magic deeper and darker. Myr pressed the back of her hand to her mouth to stifle her gasp, and then, when she heard Red-Boar's footsteps moving in her direction, ducked and scuttled away, around the corner of the next cottage over. She flattened herself up against the siding as there was another low murmur of conversation, then the sound of the kitchen door, and footsteps heading away. One set. Risking a glimpse, she confirmed that Red-Boar was stumping off, alone. Rabbit had stayed behind.

Rabbit . . . who was no longer sworn to obey his king or keep from harming his teammates.

Rabbit . . . who hadn't told her he'd made a deal with his father. And not one Dez would approve of.

"Gods." She turned back to slide down the wall and

sit on the ground while her head spun. "Oh, holy shit. What's going on here?" And, more, what was she supposed to do about it?

Realizing that her recorder was still going, she clicked it off. Somehow knowing she had actual evidence made it worse, because logic, her instincts and just about every other piece of her sane and reasonable mind said she should take it straight to Dez.

Instead, pushing back upright on shaky legs, she headed for the cottage, hoping to hell she wasn't about to make the biggest mistake of her life. She had to, though; she just had to. This was Rabbit, after all.

Rabbit held himself stiff and still until he couldn't hear his old man anymore, couldn't sense the skin-crawl of Red-Boar's presence. Then he took a huge, gaping breath.

Oh, shit. He was free. Not just of the Boar Oath, but from the threat of his old man sabotaging up the renunciation ceremony. More, he had managed to keep the vault intact while doing it. By the skin of his fucking teeth, granted—he'd missed his a.m. mental mortaring session, and the old man without fail dialed in to his inner Pissed-off Teenager. Add in the oh-holy-shit magic of the doomsday solstice, and he was seriously on the fucking edge.

He had managed it though. He'd held it together, and he'd maneuvered Red-Boar until the bastard had wound up exactly where he'd wanted him.

He had finally done something right.

"Thank Christ." He rose, not quite steady, and rinsed the blood off his healed palms. The water was cool and somehow very real, making him conscious of the press of his boots into the floor, and the possibility that none of it would be around tomorrow if he didn't keep doing things right. Sticking his head under the faucet, he took a drink and splashed his face. Then, knowing he had just enough time to hit the spare room and do some "ommmm"-ing, he straightened, finger-combing his hair back with the moisture, and—

His stomach dive-bombed at the sight of Myr standing in the doorway. Not just because his control was seriously shaky, but because her expression left no doubt that she had heard him and his old man.

She stepped into the kitchen and slammed the door. "Give me one reason not to tell the king what I just saw. And make it good."

Fuck me. "Dez already knows."

"He . . ." She leaned back against the door, expression going from confrontational to hurt, confused. "Did he order you to keep your mouth shut?"

"The two of us were the only ones who knew. And now you." Which they both knew wasn't the same thing. He could've told her, but he hadn't.

"And he approved of you breaking the Boar Oath? *Why?*"

"I needed to trick Red-Boar into burning the last of the three orders before we got to Coatepec Mountain, or else I knew he would use it to make me defy Dez, or worse." He paused. "He can't let go of his gods, and I think it's making him crazier than he started."

"But you swore you'd stick with the sky gods. How is that not going against Dez?"

"I swore that I would refuse the false gods. As far as I'm concerned, the sky gods are the false ones, not Bastet, Osiris and the others."

"You . . . damn. You're right. Okay. Okay, yeah. I get it. But . . . shit, that was risky."

"The wording was Dez's idea." But Rabbit was the one who'd pulled it off, using his old man's fanaticism against him. If it hadn't been for the sharp hurt in her eyes, he would've been feeling pretty damn proud of himself. As it was, he wished to hell he'd just told her. So much for him getting everything right this time.

He just hoped this wasn't as bad as it felt. Not when just a half hour ago they'd been in bed together, almost talking about love, about the future.

"Why didn't you just tell me?"

Because he's already threatened you. Because I was afraid you would get involved, get in trouble. Because I didn't want you looking at him in full-on crazy mode and thinking that I have the same potential. "He's a mind-bender. I didn't want him picking up anything from you." He paused. "I still don't. Promise me you'll stay away from him."

She narrowed her eyes. "I swear I'll watch out for him."

Which just went to show that he wasn't the only one who could twist a vow to suit himself. Frustration sparked, though he wasn't sure if it was coming from him or the magic that hung thick in the air between them. "I'm just trying to keep you safe, Myr. If anything happens to you—" He broke off, not wanting to imagine his world without her in it . . . or there being no world at all.

"I feel the same way," she said softly. "But, Rabbit, you're not giving me enough credit."

"It's not you who I don't trust, Myr. It's him." And that was the gods' honest truth.

After a moment, she nodded. "Okay. Given the history between the two of you, I guess I can accept that. I don't like it, but I can accept it." She paused, then fixed him with a look. "Is there anything else you're not telling me? Anything else that Dez knows that I don't?"

Yes. No. Shit. He hesitated, then said, "I've had a couple of dreams. They're like the vision we shared, with me in the old king's head, you as the queen, and the two of us ready to open the intersection beneath Chichén Itzá." When she drew back, stung, he added, "There wasn't anything new in them, really."

"Dez knows? Of course he knows," she said, more to herself than to him. "That was why he asked me about my dreams." Twin spots of color rode high on her cheekbones. "Damn it, Rabbit. Why didn't you tell me?"

"It wasn't intentional. It was just that what little time we've had together this past week, I've wanted it to be just us. Not the war, not even the magic. Just us." That, and he hadn't wanted her worrying that he was hearing voices again, and thinking back to what had happened before. Hell, he hadn't wanted to think about it himself. She didn't look worried, though. More like she wanted to drop him in the nearest cenote. "You're mad."

"I'm . . ." She blew out a soft breath. "I don't know what I am. Part of me says that I'm the one who said we shouldn't go back to the way things were between us, which means I don't get to get pissed that you didn't tell me everything that's going on in your life. We're just sleeping together, right?"

"Ah, baby—"

She held up a hand. "I'm not finished. Because here's the thing—there's another part of me that says the last time you hid things from me, it was a really, really bad sign. I'm trying not to worry that the same sort of thing is going on here." Her eyes filled suddenly; her voice broke. "Tell me it's not happening again."

"Gods, no!" He pulled her into his arms and held on to her while she gave a token protest. "I promise. Any oath you want, any sacrifice. Phee is gone. Anntah's gone. It's just me, I swear." Which was true. And it would be good enough, as long as he kept his shit together.

She held herself stiff against him for a moment, then softened on a sigh. "I know. Damn it, I know." Her arms came around him. "I know you're not that guy anymore, and it's not fair for me to keep going back there when we're supposed to be moving forward."

"Shh." He wrapped himself around her. "I don't blame you. I should've said something." When her body shook with a sob, he stroked her nape, her back, any part of her he could reach.

She burrowed into him, her breath hot on his throat. "I just . . . gods, I'm a mess. I'm scared, and I don't want to be scared."

"It's all going to be okay," he said into her hair, though they both knew those were empty words. He tightened his grip on her, suddenly all too aware that the next time they saw each other, it would be time to 'port to Coatepec Mountain, signaling the beginning of the end. "Promise me you'll take care of yourself." She wouldn't be beside him, but she would still be on the frontlines. He hated knowing that, even though he respected it. But, gods, he needed to believe she was going to be okay.

It terrified him how much he needed that, needed her.

She pulled away to look up at him. "Only if you'll promise me the same thing."

"You've got it," he said, and kissed her before she could make him swear it in blood. The kiss was deep, warm and wet, with a sharp edge that he didn't let himself think was good-bye. And after a moment, they drew apart, knowing there wasn't enough time for more.

She glanced at her wristband. "We're down to a half hour."

"Better hurry if you want that shower." And he needed all the time he could get to lock his head down tight.

"Yeah, I . . . yeah." Reaching up on tiptoes, she kissed his cheek, and slipped through the door without looking back.

He moved to the window and watched her go, trying to memorize all of it: her curves, the swing of her hair, the natural swagger that had gotten more pronounced as she had gained confidence with the magic, and with herself. And, watching her, he knew the sad truth. She said she wasn't brave, but of the two of them, he was the coward. Because only a coward would keep secrets from the woman he loved.

It was just that he'd fucked up so many things in his life, he didn't want to fuck up the doomsday, too.

Myr cut through the rock garden behind the mansion, hoping to slip into the mage's wing unseen. She didn't notice Anna sitting there with her eyes closed and her amulet cradled in her palm until she had tromped halfway across the stonescape, totally disrupting the peace and quiet.

She crunched to a stop. "Shit. Sorry."

Anna raised an eyebrow. "Problem?"

"Rabbit," she said, figuring that was explanation enough. "But it's stupid to be upset over him today of all days."

"Maybe not. Maybe this is exactly when we need to be thinking about ourselves."

"Hello, blasphemy." But part of Myr thought she was right. At the same time, though, she was afraid that thinking about her own problems would only confuse her more right now. She wasn't sure which was worse—how hard it had hit her to realize Rabbit was keeping secrets from her, or the fact that she'd gone from "what the hell" to "okay, I understand" in two minutes flat, and wasn't sure if it was fear or logic talking.

Anna let her amulet fall to hang from its chain. "Look, I know I've told you to use your head and be careful you don't confuse leftover emotions with the real thing. But I've seen you and Rabbit together, and it doesn't look like leftover anything to me. And as for using your head? I'm starting to think there's a lot to be said for following your heart, too."

"Are you talking about me and Rabbit or you and the outbreak doctor?"

"I don't have a clue. And you know what? I'm okay with it."

"You're not worried about being distracted today?"

"No. I'm giving myself something to fight for. The potential for things. Maybe nothing will happen between me and David. Maybe we'll ride off into the sunset together, maybe we'll fizzle out. Who knows?" She made a face. "I'm sorry. You've had a fight with Rabbit, and I'm going on about my new crush. That's not cool."

"It's okay. And we didn't fight. We just . . . I don't know. Things don't feel right."

"Nothing's going to feel right today. Not until it's all over."

"Good point. And thanks." Myr was suddenly reminded that Rabbit wasn't the only one she might not see again after today. "I mean it. Not just for this, but for being there for me the past few months. I've liked . . . well, I haven't had many friends. It's been nice."

"Same goes. Seriously." Anna stood and came over to hug her, squeezing tight enough that Myr felt the hard bump of the crystal amulet between them. Then Anna drew back and tipped her head toward the side door. "Now, go. You've got twenty-five minutes before we meet for the 'port."

CHAPTER TWENTY-TWO

Four hours to the Great Conjunction
Skywatch

Dez had been afraid to hope for a full army, but that was what he got. And as more and more of his fighters showed up at the ball court meet-up point, striding in wearing their full combat gear and holding their heads high, his chest tightened with emotion.

"They're all here," he rasped as the crowd grew, eddying among the piles of equipment.

Reese nodded, but since she was the one who'd been keeping tabs, she said, "Carlos, Shandi and Sebastian left. That's it as far as I know."

"Three out of almost eighty. That's good." And two of the three were older, more tradition-bound *winikin* who hadn't been granted their magical shadow-familiars, and likely wouldn't have been much use in the actual fighting. As for Sebastian . . . well, he'd always been on the borderline. He'd had a tougher life than most, even among the survivors of the massacre. Apparently he'd decided to go it on his own.

To Dez's mild surprise, he wished them luck.

"Red-Boar stayed," Reese said, making a face.

"No surprise there. I didn't expect him to go quietly." When she raised an eyebrow, he added, "Don't worry. I've got him covered." At least he hoped he did, just like he hoped he wasn't about to trigger a second, even more devastating Solstice Massacre. Scarred-Jaguar had followed a message from the gods and led his teammates to their deaths. What if he was doing the same damn thing, just dressed up to look different?

Problem was, there wasn't really a plan B. This was it. This was the war.

Taking another look around, he said, "Looks like they're all here." And they were burning daylight.

She squeezed his hand. "We're behind you one hundred percent, and this is the right thing to do."

"Gods, I hope so."

"I know so."

He looked down at her—tiny, compact, kickass, and armed to the teeth, his mate and his beloved wife, 'til death did them part—and he felt his *I'm in charge* face falter. "Reese—"

"Don't." Eyes flashing, she caught his collar and hauled his face down to hers. "Don't even try to leave me behind."

He pressed his forehead to hers, taking strength

from her fierceness. "I wish I could." It killed him that he couldn't protect her the way he wanted to, and he knew he wasn't the only one. All throughout the gathering throng, the mated pairs were huddled together, eking out the last few minutes here on home ground.

She gave him a shake. "I wouldn't let you. We're a team, Mendez. You and me, always and forever." She eased back and held up her left hand, so the light glinted off the coiled serpent ring, with its gleaming ruby. "See? I've got proof." And, bless her, she cocked an eyebrow and grinned.

Warmth washed through him like sunlight finding its way into the shadows. Gods, he loved her. He kissed her softly, and then again deeper, with more heat than finesse, until she made that sexy noise in the back of her throat and stopped holding him down by his collar and started using it to hold herself up. Then, he drew back. "You really don't think I'm repeating history here?"

"No," she said, and he didn't see a shadow of a doubt in her eyes. "I think we're breaking new ground. We're all here voluntarily; we're undoing five millennia of corruption by the *kohan* and the *kax;* and we're putting things back the way they were supposed to be, back the way your long, long ago ancestors meant for them to be."

"Then why am I afraid?" He hadn't meant to say that, not even to her.

She didn't bat an eyelash. "Because you're not a fucking moron."

He snorted. "Thanks, I think."

"No problem. Oh, and for the record? If you try to say good-bye, now or at any point today, I will kick you in your royal jewels. We're going to make it through today, we're going to get back here in one piece, and when we do, we're going to lock ourselves in the bedroom and fuck like minks on crack."

He laughed in spite of himself. "It's a date." He leaned in and kissed her one last time, then turned away. He was still chuckling—and on the borderline of squeezing out a tear—as he moved away from her to hop up on top of a stack of equipment crates, putting himself above the crowd, and pitched his voice to project. "Okay, gang, listen up!"

The crowd quieted instantly, leaving behind an eerie hear-a-bullet-drop silence.

He continued. "I know that right now I'd usually go over the op, battle plans, contingencies and that sort of thing. I'm not going to, though, because we all know the plan." He paused. "This is it, folks. It's the day we've been training for, the one we were bred for, down through generations going back way farther than I can really comprehend. All leading up to this."

He took a long look around, trying not to think that he was memorizing faces. "What I *am* going to say is this: Thank you. Thank you all for being here, for choosing to do this. Some of you may be here because I'm your king, some because you believe Bastet's message, some because you couldn't turn away from your teammates. But you're here, and that's what matters."

He paused. "I don't know what's going to happen out there today. I wish I did. But I do know that if you look to your left and right, if you look in front of you and behind, those people are going to be there for you, no matter what. Human, *winikin*, mage, the distinctions don't matter worth a godsdamn. We're all going to have each other's backs, and we're going to fight until we can't fight anymore. And then we're going to keep fighting, because there isn't anybody else to do it. We're it, gang. We're going out there to save the fucking world."

He tried not to see how pitifully small the group really was, tried not to think of how many more of them there should've been. Tried not to think that there might be far fewer of them in four or so hours . . . if hours even existed by then.

Lifting a hand, he pointed at the mansion in the distance. "And after we're done fighting . . . after we've defeated the *kohan* and the *kax* and sealed the barrier for good, we're going to meet back here, up at the mansion. And we're going to have the biggest fucking party this place has ever seen!"

There was a moment of silence, like an indrawn breath. But then somebody gave a whoop; someone else started clapping. Then things got rolling with a cheer that started out ragged, but then gained and grew, until it was loud and raucous, with lots of waving hands and promises of mayhem. Maybe there was an edge of desperation to the war cry, but he would take it. He would fucking take it.

"Okay," he said, "everybody ready to synch up?" Lifting his wrist, he programmed the countdown that would be sent to their comm devices. It read 3:45:30. Three hours and forty-some minutes until the hard threshold, when they would really feel the magic of the Great Conjunction and the barrier would start coming apart. Ten minutes after that, according to legend, the barrier would fall, beginning at the intersection.

Which meant that in four hours, one way or the other, the world would be a very different place.

He waited until it read 3:45:00, then hit "send." Seventy-some units beeped and seventy-some read-outs lit, then flickered as the seconds counted down.

Shit. This was really happening.

Gesturing for Strike and Anna to take their positions on opposite sides of the group, Dez said, "Everybody link up. It's time to go."

Coatepec Mountain

The temple atop Coatepec Mountain was open to the air, with jaguar pillars at the corners symbolizing that Strike, Anna and Sasha were its guardians. But where before the site had thrummed with the deep, sustained magic of a hotspot, now there was only the background hum of solstice power. The Nightkeepers had looked long and hard to find another intersection after Iago destroyed the tunnel system beneath Chichén Itzá, knowing that when the Great Conjunction hit its zenith, the barrier would fall at the intersection and the

Nightkeepers would go to war. But this sure as shit didn't feel like a battlefield.

"Something's not right," Rabbit muttered. "There should be way more juice than this. It doesn't even feel like an intersection." Which put a nasty churn in his gut, matching the one that came from knowing he hadn't had nearly enough time to work on his mental vault. His head buzzed with a faint rattle of dark magic and his emotions were way too close to the surface, leaving him feeling snarly and reactive, and way too ready to blow something up.

And now this . . . they had been expecting to 'port into the middle of a magical hotspot like he'd never felt before, maybe even into an ambush. But the mountaintop temple was throwing off less power than the average Denny's, and there was no sign of the *kax* or *kohan*. Not even a *xombi* guard or a couple of *'zotz* to use for target practice.

He glanced at his wristband. The conjunction was just over three hours away. Maybe they were massing behind the barrier, waiting to attack all at once.

It didn't feel right, though.

"Do you think they're going to come through the barrier somewhere else?" Myr asked. Wearing combat black and bristling with weapons, she looked every inch the sexy, kickass warrior he'd fought beside so many times before. Now, though, there was an added sheen of magic surrounding her, a subtle sparkle of power that stroked along his own. But there was also a hint of shadows in her expression, an unusual reserve.

He didn't know if she was still upset about what happened earlier, or if this was her war face, didn't know if he dared ask when he was feeling so twitchy. So he said, "It's the only intersection that's left. Where else would things go *boom*?"

"Maybe this is just the calm before the storm," Brandt said, speaking up as the others muttered the same questions, the same concerns.

"Or maybe the *kohan* are already here, waiting to see if we're going to renounce them or not," Dez added grimly. An uncomfortable silence followed that statement, but no lightning bolts came down to blast the temple, no tornadoes dropped down to do a *Wizard of Oz* on them. And after a moment, the king said, "Okay. It's time."

"Let's go." Rabbit caught Myr's hand, and together they moved into the shadows of the temple, where he would summon the sacrificial fire.

The others formed a big, loose circle—Nightkeepers, *winikin*, and humans all mixed together, all of them ready to renounce their gods.

All except one.

"Where's Red-Boar?" Myr asked, like she had read his mind.

"Gone," Rabbit said flatly. "He slipped away right after we 'ported in." He paused. "Dez saw. He's got our backs."

She stared toward the scrubby tree line. "Maybe he's running."

"I wish." Rabbit shook his head. "He's still here. I

can feel the blood-link." Along with Red-Boar's rage against the king, and his mad glee at the thought that Rabbit was going to back out of the ceremony at the last minute, screwing over his teammates and throwing the crossover's power onto the other side.

After all these years, his old man finally thought he was about to do something right.

Well, fuck him.

"Ready?" Dez asked, taking his position next to him in the circle.

"To set a fire? Definitely." Rabbit shot a last "it's okay" glance at Myr, hoped he wasn't lying to both of them, and then faced forward, blocked off the darkness and summoned his Nightkeeper magic. Spreading his fingers, he said, "*Kaak*."

Brilliant red fire speared from his fingertips and filled the middle of the circle. There was no rattle, no dark magic, thank Christ.

The others backed off a little, expressions frozen in dread, horror and resignation as the heat flared.

Dez, though, stepped closer, palmed his ceremonial knife, cut a deep furrow through his bloodline mark, and grated, "*Pasaj och*." The magic amped as he jacked in to the barrier flux. Then, stone-faced, he held his arm out over the fire, so the blood sacrifice rained down into the flames. Sparks erupted when the droplets hit, then sizzled as the blood burned off to acrid smoke. Sounding as if the words were being ripped out of him, the king recited the renunciation spell: "*Ma' tu kahool tikeni*." *I no longer recognize you.*

Boom! A shock wave of red-tinged energy flared away from Dez, leaving golden sparks behind. The wave rolled through Rabbit like a tsunami in deep water—it rocked him but kept going without doing too much damage to his equilibrium. He was aware, though, that if something like that hit him in the shallows, he'd be fucked. They all would.

This was big magic, a big move. And he hoped to hell they were doing the right thing.

The king steadied himself against Reese and straightened, expression smoothing to relief. "It's okay," he said. "I'm okay . . . and it's done." He showed the others his forearm. "It's over."

There was a collective gasp—his bloodline mark had healed over and gone from black to gold.

"It fits," Lucius muttered. "The Egyptians mined gold, but not the Mayans. I bet that was another way the *kàx* and the *kohan* steered our ancestors away from the true gods."

Dez wiped his knife and returned it to his belt. Then he looked around the circle. "Okay. Your turn." And he didn't just mean one at a time.

Rabbit kept the fire going, holding himself apart as the others pulled their knives and blooded their palms. Some of them hesitated; others moved quickly, slashing and getting it done. Beside him, Myr stared at her knife and whispered, "Please."

She wasn't talking to him, but he said, "I've got you. And tomorrow it's pancakes for breakfast. Be there."

She shot him a sidelong look, but didn't say anything. Then, pressing her lips together, she drew shallow slices through each of her talent marks, because she didn't have a bloodline. Moving forward with the others, she let her sacrifice fall into the fire, which sparked and smoked in answer.

"*Pasaj och,*" they all said in a ragged chorus, and then, "*Ma' tu kahool tikeni.*"

BOOM! A stronger shock wave blasted over them, away from them, nearly blowing out the fire and sending up a billow of smoke. Rabbit was ready for the tidal wave this time, and kept a sharp eye on Myr, but although she gasped and went pale as the spell took effect, she stayed on her feet.

When the smoke cleared, she and the others stood, shaken, with gold bloodline marks in place of black. All four of Myr's talent marks had gone gold.

"You okay?" he asked her as a buzz of similar questions rose up around them.

"Yeah. I guess I am." She stared down at her forearm, then glanced up at him. "We're really doing this, aren't we?"

"We sure are." And he would be going last, just in case all hell broke loose.

It was the godkeepers' turn next—they had broken their allegiance to the *kohan*, but still needed to renounce their godkeeper bonds. He tightened the fire to a small, hot blaze in front of the temple as Strike, Leah, Alexis and Sasha took up their positions. Their ceremonial knives flashed and their faces twisted as they carved the godkeeper marks out of their arms. Leah whimpered and Strike went gray, more worried for his mate than himself. Myr made a muffled noise and looked away as blood dripped into the fire, turning the smoke to murk. Then the four intoned, *"Ma' tu kahool tikeni. Xeen te'ealo!"* *We no longer recognize you. Leave us!*

Power surged, but this time the explosion wasn't a shock wave—it was fire. Rabbit shouted as the blaze flared, engulfing the godkeepers and bathing them in brilliant red flames. Leah gave a shocked scream that cut off ominously.

"No!" Nate surged forward with Michael on his heels. "Douse it!"

Rabbit yanked back on the out-of-control fire magic, reeling it in, suddenly afraid that the near-death-by-drowning of the godkeeper spell needed to be counteracted by near-death-by-flames. "Godsdamn it, I—" He broke off as the blaze died back abruptly.

The four godkeepers stood there, unscathed.

Thank fuck.

"Holy shit," Strike said, voice shaking, reaching for his mate as the two other men closed in on theirs. "Leah, are you okay?"

"I'm fine," she said. "I'm good." But her voice was sad, her eyes fixed on her wrist, where there was a bare, scarred patch in place of her mark. The bonds had been broken. She wasn't a godkeeper anymore. None of them were.

Prophecy said that the godkeepers would be key to winning the war. They could only pray that had been another of the *kohan's* lies.

"Still nothing," Myr said, looking up at the sky. "Where are they?"

Rabbit doused the last of his fire. "Not even a fucking thundercloud. I don't like it." His wristband showed two and a half hours on the clock. They were missing something. But what?

Sasha leaned against Michael. "It's like breaking up with someone you really loved, someone you've been agonizing about dumping, and then having them shrug and say, 'Yeah, okay. Whatever. No biggie.'"

He hugged her to his side. "They're leaving us alone because they know we've figured out their lies, so there's no point in trying to keep us."

"Or because they're planning something else," Myr said softly. She pulled her wand from her pocket and gestured with it, and green flames kindled where Rabbit's blaze had burned moments earlier. She looked up at him. "You ready?"

Her magic brushed along his skin like a touch, bringing an echo of the shadows he saw in her eyes, and a tug that came from light magic rather than dark. *Ah, baby*. Like the king in his recurring dreams, he wished he could bubble wrap her and lock her someplace safe. But, also like Jag, he knew better than to try to leave a warrior behind, and that if they didn't succeed here and now, there wouldn't be anyplace safe.

So he leaned in, brushed his lips across hers, and nodded. "Ready."

Then he pulled his combat knife, and dragged the tip across the bloodred hellmark, and then the black glyph of the boar bloodline. *"Pasaj och,"* he said. Magic surged around him, inside him, filling him with solstice power. When faint rattles leaked around the edges of the vault, he clamped down on it, determined to stay in control, get this right. *"Ma' tu kah—"*

"No!" The blow came without warning—a hot, heavy body in sweat-laced brown robes flying at him from the side. "You can't!"

Red-Boar! Rabbit didn't know where the old bastard had come from, how he'd gotten so close without being seen. Shouting, "Dez, *now*!" he went down and rolled with the attack, kicking his father off him. The combat knife skittered out of his hand. When he reached out to grab it with his mind, though, nothing happened.

I've got your magic, you disloyal fuck, the hated voice said inside his head. *I'm going to make you—* "Aaah!" Red-Boar flew backward as if he'd been yanked by an invisible giant, sailing thirty feet and hitting hard. A shield spell slammed down around him, sparking with Dez's lightning powers and threaded through with Michael's silver death magic. "No!" he shouted, scrambling to his feet and slapping his hands against the impenetrable shield. "You can't do this! You swore on your blood!"

Rabbit came to his feet and faced his old man as wrath and righteousness pounded through him. "You screwed up, old man. I swore not to follow the false gods. And as far as I'm concerned, your gods are full of shit, and so are you."

Red-Boar flushed an angry, ugly purple. "No! You

can't do it. You can't—" The rant cut off abruptly, though his mouth still moved, screaming spittle-flecked imprecations.

"Volume control," Michael said with grim satisfaction. "Shield magic is my friend."

"Thanks." Rabbit looked past him to Dez, knowing that the two of them together were strong enough to hold his old man, no matter what. "Seriously. Thanks." And he didn't just mean for the shield spell or the silence. If they hadn't trusted him, hadn't backed him up, there was no telling what would've happened. Red-Boar brought out the darkness in him.

Even now it stirred inside him, seething and whispering, *You're stronger, better than he is. You can show him, show them all.*

Yeah, he could. By fucking holding his shit together.

The king nodded. "Hey. You can't pick your family."

"Amen." But to Rabbit's surprise there was no satisfaction in seeing Red-Boar trapped and silenced, either. There was only the blink of his chrono: 2:50:36. And still nothing from the enemy.

"Here. You're going to need this." Myr levitated his combat knife and sent it winging toward him.

He caught it on the fly. "Sorry I didn't tell you the whole plan."

"Like you said earlier, he's a mind-bender. He could've read me." But she didn't quite meet his eyes as she restarted the fire.

Damn. Rabbit's heart thudded with dismay. He didn't want to shut her out like this. He wanted to kiss her, hold her, make everything okay. *Later,* he promised himself, just like he'd promised her pancakes. Later, when the solstice magic wasn't gnawing at him. Later, when he'd proven himself once and for all.

Later, when they'd won the war.

Facing the fire, he used his knife to freshen the half-healed cuts, leaned in so his blood fell into the fire, and said, *"Ma' tu kahool tikeni."*

The shock wave didn't flare out this time; it flared in, turning his vision suddenly to gold. He hissed out a breath and fought to keep his balance, heard shouts but couldn't understand the words. Then he fell and hit hard, launching himself into a vision, into the same dream he'd been having for weeks now. Except it wasn't the same anymore.

Rabbit stood in front of the chac-mool, *watching the barrier writhe in the air above the altar. Only this time he was alone . . . and he wasn't underground. Instead, he stood at the edge of a huge sinkhole, which was sixty feet across and plunged a hundred feet down to a huge, circular pool of blackish water.*

Oh, gods. He knew this place.

And, as he felt himself lift his bleeding palms, heard himself chant Scarred-Jaguar's spell and sensed it burning its way into his mind, he knew what he was supposed to do, what the dreams—or, rather, the true gods—had been trying to tell him all along.

The Nightkeepers were going to shit a fucking brick when they found out.

CHAPTER TWENTY-THREE

Ninety minutes to the Great Conjunction
Coatepec Mountain

"Rabbit?" Myr's face was the first thing he saw in the too-bright sunlight when he awakened, her hand the first thing he reached for. Relief flooded her features and she gripped his fingers for a moment, then pulled away to call over her shoulder, "Hey! He's back!"

There was a shuffle of movement around him, and then Dez appeared in Rabbit's field of vision. After a quick once-over, the king grabbed his arm and hauled him up. "What happened?"

Irritation rattled. "Jeez, give me a . . ." He trailed off at the sight of an armed encampment surrounding him. The equipment had been broken out and dug in, surveillance was up and running, and there were warriors positioned along the perimeter, watching the temple, the tree line, the sky, and Red-Boar, who sat near the temple with his hands tied behind his back, tethered to one of the jaguar pillars. More, the air sang with power . . . and Rabbit's chrono said 1:28:08. "Fuck me."

He'd been out for more than an hour.

Myr said, "Talk to us. Did you have another vision?"

"Yeah. This time it was different, though. This time, I got what the true gods have been trying to tell me." To Dez—to all of them—he said, "We're in the wrong place. We need to go to Chichén Itzá. . . . and when we get there, we need to use Scarred-Jaguar's spell to seal the barrier."

Myr gasped and took a step back, and a ripple of "Oh, hell, no" flung away from them and raced through the encampment, like he'd just dropped a boulder in a kiddie pool. Which he pretty much had.

Dez froze for a split second, but then his face went thunderous. Moving in, he grabbed Rabbit's shirt and got in his face to hiss, "Godsdamn it, don't you dare. Not fucking now."

Rabbit snapped, "You think I want this? You think—" He broke off, seeing that the other man's anger was more defensive than anything. Dez didn't want to believe he was going to be the second king to lead the Nightkeepers into battle at Chichén Itzá on the strength of some dreams, didn't want to think about enacting the same spell that had wiped out their parents. *Let the brick shitting begin.* "Think about it," Rabbit said, taking it down a notch, but all too aware of the seconds flickering on his wristband. "That's why the *kohan* haven't attacked us here. They don't give a damn what we're doing as long as we're not at the intersection."

"This *is* the intersection."

"It's a decoy. They wanted us to think Iago destroyed the real intersection at Chichén Itzá, but he didn't. The sacred chamber is still there, sunk deep in the cenote." Rabbit paused. "I think that's why I'm so important. I'm the only telekinetic left. It's my weakest talent, but if I give it everything I've got, I should be able to bring the altar back up to the surface." He looked at Myr. "I think the dreams—"

"Bullshit!" JT shouted from the edge of the crowd. "This is bullshit! *This* is the intersection. *This* is where we're supposed to be." There were a few angry nods and a holler of "We didn't sign on for this!"

Dez's hackles rose. "Renouncing the *kohan* was optional, not the rest of it. This isn't a fucking democracy, and when you agreed to come here, you put yourself under my orders. There's only one leader in this army, and it's me."

"They're not your orders. They're his." JT glared at Rabbit. "And none of us signed on to follow him." The two of them had fought together, hung together, had some good times together, but the rebel *winikin* was looking at him now like he was the enemy.

Rabbit tried not to blame him, but anger kicked in his gut, dark and ugly. "I'm not ordering anybody to do anything. I'm just telling you what I know."

"You don't know dick. You dreamed it, just like Scarred-Jaguar."

"It was a vision; there's a difference. And I wasn't in the king's head this time. I pictured myself standing at the edge of the cenote, and it was like I could see down to the very bottom. I saw the altar down there, felt its magic. More, when I heard the spell, I understood it." He paused, voice going urgent. "The magic doesn't just seal the barrier, it connects the other two realms to each other, so the *kohan* and the *kax* can duke it out themselves, leaving the earth out of the mix completely."

"This could be another *kohan* lie," JT said, almost desperately, "another distraction."

Myr said, "Rabbit didn't hear the spell until after he renounced the *kohan*. What if the dreams have been the true gods trying to reach him, but they couldn't get through because the *kohan* were interfering? Maybe the true gods were trying to get through to Scarred-Jaguar, too, but since he was still bound to the *kohan*, still praying to them, the interference was even worse. More, the *kax* and the *kohan* knew the king's plan. They were waiting for him."

JT made a face. "If Rabbit said the sky was purple, you'd back him up on it."

"Hey!" Rabbit took a step toward the *winikin*, fists clenched, anger pumping suddenly through him, looking for an outlet. "Don't you dare—"

"Enough!" Dez bellowed, cutting through the rising din. In the sudden silence, he seemed huge and golden, every inch their king. "You," he forked a finger at Rabbit. "Dial it down. You"—this time he pointed at JT—"either shut up, or get the fuck out of here." He glared around the muttering crowd. "Same goes for the rest of you. I said this isn't a democracy, and it's not. But I'll be damned if I go into battle with soldiers I can't trust." He paused. "Look, I know you're scared. We all are. But pretending this is where we're supposed to be isn't going to save us. We need to move, and we need to do it now. So go if you're going. Otherwise, link up. Next stop: Chichén Itzá."

Rabbit exhaled a tight breath. *Thank fuck.*

"No!" Red-Boar surged to his feet and flung himself to the end of his rope. "This is the intersection! This is where the gods are going to meet us!"

"Don't worry. You're staying." Dez grabbed Red-Boar's ceremonial knife off a nearby stack of ammo, and tossed it to the mage. It fell at his feet, pinging on the stones. "It shouldn't take you too long to cut yourself free." Waving for the others to join hands, he checked his chrono and swore. "Hurry up. We're burning time."

"Nooo!" Red-Boar howled, raising a booted foot over his knife. "Gods help me! Please!" Then he slammed his foot down on the etched stone blade, shattering it.

Magic detonated from the powerful sacrifice, and the air tore with a sickly *rriiip*, showing the gray-green of the barrier beyond.

"*Shit.*" Rabbit put himself in front of Myrinne, casting a shield around them both. She readied a fireball, and he did the same as other spells sprang to life.

A figure came through the gap, solidifying when it stepped onto the earth plane. Fully eight feet tall, it was a giant Mayan warrior in full regalia, wearing a cape of woven leaves and a huge headdress of cornstalks and silk.

"It's the maize god," Anna cried. "A *kohan*!"

The king didn't hesitate. "Fire!"

A salvo of fireballs seared toward the maize god, but they deflected, slamming into the earth around the creature.

Red-Boar didn't notice. "Tell them!" He begged the *kohan*, spittle flecking from his mouth. "Tell them they have to stay here and have faith! I tried. You saw how hard I tried, but—" He broke off, eyes bugging as gray-green fog erupted from the ground beneath him. His face blanked with horror. "No! You promised! You told me I could have my family back if I did what you said."

"You failed . . . and we lied." The words sounded in Rabbit's head, as Bastet's had done.

Red-Boar went to his knees in the fog. "Where's my Cassie? Where are my sons? Please. Give them to me."

"They are in the barrier, imprisoned along with generations of their kin. As you shall be, held ready to march for us when the barrier falls." The rip in the barrier grew wider and the fog began drawing back inward.

"The *nahwal*," Myr whispered in horror. "Your ancestors' souls didn't stay in the barrier to be your advisers. They're prisoners of the *kohan*!"

"Fire again!" Dez shouted, and the Nightkeepers blasted another concerted volley. But it was no use. Their magic couldn't penetrate the *kohan*'s shield.

"No!" Red-Boar shouted. "Don't! Please, gods,

don't!" He surged up, tried to run, hit the end of his bonds, and fell. He screamed as the fog covered him, flowing through the tear in the barrier. For a second, the *nahwal* were visible beyond the gap—naked and genderless, with shiny skin and eerie black eyes. Always before, the ancestral beings had looked peaceful, otherworldly and faintly disdainful. Now, though, their eyes were wide and their mouths gaped open as they reached for the earth plane. Then the fog surged back through the opening, obscuring them.

When it cleared, the *nahwal* were gone. And so was Red-Boar.

A cry rose up from the Nightkeepers, and something tore inside Rabbit, sharp and vicious. He didn't want to give a shit about his old man, but he did. Worse, there were other, far more worthy souls trapped in there with him.

Rage soured the back of his throat and he stepped away from Myrinne. "Get back and shield yourself."

"Rabbit—"

"Just do it!" he snapped. Then, dropping his shield spell and blocking her from his thoughts—blocking out everything except the *kohan* and the gray-green tear in the sky—he braced himself and shouted, *"Cha'ik ten ee'hochen!" Bring the darkness to me!*

Wham! The tsunami hit him in the shallows this time, pummeling him not just with its own force, but with all the garbage that came with it. Frustration, resentment, impotence, fury—the dark magic rose up and hammered him with the flotsam of his life. But he knew what to expect this time. Maybe he wasn't armored against it, or for the way some of it still resonated, but he could tamp it down enough to function.

Concentrating on the spells rather than the dangerous impulses that had gotten him into trouble so many times before, he called two fireballs, one in each hand—the left was dark, oily and rancid; the right was brilliant red and threaded through with sparks of gold. Then he brought his hands together, and the light and dark magic slammed into each other and glommed into a seething ball of red and brown.

With mad power singing up his arms, Rabbit shouted, "Cross this over, motherfucker!" And he launched the bolt at the *kohan*, which was still gloating in the rift, mocking Red-Boar and the *nahwal*.

The fireball shattered the shield spell, leaving the maize god suddenly unprotected. It whipped around with a hiss of shock and rage, its tasseled headdress flaring out in a spray of silken strands.

Rabbit summoned more magic, a killing blow of light and dark energy, and drew back his arm to—

The *kohan* speared its fingers at him and shouted, "*Freeze!*"

And he fucking froze. The spell surrounded him, locking him into place and boxing the magic in with him. The red-brown fireball spun and churned, caught in stasis.

"Rabbit!" Myr's cry was anguished.

"Fire!" Dez ordered, and the Nightkeepers and their allies hammered the unshielded *kohan* with everything they had—fireballs, ice, lightning, and exploding jade-tipped rounds.

The maize god swatted aside the attack and cast another shield around itself. Then, glaring at Rabbit, it sneered, *"Stay."* Like he was a fucking house pet. *"You will come with me to the sacred well, to take control of the* xombis. *Then the* kohan *will control both of the armies of the undead."* It turned toward the others. *"As for the rest of you . . ."*

The leaves of its cloak rustled as if coming alive, and the silken strands atop its headdress lifted like cobras preparing to strike as the *kohan* forked its fingers and rattled off a spell. The magic flung toward the Night-keepers' gleaming shield. For a moment, nothing happened. Then the ground shook suddenly, and green tendrils erupted *inside* the shield.

The Nightkeepers shouted and fought, defending themselves with magic, guns and knives as the vines whipped up and wrapped around the teammates—arms, legs, weapons, everything—and then thickened, sprouting leaves and then small, wispy ears of maize. But for every vine they destroyed, three more sprouted and attacked.

`At the edge of the group, green fire flared as Myrinne burned one off her left thigh, only to have another latch on to her right ankle and yank. She stumbled and nearly went down.

"Godsdamn it!" Rabbit's throat tore with the shout. *"Myr!"* He struggled against the grip of the *kohan*'s magic as rage grabbed him by the throat, cutting off his air. He couldn't move, couldn't fight, couldn't do a damn thing right.

He was a boy again, eleven years old and caught stealing booze from the gas station around the corner from his and Red-Boar's apartment; fifteen and crashing his old man's Jeep in a flooded river during a joyride gone bad. He was eighteen and watching Jox's warehouse burn; nineteen and watching a seedy corner of the French Quarter burn; twenty-two and watching Oc Ajal burn, proving over and over again that his old man was right. He was a fuckup, a loose cannon, the Master of Disaster. Everything he'd been called over the years. Everything he'd called himself.

"Not anymore," he grated, fighting off all the anger and hatred that came from the boy he'd been, and pouring all the power of his better self—his more mature, more controlled self—into the seething fireball instead, trying to break through the *kohan's* spell.

Please gods, he whispered inwardly. *A little help here.*

Then, suddenly, he wasn't alone in his own skull anymore. There was a presence inside him, filling his head, and an almost familiar voice boomed, *The things you are rejecting are all part of you, son of chaos. They are not flaws when they are balanced by the other half of you.*

"Jag?" It sounded like the voice from his visions, only not.

You're hot-tempered, impulsive and stubborn . . . but your temper makes you a fierce warrior, your impulsiveness gives you moments of brilliance, and your stubbornness means you refuse to give up. There was a pause. *You punish your-*

self for your past sins, but do not credit your successes. You need to accept yourself—every part of you—if you mean to be the crossover.

There was a jolt and the presence disappeared as quickly and thoroughly as it had come. It didn't leave Rabbit empty, though. Instead, his senses vibrated in its wake, his mind spun.

Yeah, it was a big foam finger moment. But did he dare trust it? More, did he dare trust himself?

And he had to decide fast, because inside the Night-keepers' shield, the vines were winning.

Wrapping his mind around the fireball that still spun and pulsed beside him, frozen by the *kohan*'s spell, Rabbit steeled himself and said, *"Ten cha'ik ee'hochen!" Bring my darkness!*

The tsunami came again, but this time it swept him up and carried him along with it. Fury, frustration, impotence, guilt, regret, revenge—familiar from every stage of his life except for the past few weeks—flooded through him, and he accepted all of it, embraced it.

Yes, he thought as the reckless intensity built, making him want to do something stupid, dangerous and fun. *Yes*. This was what he had been missing without realizing it.

No longer contained by any vault or vain attempts to be what he thought he should be, the chaos flowed free, filling him with crazy thoughts, then soldering them into place. And once that happened, the impulses didn't seem so insane anymore. They felt sharp and edgy, yet contained. Balanced. And he felt more like himself than he had since he first heard Phee's voice in his mind. He was the wild half blood, the pyro, the Master of Disaster . . . but he was also the guy who had turned back the first *xombi* outbreak, and who had stayed with the villagers in the aftermath. He had tracked down his mother, faced down his grandfather and made sure his old man didn't hurt the Nightkeepers. He wasn't all good, but he wasn't all bad, either.

He was the crossover, damn it.

Chest tightening with fear and hope as magic crackled along his skin, he said, "*Pasaj och.*"

The barrier connection formed instantly, but the magic that raced into him wasn't like anything he'd ever felt before. Power flared, huge and incomprehensible, and the fireball gleamed suddenly from within. The red and brown powers bled together, becoming one . . . and then they turned to pure gold.

Suddenly, the *kohan*'s spell dissolved. He could move again!

The maize god stood near the temple, still fully shielded. It hadn't noticed that Rabbit was loose, but that could change at any second. He had only one chance.

Hit him hard, he told himself. *No fuss, no bullshit, just bust through that shield.* But beneath his warrior's determination, a wilder, crazier part of him had a better idea. He started to push it away, but then hesitated. And went with it.

Be brilliant.

With molten gold searing through his veins, Rabbit

shouted and unleashed a bolt of terrible fury . . . straight into the Nightkeepers' sacred temple. The two-thousand-year-old structure shuddered then exploded in a con-flagration of stone shrapnel and golden magic. The *kohan* spun with a shocked roar, its shield disintegrat-ing under the onslaught.

"Eat this!" Rabbit didn't even gather the power this time; he just pointed. But that was more than enough—the golden magic flew from his hand in a lethal bolt. It hit the maize god, wreathing it with golden flames.

The *kohan* screeched, spun and fell.

Rabbit poured more power into the fire, which roared like thunder. "Die!" he shouted, closing on the fire and watching the maize god's headdress blaze. Fury boiled in his blood and spurred him on. This was the enemy as much as Phee, Anntah, or the *kax*. Worse, even. "Fucking go to hell."

Golden flames detonated, sounding like a dozen buses crashing together, and the god disappeared. The vines vaporized. Even the tear in the barrier blinked out of existence.

In the aftermath, there was silence. Normalcy, even. Except for the temple's destruction, it seemed as though nothing had changed.

Rabbit, though, had been through the change of his life. He stood, shaken, staring at the ruined temple while his mind spun.

He was the fucking crossover.

Anntah was right. The magic had been inside him all along.

His throat was scorched, his ribs hurt, and his eyes burned as if they were being eaten from the inside by acid. But for the first time in a really long fucking time, maybe ever, he felt whole. And not because Red-Boar was gone, either. He might've cleared up some of the questions surrounding Rabbit's birth, but he'd still been an asshole. And besides, it hadn't ever been about Rabbit missing a twin, a parent, or a part of the magic. It had been about him missing a part of himself—not because it had been taken from him, but because he'd been rejecting it, trying to be what everybody else wanted him to be, what he thought the Nightkeepers and the gods needed him to be.

What a fucking relief to discover that they needed him to be exactly who and what he always had been— a former juvenile delinquent who had learned some manners over the years.

But as he turned away from the temple, that relief vanished in an instant. Because Myr stood there, staring at him with fear in her eyes, with the others ranged behind her. And his heart fucking sank, because while most of them—maybe all—would be grateful they finally had their crossover, she already looked devastated.

She didn't want the crossover. She wanted the self-contained, well-behaved guy she'd had for the past couple of weeks . . . and he didn't exist anymore.

And whoever he was now, his wristband read 1:01:34.

"Rabbit?" Myr didn't care that her voice shook. Her arms and legs throbbed where she had wrestled with the vines, but that was nothing compared to the pain and fear that was suddenly lodged deep within her heart. "Are you okay?"

It should've been a dumb question, because he certainly looked okay. Hell, he looked amazing, standing there with the ruined temple at his back, looking bigger and badder than he ever had before. His hair moved in the faint breeze, but other than that, he was utterly still.

She stopped just a few feet away from him. *Tell me you're okay. Tell me what I just saw wasn't as scary as it looked.* Because even as she and the others had fought off the maize god's attack, they had seen the golden magic and felt Rabbit's new power.

He had become the crossover . . . but she wasn't sure what that meant.

"I'm not hurt," he said. His eyes, though, were bleak.

"Talk to me," she urged. "You're scaring me." More, he was shutting her out again.

He looked beyond her to where the others had dispersed to gather up the equipment. After what just happened, it was a no-brainer that they needed to head for Chichén Itzá. "We should go."

He's right, she told herself. *Deal with it after. This isn't the right time.* Or maybe, like Anna said, it was exactly the right time to focus on the personal stuff and remember what they were fighting for. More, Myr was still the one who knew him best, the one who needed to warn the others if he was going off the rails.

"What happened to you?" she pressed, stomach

knotting at the sight of a strange new light in his eyes. "What aren't you telling me?"

He hesitated, then held out his hand. "I'll show you. It's probably better this way."

Which sounded ominous and put a new quiver in her belly. But there was no time to hesitate, no time to shore up her inner defenses. She would have to be strong enough to deal with whatever came next.

Taking a deep breath, she clasped his fingers in hers, and opened herself to the mind-bend.

Emotions poured into her—determination, fear, grief, regret, relief, all the things she'd felt from him when he'd first returned to Skywatch. Now, though, there was also an edge of instability, of volatility. As she saw things unfold with rapid-fire in his mind—the stasis spell, the voice, the dark and twisted emotions he'd let back into his head—her heart leaped up to clog her throat. And then it broke.

He had hidden the anger from her, hidden the danger from her. Hidden *himself* from her.

She reeled back, breaking the connection. "Oh, Rabbit." She didn't know what to say, or even what she was feeling, except that it was huge and terrible, and it made her want to weep.

"I was trying to protect you."

Anger flared, bright and righteous. "Bullshit! You were doing what you always do, which is exactly what you want to do, when you want to do it. You were afraid I would be mad because you've gone back to being your old self? You're damn right. More, from where I'm standing, it looks like you never stopped being that guy. You just camouflaged it better for a while." And if the words didn't feel exactly right, the fury did. The panic did. He was back to being the man she feared, the one she couldn't trust.

His face blanked. "You used to love that guy."

"I outgrew him three months ago, when I regained consciousness and remembered what he had done to me."

"Two minutes to 'port," Dez bellowed. He made it sound like he was announcing it to the entire team, but his eyes were on the two of them.

Rabbit reached for her. "Give me another chance, later."

She backed off and shook her head as a tear tracked down her face. "I can't. I won't." She took a shuddering breath. "I'm sorry, but I waited too damn long to run away from the Witch. I refuse to make the same mistake again."

"Myr—"

"No. That's it, we're done. I can't do this anymore."

"Myr, please, for the love of the gods, don't. I love you." His throat worked. "And that's not leftover from before, and it's not just because we've been great together these past few weeks. It's all of it. I never stopped loving you, damn it."

She choked on a sob. "I don't . . . I can't. I'm sorry." And she was. So sorry that it felt like green flames were burning her from the inside out.

But just because it hurt didn't make it the wrong decision.

Nearly blinded by tears, she turned and headed toward where the others were finishing up packing the essentials, and she didn't let herself look back, even when he called her name. Because he'd been right all along when he'd said they needed to move forward. She just hadn't realized until now that in order for her to move forward, she was going to have to leave him behind.

CHAPTER TWENTY-FOUR

Chichén Itzá, Mexico

The Nightkeepers 'ported into the shadow of the main pyramid, heavily shielded and weapons hot, but there was no attack, no sign of the enemy.

The atmosphere crackled with magic, though, making Rabbit feel itchy and twitchy, and like he was going to jump out of his damn skin if he didn't get to fight, and soon. But at the same time, there was a deep darkness inside him, a chill that was impervious to the magic.

He looked over to where Myr stood beside Anna, the two of them talking with their heads together, carefully not looking at him.

He didn't blame her—or he was trying not to.

Trying really fucking hard.

"This is definitely the right place," Dez said, but his eyes were on the empty sky, his brows furrowed.

"The maize god needed Red-Boar's sacrifice to ma-
terialize," Lucius said. "That suggests that the big guns
still can't get through the barrier, at least not yet."

"Why not send *makol*, then, or the *xombis*?"

"No clue."

Dez glanced at his wrist. "Fifty minutes to the hard
threshold." He directed the *winikin* to summon their
totems—the ghost animals they commanded—and put
them on outer surveillance. Then he waved toward the
raised limestone road that led to the sacred cenote.
"Eyes open, people. We can't be alone."

Rabbit found himself walking alone as the others
hung back or shifted away. He didn't know if they were
afraid of what he *could* do, or wondering what he *would*
do, but that was nothing new. If anything, it felt too
fucking familiar.

*The prophecies had said the crossover was supposed to be
a lone warrior*, he thought. *Guess they got it right.*

As they moved out of the pyramid's shadow, they
saw scorched earth, splintered wood and other garbage, seeming very out of place on the grounds of the
normally groomed tourist attraction.

"Riots," Anna said grimly. "The believers are making illegal sacrifices, the nonbelievers are trying to stop
them and get them to shut the hell up, the cops are trying to keep people out of the hot zone, and everyone
wants the outbreak to be over, one way or another."
Her eyes went to the tent city she could just see in the
distance. Twin columns of smoke rose up from one end,
but the camp itself looked intact.

Beside her, Myr had her shields up and her magic at the ready, and was staring intently into the shadows of each ruin they passed, then the jumbled pile of rocks that marked where the roadway led out of the main city and continued on to the cenote. She caught Rabbit's eye in passing, hesitated and then nodded, like one teammate to another. Like she was already living in Let's Just Be Friends Land.

"Well, fuck that," he muttered under his breath, suddenly pissed at himself, at the situation. How had he let this happen? How had it come to this?

You don't give up, even when the battle seems lost, Jag's voice whispered in his mind. But if that was true, why hadn't he argued with her when she said it was over?

Then again, that was one of the things he did, wasn't it? He coasted, at least when it came to her. He hadn't worked hard enough to fix things when they went off the rails the first time, and he hadn't fought hard enough just now. Maybe because things had happened too easily with her in the beginning he'd never learned how . . . or maybe because he still wasn't really sure what she was doing with a guy like him.

Yeah, that resonated.

She doesn't want you, not like this. The whisper came from the parts of himself he'd just taken back—the frustrations and insecurities that had hamstrung him too many times before, making him do dumb-ass things. *She dumped you. She walked away. She didn't look back.*

But she'd been crying as she did it. More, she wasn't

just the warrior she'd become over the past few months. She was also the Goth chick he'd gone to college with, and the skinny girl who'd tried to barter a knife for her freedom from the Witch. And those people had loved him despite his temper and impulsiveness. Hell, in the beginning, she had loved him *because* of it—she had been as much a rebel as he was, if not more. That was what he'd first seen in her, what had brought them together. It was still there, he knew. Maybe right now it was buried beneath duty and fear, but it was there.

And he'd be damned if he gave up on her. He loved her, and he wanted her at his side for the rest of their lives, whether that was five minutes or fifty-five years.

"Hold." Dez raised a hand, stopping the group as the pathway ahead of them shimmered and then solidified to reveal Alexis astride Nate in his giant hawk form. "Anything?" the king asked the forward scouts.

Alexis shook her head. "Not a damn thing. Either the cenote is clear, or they're hiding behind magic that I can't sense."

The teammates moved off again, cautiously, as the low trees opened up to reveal the uppermost level of the Cenote Sagrada, where a hundred-foot pit gaped in the earth and plunged down to a green-blue pool at the bottom.

Rabbit's head said to get up to the small temple and start the spell.

"Fuck this." He turned back and headed for Myr,

knowing that his magic—and his heart—would be stronger if he said what he needed to say to her.

He had gone three steps when JT shouted, "Incoming!"

"Son of a—" He twisted too late, saw wide brown wings and a puke-ugly face headed straight for him, and threw all of his power to his shield. The 'zotz crashed into it at full speed, driving him back, off the edge of the raised roadway. He tripped and fell, and the impact jarred the shit out of him, just enough that he lost control of the shield spell for a split second.

The 'zotz screeched, lashed out with its barb-tipped tail, and sliced him to the bone. "Motherfu—"

Darkness.

Within seconds, a dozen *camazotz* swarmed the spot where Rabbit had been, tearing at him in a frenzy. There were others nearby, blackening the air and screeching as they attacked, but the Nightkeepers' shields held them off.

Rabbit's shield was down, though. *He* was down.

"No!" The world blurred as Myrinne screamed and unleashed a massive bolt of green fire into the flock, aiming high so she didn't hit him. The fireball detonated and the fire magic clung to the creatures, eating into them and driving them to the ground as she raced to where he lay in a bloody heap. *"Rabbit!"*

He was sprawled in a spreading pool of blood; she wasn't sure where it was coming from, but there was too much of it. And there was no sign of the golden magic, no sign of life.

The nearest *'zotz* began to move again, regenerating even as its flesh smoldered, but before she could react, Strike and JT closed from opposite directions, knives out, ready to dispatch the *camazotz*. "We've got this," the *winikin* said. "You take care of him."

Around them, the battle raged on. She saw the Night-keepers bringing down *camazotz* and strange, fishlike creatures that sliced through the air with sharp fins and tails, and snapped with piranha jaws. They weren't the *kax* or *kohan*, though, just minions, guards put in place to stop the Nightkeepers from getting to the cenote.

That had to mean they were in the right place. But now they were missing a key player.

"Come back, you hear me?" She clutched Rabbit's bloodied hand and sent her energy into him through the mind-bender's magic. "We need you." *I need you.*

The truth was stark and real: she wasn't all that mad at him about hiding the truth about the dark magic. Instead, she was terrified of him, terrified for him, and just plain terrified in general . . . He hadn't just claimed the magic, he had reclaimed the part of himself that scared her the most, not because she was afraid he would hurt her, but because she knew that it would put him in the worst sort of danger.

So what had she done? She panicked and bolted, even though she'd promised herself she wouldn't ever run away from him again.

"Come on, come on." She clutched his hand and sent her magic flowing faster, but his skin was chalky and cool, and there was no echo of his conscious self inside his skull. Panic sliced through her. "This isn't working. I need Sasha!"

"I'm here." The healer skidded to a stop on the other side of Rabbit and dropped down, breathing hard. She was sweating, and had dark spatters on her sleeves.

"He's lost a lot of blood," Myr said. "And I can't find him with my magic."

"I'll see what I can do."

As Sasha bent over him, Myr looked beyond to where the Nightkeepers fought against the enemy's thinning ranks. As she watched, Michael fried a fish-thing out of the sky with a stream of silver death magic, and hawk-Nate brought down a *camazotz* on the fly and then backwinged while Alexis fried it to dust. All of the Nightkeepers and their teammates seemed to be up and moving.

Except Rabbit.

Holding his too-cool hand against her face, she said, "He was so worried about what would happen to me when the demons zeroed in on the crossover, but he forgot to worry about himself."

"That's because he loves you," Sasha said, not taking her eyes off her patient. She said it with a "duh" tone in her voice, but not unkindly. More like she'd been there, done that, and come out the other side of it.

Myr ducked her head to hide the tears, and also so

Sasha wouldn't hear her whisper in his ear, "Don't you dare leave me."

Her voice caught on the words, her heart twisted, and pain bit so deeply that she sucked in a breath. Sudden panic crushed in on her, and she tightened her grip on him, afraid that if she didn't hold on to him, he would disappear. *Don't leave me.* Her parents had dumped her in a strip club. The Witch had disappeared, leaving her locked out of her home. At the time, Myr hadn't known that Iago had killed her; all she had known was that she was alone and didn't have anywhere to go until she found the Nightkeepers. But while they had given her a family of sorts, the team was poised to break up after today, one way or another.

Don't leave me. Everyone she had depended on over the years, right or wrong, had left her. Except for Rabbit. Because this time, she had left him before he could leave her . . . but that had been a stupid move, a coward's move. She loved him. She always had. And she was going to lose him . . . unless he came back, so she could tell him that she was sorry, that she loved him, that she'd been afraid.

"It's not working." Sasha shook her head. "His magic and mine just aren't compatible."

"Keep trying," Myr said. "There has to be something else you can do. Some spell or incantation, or . . . oh." She stopped, suddenly very aware of the green-threaded shield she had been automatically maintaining around her and Rabbit, the mind-bender's magic that linked them, and the fireball spell that shimmered at the surface of her soul, ready to attack at a moment's notice.

It was her magic . . . but it was his, too.

"I know what to do. Stand back." She took a breath, knowing this was the only way. And, more, knowing that she was okay with it—he could have every last spark of her magic, if that was what it took to bring him back.

Pulling her knife, she bloodied her palms, took his hands in hers, and whispered raggedly, *"Pasaj och."* Then as the barrier connection formed—feeling suddenly unsteady—she said the transfer spell and opened herself up to it, to him.

I love you. She sent the words into him on a wave of green-tinged magic. *Come back to me.* Magic poured through her, and from her into him. Something inside her tore loose, just as it had the last time they used the spell. This time, though, nothing stayed inside her—all of her power drained. All of her magic left her. And she let it.

"No." It was a moan, a soft sound of denial, but she didn't pull back or block the magic from leaving her. This was her choice. Her sacrifice.

Sasha gasped. "Look!"

Myr's eyelids felt heavy, but she cranked them open, then stared as a pair of butterflies flitted down toward her and Rabbit—one green, the other streaked red and orange. It couldn't be the same two from Oc Ajal . . . but it sure looked like them.

As the last of the magic drained from her and the spell died away, they landed on Rabbit's chest. The moment they made contact, he took a convulsive breath, opened his eyes, and locked on her. "Ah, baby." His voice was low, and ragged with emotion. "That's what I wanted to tell you. I'm not giving up on us this time. I'm going to fight. I'm going to do whatever it takes."

Myr gave a low cry of joy and relief. He shoved himself up and reached for her, and she met him halfway. The move startled the butterflies, which flitted upward as they embraced.

His arms went around her, strong and sure; she almost couldn't believe it—couldn't believe that he was alive, that they were kissing.

"I'm sorry," she said against his lips. "I didn't mean what I said. I was scared and I lashed out. I love you. Oh, how I love you."

He silenced her with his lips, with his kiss, and when they parted, he said, "I was coming back for you. I need you so damn much, and I'm not letting you go. Never again. Because I love you."

A delicious rushing sensation suddenly flared inside her, and, as if that had turned the key in a lock, a connection bloomed open at the back of her mind. Suddenly, the magic raced through her once more. It had come back!

"Rabbit!"

His face lit with fierce joy. "I feel it!" It was the same as before, only not. Because this time, she was sharing his magic. And, more, this time she didn't resent the connection that forged itself between them. She gloried in it, loved it.

Loved him, and was loved in return.

The butterflies circled them, drawing their attention up, and together, they watched the creatures flit away into a sky that was free of the enemy now, but buzzed with magic and anticipation.

Her wristband ticked below the ten-minute mark, but she gave herself these last few seconds of joy. Of love.

Then, when the butterflies had disappeared into the trees, he turned and held out a hand to her. "Come on. We have a sacred chamber to salvage, a barrier to seal, a shit ton of demons to defeat, and two undead armies to save."

Incredibly, impossibly, she found a lopsided grin. "What are you planning for an encore?"

He smiled back with the devilish glint she had so missed in him, without even realizing she had missed it. "I was thinking of getting really wasted, making love to you, and then sleeping for twenty or so hours, possibly not in that order, and definitely including pancakes somewhere in there. But I'm open to suggestions."

Finally feeling like he was exactly where he was supposed to be, doing what he was supposed to do, Rabbit led Myr to the temple, and then beyond it, to where a rocky outcropping speared out into thin air, hovering a hundred feet above the murky water of the Cenote Sagrada.

She balked. "Wait. Should you go alone? The crossover is supposed to be a lone warrior."

"That's the nice thing about being a rebel. I can pick and choose my rebellions. And this is one of them." He tightened his grip on her hand. "Besides, we were together in the visions, like Jag and Asia." And he could protect her. More, she could protect herself.

"Okay." She nodded and stepped up beside him. "Let's do this."

His chrono said 00:05:32. Five minutes until the magic of the Great Conjunction would kick on, another ten after that until the barrier fell all the way.

It was time.

With the Nightkeepers behind them, shielding and protecting them, Rabbit and Myrinne faced the cenote. Heat flared in his veins as he called on his magic, and the world went gold. And Myr was right there with him, joined through their shared magic.

"Oh," she breathed, tightening her fingers on his. "Yes."

Almost instantly, the huge pool below them bubbled and churned, foaming up with dark leaves and muck, and brighter objects that glinted in the light—artifacts, maybe, or bones. Then the waters parted and fell back as a huge, ominous shape broke the surface. At first it looked like something strange and alien, a hidden spaceship. Then the water and weeds fell away to reveal a circular platform that was rising on some ancient mechanism, traveling up along the side of the cenote, drawn by their magic.

"It's the floor of the sacred chamber," Lucius confirmed. "I see the *chac-mool* altar!"

They had found the intersection where Jag and Asia had triggered the massacre. Rabbit only hoped to Christ—and the six true gods—that he and Myrinne didn't do the same.

The chamber was huge and heavy, but it rose up like a pebble falling in reverse, until it was level with the stone outcropping. The moment it made contact, magic flared and it fused with the surrounding stone, which meant that he and Myr didn't have to keep lifting. It also meant that the ancients knew this was going to happen somehow. Then again, so had his dreams. Because suddenly he was standing just as he had been in that last vision . . . with one very important difference.

In the vision, he'd been alone. Now, he had Myr by his side.

He glanced at her. "You ready for this?"

"I'd better be."

A glance at Dez got the go-ahead nod. The Nightkeepers had a shield around the cenote and weapons primed. This was as good as it was going to get.

"Please gods," Rabbit said, and meant it. And then, united in every way possible, he and Myr lifted their bloodied hands, and began Scarred-Jaguar's spell. *"Uxmal'aach tul—"*

Wind whipped suddenly and a terrible ripping

noise tore the air around them. The ground heaved, the nearby temple shuddered, and then the barrier tore at that spot, sending gray-green fog gushing out, pouring toward Rabbit and Myr. Figures appeared in the fog, racing toward the Nightkeepers.

"Fire!" Dez shouted, but Rabbit shouted in the same second, "Hold! It's not the enemy!"

It was the *nahwal*. They were free!

Incredibly, impossibly, the ancestral beings were scrambling through the rift and beelining for their bloodline warriors.

The one that made for Rabbit was walnut-skinned, dark eyed, and wore the mark of the boar bloodline on its wrist.

Thoughts racing, Rabbit said, "Are you—" His chrono beeped, interrupting. It read: 00:00:00. The magic of the Great Conjunction was online.

Throom! A pillar of dark magic burst from the sacred well and speared up into the sky just as a huge bolt of lightning cracked down, bringing a matching pillar of sunlight and rainbows. The light and dark magic *whoomed* together in the middle, and the earth plane shuddered. Dark shapes poured up out of the Cenote Sagrada and bright, brilliant forms plummeted down from the hole in the sky, chilling Rabbit's blood and making his instincts hiss *enemy*. But at the same time, mad joy sang in his veins. He had been bred for this, born for it.

"They're coming," Myr said, and clung into him for a moment before she pushed away. "It's time." She looked up at him, face etched with determination. "I love you. And when we get out of here, I'm buying the first round tonight."

He kissed her hard and fast. "I love you back. And I've got the second round for the whole damn army."

Suddenly, from behind him, a whole lot of voices all said at once, "Son of the boar bloodline. *We* are your army."

"What the fuck?" He spun. And his jaw hit the deck at the sight of a hundred or so Xerox copies of the boar *nahwal*, standing rank and file, staring at him with their creepy black eyes. "Where the hell did you come from?"

Okay, dumb question. But he was in shock here. And when Myr grabbed his arm hard enough to cut off circulation, he knew he wasn't the only one.

The *nahwal* said, in a hair-raising chorus, "You called us from the barrier, helped us cross over from un-death to the earth. While we are here, we have your powers, your magic. Command us."

Cross over. Crossover. Rabbit froze in place, because oh, holy shit, this was it. This was the fighting force the Nightkeepers had needed all along, the numbers they lacked.

"Look!" Myr said, pointing at a cloud of winged shadows that were leaving the ground and flying up into the air. At first he thought it was the animal familiars of the *winikin*, but these were all the same size, huge and winged, and for all the world resembling—

"Holy fuck, it's Blackhawk." Or, rather, it was a hundred Nates, all in his hawk-shifter form, blazing up into the sky to challenge the *kohan* as they flew out of the rainbow.

Off to the other side, silver bolts flared from the ground, launching up into the sky to slam into *kohan* and *kax* alike, as Michael and his *nahwal* soldiers attacked the enemy. Jade and her *nahwal* threw ice magic; Sasha's battalion commanded plants that reared up, grabbed at the *kax* and dragged them back down; and suddenly there were teleporting *nahwal* everywhere, zapping in under Strike and Anna's orders to throw vicious fireballs and then disappear before the enemy could launch a counterattack.

The fire and ice were failing, though. "Their shields are too strong!" Myr cried.

Rabbit grinned viciously. "Not for long, they aren't."

Forking his fingers, he called on the golden magic. And, using what he'd learned from the *kohan* back at Coatepec, he brought down the enemy shields.

Screeches and screams rang out over the battlefield as the *kax* and *kohan* found themselves suddenly vulnerable, followed by the Nightkeepers' cheers as they regrouped and attacked.

Fierce joy exploded through Rabbit and he shouted to his *nahwal*. "Let's fight these fuckers!" At the edge of the cenote a huge, smoky *makol* was climbing up and out. Behind it there were two more, four, a dozen. Rabbit pointed and bellowed, "Get them!"

His battalion shouted and charged.

The next few minutes were a blur of shields and fire as the boar army tore into the *makol*. Green flames burst amid the red as Rabbit and Myr fought shoulder to shoulder, back to back, however and wherever they could. The magic flowed between them, solidly intertwined, giving him an extra kick of power, an extra layer of fierce protectiveness at the sheer joy of her being his partner. His mate.

They were going to make it through this war, he promised himself. And they were going to make for themselves the kind of family neither of them had grown up with.

A *makol* attacked, then spun and screeched in triumph as a translucent, fiery red creature reared up and over him, swiping with its six-clawed paw and turning solid in the last second before it hit.

"Down!" he shouted, and he and Myr pancaked as the *boluntiku*'s slash whistled over their heads. Rabbit came up as the *'tiku* reversed for the backswing, and blasted the back of its head with a golden fireball that clung like napalm, eating into the creature. It screeched and fell back into the cenote, leaving the area around the altar momentarily clear.

Now, said the booming voice inside Rabbit. *It is time.*

"Dez!" Rabbit shouted. "The spell!"

The king looked at him for a heartbeat, then nodded. He leaped to the top of the temple, filled his lungs and bellowed, "Everyone get under a big-ass shield and link up! And I mean *everyone*! Pass it on!"

There was a mad scramble, a huge flare of shield magic, and the frustrated fingernail-on-blackboard screams of new *kax* and *boluntiku* erupting from the sacred well, new winged gods dropping down from the sky. The enemy lashed at the shield with flames, claws and acid, but the shield held, by the gods, it held!

Beneath it, the Nightkeepers, *winikin*, human and *nahwal* all cut their palms and connected with each other, blood to blood. Rabbit found himself linked to Myr on one side and one of his own *nahwal* on the other side, and felt the uplink gain strength as more and more links were added. Boars, jaguars, eagles, iguanas, smokes, stones, harvesters . . . the powers of the different bloodlines flowed through the uplink. And as the magic passed into them, Rabbit and Myrinne smoothed it into a single flowing stream of power, blended and wonderful.

"Ready?" Dez called to him.

Rabbit took a look around to confirm.

A *nahwal* caught his attention; it was staring at him intently. More, it was distinguished from the others by the wink of a ruby earring in one ear. *Jag*. The former king nodded to him, man to man, and sudden certainty filled Rabbit. This was how it was supposed to have been. This was what Scarred-Jaguar had been destined to do, only he'd tried to do it thirty years too early, and without the help of the crossover and his earth-mage mate.

Now, though, things would be as the true gods had meant them to be.

"Yeah," he said, tightening his grip on Myr's hand. "We're ready."

They sent the spell words around the blood-link, so

the entire Nightkeeper army, more than a thousand strong, spoke in synchrony, like the biggest, baddest *nahwal* ever made.

As they began the spell, two earth-shuddering roars rose up in response—one from above and one from below—and the fabric of the air around them shivered and started to tear.

Hurry! Myr's mind spoke in Rabbit's head, in his heart, but the spell was complicated, couldn't be rushed. He kept going as a huge winged creature, black as night, came up from the depths while another, identical but pure white, dropped down from above. They were enormous, monstrous, and power crackled around them like storms. They landed together, *thud-thud*, on the Nightkeepers' shield and started tearing at the magic with teeth that glinted like diamonds. The shield gave and made a wretched crackling noise.

Behind the creatures, though, the pillar of dark and light magic shuddered and began to rotate, moved by Rabbit's spell.

"It's working!" he ordered. "Give it more power!" They had finished the incantation, but the momentum was slow, the barrier frail. The Nightkeepers and their allies dug deep and gave it everything they had, and as the power amped its flow through the uplink, the pillar spun faster and faster. "More!" he shouted and then, through the uplink itself, he sent into their minds, *Think of your mates, your children, your families.* It went against the writs but he didn't give a shit. Not when he'd learned firsthand that love was everything.

Let your magic flow. It doesn't matter what talent, big or small, just send it to me and Myr and we'll make it come together.

The stream of power coming into him became a river, then a flash flood. And beyond the shield and the monsters on their roof, the pillar went into overdrive, split apart, and started tornadoing. The twin funnels cranked and whirred, sucking in everything that had come out of the sky and underworld.

Rabbit saw a *boluntiku* go, more *'zotz*, a *makol* or three. But the huge winged beasts above them hung on and dug in. A section of the shield caved, and a clawed foot broke through. They were so fucking close, but they weren't going to make it!

"Myr," he said, the word coming out broken. "Jesus Christ, Myr."

She looked up at him, and found a way to smile. "What a perfectly wonderful disaster this is turning out to be."

And, holy shit, he laughed out loud at that, and somewhere, somehow, let go of the last little thread of control, giving himself over to the chaos. The golden magic flared through him, into the uplink and from there to the funnel clouds, and the damn things *exploded*, expanding to suddenly wrap around the winged creatures, which growled and snapped, then howled as they were torn away and sucked into the vortices, one to the sky, the other to Xibalba. The one headed to hell was joined by dozens of little flickers of red and green, hundreds of them.

"The *xombis*!" Anna cried. "You're banishing the *xombi* magic!"

Rabbit let his head fall back and let out a whoop. "It's working!"

He wanted to dance and sing, wanted to spin Myr around and around, but he held on to the spell instead, pouring himself into it, feeling the strength of the Nightkeepers' uplink. The last of the *xombi* flickers whipped past them and down, and then, with a final roar, the funnel clouds folded in on themselves and sucked back to where they'd started.

And *pop*. They were gone.

It was over.

Only it wasn't.

The storm was gone, the *kohan* and the *kax* were gone, and everything was the same as it had been when they got there . . . except for the *nahwal*. The Nightkeepers' armies of the dead stood clustered near the last members of their bloodlines, waiting to cross over to the afterlife.

Crossover.

The golden magic pulsed inside Rabbit, chaotic and disordered, just like life itself. And, going on instinct, he looped an arm around Myr's waist, pointed to the sky, and sent a stream of the magic winging up, up, and up some more, until it hit a cloud.

Sunlight flared, bright and unexpected, and a beam speared down, descending along the stream of golden magic until it reached the ground.

"Oh," Myr breathed.

Once the sunbeam was on the ground, it moved with a magic of its own, seeking out the *nahwal*. Some flared quickly bright and then disappeared, becoming golden glitters that flowed up the sunlight shaft and headed for the sky. Not to the realm of the *kohan*, but to the true sky. The reward for brave warriors.

The few *nahwal* who didn't disappear, though, grew solid. More, their eyes turned normal, clothes glistened into being around them, and they suddenly looked like real people.

Rabbit's heart thudded in his chest. "Holy shit," he whispered, and felt Myr squeeze his hand.

Anna gave a soft cry and moved toward one of them. "Mama!" She hesitated as the gold dust swirled, but when it cleared, it revealed a woman who was very familiar to Rabbit from his dreams. Asia. Scarred-Jaguar's queen. Gods.

The two women embraced while Sasha moved toward them, eyes alight. Strike, meanwhile, faced the *nahwal* with the ruby earring as the old king's features became clear, and father and son saw each other for the first time in thirty years. And it would be the last, Rabbit saw, because after a brief exchange, the shimmers intensified and the old king streamed up into the sky.

"Do you see?" Myr's voice cracked and her fingers dug into his arm. "Are you seeing this?"

It was happening all around them, for each of the Nightkeepers. Which meant . . .

Stiffening, he turned. And found himself facing not one *nahwal* . . . but four of them.

Red-Boar stood beside a pretty, perky-looking brunette with a wide smile. And in front of them, wrapped in their arms, were twin boys who looked up at Rabbit with eyes so much like his own that his heart clutched.

He had hated them, he realized. All along, he had hated them.

"Go on," he told them now. "Go be together." And he sent the crossover magic toward them.

As the sparks gathered and surrounded the four, Red-Boar raised a hand in farewell.

Then the golden magic streamed airborne and up onto the sunbeam, and Rabbit's old man was gone. For real this time.

He had been the last of them, Rabbit saw. The *nahwal* were all gone, and the *winikin*'s animal familiars were streaming up along the sunlight as well, being waved off with cheers and tears, and cries of thanks. When they were gone, figuring it was over, Rabbit let his magic die away. He held Myr close to his side and said, "Well, as disasters go . . ." He trailed off as the sunbeam intensified once more. "This one may not be over."

CHAPTER TWENTY-FIVE

Myr pressed close to Rabbit's side as the golden sparks flitted down from the clouds, then spun, dipped and formed the head of a giant creature, one that had the pointy features of a Doberman, but with a drooping, anteater-like nose and wide, squared-off ears that stood high at attention.

Seth, the lord of chaos, looked down at the Nightkeepers and their allies, and smiled. Which in itself was pretty damn terrifying, she decided. But at the same time, her blood thrummed.

They had survived the war! They could handle whatever came next.

"Well done, children of the Earth plane." Seth spoke, as Bastet had, in all of their minds at once. But then he turned, sweeping the crowd and zeroing in on Rabbit. *"Especially you, son of chaos."*

Rabbit had gone still. "I know that voice."

Myr did too. It came from the vision, from Asia's king. Only it hadn't been Jag's voice, she realized now. It had been the god's.

The great head inclined. *"I spoke to you as I could, and told you what you needed to hear. You are the crossover, the embodiment of random chance. My son on this earth. You are risk and danger, change and invention. Your blood will reinvigorate the Nightkeepers, keeping the magic alive for another twenty-six thousand years, until the next Great Conjunction."*

"We get to keep the magic?" Myr blurted. She had assumed that it would disappear now that the barrier was sealed once more, quiescent until the next cycle, like a zillion generations from now.

Those golden eyes locked on her. *"Yes and no, earth daughter. The magic still exists, but it is hidden. It will work only on the Cardinal Days, or if the earth should need its Keepers and their allies again in the future."* Seth's eyes swept the crowd again, touching on each of them. *"So teach your children well, and your children's children, and down the line. Protect them. Hide them if necessary. And do not forget the lies of the other realms . . . or the power of love."*

Magic hummed in the air and the golden pixels swirled and spun, beginning to break up. As Seth's face melted away, though, he looked at Rabbit again, and sent him another of those terrifying smiles. *"You are my pride, son of chaos. Never forget it."*

And then the god was gone, leaving utter silence behind.

Myr's heart was lodged somewhere south of her tonsils, her fingers digging into Rabbit's arm. He was the first one to move, taking a shuddering breath and unlocking his body to drag a hand down his face.

"Jesus Christ," he said raggedly. "Jesus fucking Christ."

The lump in her throat turned into a tickle. "I'm pretty sure he's the son of a different god." The tickle turned into a laugh that was more than a bit hysterical.

"Wow." Strike shook his head. "Seriously. That was. Wow."

Conversation rippled outward from there, with a whole lot of "holy shit" and "did you see that?" Then Rabbit threw back his head and let out a howl of "Ya-hoooo!" It echoed off the confines of the sacred well and the distant ruins and came back to them.

"Awoooo!" caroled one of the coyotes, and the second one joined in a beat later. And then everyone joined in, shouting and screaming, and making noise as it started dawning that they had survived—every one of them, with not a single fatality—and the barrier was sealed.

"We won!" Rabbit swept Myr up and spun her around. "We won!"

"Damn straight!" She kissed him on the lips—her beautiful, wonderful, chaotic man—and raised her hands in the air as he spun them both around. "First round's on me!" she shouted to a chorus of cheers. "And the second one's on Rabbit here, so save the expensive stuff for him!"

*   *   *

While the others whirled and cheered, shouting plans for a party to end all parties back at Skywatch, Anna stripped off her weapons belt and slipped away, heading for the fringes of the excitement.

"Hey, sis." Strike's voice stopped her, had her turning back.

"I'm just . . ." She made a vague gesture that wasn't quite in the direction of the quarantine camp. "I'll be back soon. If you need me to 'port before then, just—"

"I just wanted to wish you all the luck in the world."

"Oh." A tentative smile caught, then spread. "Thanks."

He waved her off. "Go on, take your time. I'll cover the transport."

She glanced down at her marks. "Do you think the 'port magic will still work?"

"While we're still in equinox and the conjunction? Yeah. Tomorrow? We'll have to see." He paused. "Does it matter?"

"Not to me." She lifted a hand. "See you in a bit, little brother."

He was chuckling and saying something along the lines of "Little, my ass" as she spun up the magic, found the golden travel thread connecting her to her destination, and made the jump.

The supply closet she 'ported into was deserted, but the hallway outside was anything but. She stepped out into a scene of utter chaos.

It was glorious and fan-freaking-tastic chaos, though, because it didn't come from doctors running around, trying to deal with some new medical crisis. Instead, it came from the johnny-clad people thronging the hallways, all talking at once in a mix of English, Spanish and Maya, and the shouts of the security officers trying to herd them along.

Over the cranked-loud intercom, a woman's voice blared, "Please follow the exit signs out to the central courtyard. Officers will direct you to the mess hall, where you will be given further information." The message repeated in the other two languages.

A bubble of joy lifted in Anna's throat, coming out as a delighted laugh. They were awake! The *xombis* were up and moving, and out of their restraints. She wasn't sure how that had happened or why, as it seemed there could've been a more organized release protocol in place. But that wasn't her call; she wasn't in charge.

And speaking of the man in charge . . . she looked but didn't see any of the volunteers she'd gotten to know, and the few scrub-wearing nurses and techs within range were wide-eyed, overwhelmed, and doing their best to keep the human tide moving. But that was okay. Anna had a feeling she knew where she could find David.

It took her a long five minutes to make it to the far patient wing, even with some subtle magical nudges, but she finally reached her destination. She paused for a moment outside Rosa's door, sudden nerves kicking. The panel was closed and the KEEP OUT signs were still posted. What if she was too late? What if . . . ?

"Knock it off," she told herself, then took a deep breath and let herself through.

Rosa was there, still curled up beneath the teddy bears. And David was there, sitting at her bedside in jeans and a rolled-up shirt, with a beard-shadow and dark circles under his eyes, looking as if he hadn't moved since last night. The lab coat tossed over the back of his chair said he'd been with the others, though, and the worry in his face told her the news wasn't good, at least in this one room.

When he saw Anna, his expression blanked for a second, then flared. He rose and crossed to her, stopping short with a move that made her think he wanted to reach out, wanted to touch her, but didn't know whether he should. And she felt the same sudden shyness, the realization that their e-mails had gotten far more intimate than their physical selves.

He cleared his throat. "I should probably snarl at you for still being in this area, but I'm not sure I've really got the right to yell at you, and, besides, it'd be a total lie because damn, I'm glad to see you."

And there it was, the e-mail voice she'd started looking for, needing. Fighting for, even. She grinned as his online and real selves merged once more in her mind. "Let's just say I didn't go all that far." Her smile faded, though, as she looked past him. "She didn't wake up when the others did?"

"How did you know about that?" He waved it off. "Never mind. Rumor mill. God knows I'm surprised the families haven't rushed the fence line yet to get to the patients, or vice versa. We need to run some tests first, make sure this isn't some weird lull before another outbreak, or . . . shit. I'm stalling. Because yeah, Rosa didn't wake up. Probably ninety percent of the patients just clicked on about twenty minutes ago, *bing*, the lights went on and somebody was home. Almost all of the ones who didn't wake up had been really far gone before they went into stasis, so starved there's a good chance they were brain-dead or close to it." He turned back to the bed, eyes hollowing out. "Rosa, though . . . I just don't know what's going on, whether it's still the disease, or if there's something else. For all I know, she's staying under because of the shock of seeing her parents kill each other. But even then, how can I help her?" His voice lowered, went soft as he said to the child in Spanish, "You can come back, little one. I know you've had a bad time of it, but you've got people here on your side. We'll take care of you. I promise."

Anna's heart tugged for them both, yet ached a little for herself. Because what she was about to do was a hell of a risk. "I brought something I think might help her."

His head came up. "More homeopathics?"

"Something like that." She reached into a pocket and came up with the sturdy stoppered bottle she had carried into battle as a talisman. The liquid inside was brown, greasy and brackish, and reminded her of dark magic. It was the good stuff, though. And maybe it would work.

She'd gotten it from Sasha early this morning, along with the basic recipe if more was needed. The healer had taken a tonic she'd had on hand, and infused it with a jolt of equinox magic and a potent mixture of cacao, maize and sacrificial blood. It couldn't cure the *xombi* virus, but Sasha had thought that once the spell was lifted—if it lifted—the potion might help bring the patients back by strengthening their *chu'ul*, their life force.

The *xombis* hadn't needed it, luckily. But would it be enough to bring Rosa back? There was no telling why the child was still out, if it was because of the virus or the shock to her system, or if channeling Bastet's message had changed her irrevocably, perhaps putting her mind partly in this world, partly in the next. Anna knew she had to try the potion, though, had to do anything in her power to break through the little girl's coma. Even if what she did was guaranteed to increase David's suspicions.

Already, he was looking at her a little sideways, like he wanted to quiz her, but was afraid to. Instead, he took a big step back, making room for her. "Go ahead."

She tried for a smile. "It's not FDA approved."

"This does not surprise me." He held her eyes, though she wasn't sure what he saw, or what he was thinking. He inhaled like he was going to say something more, but then waved her forward. "Do it. I trust you not to hurt her."

"I don't want to." But she whispered an inner prayer as she sat and leaned over the tiny form. *Please, gods, let your messenger awaken safely.*

Holding her breath, she unstoppered the small bottle and squirted a healthy dose into Rosa's mouth, then used a finger to close her jaw and tip her head back. "Come on, sweetie. Swallow."

Nothing happened. And for a good two minutes, nothing kept happening, leaving Anna sitting there, staring at Rosa, all too aware of the flop sweats starting on her palms and the man standing behind her, waiting for a miracle.

Frustration welled. *Come on, come on. Please.*

And, suddenly, it felt way too much like all the times she'd tried to call on her *itza'at*'s magic. Back then, it had been a blessing in disguise that she'd never been able to make her own magic work properly—that was what had let the true gods contact her, after all. Now, though . . . there was no blessing here, no upside. This had to work, she had to *make* it work.

Wake up, damn it!

Sweat prickled down her spine as she filled another stopper. Then she tugged at her chain and brought out the yellow quartz skull, which felt heavy as it swung free, glinting in the light.

"What is . . ." David trailed off, exhaling. "Never mind. Sorry. Keep going."

He moved, but she wasn't sure if he was leaning closer or edging away, and she was afraid to look, didn't want to know which it was. Not when she would need all her concentration and confidence to pull this off. Already, she could feel the conjunction moving on, the magic starting to fade.

"Fuck it," she said under her breath, and went for her worn pocketknife. She heard his startled oath when she carved sharp slices across her palm scars on both sides, but she ignored it, ignored him, and focused on the child lying there, motionless. Helpless. *She's there because of me. I can get her back.* "Pasaj och."

The magic came at her call, flaring through her veins and lighting the air red and gold. She hoped to hell he couldn't see the glimmer—most humans couldn't. But she couldn't turn back now. *Come on, come on.*

The power was sluggish, thick and syrupy, but it was there. More, it reached out to wrap around the dropper containing Sasha's potion, which started to throb with a low yellow glow, just as it had when the healer had first mixed it together.

"Please gods," Anna whispered. And dripped it slowly into Rosa's mouth.

This time, incredibly, something started happening. First the yellow glow spread to the little girl's face, which flushed and pinkened, looking healthier than it had since the child's arrival. Then it moved down, flowing through Rosa, warming her. Her breathing changed, deepening and speeding up, and Anna's pulse jumped in response. "That's it. Come on back. You can do it."

"Jesus Christ," David muttered. She thought he might even have crossed himself.

Her stomach hollowed out, but she couldn't worry about him right now; she had to focus. "Wake up, sweetie. It's okay. You're safe now."

The girl stirred and straightened beneath the blanket, working her feet for a moment to kick free. Then she sighed, rubbed her cheek against the pillow, and opened her eyes.

Holy gods. Anna stared, transfixed, as Rosa blinked up at her, puzzled. Then she focused, and there was acceptance in her eyes, not fear. "I know you," she said drowsily in Spanish. "You're the lady who sat with me at night and told me stories."

Anna's breath left her in a soft whoosh. "You heard me," she said in the same language.

"Mostly just you and the nice doctor." She didn't seem to see David in the background. "And the cat-woman. But she wasn't really here, was she?"

"Only in your dreams." Anna paused, wondering how much to say, and how. Not too much, she decided, as the little girl looked like she was already fading. "You've been sick, but you're going to be okay now."

"I know. The cat-lady told me. She said . . . she said . . ." The child's eyelids fluttered and eased shut. But this time her sleep was a more natural one, coming from her body issuing a shutdown command so it could have time to heal the physical damage.

The emotional damage would take longer, Anna knew. Even the best support system in the world couldn't undo the horrific loss of her entire family, or the trauma of watching it happen. *Been there, done that.* She had fought through it, though, and could help Rosa do the same, and do it better than she had. But although she could do that alone, could do all of it alone . . . she didn't want to, damn it.

And she couldn't put off looking up at him any longer.

She braced herself to see David all the way across the room, plastered to the back wall, staring at her like she was off her fucking rocker—or, worse, something he should be afraid of. Gods knew that most human scientists didn't like the unknown.

Already planning on hitting him with a sleep spell, bringing Rabbit back to do some mental remediation, and never seeing her doomsday crush ever again, she turned—

And found him very close, practically breathing over her shoulder, his eyes full of awe, excitement and wonder. When their eyes met, his lips turned up in a perfectly approving smile. "You did it," he said softly. "You . . . I don't know what you just did, but you did it."

"I want her," she said in English. All the other things she'd planned to say suddenly backed up in her lungs, trapped there by the look in his eyes and the knowledge that this moment, here and now, was as important to her as facing off opposite her parents' spirits and sending them to the sky. That had brought the past full circle. Now she wanted to start the future of her choosing. "If her family won't take her back—"

"They won't. Her uncle signed her over when she first came in."

"Then I want her. I can provide for her, love her. I

know what it's like to lose both parents the way she did, and I can help her through it." She looked down at her wrists, with their crisscross scars and the line of tattoos, saw the gleam of yellow as the crystal skull swung into view, and wondered just how crazy this all sounded to him, how crazy she looked right now. "I know I may not seem like the stablest bet right now from your perspective, but I promise you—"

"Stop," he said. "Anna, stop. Christ, you don't need to sell me. I've seen you with her. I've seen . . . well, what I've seen. Anyway. I can pull some strings, get the paperwork expedited." He hesitated, searching her eyes. "Though I get the feeling you could handle that on your own, too." And now he really did take a big step back.

She reached out to him. "David. Don't."

"I won't. I don't mean to. But . . . Christ, Anna. That was . . . it was . . ."

"An herbal remedy with a little bit of faith-based healing thrown in for good measure. It was the tonic that did the trick. The prayer just made me feel better." She let her hand drift back to her side, unclaimed. "Don't," she said again, softer this time. *Don't look at me like you're debating between a psych consult and an exorcism.* "It wasn't anything weird. I'm just me."

"You're not 'just' anything, are you?" But his eyes were regaining some of the wonder she'd seen in them earlier.

Hopefully not too much of it. The last thing she wanted was for him to put her on a magical pedestal of some sort. "You said it yourself: Even Western science is starting to recognize the validity of some native remedies."

"That was more than some herbs. And the things Rosa was saying . . ."

"I snuck in to visit her sometimes when you weren't here, that's all."

"What about the cat-woman she mentioned?" He looked around as if searching for something hiding in the shadows.

"It was nothing. Probably just a dream." *Or a god.* It seemed that Bastet, too, hadn't been able to leave the child to wander the darkness alone. Now there was a god Anna would be proud to serve, one she would be happy to pray to on the Cardinal Days. But oh, how she hoped she wouldn't have to spend the other three hundred and sixty-something days of the year without the dream she'd just started allowing herself. The dream of a daughter and a lover. A family. "Please," she said softly. "Don't make what I did seem like more than it really was."

"I won't. I'm not. It's just . . ." He moved back toward her, and now it was his turn to lift a hand and let it fall, like he wanted to touch her but didn't quite dare. "Who are you?"

She didn't let herself wince. "I'm exactly what you've seen, exactly what I've written to you. None of that has been a lie."

"But there's more to you, isn't there?"

"Not anymore."

She expected him to push harder, was thrown a little off balance when he didn't. Instead, he took the last step separating them, and lifted his hand to brush the back of one finger softly down her cheek. "I thought you might disappear after today."

The shiver that ran through her body wasn't just from the caress. "Not unless you want me to."

"No," he said. "That's exactly what I *don't* want you to do. In fact, I want you to stick around for a long, long time."

Something eased inside her. "Right here?"

His eyes lit and he smiled a slow, sexy grin. "Actually, darlin', I don't give a shit where, as long as it's with me."

They were both smiling when he cupped her face in his hands, and kissed her.

His lips were warm and firm, his beard-shadow a bristly, masculine contrast as his mouth claimed hers, his tongue invaded, and heat pooled low in her belly. Anna leaned in, opened to him, and breathed the softest of moans.

How long had it been since she'd been kissed? Had she ever been kissed like this? She didn't think so, didn't remember this kind of hunger, this kind of combustion. She caught his wrists, not to pull him away, but to hold him close. His pulse thudded beneath her thumbs, bringing an electrical charge that flared from him to her and back again. There was magic in the moment and the man, she thought, but of the purely human variety. And she was very okay with that.

He eased the kiss, still cupping her face as he pulled back to take a long look around the room, as if suddenly seeing where she had hidden behind the shield, or the fading sparkle of magic in the air. "Seriously, though. What happened here?"

"What if I say that I'll tell you the whole story one day?" she said, and was surprised not to feel the slightest twinge from her conscience.

She hadn't ever told Dick the truth, hadn't even considered it. And maybe that had been part of their problem, because as much as she had wanted to be truly human, it had been a lie. Now, though . . . yeah. Now, she thought she could talk about her childhood, the massacre, the magic, the war, all of it. And she thought David would believe it, even understand. He wasn't like anyone she'd ever met before, not like anyone she could've imagined meeting.

"Okay, I'll take that." His grin was a lightning flash of perfect teeth. "No rush, by the way. We've got time." He paused, searching her eyes. "Right?"

"Yes, we do." Her smile felt like it lit her from within. "In fact, as of today, we've got all the time in the world."

December 22
Skywatch

Myr came awake feeling warm, fuzzy, a little headachy, a lot dizzy, and so damn comfortable cuddled up with Rabbit on a wide, squishy couch that she didn't ever want to move. But at the same time, there was a part of her that was buzzing with excitement and anticipation, telling her that something wonderful was coming, or had already arrived.

Snuggling in, she cracked an eyelid, and for a moment thought she was still dreaming, or that she'd gone back to college or something. That was the last time she'd awakened borderline hungover, to the sight of a battlefield of a living room strewn with empties, plates, cups, streamers and other unidentifiables—and, hello, was that a blow-up doll in the corner?—along with bodies of both sexes lying asleep in a variety of positions ranging from comfortable to "oh, hell, that's gonna hurt when he wakes up."

But as she came all the way back to consciousness, she recognized the bodies and the room, and knew this wasn't college. It was Skywatch . . . and it was the Day After.

"Holy crap." Her voice cracked. "We saved the world."

"Yeah, we did, didn't we?" Rabbit's voice rumbled in her ear and his lips cruised the back of her neck. "And we capped it off with a hell of a party. Really wrecked this place." His hand shifted from her hip to her stomach, where he spread his fingers and pressed, pulling her back against him so she could feel his morning wood through several layers of clothing. "Got a party going on in here, too."

A laugh bubbled up. "Classy."

"That's me, baby. Classy, elegant and all yours."

She turned in his arms, rearranged her legs to dovetail intimately with his, and grinned into his sleep-fuzzed, beautiful, beloved face. "Yeah, you are. And I'm not gonna let you forget it again."

"Won't happen." His hand had migrated to her ass, and urged her close as his lips found her cheek, her ear. "I'm yours, Myr, and you're mine." And there was nothing sleep-fuzzed about the look in his eyes as he drew her in for a kiss that heated her blood and made her head spin in a very different way.

"Love you," she whispered against his lips, not afraid to say it now. Not afraid to feel it.

"Love you back, Myr. Love you back."

"Hey, you two, get a freaking room," called a voice from the other side of the sofa, down by the vicinity of the floor. "Trying to slip into a coma here."

Rabbit chuckled. "Sorry, Kev. Hey, that your doll over there?"

"Bite me." But there was a laugh in the *winikin*'s party-roughened voice.

Heavy, shuffling footsteps sounded from the direction of the kitchen, and Strike called. "Coffee?"

"Are you asking if we want some or if we'll make you some?" Rabbit retorted. "That would be 'yes' and 'no', respectively, by the way. Black for me, warmed-over coffee ice cream–style for Myr."

"Lots of cream, lots of sugar. Got it."

As the smell of brewing coffee spread across the great room, the bodies started coming back to life. Rabbit and Myrinne got vertical and cuddled on the couch, not in any real hurry to do anything, even make pancakes. Some of the partiers grogged off to their beds, while others wandered into the big kitchen and started rummaging for leftovers. Pretty soon, there were a couple of different breakfasts going and a buzz of conversation, heavy on the good-natured ribbing.

"Feels like Christmas morning a few days early," Rabbit said. "Or pick the celebration of your choice. It's that lull after the presents and before the big feast, you know?"

Myr just nodded, but along with the satisfaction of a job very well done and the deep, warm happiness of being there with him, and knowing they were together for good this time, came a quiet sort of sadness as she looked around the party-blasted great room, and beyond the glass sliders to the tarped-over pool. "Everything's going to change now. Isn't it?"

She had lived here with the Nightkeepers for almost three years. She had trained with them, fought with them, sometimes argued with them, and while she might not have appreciated all of them—or their rules—right off the bat, they had been far more of a family to her than she'd ever had before.

Rabbit's arm tightened around her. "We'll still see each other on the Cardinal Days."

The mention brought another stab of regret. She almost didn't want to try it, didn't want to know, but she made herself cup her hand, palm up, and whisper, *"Pasaj och."*

There was a faint lift beneath her heart, but there was no magic.

It was really gone.

"Not gone," Rabbit said, as if he could still read her thoughts. He rubbed his roughened cheek on the top of her head. "It'll still be there if we need it."

"And different isn't bad," Strike said, setting down their coffees and taking the love seat opposite them with a gusty sigh. "It's just different."

"Being waited on by the former king," Rabbit said, reaching forward to hand Myr her coffee and then snag his own sludge-black brew. "Now that's different."

Strike grinned. "I'd tell you to bite me, but it sounded like Kev got there first."

"He's just pissed that his little secret floated out last night." Rabbit nodded in the direction of the blow-up doll, who was deep-throating a beer bottle.

They kept going like that, in an easy man-cave banter that flowed over Myr, smoothing the sharp edges and reminding her that this was why she didn't party hard all that often—she got pretty damn melancholy when she was hungover.

"Look at it this way," Rabbit said into her ear. "Things could be a hell of a lot worse."

That startled a snort out of her. "Understatement of the year." But she took a deep sip of her coffee, hoping that the sugar and caffeine would give her the kick in the ass she needed. "Sorry. I'm just . . . it's so weird to think that we're all going to go our separate ways now, and that's got me feeling . . . I don't know. Clingy, I guess."

"We're sure as hell not going our separate anything,

babe." Rabbit nipped her ear. "You said you loved me, remember? I've got witnesses."

She chuckled and poked him in the ticklish spot over his ribs, making him twitch and grab her wrist. The exchange sloshed her coffee, but it made her feel immeasurably better.

"Call it clingy if you want." Strike shrugged. "I call it love. Family. And there's nothing wrong with that—in fact, it's exactly right as far as I'm concerned." He was sprawled back in the love seat with his feet up on a detritus-heaped coffee table, but his eyes were suddenly intense. Suddenly those of the one-time king. "You guys know we're family, right? I don't care about blood, your parents, or what-the-fuck-ever, Rabbit's my little brother, and that's never going to change."

"I . . ." Rabbit cleared his throat. "Yeah. Thanks. Love you, man."

"Same goes. And being family, I want you to come to me and Leah if you need anything—a place to land, a sounding board, a kick in the ass, whatever." His eyes flicked to Myr. "You, too, kiddo. You'd be family even if you hadn't hooked up with this one." But his grin said he was glad they had worked things out, that they were in it together for the long haul.

"What does that make her," Rabbit said in a teasing tone, trying to reassemble his tough-guy image. "An in-law?"

"I've always liked the idea of being an outlaw," she put in, ignoring the faint, unexpected tug. There would be time to get into the marriage-and-future stuff later.

It surprised her a little, though, to realize it was something she wanted with him—something normal and official, and just about the two of them.

"Family is family," Strike said, wisely avoiding the topic.

A sudden burst of noise and energy from the Nightkeepers' wing brought her eyes around just as Patience and Brandt hustled through the archway, dragging wheeled carry-on suitcases.

"We're ready," Patience announced breathlessly. Her cheeks were pink and her eyes shone with excitement. "We're leaving."

"I suspect they picked up on that," Brandt said dryly. But he was grinning, looking more relaxed and easy than Myr had ever seen him. To Strike, he said, "I just talked to Jox, confirming everything. He said to say 'hi' and that he'll see you soon, with Hannah, Harry, Braden and the dog all in tow."

In other words, the *winikin* and the twins were fine, and there hadn't been any unexpected end-date happenings on that end. No doubt the *winikin* had been equally relieved—if not more so—to learn that the Nightkeepers had made it through without any real casualties except their magic. Which was a worthwhile sacrifice, Myr supposed, even though it was going to take some time to get used to the loss.

Strike closed his eyes and exhaled a long, relieved breath. "Good, good. I'm . . . that's good." Then he cracked one eye. "What dog?"

For some reason, Brandt's eyes went to Rabbit and

danced with glee before he said, "Long story. Tell you when we get back."

"Let's go, let's go!" Patience nudged her husband toward the garage. "We've got a plane to catch."

Amid a chorus of "Good luck," "Congratulations" and "See you soon," Patience and Brandt headed off, dragging their luggage and looking like any other couple headed off for a few days away. Well, any other couple made up of two huge, incredibly attractive people who drew the eye and exuded an aura of power. It seemed that Seth had been as good as his word, letting them keep some of their lower-level magic.

"Damn it's going to be good to have Jox home," Strike said with a broad grin.

"And the rug rats," Rabbit added, eyes gleaming at the prospect of once more being Unc' Rabbit.

When they said it like that, acted like that, Myr finally relaxed all the way, realizing that things at Skywatch weren't going to break up right away. There were reunions yet to have, plans yet to make. And no matter what else was going on in their lives, they would meet back every three months for the Cardinal Day ceremonies, year after year, generation after generation.

"Puppies!" a new voice said from up near the kitchen, and Sven shuffled through the archway with his hair standing straight up, wearing nothing but boxers and an utterly disconcerted look.

"The twins got puppies?" Strike asked.

Sven frowned. "No clue. But if they don't, I've got

some they can have. Eight, in fact. Eight coyote puppies in the back of my freaking closet." He headed for
the coffee like it was the answer to a prayer, muttering
to himself, "We didn't even realize Pearl was preggers.
How the hell did she hide that? Why? She was *fighting*
yesterday, for crap's sake."

One of the *winikin*, Ritchie, looked over from cooking up a mess of eggs. "Why are you in your boxers?
Aren't you cold?"

"Shit, yeah. But Mac won't let me near my clothes."
Sven sucked back half his coffee, then looked into the
mug. "My own familiar. Sheesh!"

"You can grab some of my jeans and stuff," Strike
offered. "Just knock. Leah's hiding out with a book,
taking some quiet time."

The corner of Sven's mouth kicked up as he took a
look around the room. "Can't imagine why." As he
headed for Strike and Leah's quarters, though, Cara
came into the kitchen—fully clothed—and he diverted
to give her a kiss and offer up his coffee. As she leaned
into him and took a sip, he asked, "How are the happy
parents? Did you get Mac to cough up a T-shirt or
two?"

She grinned and shot him a sidelong look. "Cut him
some slack. He's her mate, and he's got to be pretty
freaked out right now."

"I guess."

"Poor guy." She patted his cheek. "You should borrow something to wear."

"So they tell me." He grinned though, and kissed

her again, more thoroughly this time, until Ritchie ordered them both to get their asses out of the kitchen if they wanted to eat any time soon. Still, though, as Sven headed off, he was shaking his head and muttering, "Puppies. Seriously?"

Rabbit's low chuckle vibrated through Myrinne, making her smile up at him in answer. He grinned down at her. "I guess the world really didn't end, after all."

"Nope," she agreed with all the joy that was bursting in her heart. "In fact, it seems like things around here are getting going."

CHAPTER TWENTY-SIX

Three months later
Spring equinox
Skywatch

Ninety days after the world didn't end, the Nightkeepers, the *winikin* and their human allies met back at the training compound for the Cardinal Day ceremony. It took a while for everyone to get there, since they had to use human-normal transport now. Anna didn't mind the long, storm-delayed flight or the dusty drive, though. In fact, she thought it was all pretty awesome.

It was funny how fast things could change.

Three days ago, she'd been in the Australian outback, eating flaky morsels of fish that she, David and Rosa had cooked on a campfire, simply because they could. The bulk of the meal had been made up of yellowbelly that she and David had landed using native-style handlines from the bank. The tastiest bites, though, had come from the little trout Rosa had caught in the shallows, using a trap she'd dug out with the help of David's six-year-old nephew. Colin had become a fixture around the cabin, and fast friends with Rosa, who had adapted to the cabin and her new friend just as quickly as she'd taken to her new life.

Loud noises still made her duck and cover, and there were times when she got quiet and withdrew inside herself. But although some things would take time, she was a bright, cheerful kid who seemed ready to thrive in any situation. She'd wrapped most of the quarantine camp around her pinkie by the time the adoption paperwork had gone through, making her Anna's daughter for real and forever. She'd taken to David's cabin—and his family—instantly, yet she'd been equally intrigued by their flight back to the States, charming the attendants and chattering in a mix of Spanish and English, the latter of which currently carried more than a little of an outback twang.

The trip to the cabin had been a delight . . . and so was the small family they were building. Anna had tried to hold back at first, not wanting to assume anything or fall too quickly. She kept reminding herself that Rosa was hers, and that relationship needed to be separate from her and David's budding romance.

On their third afternoon at the cabin, though, he had gotten a couple of cousins to babysit and took her out for a long ride to an Aboriginal site, where Anna delighted in the pictograms carved high on the weathered stones. They were painted in hidden clefts in colors that were still bright and vivid, and made her feel like the artists had just packed up their paints and moved on only moments before their arrival.

After exploring, they had camped and drunk home-made wine until they were giggling like little kids, then made clumsy love for the first time, in a sleeping bag that wasn't quite built for two. Then, later, drunk only on each other, they had made love again, lying atop the sleeping bag, naked under the stars and moon. When morning came, there was no question that they were a couple, and that they were in it for the long haul.

As for the rest? They would figure it out as they went. For now, they were taking each day as it came, and enjoying the hell out of life. With David's time off coming to a close, though, things were going to change. As much as Anna would've liked to go with him to every new outbreak, new adventure, she had Rosa to think about—school, friends, that sort of thing—so she had started looking around for a place to live, and had surprised herself by gravitating toward the Albuquer-que area.

David had taken a laid-back "when I'm not off on assignment, home is where you two are" attitude about things, so he and Rosa were going to spend the next few days checking out the city and its 'burbs, and thinking about putting down roots there. He'd been curious about Anna's trip into canyon country, but hadn't pressed. He would someday, she knew. But not yet.

A year ago, if someone had told her that in twelve months she would be part of a mom-dad-kid trifecta and thinking about getting a job at one of the universities in the city nearest Skywatch, she would've laughed her ass off. Hell, she wouldn't have believed it even if she'd seen it in a vision. But it was her new reality, her new life. And she was freaking loving every minute of it.

She'd earned this reprieve. They all had. For her—and, she hoped, for all of her teammates—it wasn't about zapping from place to place anymore, wasn't about training and prepping for the next equinox or solstice, the next attack. It wasn't about saving the world—it was about living in it, and enjoying every moment.

And as she pulled through the wide-open gates of Skywatch, she was surprised to realize that she was enjoying the hell out of this particular moment too.

She'd been sad to leave David and Rosa behind, and had figured she would treat the ceremony more like a duty visit to her relatives than anything. But her spirits lifted suddenly when she saw the front of the mansion jam-packed with a dizzying variety of conveyances, and it hit her that she might be back at Skywatch, but it was nothing like it had been before.

The vehicles ranged from Harleys, Victories and other two-wheelers leaned up in the rock garden to the right of the main entrance, to a wide assortment of banged-up jeeps and random rentals, all the way up to the sleek black Jaguar that Leah had bought for Strike, partly as a joke on his bloodline name, and partly because she liked going fast. The narrow-nosed helicopter off to one side probably belonged to Nate, who'd always had a thing for techware and had undoubtedly needed to get back in the air. He and Alexis had loved flying together, after all.

Oh, and of course, there was Sven and Cara's windsail, a flimsy wheeled surfboard thing that cruised along the hardpan at stupid speeds. They had surprised everyone by staying on at Skywatch when Reese and Dez relocated permanently to Denver, taking a goodly number of the *winikin* with them to found a bunch of nonprofits and see about spreading out the Nightkeeper Fund.

Despite Sven's former footloose tendencies, he and Cara had decided Skywatch was the best place for Mac, Pearl, and their pups, at least for the time being. So they had stayed to oversee things, and were helping Jade and Lucius fully catalog the library and figure out how to keep the Nightkeepers' records secure for the next twenty-six millennia or so. They all wanted to believe that Rabbit's magic had barred the *kax* and the *kohan* from the earth for good, but they weren't taking any chances.

No doubt Sven had parked his toy out front as a reminder that these were his digs now, a way of marking his turf that was a little more subtle than taking a whizz on the pillars that ran on either side of the covered overhang leading up to the front door.

Then again, Anna wouldn't put it past him to have done that, too.

She was grinning at the thought as she parked at random amid the vehicular mob scene, killed the engine, and just sat for a moment, looking up at the mansion. It was the same white-trimmed stone as before, with its sprawling wings and low-maintenance landscaping, but somehow it looked different to her now, as if it had changed.

Or maybe—probably—she was the one who'd changed.

Then the door swung open to reveal Strike, Leah and Jox jammed into the opening, waving and shouting for her to get her ass inside already, looking like they were so damn glad to see her they couldn't stand themselves.

She was out of the car in a flash, leaving her luggage behind, and dodging through the jammed parking area to meet them halfway.

Leah got to her first. "You look amazing!" Hauling Anna into an energetic hug, she whispered, "I'm so happy for you!" She broke away with a grin and a wink as Strike and Jox reached them, and passed Anna off for more hugs, more exclamations.

"Come in, come in." They urged her up the walkway so quickly that she didn't get a chance to hesitate, as she had done almost five years earlier, when she'd first come back after so long, and found only bad old memories.

Now there were new memories—not all of them good, granted, but enough good ones to balance off the bad. And, really, she couldn't regret the things that had made her the person she was today, living the life she had now.

Better yet, as she walked through the front doors, past the engraved sign that showed the world tree and reminded her to fight, protect and forgive, she felt for the first time since she was a teenager that she really had come back to her childhood home, and she was safe there. And, better yet, she was happy to be there for a while . . . though she'd be happy to get back to her family, too.

Maybe, hopefully, the teammates would eventually find a way to bring their human families into the compound and include them in the Cardinal Day celebrations. Because gods knew there would be human families and more celebrations—there were too few of them to intermarry, and they had vowed to keep the traditions alive, one way or another. There would need to be changes, of course, ways of explaining the teammates and their gatherings so the humans wouldn't find them too strange, but one day soon, Skywatch would be filled to its seams once more, would be alive once more, as it had been in their parents' times.

For now, though, this was good. It was right.

And it was time to party.

As the quick spring dusk descended on Skywatch, the teammates gathered beneath the ceiba tree; they had decided to start a new tradition of meeting out there, at the center of their little village. Where once the area had been shadowed with the ashes of the fallen and packed hard by countless feet coming and going from the training hall, now it was softly carpeted with a faint, fuzzy green, suggesting that while the Nightkeepers' magic might've ramped down, the earth magic that sustained their rain forest grotto was still going strong, keeping the ground unusually fertile.

And the grove apparently wasn't the only thing benefitting from some fertility dancing, Myr thought with a sidelong look at where Sasha, Reese and Cara were sitting at a picnic table comparing notes; all three had announced their pregnancies at lunch, and gotten a raucous round of applause. Cara was the only one with a visible baby bump, suggesting that she and Sven had gotten a jump on things prior to the end date, intentionally or not. The other two weren't showing yet, but they freaking glowed.

She was a little surprised to feel a harmless tug of envy—look at that, maybe she had a bio-clock, after all. *Down girl*, she told herself with a grin, tamping down on her link with Rabbit so he wouldn't catch the direction where her thoughts were going and do a deer-in-headlights impression.

At the moment, he was over with Dez, Sven and Michael, stacking wood for the bonfire, their efforts overseen by two adult coyotes and their perpetual-motion puppy pack.

Even that tugged, making her laugh at herself. Really, it wasn't like she wanted to do the home-and-baby thing any time soon. For one, she and Rabbit had a few things to knock off the to-do list between now and then. Like finishing up their degrees—something environmental for her, engineering and physics for him, along with some business courses and international relations, with the plan of heading up the emerging Nightkeeper Foundation's interests in the Mayan highlands. They both loved it down there, and wanted to help the locals recover from the outbreak. At least that was their current game plan.

And that was the awesome thing. They didn't need to know for sure right now. They could explore for a bit. Or, heck, for the rest of their lives. Because, hey, howdy, they had a future now. A beautiful and totally blank-slate future. The only thing they needed to know for sure was that they were going to be spending it together. Period. Full stop. She didn't care if the gods had meant for them to be together, or that they hadn't ever gotten their mated marks. Okay, she cared a little, but only because it had once been important to him. Now, though, he seemed content for them to go on as they were, living together and loving each other while they started really figuring out what their lives were going to look like for the next few years.

And after that? Marriage, she hoped. Kids. The family neither of them had gotten when they were growing up, but could give to the next generation.

"Gather round!" Dez called, tossing a last few sticks on the huge mound of pallets, kindling and other flammables he and the others had built. "It's time."

The former residents of Skywatch formed a horseshoe, with the open end facing south, the direction the wind was blowing, leaving room for the gods to join them, at least in spirit if not in practice.

What do you say? Ready for some action? The words formed in her mind, accompanied by a phantom brush of warmth across her lips, stirring her blood.

She looked up to find Rabbit standing at the center point of the horseshoe, with an open spot beside him. Her spot. With her head up and her eyes on him, she swaggered over, feeling good in black jeans and a tight black top, with high black boots that had a glint of silver at the edges. When she reached him, she leaned in and kissed him with a little nip of his lower lip that had him sucking in a breath.

Then, as the magic gathered in her head and heart, making her feel like she could do almost anything, she took her place beside him, and grinned around the horseshoe at the others, at her friends and teammates. "Okay. Now I'm ready for some action."

That got a chuckle, the loudest from Rabbit, as Dez cleared his throat. "Then by all means. Let's link up!"

She and Rabbit could've lit the bonfire on their own, given the magic that was zinging through them, re-awakened by the equinox. But the ceremony belonged to all of them, so they joined hands—Nightkeeper, *winikin*, human—and opened themselves to the magic. Where before the uplink would've been a huge, roaring upswell of power, now it was a softer, mellower heat. Still, though, it was magic. And it was beautiful.

He squeezed her hand. "Do you want to do the honors?"

"You do it." She didn't need to prove anything, not anymore.

Nodding, he spread his fingers toward the stacked wood and said, "*Kaak!*"

A soundless shock wave detonated from them both, and red and green fire exploded from his fingers and curled around the beehive-shaped stack. It whirled around once, twice and then a third time—and *whoomp!*—the bonfire lit with a crackling roar, sending a pillar of red and green flames twenty feet in the air, then thirty.

Heat drove everyone back a couple of steps, but nobody seemed to mind, given the show.

"Whooo!" Reese called, bending back to watch colored sparks swirl up on the breeze, and the others joined in with a chorus of *ooh*s and *aah*s.

Getting into it, Rabbit made the flames spiral and then curl around themselves. Myr laughed and added a little more blue to the mix, dropping fire bursts that looked like flowers on the curling vines of flame.

"Show-offs!" Dez called, but he was laughing.

"Sorry," Rabbit said, totally unrepentant.

After another minute, though, they let the pyrotechnics die down, so the heat subsided a little and the bonfire became just a normal bonfire, the magic just a background hum. The teammates were still linked, though, and their power sang a sweet note in the air as Dez led them through the first Cardinal Day prayer of the new age.

There was no bloodletting, no sacrifice, no prophecies or threats of dire retribution. Instead, the teammates thanked the true gods for their help, for the victory, and for their lives. It still seemed impossible that they had all survived, yet they had. Now they would go on to live as they chose. And thank the gods for that.

There was a soft upswing in the magic, as if the gods had heard them. Or maybe it came from the prayer itself; Myr didn't know. But she knew that she was happy, here and now, standing beside Rabbit in the center of a community that her childhood self never would have dreamed existed, never mind that she would become part of it. These were her people, her friends. And Rabbit was hers, always and forever.

"Before we break for games and food," Dez said, "I believe someone wanted to say something?"

Myr frowned with the others, looking around. "What the—"

"That'd be me," Rabbit said, and stepped out of line, then turned to face her.

And got down on one knee.

She caught her breath at the sight of him down there—Rabbit, who wouldn't willingly get on his knees for anything or anyone. Rabbit, who pulled a ring box out of his pocket and flipped it open to reveal a blaze of ruby and emerald, two perfect stones set atop a diamond-studded ring.

"Oh," she said, the word barely a breath as all the oxygen suddenly left her body.

His eyes gleamed as he said, "I've never loved anyone but you, and I'll go on loving you forever, with or without this. But this is what I want, and I hope it's what you want, too." Then, with him on one knee and everyone they cared about watching, he levitated the ring and sent it floating into the air, so it hovered between them, wreathed in red-gold magic. "What do you say, Myr? Will you marry me?"

Now it was her turn to go deer-in-headlights. Not because she was horrified or steamrollered or anything, but because she hadn't expected this. Not in a million years—or at least not for a few more years, anyway. Her pulse drummed in her ears and her hands shook. She was overwhelmed, she was shocked, she was—

She was supposed to say something.

Everyone was waiting.

The ring was waiting. The magic was waiting.

Yes, of course, yes! she shouted inside, but even if he heard her through their link, it didn't count. This was the sort of thing she needed to say out loud to make it real. And she would. In a second, when she remembered how to breathe.

Behind him, the bonfire grew hotter and bigger, going the pure orange-red of his magic now. For a moment, she thought he was letting off some steam into the magic, channeling his hidden nerves. But then the flames rose up from the bonfire, curled in on themselves, and made a perfect heart. It hung there behind him, living, beating in time with her pulse, then dissolved to the words "I love you."

Suddenly she could breathe again. She could even

laugh again, though the sound was breathless and a little wild. "Only you," she said on a rush. "Only you could propose by writing it across the sky in flames."

"And?"

"And yes, of course. Of course I'll marry you. Only you, Rabbit. My one and only." She held out her hand and watched it tremble as the ring floated onto it and snugged into place.

He exhaled in a rush and bowed his head for a second. "Thank fuck. For a second there, I thought . . ."

"No," she said, tugging him to his feet. "Don't ever think it." Then they kissed, triggering a chorus of whoops and applause, along with shouted suggestions that ranged from cute to borderline obscene, though all in good fun.

Rabbit chuckled against her mouth. "Hope you didn't want me to do that in private."

"It's perfect. You're perfect."

"That's pushing it."

"Okay. You're perfect for me, which is why I love you. It's why I'm going to marry you. And it's why, as soon as I get you alone, I'm going to . . ." She put her lips to his ear and started whispering.

Her skin heated as she got to the nitty-gritty and heard his breath quicken, felt his fingers tighten on her hips. The air around them hummed with equinox magic and the blood began to roar through her veins like—

"Whoa!" Rabbit pulled away and put himself between her and the bonfire, which suddenly flared higher and hotter, reaching up into the night sky. "Sorry. Got a little carried away there."

But when he gestured to bring the flames under control, the bonfire didn't respond, even when Myr added her magic to his. Instead it burned even brighter, flaring into strange shapes and moving like a living creature. It wasn't under their control anymore!

"Wait!" She grabbed his arm. "Look!"

The flames curled into the shape of an animal's head on a man's shoulders. It wasn't any critter that'd ever done a cameo on Animal Planet, though.

It was Seth.

The god didn't speak, but it moved within the flames and the smoke, turning to peer down at Rabbit and Myrinne. Its eyes shimmered, and the radiance of golden magic emerged from the flames and snaked to wrap around them, touch them, twine around their wrists.

Myr gasped as her skin heated, then burned, and something shifted inside her, soldering into place with a click that she felt more than heard. Then the burn faded and the smoke withdrew.

"Gods," Rabbit whispered. "Father. Thank you."

The giant head of flame tipped once in acknowledgment, then shimmered and disappeared. Moments later, the fire died down to normal once more, leaving a stunned, awed silence behind.

"Did that just happen?" Leah whispered. Her face was lit with wonder and her hands were wrapped around Strike's arm as if she'd had to hold him back from coming to Rabbit's aid.

Rabbit hadn't needed help, though. And Myr had a feeling he'd finally gotten what he wanted. What they both wanted, though they had trained themselves not to care.

Now, though . . .

Holding her breath, she put her right forearm near Rabbit's, both of them facing down. "You ready?" she whispered as her heart drummed against her ribs.

He swallowed hard. "Yeah."

"On three. One . . . two . . ." On "three" they both flipped their wrists over to show their marks. And sure enough, they both had a new golden glyph: the intertwined curlicues of the *jun tan*. The mated mark that signaled the gods' acceptance of their paring.

Finally, Myr thought. Or maybe she said it aloud, because Rabbit looked at her with a quick grin that did nothing to wipe the awe from his face.

"Myr . . . gods. I love you."

"I love you too."

Tears were running down her face, but she didn't care. She hadn't thought the *jun tan* would matter, but it did. It really, really did. Because as she held him, kissed him, she could feel the magic of their new connection, feel the love washing from her to him and back again. More, she felt *him*. He was tough and solid, and ready to go to war for her, for what he thought was right. He was her soldier, her lover. More, he was Rabbit. Her man. Her mate. Her one and only.

And her husband-to-freaking-be, thankyouverymuch.

* * *

The next twenty minutes or so were pretty much a blur to Rabbit. He got his hand shaken and his back thumped enough that his shoulder started to tingle. Or maybe that was just part of the whole-body sizzle that'd hit him about three seconds after he got the ring on Myr's finger and the first wave of *Oh, holy shit, I'm getting married!* hit him for real.

He'd known what he wanted, had known he was going to ask her, of course; hell, he'd had the ring for nearly a month, burning a hole in his frigging pocket. He'd wanted to wait until today, though, to share the moment with their teammates and the magic of the equinox. No way he'd expected Seth's trick with the fire, though, or for the god to give them their mated marks. That added a whole 'nother layer to the tingles, that was for sure.

As the crowd around him thinned a little and the congratulations died down, he took her hand and brushed his fingertips across her mark, feeling a skim of heat shiver through his own forearm.

He grinned. Oh, yeah. This was going to be very cool.

"Happy?" she asked with a sassy, knowing arch of one eyebrow.

"Very. You?"

"Duh."

He chuckled and tucked her close against his side, "Yeah. Duh." Their style might not work for everyone, but it was perfect for the two of them, and that was what mattered, wasn't it? He didn't think he'd ever find someone else who got him the way she did, or who made him want to protect the hell out of her on one hand, while challenging her to go faster, farther and hotter on the other. And the thing was, as he looked around, he saw the same kind of love in each of the mated pairs—and in the family joy of Patience, Brandt and the twins—as they leaned into each other and laughed, touched, looked. There was love in every small gesture and moment, reaffirming the bonds that they might have discovered in the years leading up to the war, but that would last for decades to come.

He didn't know if it was because the magic-users were wired to love so deeply and fiercely, a trick of the *jun tan*, or what, but he got it now, more than he ever had before.

Looking up at the sky as the fire started to burn low, he let out a long, slow breath. "It doesn't excuse everything you did, you know."

"What?" Myr had been talking to Anna—he had tuned out at the first mention of bridesmaids—but now she zoned back in on him and followed his eyes to the sky. "Are you looking at the moon?"

"No. Those five bright stars over there." He pointed. "They make up the great boar constellation."

"Your place in the sky."

"And the old man's."

She tightened her grip on him. "He's gone."

He shook his head. "Not really. He's still stuck in here." He tapped a thumb on his chest. "I can't . . ." He glanced off to the side, to where the ceiba spread its huge branches far overhead. "I've fought and I've protected, but I haven't really forgiven, until now." Looking back down at the others, he swept a hand toward the mated pairs. "Look at them. Hell, look at us. What we've got is special. It's *everything*. If you had died—"

"I didn't."

"But if you had, that would've been the end for me. I would've . . ." He trailed off, not wanting to say what was in his heart. Not with the gods so near, with their gift so fresh. "Anyway. I understand better now what happened to the old man, how it must've felt to watch Cassie die, then see the *boluntiku* race off to Skywatch, knowing they were going to kill his sons and not be able to do a damned thing about it. Look at Brandt." He pointed to where the big Nightkeeper had Harry on his shoulders and Braden swinging from one of his arms, the three of them laughing like loons while the puppy barked like crazy and jumped up, trying to nip at the boy's sneakers. A few feet away, Patience stood back with Jox and Hannah, and tried to look like she thought they were a bunch of idiots. Her eyes danced, though, giving her away. "Think of what he'd be like if he'd lost that. If any of us had lost each other."

"It didn't happen." She pressed her face to his arm. "We're all here. *I'm* here."

"I know. But the old man didn't have that, he hadn't had it for a long, long time." Looking up at the Great Boar, he said, "I owe you, old man, for getting me away from Oc Ajal, away from Phee and Anntah. I owe you for raising me on your own, and when you couldn't handle that anymore, for bringing me to live with Jox and the others. I owe you for coming back and helping the others find me, and for telling me the truth about who I am. I'm grateful for all of those things, even if you didn't really do them for me. And I get it now. I understand why you were the way you were. That didn't give you the right to be an asshole or a shitty father, but it gives me a reason to let it go. So there it is. I forgive you, Father. It doesn't matter whether or not you give a crap, because I do. I forgive you, and I hope you've found your peace up there with your family."

It wasn't until he finished that he realized the others had all fallen silent, that they'd heard what he'd said. But as he looked around at them and shrugged a little, suddenly uncomfortable, he caught Patience giving him a thumbs up. Then Jox. Then Strike and a few of the others. And that made it okay, somehow. Better than okay, even.

It made it right, finally.

"Well," Dez said into the silence. "I think this calls for the newly traditional Cardinal Day feast . . . Who's up for some football, beer and wings?"

A laughing, ragged cheer rose up from the group, gaining ground and volume as it went, and the others dispersed to grab the coolers and other essentials from the *winikin*'s hall.

When Rabbit started to follow them, though, Myr tugged him back. "Not so fast, buster."

"Wait, what? Did I do something wrong?"

Her flashing eyes softened. "No, baby, you did something very right." She pressed her hand over his heart, which thudded double-time when she leaned in and kissed him softly. "I'm so proud of you." She kissed him a little harder. "I love you."

This time when she kissed him, he closed his hands on her hips and took it deep, whispering through their new bond, *Thank you*, and, *I love you, too*, and *Gods, I'm so glad you're mine*.

Heat rose as the kiss continued, tightening his skin and making him think they should slip away for a half hour or so and nobody would notice. But when he started to urge her off toward the shadows, she twisted away, shot him a sidelong look and headed for one of the coolers to snag a couple of beers, then skipped toward where a game of touch football was forming up, cocking a "come hither" finger at him as she went.

He laughed aloud and followed, joining her in the huddle, grabbing his beer and letting his body bump against hers, amping the anticipation that was growing steadily between them.

The night was young, after all, and they didn't need to rush. There was a whole world of trouble for them to get into . . . and they were going to have a lifetime together to do it.

ABOUT THE AUTHOR

A series of childhood trips to the Yucatán left **Jessica Andersen** with an enduring love of Mayan myths and legends. Since leaving academic science for a career as a novelist, she has written more than twenty science-based romantic suspense novels. Now she's thrilled to bring her research background to bear on one of her earliest fascinations, the Mayan 2012 doomsday. Jessica is a lifelong New Englander; she and her critters currently live in eastern Connecticut, on the border where Yankee country intersects with Red Sox nation (go, Sox!).

Connect Online
www.jessicaandersen.com
facebook.com/docjess

Don't miss the brand-new contemporary series
by Jessica Andersen, writing as Jesse Hayworth,
beginning with

Summer at Mustang Ridge

Available in summer 2013 from Signet Eclipse!
Read on for a special preview.

Foster grinned as he led Brutus in from the geldings'
pen, where a dozen or so mustangs were munching
hay and snoozing in the sun.

The chestnut snaked his head around, feinting for a
nip.

"Quit that." He nudged the horse out of his space,
reminding him how the pecking order went: without
Brutus at the top, despite his delusions of grandeur.
The mustang had been at the ranch since last fall's
gather and had been under saddle for nearly six
months. He'd been in the working string for only a few
weeks, though, and was still reserved for the wran-
glers' use because his better-than-average smarts were
paired with an unpredictable streak wider than the
stripe running down his nose. He wasn't dangerous,
but Foster wouldn't exactly call him reliable, either.
And given his quick mind, big feet and smooth gaits,
he was worth putting some time into.

Annoyed that his nap had been interrupted, the gelding rolled an eye back at Foster.

"Yeah, yeah, life's tough. You think this is hard work, try being a real cow horse. Compared to them, you're just a glorified trail pony."

Then again, what did that make him? Head trail-pony wrangler? Executive greenhorn herder? Overlord of make-sure-the-dudes-don't-kill-themselves?

It made him employed—that was what. And saving for better days.

He gave the gelding a nudge as they reached the barn, where the bright sun turned to murky shadows at the doorway and a nervous horse—or one with a questionable sense of humor—could spook. "Don't even think about it," he warned conversationally. "This is supposed to be my day off, and I'm not in the mood to deal with your—"

Movement flashed in his peripheral vision as they stepped from light into dark, and Brutus gave a sudden elephant snort and exploded in a spook that was part pent-up energy, part *Aieeeee, mountain lion!* The big gelding's shoes struck sparks on the cement as he tried to wheel and bolt, dragging Foster around with a thousand pounds of momentum and a cement-strong neck. Vader got in front of him and splayed all four feet, barking, trying to head off the runaway.

Foster hauled back on the lead. "Whoa, dang it! And, Vader, git!"

As the dog scurried out the back, Foster caught a flash of brown hair and wide, scared hazel eyes in a triangular face. He had only a split second to think *Oh crap* at the realization that the little girl was about to get flattened. Then Brutus swung his haunches around and bumped her hard, and she went flying across the aisle.

She hit the wall and went down in a pink-and-denim heap.

Oh crap turned into an inner *nine-one-one*, but Foster's body kept reacting, using thirty-some years of experience to juggle the gelding away from the kid and down to the other end of the aisle.

"Knock it off!" he growled, getting right up near one of Brutus's white-rimmed eyes. Where normally he would've soothed, now he muscled the blockheaded chestnut under some semblance of control, then kicked open a nearby stall and sent him into it still wearing his halter. "Don't you dare get tangled in that lead," he ordered, then ran the door shut and latched it tight.

He spun back, expecting to find the little girl still down. She wasn't, though. She was on her feet, plastered in the corner where the tack stall jutted out a few feet into the aisle. Her pink T-shirt and jeans were streaked with dust, her face sheet white. All arms and legs, with a long torso and those big hazel eyes, she reminded him of a long yearling in the middle of a growth spurt, when all the pieces didn't go together quite right.

She hadn't made a sound, wasn't crying now, just stood there staring at him.

"You okay?" When she didn't say anything, he took a step toward her and reached out a hand. "Are you hurt?"

"Lizzie!"

Foster's head whipped around as a dark-haired woman in a ridiculous black pantsuit raced into the barn wearing the same sort of look he'd seen before in a half-wild heifer's eyes when he'd made the mistake of getting between her and her newborn calf. The kind of look that said she didn't care what happened to her or anything around her as long as she got up close and personal with the little one, pronto.

He did what he should've done back then, which would have saved him a whole bunch of black-and-blues. He got the heck out of the way.

"Are you okay?" Shelby dropped to her knees, hitting so hard that the cement grated through her pants. Not seeing any blood or obvious injuries on her daughter, she whipped a look over her shoulder at the stranger. "What happened?"

"She spooked one of the horses, zigged when she should've zagged and took a tumble. By the time I got Brutus in a stall, she was up and moving." He was straight out of central casting, filed under "cowboy, circa twenty-first century" in worn jeans, scarred brown boots and a black felt hat that was flecked with hay and dirt and sat low on his forehead. Compared to the guys in the dining hall, he looked faded and authentic. And concerned. Points there.

Focusing on Lizzie, she brushed at the dirt smudges on her daughter's clothes and tried to remember how to breathe. *She's okay. It's okay.* But it wasn't, not when Lizzie could've gotten seriously hurt because her idiot mother had stopped paying attention for a few minutes. "Why did you leave the dining hall? I *told* you not to go near the horses without a grown-up!"

Lizzie didn't answer, didn't meet her eyes, didn't give her any sign to indicate that she'd heard or understood.

"Is she okay?" He sounded dubious. "I didn't see her hit her head, but she seems kind of out of it."

Shelby stood and faced him, tucking her daughter behind her. "She's fine."

"Maybe somebody should take a look at her. It's Stace's day off, but Gran has doctored more banged-up riders than your average ER."

She's seen plenty of doctors. "We don't need anybody, but thanks. And thanks for containing the situation." She had some idea of how fast things could get out of control when horses were involved and shuddered to think how much worse it could've been. "I'm very sorry she got underfoot. It won't happen again." She tightened her grip on Lizzie's shoulder. "That's a promise."

"But she's—"

"Perfectly okay just the way she is."

His eyes snapped up to hers, as if she'd just said more than that. "Oh. Sorry. I, ah . . . Sorry."

"Don't be. I'm not." *Don't you dare pity us.*

He frowned at her instead and then looked at Lizzie. "What is she, seven? Eight? And you brought her to singles week? There isn't going to be our usual family-vacation vibe, you know."

It wouldn't have irritated her so much if she hadn't already been thinking the same thing. "She's nine. Not that it matters, because we're not here for guest activities. I'll be working in the kitchen."

"You're . . ." He trailed off.

"The new assistant cook," she filled in.

"What happened to Bertie?"

"The doctor wants her on bed rest until she has her baby." Which was why she and Lizzie had hit the road a week ahead of schedule, arriving in the middle of speed dates rather than next week's thirty-person family reunion.

"You're a chef?"

"Nope. I'm in advertising, but a friend of mine knows Krista and the ranch. When she found out I wanted to get Lizzie away from the city for the summer, she set things up. The next thing I knew, I had a summer job and a place for us to stay." It was such a simple summary for what had been in reality a really tough choice involving dire warnings from both her boss and Lizzie's doctor, and the inner fear that she'd come into September with Lizzie no better and her clients having forgotten who she was. In her line of work, you were only as good as your last campaign.

"A summer job." His face was deadpan.

"Yep. Now through Labor Day. Three months, give or take." She tipped her head. "Problem?"

He gave her an up and down just like the guys in the dining hall, only he didn't look nearly so appreciative of her round-toed shoes and clingy pants. "Nope. No problem at all. I mostly do my own cooking anyway. What Krista does up at the main house is her business. What happens in the barn is mine."

Shelby wasn't sure which annoyed her more: the way he'd zeroed right in on Lizzie's issues, the implication that she wouldn't be able to handle herself as a ranch cook . . . or how she was way too sensitive on both fronts. Points-wise, it was a draw.

Refusing to dwell on it—or on him—she snagged Lizzie around the neck in a fake headlock they'd learned from watching too much TV wrestling for a pitch that hadn't gone anywhere—*Women's Xtreme Wrestling. Fight like a girl!*—and tugged her toward the door. "Come on, kiddo, it's back to orientation for us. And consider yourself lucky if I don't tattoo a couple of those rules on the insides of your eyelids."

Foster watched them leave, telling himself it was because he wanted to be sure the little girl was moving okay. He wasn't sure whether she'd been shell-shocked or if there was something else going on, but it seemed like her mother had it covered either way. Still, though, he'd had a fall or two that he'd walked away from, only to feel it later.

"Kid's fine," he muttered, and it didn't take Brutus's snort to tell him that his eyes had wandered. Okay, so little Lizzie's mama had a fine rear view, with nice curves and a feminine wiggle. And the front view was just as good, all sleek and pretty.

So, that was Bertie's fill-in? Huh. Wouldn't have been his choice . . . but then again, it wasn't his choice, was it? And while Krista was whip smart, she had a soft heart and a penchant for good deeds. He should know; he'd been one of them. He only hoped she didn't get burned by this one.

"Ah, well. Not my problem." Besides, Gran might be a little nutty around the edges, but she was plenty sharp when it came to her kitchen, and she had Tipper, Topper and Krista to back her up. They'd be okay, even if Ms. Fancypants flaked on them.

Whistling softly, he bent to pick up Brutus's chipped-up foot, determined to enjoy the rest of his so-called day off. Because starting tomorrow, he'd spend the next six days being the cowboy the guests wanted to see, the wrangler they'd *ooh* and *ahh* over, the horseman they needed to have making sure they didn't kill themselves or any innocent bystanders. They would ride, laugh, drink, dance, pair off—some of them two or three times—and have a good time, thinking they were living the Wild West experience, when really they were getting the Disney version. In this case, the R-rated version. And then next week Mustang Ridge would do it all over again, starting fresh with a whole new cast of characters and a different theme.

Rinse, repeat and be grateful for the work, he thought, casting another look up toward the main house. He

wasn't looking after the new assistant cook and her daughter this time, though. No, his eyes were on the house itself, and everything it represented, reminding him that fancy females were a distraction he couldn't afford when he had his sights set on more important things.